JUPITER'S DAUGHTER
A Katy Klein Mystery

◆ ◆ ◆

KAREN IRVING

POLESTAR
BOOK PUBLISHERS

Polestar Book Publishers and Raincoast Books acknowledge the ongoing support of The Canada Council; the British Columbia Ministry of Small Business, Tourism and Culture through the BC Arts Council; and the Government of Canada through the Book Publishing Industry Development Program (BPIDP).

Cover design by Val Speidel.
Cover image by Les Smith.
Author photo by Mitchell Beer.
Book layout by Bamboo & Silk Design Inc.
Printed and bound in Canada.

CANADIAN CATALOGUING IN PUBLICATION DATA

Irving, Karen, 1957-
Jupiter's daughter
ISBN 1-896095-54-2
I. Title.
PS8567.R862J86 2000   C813'.54   C99-911334-8
PR9199.3.I688J86 2000

LIBRARY OF CONGRESS CATALOGUE NUMBER: 99-69301

Polestar Book Publishers/Raincoast Books
9050 Shaughnessy Street
Vancouver, BC
V6P 6E5

5 4 3 2 1

For Mitchell,
with all my love.

Jupiter, ruler of Mount Olympus, was the ancient symbol of power, rule and the law. He was also infamous for his libidinous rampages among immortals and humans alike. He fathered many children, including Athena, aka Minerva, who is said to have sprung fully formed from his forehead; Artemis, aka Diana, twin sister of Apollo, who assisted her own mother in birthing her twin; and the Three Fates, Klotho, Atropos and Lachesis, who spun, wove and cut the thread of life.

Astrologically, Jupiter is known as the Greater Benefic — it governs expansion, success, achievement and integration, but also excess, arrogance, waste and abuse of power. In an individual's horoscope, Jupiter snows where the person's greatest potential lies and where they are most vulnerable to overweening pride — which, as we know, goeth before a fall.

1

SATURDAY, DECEMBER 11
Moon opposition Jupiter ✦
Sun square Jupiter ✦
Mars trine Uranus ✦
Saturn square Neptune ✦

The thing I have always hated most about winter is not the cold. It is the darkness. Early December is the worst time, and this particular December seemed even more sombre than most. The snow had not yet begun to fall in earnest, but the brilliance of autumn had faded to a uniform grey, lit feebly by the weakened sun as it died its long death.

Each year there is one bright spot, though — an antidote to the gloomy days and wintry nights: the gala Christmas party my friend Carmen Capricci throws on the second Saturday of December. It's always a brilliant, effervescent affair, complete with twinkling lights, sophisticated food and drink, and of course, fascinating gossip. This year was no exception.

Carmen held the event in the reception area above her suite of offices on Sussex Drive, where she had founded Ottawa's most exclusive interior design company fifteen years ago. Her work is in high demand among those who can afford to pay someone to tell them to buy five-thousand-dollar couches, hand-knotted Persian rugs, inlaid desks made of three or four precious woods, and scalloped pelmets. Whatever a pelmet is.

As usual, I arrived late; the party was already in full swing. I slipped into the room more or less unnoticed, which was fine by me. I have a love/hate relationship with Carmen's parties — I'm drawn like a magpie to the sparkle and flash, but these huge gatherings intimidate me more than they should. Was I under- or over-dressed? Would I put my foot in my mouth — again? I blanched at the memory of having blithely informed one of Carmen's most obstreperous clients that she didn't seem nearly as difficult as Carmen had reported. That was three years ago, and Carmen had assured me she'd forgotten all about the episode. I haven't.

I squeezed past several clusters of chattering merrymakers to the bar, where a very nice young man poured me a Heineken. Then I tried my best to mingle in a sociable yet unobtrusive manner. Easier said than done: everyone else, it seemed, had found someone to converse with. The room was a bubbling mass of bright, high-pitched voices, and I hovered awkwardly for several minutes, trying to find a place to fit in.

It seemed like everyone in Ottawa had been invited to Carmen's party. In the corner, near a huge plant, I glimpsed an elderly senator leering at the swelling bosom of a computer mogul's wife. She punctuated each sentence by tossing her teased mane of blonde hair over her bare shoulders. I recognized a couple of city councillors milling around the bar, slapping the owner of Ottawa's big league hockey franchise on the back. Ottawa doesn't exactly have a glitterati set, but at Carmen's party, you could be fooled.

"I can't believe you wore that dress — you look like some kind of a slut," someone hissed directly behind me. I whirled around, preparing to defend my honour (and that of the outfit I'd splurged on last week), but the man wasn't addressing me.

The object of his derision, a plump auburn-haired woman who looked no more than thirty, stood frozen, a glass of wine suspended midway to her mouth. Her full lower lip started to tremble and her huge brown eyes welled with tears. The dress in question was forest-green velvet; it hugged her curves beautifully, the scooped neck revealing a hint of bosom, the skirt flaring out over ample hips from her tiny waist.

"Actually, I think she looks perfectly lovely," I butted in, forgetting my vow to remain discreet. The man, a tall, bearded guy whose knobby wrists extended a good inch beyond the shiny cuffs of his obviously rented tux, narrowed his eyes at me, warning me off. I pretended not to notice, and turned to talk to the woman.

"That colour looks wonderful on you," I said. "It makes your skin glow. Where did you get it?"

The man shot me a foul look, growled something under his breath, then turned on his heel and disappeared toward the bar. The woman ventured a timid smile.

"Thank you," she whispered. "When he does that, I just don't know what to say to him. It's like I freeze, you know? And he does it all the time ..." She lowered her eyes, flushing painfully.

"Well, never mind what he says. You do look great.

Are you a friend of Carmen's?"

Her face brightened. "Oh, well, not a friend, exactly, but I like her a lot! She's a lovely lady. We met a few weeks ago, and she's been just wonderful to me. I couldn't believe she'd actually invite me to a party like this ..."

Bib-bip-bip-beep ... The high-pitched beeping made me jump, but the woman reached into her velveteen handbag and pulled out a digital watch. With a practised flick, she switched off the alarm.

"Time for my medicine," she explained with a rueful smile. "Sorry. If I miss a dose, my brain fries."

I nodded as she popped a green-and-yellow capsule into her mouth, washing it down with her drink.

"I'm Marion," she said, when she was done.

"Katy Klein. Nice to meet you." I extended my hand, and she took it.

"To tell you the truth, I've never been to a party as big and fancy as this," she confided. "It's a little intimidating, isn't it? I mean, all these famous people ..." She gestured toward the crowd.

"I know what you mean. Carmen's set is a bit rich for my blood, too. Fun to watch, though."

Marion nodded. "I think Phil — that's my husband — is feeling a bit out of his depth here. He gets mean whenever he feels that way. Which is often." She gave an impish smile.

"Is Phil the guy who was putting your dress down? He's your husband?"

She smiled ruefully. "Not for much longer. He — he did something I just can't reconcile, you know? It was the final straw. I didn't want him coming here, and he didn't want to come either, at first. But then he thought there was a chance I might have fun without him, so he rented that tux this morning. I wish he'd just leave me alone."

"Well, if I were you, I'd go ahead and have a blast. Don't let him stop you."

Marion had stopped listening to me, though. She stared past me with an expression I couldn't interpret.

"Oh, dear," she said. "Could you possibly excuse me? There's someone over there ... I need to talk to them. Maybe we can chat a bit more later? Nice meeting you!"

She scurried away, and I sipped my Heineken, leaning against a pillar. The tinkle of glasses, the buzz of conversation and laughter swirled around me, and I scanned the faces near me, looking for a familiar one.

"I hate these things, don't you?" A woman's voice cut through the hubbub, low and husky. "Such a load of hypocritical crap."

The young woman was tall and poker-thin, her nearly black hair cropped short above a fine-boned, angular face. She wore a black silk pantsuit, just this side of severe, but very elegant. She fingered the small silver cross that glinted at her throat, and glared as though expecting me to disagree.

"Well, I -" I started, but she cut me off.

"It's the fakery of it that gets to me," she said, as if I weren't there. "Everyone all lovey-kissy, when underneath it all they're thinking about how to stab each other in the back. Half the people here hate each other, you know. Some way to celebrate Christ's birthday, don't you think?"

I nodded, not sure how to respond.

Suddenly she shook her head, as though to clear it. An uncertain smile illuminated her stern features, and she looked at me as though she'd only just seen me.

"I'm sorry. Where are my manners? Are you a friend of Carmen's?"

"Actually, Carmen and I have known each other since kindergarten," I said. "What about you?"

"We've met a few times. Through my brother, mainly. I really hate these things — I don't know why I let her talk me into coming."

"I know what you mean," I sympathized. "It took me fifteen minutes just to get to the bar. I'm Katy Klein, by the way."

"Diana Farnsworth. Nice to meet you." She extended her hand, and I shook it. It was cold. "Oh, look, here's Carmen -"

"Katy! When did you get here? I didn't even see you come in!" Carmen pounced on me, gripping my elbow. I nearly spilled my drink. "Oh, my God, you look just fabulous — that outfit is so flattering on you! It drapes so well, I'd swear you've been on a diet. Stand back a second. It's perfect! You see, I told you you'd look good in crimson. Diana, doesn't she look great?"

"Terrific," Diana agreed with a tiny smile, already starting to turn away.

"Hey, Carmen." I checked the front of my V-neck swing-top to see if I'd managed to dribble anything on myself during her surprise attack. "No fair sneaking up on me like that — I didn't even see you coming. Great party, though. As usual."

"Isn't it?" she dimpled. "Nearly everyone I invited is here. Not to mention a few I didn't. But that's okay. Just makes it more interesting. What do you think of the hors d'oeuvres? D'you think the pear and Gorgonzola bruschetta is a bit much? After all, this isn't Toronto."

"Carmen, settle down. Everything's fine. Your parties

are always fine, you know that. I like the string ensemble — nice touch." I stooped to give my friend a quick hug, but she wriggled away from me.

"Sweetie, I just got my hair done. Oh!" Carmen's eyes widened, and she tugged on my arm again. "Katy, there's someone here you must meet. Diana, honey, your brother is right over here. He was just asking whether you were here yet — you really should come and say hi."

Diana, who was now moving away from us, looked less than enthusiastic, but Carmen seemed not to notice, steering me instead toward a tall, raven-haired man who stood in the centre of a group of women. Apparently whatever he was telling them was vastly entertaining; each time he paused, he was rewarded with a chorus of high-pitched giggles.

"Nigel! Nigel, I'd like you to meet my absolute best friend in the whole world, Dr. Katy Klein. Katy, this is Nigel Farnsworth."

I stuck my hand out, but a woman chose that moment to walk between us. Over her head, Nigel raised his drink to me in a mock salute. His deep blue eyes crinkled at the corners and the warmth of his smile radiated across the space between us.

"Katy, it's wonderful to meet you at last. Carmen has told me so much about you." Though he had to shout to make himself heard above the laughter and clinking of glasses around us, his voice was deep and mellifluous, a natural baritone. Nigel Farnsworth — the name was familiar. Was he a singer? Maybe with the National Arts Centre ... In any case, he was gorgeous, though he seemed entirely unselfconscious about it. No wonder his impromptu groupies were hanging on his every word.

"Nice to meet you." I smiled back, trying to place Nigel. In a town the size of Ottawa, it shouldn't have been hard, but my aging brain was refusing to co-operate.

Nigel eased his way closer to Carmen and me and rested his long, tapered hand with easy familiarity on my friend's silk-clad shoulder.

"Katy, Nigel is going to be getting his own television show next month," Carmen said. "Isn't that marvellous? I don't think I've ever been this close to a TV star before!" She twinkled up at him, all girlish adoration.

Nigel looked embarrassed, but there was a smile in his voice. "Not exactly a star, Carmen. It's not even a nationally syndicated show. I'm hardly a household name."

"Never mind. You soon will be, we all know that."

"What kind of television show will you have, Nigel?" I asked.

"It's an inspirational show, for the Sunday evening audience. I've had a small early morning program for several years, on the local cable station," he said, "but this is our first crack at commercial television. I'm hoping to really broaden our audience share, maybe even expand to a national base."

"Wow, that sounds interesting," I said, trying to infuse my voice with enthusiasm. I'm not much of an inspirational TV watcher, myself.

Nigel leaned toward me, and the crisp smell of his aftershave tickled my nostrils. "May I ask, Katy — are you a Christian?"

"God, no!" I blurted. "I mean, no, I'm not. That is, I'm Jewish."

"Ah! Well, I know the rabbi from Beth Israel here in

Ottawa — we were just at an ecumenical session last week, talking about problems with the justice system. Very fine gentleman. Perhaps you know him? Rafael Tanner. He struck me as highly intelligent and very dedicated."

"Sorry, I'm not much of a joiner when it comes to religion. I haven't set foot in a *shul* in years."

"*Shul?*" Nigel frowned at the unfamiliar word. Then he brightened. "Ah! Synagogue, you mean! Well, we all relate to God differently, don't we?"

I couldn't think of an intelligent response to this; I've been an atheist since I can remember. I just flashed him my brightest smile, hoping he'd take it for assent. Carmen interrupted, and just in time, too.

"Well! Oh, my dears, I just abandoned poor Diana! Nigel, she's right over there, she said she'd catch up with you as soon as she could. I must go introduce her around. Nigel, why don't you refill Katy's glass? You're drinking beer, aren't you, Katy? Nigel's a teetotaller, but he's very broad-minded, isn't that right, sweetie? You'll never believe it, Katy, but he and Diana have actually had me on the wagon for nearly a month now!"

She was right — I didn't believe it. But my admiration for Nigel Farnsworth and his sister took an upward leap. I wondered what their magic technique was.

Without a backward glance, Carmen darted through the crowd. Nigel and I stood awkwardly for a moment as I scanned frantically through my Conversational Gambits file for something intelligent to say to him. He got there first.

"So, ah, tell me, Katy, what do you do?" he asked. "For a living, that is."

"As it happens, Nigel, I'm an astrologer." I'm not

sure what kind of response I expected to this announcement, but it was not the one I got.

"Dear God in heaven!" Nigel exploded. Imported beer sloshed over the brim of my glass, and I held the drink away from me, hoping to spare my outfit.

"What? You don't like astrologers?" I tried not to sound overly defensive, but the words were out before I could stop them. However, Nigel didn't seem to have heard me. His gaze was riveted on something a few feet away, behind the small cluster of women who'd surrounded him earlier. I couldn't quite see what had captured his attention.

Then I heard the scream.

"Oh, my God — someone help her!" a woman cried, and all conversation in the room suddenly hushed. The musical ensemble stopped playing, right in the middle of "Eine Kleine Nachtmuzik."

There was a gurgling, choking sound, and then a man yelled, "Marion! Goddammit, stop this! Get up!"

"Hey! Get him off her!" someone else shouted, and the room erupted into pandemonium.

I elbowed my way mercilessly past Nigel and his fan club, taking advantage of my height and weight to jab and thrust my way toward whatever was happening to Marion. It was the smell that halted me. Sour, acrid — someone had vomited, all over the polished pine floors. I peered over the head of a tiny, perfectly coiffed woman dressed in a very expensive-looking leopardskin catsuit.

Marion, the woman I'd spoken with earlier, lay on the floor in a puddle of vomit. Her long, dark auburn hair was a tangled mess and her handbag had flown out of her hand, landing a few feet away. Her husband, Phil, had grabbed her by the forearm and was trying to yank her upright, but she kept arching and flopping backward, her head cracking against the floor. A young man, possibly the bartender, had hold of Phil's collar and was trying to haul him away from the woman. Phil paid him no attention.

"Marion! Marion, I've had about enough of this! Enough, do you hear me? Snap out of it and get up, dammit!"

Marion was in no condition to snap out of anything. Her body heaved and buckled, neck arching and spasming, eyes bulging. The rest of Carmen's guests stood frozen, horror and shock winning out over common sense. I forced my way into middle of this bizarre tableau and grabbed Phil by the shiny sleeve of his tuxedo.

"What the hell is the matter with you? She's having a seizure, you idiot!" I screamed. "Get away from her! Someone, get this guy out of here. Now!"

Two men obliged, springing forward and helping the bartender. Phil struggled and swore, but they pushed him away from Marion, and eventually he retreated toward the bar, muttering to himself. After that, no one paid him much attention.

"Someone call an ambulance," I commanded. "Back off, people, give the woman some air. Carmen, can you open these windows?"

I wasn't certain that someone having an epileptic seizure actually needed air, but it seemed to make sense at the time.

Carmen hovered near the woman, her mouth opening and closing wordlessly.

"Carmen!" She jumped at my voice. "Carmen, someone has to call 911. Does anyone here have a phone?"

"D-don't know," she gulped, and looked around beseechingly. "No, wait, I have one ..."

"Where? Come on, this is an emergency!"

"Purse. In my purse. I'll get it."

The woman on the floor had stopped spasming and now lay quiet, her eyelids fluttering lightly. Her simple green velvet dress was stained and rumpled, and her face was the colour of putty. I stepped closer, repulsed by the foul odour of vomit and something else — had she emptied her bowels? My stomach heaved, but I knelt beside her and gingerly picked up a limp wrist, feeling for a pulse. There it was, weak and thready.

"Is the ambulance coming? Good." I tried to sound like the voice of calm authority. Then, "Oh, God — I think she's starting again." Sure enough, the woman's body arched away from the floor, then dropped, only to spasm again. "Someone give me a hand here — we've got to turn her on her side to keep her from aspirating her own vomit."

The paramedics arrived within five minutes. By the time they'd strapped her to a board and loaded her into the ambulance, the party had begun to break up. As I left, the musical ensemble was packing their instruments.

✦

"So what happened to the lady, Mom?" Dawn, my fifteen-year-old daughter, lay sprawled across my bed. I stripped off my vomit-stained outfit, balled it up and stuffed it into a plastic laundry bag.

"Damn — this thing cost me nearly a week's pay," I complained. "I hope the cleaner can get this guck out of it."

"Mom!"

"Sorry, honey. I don't know. They took her away, and we all just left. There wasn't much more anyone could do. Carmen was in tears, of course — you know how she makes such a big deal out of these parties every year. I don't know how well she knew the woman, but you'd think the poor thing decided to have a seizure just to spoil Carmen's fun. When I left, Nigel was talking to her, and she was clinging to him like he was the last liferaft on the Titanic. I couldn't catch her eye, so I took off."

"I didn't think Carmen even went to church," Dawn said. "What's with the televangelist? Is he her new boyfriend, or something?"

"Who knows?" I yawned. "She never tells me who she's going out with anymore. She thinks I'll judge her, or something."

"Well, she's right!" Dawn laughed. "She's not exactly the queen of good taste in the men department, you know."

"Hey! That's my oldest friend you're talking about, kid!" But I laughed too. Dawn was right — Carmen had a habit of choosing wildly unsuitable men, then being devastated when it didn't work out.

"Anyway, this is an about-face for her, isn't it? Wasn't she the one who told me religion was the something-or-other of the masses?"

"The opiate? Yeah, she probably did. But you know how she is — she goes through these cycles. This time she's found religion, that's all."

"Well, I wonder how long this one'll last?"

"Dawn, since when have you started being so judgmental about Carmen? You know she adores you."

"I don't know. There's just something ... odd about

it. It's like, she says one thing, then does the opposite. What am I supposed to think?"

I sighed. "I don't know. It's really none of our business, though, is it?"

"Maybe not. But I'll tell you one thing, Mom. I'm no astrologer, but even I can see that this relationship is headed for disaster."

2

MONDAY, DECEMBER 13
Sun square Jupiter ✦
Mercury conjunct Pluto ✦
Mars trine Uranus ✦
Saturn square Neptune ✦

Many people think astrologers live exotic, glamorous lives, consulting to the rich and famous, flitting from private dinners with Ronald and Nancy Reagan to interviews with Rosie O'Donnell and Oprah. Those people would be wrong.

My cramped office over the last remaining crunchy-granola style bakery on Bank Street was freezing when I got in. The landlord had presumably decided that since I was not likely to actually expire on him, presenting an inconvenient corpse to haul away, he might as well save some money by leaving the furnace at its lowest setting. Either that, or he'd forgotten to pay the gas bill. Again.

Still, despite the drafts whistling in through the leaky windows and the fact that I looked like the Michelin tire lady, bundled up in sweater upon sweatshirt upon turtleneck, I wasn't seriously thinking about moving my business elsewhere. For one thing, this place is cheap, and I'm kind of used to it.

As I ate my lunch on this particularly grey and chilly December afternoon, the chart in front of me got less than its full due. I couldn't seem to keep my mind from poking away at the events of Saturday night, the way you can't keep your tongue from prodding at a painful tooth. I kept wondering what had happened to Marion. If I knew which hospital she'd been sent to, I'd have called to check on her. Maybe Carmen would know? I should give her a call. Okay, as soon as I finished my sandwich, that's what I'd do. Pushing away from the desk, I closed my eyes and leaned back in my chair, trying to relax. Muffled Christmas music drifted upward, piped out from one of the small shops that line the street below my office. I turned up the volume on my radio and let a Mahler symphony drown out "Jingle Bells." I've been trying to get more cultured lately.

I was jolted out of my lunchtime reverie by the phone.

"Star-Dynamic, how can I help you?" I tried to swallow my mouthful of half-chewed whole-grain bread without choking on it.

"Yes, ma'am. Are you an astrologer?"

Young, male — I'd estimate late teens or early twenties. There was a slight quaver in his voice.

"Sure am," I said. "What can I do for you?"

"Well, ma'am," he coughed nervously, "are you aware that astrology defies the natural laws of God and Jesus Christ? The Bible, the sacred Word of God, specifically states -"

Oh, bloody hell. I hate these calls.

"Excuse me. Could I ask you to do me a favour?"

"What's that, ma'am?"

"Could you take me off your list? You guys spend way too much time calling me, and I keep telling you, I'm not interested."

The kid didn't seem to have heard me.

"Well, see, ma'am, I'm just calling to let you know that there are alternatives for people like you. If you just accept God's Word, you too can come into the fold and be embraced by Christ ..."

"You're not listening to me," I interrupted, louder this time. "I really don't care about your God, okay? Why don't you go harass someone else?"

I heard the rustle of paper; just as I suspected, he was reading from a prepared script.

"I think you should know, ma'am, that people such as yourself can expect to burn in hell for all eternity, unless you decide to for- ... forswear your Satanic practices now. It is the task of all right-thinking Christians to wipe your kind off the face of the planet. In the coming holocaust ..."

I hung up, wishing I'd done it earlier. This is what comes of trying to be nice.

These crank calls tend to come in clusters. I had gone maybe two months without a single one, and now I could probably expect ten in the next two weeks. Maybe I should consider getting a phone with call display so I'd know who was calling. On the other hand, I couldn't afford the additional expense. My monthly overhead was about all I could handle right now.

The air was growing ever more frigid in my office, although I had pried open the valves on the ancient radiators that sometimes, in the coldest weather, condescend to emit a faint warmth. No dice today, however. I used to use a small electric space heater, but when my father the engineer found out, he went into orbit about overloaded circuits and electrical fires and so on, so I gave it up. With a new client due to arrive soon, I decided to take my life in my hands and call the landlord.

"Yeah?" This is Keon's standard greeting when he sees my number on his phone display.

"John? It's Katy Klein. It's a little cool in the office today, and I've got clients due this afternoon. Do you think you could turn the furnace on?"

"It's on already."

"No, I don't think it is. The radiators are cold to the touch, John. It's close to freezing in here. I really don't want to have to call in the city inspectors again, but ..."

"Look, I said the furnace is on. It's on, okay? You don't like it, you can find another place to do your goddamn palm reading or whatever. For the rent you're paying, I don't need your shit."

I struggled to keep my voice calm. "So you're saying you aren't going to do anything about this?"

"You got it."

I sighed regretfully. "Then I'm afraid I'll have to have the city inspectors come in and check it out, because the furnace obviously isn't working. Shall I just have them send you the bill?"

Under the circumstances, I thought I was being remarkably calm and non-adversarial, but that didn't stop Keon from banging the phone down in my ear.

My next call was to the city inspectors' office. They agreed to have someone here within the hour, and I decided to warm myself in the interim by running downstairs to the bakery.

One of the foremost selling points of my rickety and cramped office is its location above Fruits of the Earth, an establishment specializing in whole-grain breads and muffins so chock-full of nutritious and delicious natural ingredients that they can actually be used as small doorstops. The smells wafting up from the bakery told me that their justly famous Whole Wheat Pesto Cheese Bread was just about to come out of the oven.

Joanie, the owner and primary baker, came to the front counter, brushing her purple hair from her eyes with the back of a floury hand. Her hair colour changes on a weekly basis; some of the local small business owners place bets on what it will be on any given Monday.

"Hey, Katy! How's things up there?"

"Freezing. My teeth are chattering, so I thought I'd get some warm bread. And do you have any coffee today?"

"Nope. I'm not selling it anymore. Poisons the system, you know. But I have some nice fennel tea, if you want it."

"The mind boggles. Never mind, I'll stick with the bread. Hey, when did you get the lip ring?"

"You like it?" Joanie grinned. "It was Shane's idea. We both got it done at the same time. We got nipple rings, too. Wanna see?"

I shook my head vehemently. "'Like' might be too strong a word," I said. "It's ... interesting. Didn't it hurt?"

"You sound just like my mom. She's all grossed out, too. But I told her she did the same thing back in the sixties — you know, long-haired hippie weirdo freaks and all that."

"Yeah, the sixties were definitely a hard act to follow. Listen, if the city inspector comes by, show him upstairs, would you? Keon is being a jerk about the heat again."

Joanie rang up my bread, and I warmed my chilled fingers on the fragrant loaf. I was halfway out the door when Joanie called me back.

"Hey — did that woman find you?"

"Woman? Which woman?"

"I dunno. Older than me, looked like a model, or something. Short black hair, and cheekbones to die for. Said she knew you."

"A model?" I didn't know anyone who fit that description. "No, no one's been by. Listen, if you see her again, get her phone number, okay? She might be a client. A paying client, if you get my drift."

I could use all the customers I could dredge up right now. Business had been slow since the summer, when everything had ground to a halt for a month or so. I'd foolishly allowed myself to become embroiled in a Nancy Drew shtick, chasing all over the countryside after a killer, and my heroics had cost me a fair chunk of business, not to mention peace of mind. Never again, I'd resolved.

"Sure, I'll try and nab her. And good luck with Keon. You're gonna need it."

I had just settled in upstairs when someone rapped at the door. It was the city inspector, a very large, extremely loud middle-aged man who assured me this was not the first Keon property he'd been compelled to visit recently. He stomped down to the bowels of the building, returning a few minutes later with cobwebs in his thinning hair. He swiped at his head with a beefy hand.

"I turned it on, ma'am." I took a step back to avoid having my eardrums blasted out. "Keon'll get our bill. Won't be too happy about that, I bet!"

"I certainly hope not. Hey, is there any way you guys can force him to keep the heat at a reasonable level? I mean all the time, not just when he feels like it?"

"Not much we can do." He shook his head ponderously. "I can serve him with a notice, but he'll just ignore it. All's you can do is keep calling us, we'll come out and turn it on for you any time you need it. And he gets the bill for our services. Fifty bucks a pop on weekdays, a hunnerd on weekends."

He winked and lumbered down the stairs, stopping at the bottom to clap a battered porkpie hat on his head.

I settled back into my chair and tried to finish my lunch. However, it was not to be.

Just as I took another bite from my sandwich, the phone rang again. This time I took a few seconds to chew thoroughly, and picked up on the fourth ring.

"Good afternoon, Star-Dynamic."

"Katy, she's dead!" It was Carmen, and she was sobbing.

"Who's dead? Carmen, what're you talking about?"

"Marion! You know –"

"You mean that woman from your party? *That* Marion?"

I dropped my sandwich onto the desk and lowered the volume on the radio. My mouth was suddenly dry.

"Y-yes," she stuttered, then took a deep breath to steady herself. "I just found out. Called the hospital to see how she was, and they said ... Oh God!" She wailed again, and I waited until her sobs died down. There

was no point trying to deal with Carmen in full histri-
onic mode.

"Carmen ... Carmen, it's okay. Tell me what happened."

"I called just a while ago, and that's how I found
out. That bastard Phil wasn't even going to tell us, I had
to find out from a complete stranger —"

"Carmen, slow down. I'm having trouble following
you. When did Marion die? What happened?"

"I don't know, exactly. Late last night, I think. She
never woke up from the seizures. They said she never
regained consciousness. Katy, it's just so awful ..."

"I know, it's terrible," I agreed. "But why wouldn't
Phil tell you about it?"

"That good-for-nothing," Carmen spat. "Weaselly
little bastard. He thought she was faking it, if you can
believe it. He told the doctor she did it all the time, just
to get attention."

"What kind of craziness is that? That was no faked
seizure, Carmen, I can tell you. You know, when I saw
them earlier in the evening, he was in the middle of
telling her she was dressed like a slut. Quote-unquote.
He seems like a real piece of work, that Phil."

"He's disgusting. And the worst of it is, she was
planning to leave him next week. He kicked their kid
out on the street, you know. Marion said that was the
last straw. She told me about it, not half an hour before
she started having that ... that seizure. Oh God, Katy, I
never even knew a person could die from seizures!
Have you ever heard of such a thing?"

"I've heard of it." My voice seemed disconnected
from me, as though someone else was speaking
through my mouth. "It's something called status
epilepticus. I had a patient at the hospital once who

nearly died from it. It can happen in a known epileptic who doesn't take their medication regularly. If you don't get meds into them really quickly, the brain starts to get deprived of oxygen. It's not a nice way to go."

Carmen was silent. I hoped she hadn't fainted or something.

"Carmen? You still there?"

"I'm here," she whispered. "Poor, poor Marion. I just can't believe ..." Her voice trailed off into a moan.

"Was she a friend of yours? I don't recall you mentioning her before," I said, trying to distract her.

"Oh, no, I wouldn't have. You remember that job I did, the church out in the west end? It was a big renovation, and they wanted the whole interior gutted and replaced. Well, Marion was the secretary there, that's all. She was always sweet to me, brought me tea and cookies. So the other day when I was out there, I thought what the hell, and I gave her an invitation. She said she didn't get out much, and I thought the party would give her a lift ..." She sniffled again.

"Oh, right, that church thing." Something clicked in the deep recesses of my brain. "And that's where you met Nigel, right?"

"Oh, him. Yes. But Katy, I was just trying to do poor Marion a favour — and look what happened! I can't help feeling a sense of responsibility."

"Responsibility? For what? Carmen, that's silly. She'd have had that seizure no matter where she was, you know. You didn't have anything to do with it." Impatience tinged my voice; Carmen had a nasty habit of making everything about her.

"What? Oh, yes, I suppose you're right." Carmen blew her nose loudly. When she spoke again, it was as if nothing had happened. "Well, listen Katy, sorry to

butt into your day like this, but I just had to tell someone about poor Marion. I was so upset!"

"Of course. But Carmen, there's something I don't
understand."

"What?"

"Well, about fifteen minutes before Marion started
seizing, I watched her take her meds. At least, she said
that's what it was."

"Are you sure?" Carmen's voice had a sharp edge.
"You saw her take the pills?"

"Yup. It's just odd, that's all. Someone who takes
their meds regularly shouldn't even have one seizure,
let alone go into status. She'd have to have been off her
meds for several hours, if she takes them on a tight
schedule. Twelve, at least, I'd say. And yet ..."

"Katy, there's probably stuff we don't know. Her
doctor told me it was just one of those things — could-
n't be helped."

"I guess. It's funny, though."

"Uh-huh. So — how's Dawn? She must be getting
ready for exams, right?"

"Actually, she's managed to get recommendations
for nearly all of them. Except geography — she says the
teacher puts her to sleep."

Carmen giggled. "Poor honeybun. Hey, wasn't that
an excuse you used when you failed chemistry way
back when?"

"Oh, don't remind me. You've known me way too
long, Carmen. Hey, why don't you come over for supper soon? Nothing special, but Dawn was asking after
you just the other day. We could catch up a bit."

Carmen checked her date book, and we settled on
Tuesday, the one day that week when she wouldn't
have a meeting to attend. Carmen is a meeting junkie,

the kind of person who just can't get along without some cause to which she can over-commit herself. So she heads the local branch of her professional organization, sits on the board of a committee to beautify the downtown core of the city, and belongs to an environmental group, a reading club and others I probably don't even know about. She spends her little free time complaining of exhaustion, but whenever she drops one commitment she instantly adopts another. She's been this way as long as I can remember.

I hung up and sat for a moment with my eyes closed. Marion couldn't have been older than thirty. Such a waste. I made a mental note to ask Carmen if there was going to be a funeral. I'd like the chance to say good-bye to Marion, even if I'd only known her a matter of minutes before she died. It seemed only right.

3

The rap on the door was so gentle that at first I thought it was just the wind rattling the windows.

"Hello? Anyone here?" The voice was soft, too, but it was directly outside my door.

I glanced at my watch. I wasn't expecting my next client until three o'clock, and it was now just past one. I pulled the door open, and my visitor jumped slightly.

"Hello!" The woman on my landing was bundled in a multicoloured jacket, handknit by the look of it, in brilliant jewel tones that set off her short black hair and dark blue eyes. This must be the woman Joanie had seen — she had the striking good looks of a model.

"Hi," I said, brushing a sandwich crumb from my mouth. "Can I help you?"

"You're Katy, right?"

"That's right. And you are ... ?"

"We met the other night. At that party ..."

Ah, now my brain was revving into action. "Of course! It's Diane, right? Come on in."

"Diana." She corrected me with a smile. "It's okay, I didn't really think you'd remember me. We only met for a few seconds. Right before all hell broke loose. Poor Marion. I heard she died in the hospital?"

"So I understand. You knew her?"

"Not well. She worked for my brother, so I saw her now and then. A nice lady."

"Well, I'm sorry. No one should have to die the way she did," I said. "Anyway, it's nice to see you again."

"Well, I'm not really here to talk about Marion. In fact, Carmen Capricci told me you're an astrologer. Is that true?"

The grey light filling my office accentuated the dark circles under her eyes.

"It is. Please, take a seat."

She dropped onto the futon couch, crossing her long legs at the ankle with casual grace. She shrugged off her jacket, but left it draped over her shoulders.

"So. Is it true what they say about astrologers? Can you really read my thoughts?"

I shook my head, laughing. "Nope. Can't even remember my own, half the time. But lots of people feel a bit nervous when they first come here. Take your time."

Diana didn't answer at first, but swept her cool glance around my office. I was aware, suddenly, of the shabbiness of the posters I'd tacked on the walls, the dust bunnies I'd neglected to harvest from under my desk.

"I don't really know why I'm here," Diana said, more to herself than to me. "Maybe this is a waste of time."

I said nothing.

"So?" She caught me in that studied gaze. "Tell me, Katy, is this a waste of my time? What am I doing here? You're the astrologer who knows all and sees all, aren't you?"

"Not exactly," I said. "But I think you already know

why you're here. That's not prescience — it's just plain common sense. Something made you think it would be a good idea to talk to me, and only you know what that something is." Ball's in your court, honey, I thought, with a degree of malicious satisfaction.

Something seemed to go out of her, and she sighed, leaning back against the futon. "You're right. There are some questions I need answered, and God knows I've tried every other way I can think of to figure them out. It's just that you don't seem very ... I don't know, I guess I was expecting someone with long red fingernails and a mole on her cheek, wearing a scarf. Someone who could tell me I'm not crazy, and everything's really fine."

"Hey, I don't even own a crystal ball," I said. "And my manicurist gave up on me a long time ago. But if you've got a question or two, I'll give it my best shot."

"You know, I'm a Christian — and we're not supposed to listen to soothsayers. Maybe this was a bad idea."

I was getting a little tired of this game. "Maybe you're right, Diana. Why don't you take some more time to think about it, and come back when you're ready? You shouldn't be here if it's making you uncomfortable."

"I'm not uncomfortable," she bristled. "It's just — no, I'd really rather stay, now that I'm here. What do you need to know?"

"Your birth date and time, and the place you were born. But only if you're sure."

"I am."

She wrote the information on a slip of paper from her purse, and handed it to me.

"Okay," I muttered, punching the data into my

computer, which rewarded me with a perfectly calcu-
lated chart. First time, every time.

Diana pulled her jacket more tightly around her
shoulders and rubbed her hands together. "Is it always
this cold in here? I can see my breath!"

I snorted. "Sorry. The guy from the city was just in
to turn on the heat. It should warm up soon."

I showed her the chart on the computer screen
and gave her the quickie overview — Aquarius Sun,
Gemini Moon. She'd need lots of freedom, but with her
Sun in the seventh house of marriage and partnership,
her need for intimacy would do battle with her wish
for independence.

"Just looking at that one set of influences," I said, "I'd
say that when you let a person get close to you, even if
it's someone you really care about, it can very quickly
start to feel like an invasion of your space, right?"

Diana eyed me suspiciously. "How do you know
this? Have you talked to Carmen about me?"

"I don't need to — it's all in the chart. Astrology is
just a language, and I'm an interpreter. Is this bothering you?"

"No. I'm fine. It's just that for years I was told
astrology was a black art — you know, a tool of the
devil. I don't believe everything I hear, though." She
gave me a tentative smile, which I returned in what I
hoped was an encouraging way. "Anyway, it feels weird
that you know so much about me, just from this little
chart." She fiddled with a button on her sweater.

"I admit, I don't understand it myself. I mean, I
have my theories, but I'm pretty sure I'm not in league
with the devil. Do you want to go on?"

"Sure." Her voice was confident, but her shoulders
remained tense.

"So tell me," I said, "are you married or in a relationship right now?"

"Can't you tell that from my chart?"

I carefully refrained from sighing. "No, I can't. I can tell how you might react in a relationship, but not whether there is one."

"Oh." She paused to digest this. "Well, okay. I've been thinking about getting involved with someone. I was hoping you could tell me whether it'll work out."

"Sure. We'll get to that in a second. But it looks like you've had trouble in past relationships already."

I pointed out Diana's fifth house, where loving Venus was ensconced in commitment-phobic Sagittarius. A notorious placement for those with allergies to long-term liaisons.

She laughed shortly. "Exactly. My ... partner and I were good together in a lot of ways, but I felt like I wasn't being heard when I said I wanted some space. People are constantly misinterpreting me."

"When all you needed was some air, right?"

"Exactly."

"Can I ask a personal question?"

"Why not?"

"The partner you mentioned — was that a woman?"

Diana shot me a strange look and hesitated a fraction of a second before answering.

"Yes — why?"

"Just wondering. It's not in your chart or anything, but you phrased it kind of vaguely."

"Well, there's a reason for that. No one in Ottawa knows about me, and I want to keep it that way, at least for now. My religious community isn't very ... tolerant."

"That must be a strain on you — with your Gemini Moon, you have a hard time keeping your ideas to yourself, don't you?"

She laughed, but without amusement. "Oh, yes. In fact, I'd say that's a major source of trouble for me. Have you ever heard of Serenity Haven?"

"I think so. It's a drug and alcohol rehab centre, isn't it?"

"Yes. My brother founded it a few years ago. I'm the new director — he hired me three months ago. The board is almost completely made up of members of his congregation, and believe me, they wouldn't take kindly to having a known pervert running their prize project. I'd be out on my ear in nothing flat."

"But that's against the law," I said, knowing even as the words exited my mouth that they sounded stupid.

"Of course it is. But they wouldn't say they were firing me because I'm a lesbian — they'd just say I wasn't handling my responsibilities well, or something. It's not fair, but it's the way things are."

"That sucks."

"It does, but it's not your concern. What else do you see?"

I showed her Mercury in Aquarius, and we talked about her original ideas, her need to keep her thoughts free of emotional baggage.

"Funny you should say that," she said. "I've always admired Mr. Spock, you know, identified with him. I want things to be rational. Feelings are just so ... so messy."

"Maybe, but don't you think they can also bring you joy?" I countered. "Emotions are part of the human equation, Diana."

"In my experience, joy is highly overrated. And rare. Sometimes it's easier to just stick to the rational. That way no one gets hurt."

We looked at her Moon/Mercury square, and I pointed out her tendency to resort to sarcasm when challenged.

"Yeah, I admit that. But sometimes people need to defend themselves."

"That's true, but from looking at your chart, I'd say you don't know your own strength — you can cause a lot of damage if you're provoked."

"Don't be ridiculous." Her voice was flat. "I've never hurt anyone in my life, and I'm not about to start. I abhor violence."

"I didn't mean just physical damage. Your tongue can be a powerful weapon, too, you know."

"Oh." She sat back, digesting this.

I waited quietly.

"All right, sometimes I do ... I mean, I get urges. To lash out. Not just with words — with force. I get so scared sometimes, because I know that if I really did hurt someone, I'd never forgive myself. I pray that God will help me stay in control, but ... it scares me. That's all."

"Sure, of course. But you've never done it, right? And if it scares you that much, you probably won't."

"What makes you think so?"

"Well, it's the people who don't consider the effects of their actions who are most likely to get into trouble. If I were you, I'd go a little easier on myself."

"Easy for you to say," she said. "You aren't living my life."

"True. But it sounds like there are more than enough people out there willing to judge you — why join the crowd?"

Diana curled her lip, and I thought for a moment she was going to say something cutting. She didn't, though.

"Let's just get on with this, okay?" She looked tired, and I noticed the purplish shadows under her eyes again.

"Are you sure? Do you want to take a break?"

"I'm fine."

"Astrology can bring up a lot of emotional stuff," I offered. "It can be hard if you're not expecting it."

"I don't know what I expected. But tell me what else you see."

"Sure. Here's Mars in the third house. I'd say you see your siblings as very powerful, driving forces. Did you have a lot of fights with them when you were younger?"

"Not just when we were younger," she said. "And I only have the one — Nigel. He's older than me, by ten years. Let's just say we don't always see eye to eye."

"Looking at your chart, I'd say he's a pretty energetic person."

"Energetic isn't the word. A fireball would be more accurate. He's only forty, but he's already started Serenity Haven, an old age home and a school, and he's on the boards of all of them. Plus, he and a group of his buddies at our old church decided they didn't like the way things were heading there, so they founded their own breakaway church. He's the minister there, and now he's getting this TV deal, too. Sometimes he makes me feel like a real slug."

"Well, you're no slouch either, Diana. Here, look at this." I pointed at her chart. "See here, you have Jupiter and Uranus right on your Ascendant. First, Jupiter is retrograde, so you need to work out your own belief system. When you pull in Uranus, the planet of radical thought, you have this urge to figure things out for yourself, no matter what anyone says. Now, put that on one of the most personal points in the chart, and that rebellion, that need to find your own truth, becomes a real driving force in your life."

"You're right on that one," Diana said. "And I think you know a great deal more about me than you should. What about the rest of my family?"

"Well here, in the fourth house — that represents your home, the family you were born into — you've got both Neptune and Saturn, so it looks as though you might have seen your mother through a kind of haze. It was hard for you to really figure out who she was. And there's a sadness, some kind of loss associated with your childhood."

No response, but Diana's cheeks blazed.

"You have Libra on the fourth house cusp, so I'd say you experienced your mother as beautiful and loving, but kind of distant or vague — like a fairy godmother."

"My mother died shortly after I was born." There was no trace of emotion in her voice.

"Oh, I'm sorry. I didn't mean to ..."

"It's fine. I've had some time to get used to it. Tell me more."

I drew a deep breath. "Okay. Wherever I see Saturn in a person's chart, that's where I look for a real sense of seriousness. As I said, that would be in your family. It's like you had to become an adult too quickly. There's a feeling of obligation there ..."

She cut me off. "Obligation, yes, that's the word. I always felt obligated. My father told me my mother sacrificed her life for me — how is a person supposed to live up to that? And now Nigel is this powerhouse, and what am I? Nothing."

"You don't think your work is important?"

"Sure, it's got its moments. Getting someone clean and sober is a great feeling, but it's not enough. And now that Nigel and I are living together ..."

"Pardon? Why would you –"

"Because I'm an idiot, that's why. Because I thought things might actually change between us. That's a laugh. When our father died last year, he left us both his house in Nepean. It's a nice enough place, but I wanted to sell it and split the profit — but Nigel wouldn't hear of it. He said Dad left us the house so we could reconcile with each other, and we had to at least give it a chance. How could I turn him down? He's my brother, after all."

She blew her nose discreetly and dabbed at her eyes with a tissue. "I just try to keep out of his way. When he asked me to move in with him, he made it sound like he really wanted to put our past behind us, but that's such a crock. I wanted to forgive him, but he hasn't changed since we were kids. And he's not going to, at this point."

"That must be ..." I searched for the word.

"Like having the life choked out of me? Yes." She grimaced. "It's hellish. He's always been controlling, but now he's constantly at me. He monitors my phone calls, vets my friends, keeps track of when I come in at night. Sometimes I'd just like to –" She stopped herself.

"Like to what?" I prompted, but she shook her head.

"It's not right. I shouldn't talk like this."

"Diana, don't you think it's better to let your feelings out than keep them bottled up?"

She smiled weakly. "Carmen did say you're a former shrink. You sound like one."

"Well, it's just common sense. If you have that many problems with your brother, you should air them out. Otherwise, someone's bound to get hurt."

"Let's stick to the astrology, okay? No offense, but I don't need anyone analyzing my life for me."

"Sure."

"Oh, now I've offended you."

"Not at all," I lied. "I shouldn't butt in where my advice isn't wanted."

Diana closed her eyes and leaned back against the futon couch, arching her back and stretching like a cat. "Well, there's one place where I could use some of your sage advice."

I said nothing, waiting for her question.

"Here goes. Everyone thinks Nigel is so damn wonderful, and I guess he is, but he's been a thorn in my side my entire life. I've never known what it would be like not to have this great and glorious older brother around, making me feel like I'm a piece of dirt. So what I want to know is — will there be a time in my life when I'll be free of him?"

"You mean, when he'll stop having such a strong effect on you?"

"I guess. Yeah, that's more or less it. The only problem is, I can't see that happening until ... until he's dead. There, I've said it. Can you tell me when Nigel is going to die and get the hell out of my life?"

I drew a deep breath and framed my words carefully. "I know you want out of this situation, Diana. I understand that completely. But astrology has some pretty well-defined limits. Predicting death is one of them. It's partly an ethical issue, but it's practical, too.

I can't say when he'll die, because death shows up differently for each person. I don't think I can help you."

"I should have known," she said, studying her long, thin hands. She stretched them out, then balled them into fists, the knuckles turning white. "Thanks anyway."

"Sorry. But I can draw up a chart of some general trends over the next little while. That might help you figure out where you're going."

"Sure, whatever," she said, glancing at her watch. "Our time must be up, right?"

She stood up. I was reminded of a cheetah, all long legs, poised and graceful, ready to dash. Turning to go, she extended her hand and I shook it.

She slid out the door and down the stairs, providentially just moments before the rock came through the window.

4

I had just closed the door behind Diana and was heading for a much needed bathroom break when I felt rather than heard the clatter of something heavy bursting through the glass behind me. Then a whoosh of frigid air swept into the room. I whirled around, my heart pounding, and stared stupidly at the hole in the window.

It took me several moments to determine exactly what had happened, and it wasn't until I saw the large chunk of granite on the floor that I clued in. Shards of broken glass littered the floor. In the movies, the rock would have had a note attached to it, something to indicate that it was not just a random visitor that happened to drop in. This rock, though, brought no clues.

I fetched a cardboard file folder and the whisk broom from under the bathroom sink and mechanically swept up the shards of glass, emptying them into my wastepaper basket. Then I found some masking tape and patched the hole in the window as best I could. It was cold enough in here already, thank you very much. Finally, I called the police.

The neighbourhood patrol officer rubbed his chin thoughtfully as he contemplated the rock on my floor.

"You say it just landed here?"

I nodded.

"And it broke that window over there?"

I nodded again.

"Where's the glass?"

"I cleaned it up. It was all over the place, and I didn't want to step on it and cut myself."

"Lady, I'll tell you something. You mess around with the evidence, we can't do our job. You know the term 'tampering with evidence'? Good thing this isn't a really big deal -"

I interrupted him. "Not a big deal? According to whom? Listen, some yahoo threw a rock through my office window. Someone could have been hurt, you know."

The officer looked annoyed. "But no one was, were they? Now, this is a second storey office," he said, as though I hadn't spoken. "Whoever threw the rock must have a strong pitching arm. And good aim."

He stepped over to the window and looked down at the street. "Look, over there." He pointed.

I looked. Across the street there is a small park, one of those treeless patches of grass and concrete where old geezers gather in the summer to play chess, gossip and smoke foul-smelling European cigarettes. Right now, the lot was empty.

"To heave that rock all the way up here, someone would have to be standing in the park," the officer said. "Just judging by the trajectory."

Sounded good to me.

"But I don't understand why someone would go to all that trouble." I tried to keep the whining undertone out of my voice. "I mean, why me?"

"Can you think of anyone who'd have a grudge? Anyone who's mad at you?"

Suddenly I felt like I was the one under suspicion. Of what? Cultivating enemies? I don't cultivate them; they just happen. I shook my head.

"I can't – Oh. There was this guy who phoned me and called me a Satanist earlier today. He said it was the task of right-thinking Christians to rid the world of people like me."

The cop raised his eyebrows. "Now why would anyone call you a Satanist?"

"I'm an astrologer. Some people get that mixed up with witchcraft or something. Religious nuts, mostly. I get these calls from time to time."

"Well, I'll put that in my incident report. Anything else happens, you be sure and let me know, okay?"

"Believe me, you'll hear about it."

"And you better call your landlord, get him to replace the window," the cop said.

"Easier said than done. My landlord's one of those guys who doesn't think much of me."

"Well, you'd better get it fixed, or you're going to freeze your ... you're going to get pretty darn cold. They're forecasting snow for tonight, you know."

When the officer had left, I sat for several minutes on my couch. Tears prickled at the back of my eyes, but I fended them off. It had been a hell of a day, so far, and it was only mid-afternoon.

My three o'clock client didn't seem particularly fazed by the boarded-over window, which may say something about how my decorating skills in general are perceived. I managed to make it through the rest of the day without any more untoward incidents, and by four-thirty, I was more than ready to pack it in.

In the waning light, I pulled on my anorak, found my fleece gloves where I had inexplicably shoved them into a filing basket, switched on the answering machine and left the office. The sky had been heavy with snow all day, and now the first few hesitant flakes had begun to spiral down. I pretended not to see them, hoping to delay winter's onset by sheer force of will.

Except in the very worst weather, I walk the fifteen or so blocks from my office to my home, an apartment in what remains of Ottawa's central core. As in most North American cities, "downtown Ottawa" has become something of an oxymoron. Each month I pass more and more empty windows, defunct shops and boarded-up businesses strewn like dominoes the length of Bank Street. Apparently, no one on our city's main drag has noticed the recent alleged "economic recovery".

Why do I live in Ottawa? This is a question I ask myself frequently. In fact, I don't understand why anyone ever settled in this part of the world in the first place. Who in hell would voluntarily set down stakes in a land where the summers are chokingly humid and hot, the winters breathtakingly cold and piled with snow, and autumn and spring last no more than three days per year?

Yet here we stay, perverse and stubborn, complaining about the weather, constantly threatening to just chuck it all and head for balmy British Columbia, or even the U.S. We speak half-admiringly, half-disdainfully of people who've actually fled for the West Coast. They're the ones who can't hack it here, the wimps. We take pride in our ability to endure, to adapt, to survive. Maybe that's a good thing.

For me, this city has been home since I was five years old, so I suppose it could be argued that I stay because I don't know better. If you put the climate aside for a moment, it's not a bad place to live. Ottawa can be viewed either as a small town with cosmopolitan pretensions, or as a city that hasn't yet figured out it's no longer a small town.

The snow was falling more purposefully now, swirling in tiny tornadoes along the street, gathering strength and volume, whisked along by a brisk northerly wind. Flakes glittered in the headlights of passing cars. At first the snow tickled my face softly, but then it began to sting as the storm grew more forceful. I picked up the pace and nearly jogged the last couple of blocks home.

Inside the foyer of my apartment building, I shook myself off, brushing caked snow from the creases in my anorak. I live on the ground floor of an old three-storey house, circa 1863, which has been converted into small yet reasonably comfortable apartments.

Peter, my ex-husband, lives on the second floor. When our marriage first ended, we worried about living so close together, but we'd agreed to chance it for the sake of our daughter. Over the years, it has worked out well, and Dawn has never felt the need to choose between her parents, the way some kids have to. This is one of the few parts of my life in which I feel I have behaved with undiluted maturity.

As I stamped and shook in the foyer of our apartment, I caught a glimpse of Sylvie, Dawn's best friend, sprawled across my ancient armchair, her short, obsidian hair contrasting strangely with her fair complexion and much lighter eyebrows. She wore beige checked polyester knit pants that looked as though her father might have sported them in better days, and a V-necked sweater in one of those vile seventies colours like burnt orange. But I was used to her fashion choices. What startled me was her silence. Sylvie is never silent, at least not voluntarily. Was she ill?

A younger girl huddled on the floor, her knees drawn up to her chin. Though the bottom half of her face was obscured by — oh, dear lord, could those be wide-legged corduroys? — her eyes, dark and sullen, stared into space. Her hair was bleached the colour of sun-dried straw and had about the same texture. It was short, ragged and straight; by my estimation, another round of peroxide might finish it off altogether. The girl's right eyebrow had been pierced in several places, the holes filled with silver hoops.

Dawn crouched next to her, speaking into her ear in a low and earnest voice. My daughter is a lovely young woman who has not yet experienced the urge to chop off, dye or otherwise mutilate her dark blonde hair. However, she has fallen victim to seventies mania recently, and I am proud to say I have kept my mouth clamped firmly shut.

She was wearing one of those gaudy multicoloured nylon knit clingy shirts, the ones that stick to the skin and flatter virtually no one. I pretended not to notice.

I cleared my throat and Dawn jumped up to greet me with a hug, pulling me into the room to meet Sylvie's young cousin, Rose.

"Hi, Rose, glad to meet you."

I held a hand awkwardly down to the young woman, who turned her head away and squeezed her eyes shut. Charmed, I'm sure. Okay, I'm cool, I can handle rejection. I tried another tack.

"How's it going, Sylvie?"

Normally, to ask Sylvie a question like that is to guarantee at least a fifteen-minute monologue, but today even Sylvie looked subdued.

"I'm fine, Mrs. Klein. How about you?" she murmured politely.

"Mom, can I see you for a sec?" Dawn looked anxious.

I cocked a curious eyebrow. "Sure, honey. Let me just get some of these layers off."

Dawn followed me into my bedroom, where I stripped off my Fair Isle sweater, last year's Hanukkah gift from my mother.

"What's up, kiddo?"

"Listen, I did something I know you won't like," she began. "I took the day off school ..."

"What!" Despite myself, I screeched. "Dawn, this is no good — you can't just ..."

"Mom, Mom, just listen, okay?" Dawn lowered her voice to a whisper. "I did it for a good reason. I meant to call and tell you, but things just got too crazy. Sylvie and I came home after homeroom because Rose needed us. She told Sylvie she was going to cut herself up — like, slash her arms up, or something! She had the razor blade all ready and everything."

"That little girl out there in the living room? Why on earth would she do that?"

"She won't talk about it. We went downtown, you know, 'cause she called Sylvie before breakfast from a payphone at some drop-in or something. Sylvie asked around a bit, and finally we found her, but she won't talk much to me. She whispers to Sylvie once in a while, and that's it. She agreed to come here, but she keeps saying she's going to leave. I've been trying to keep her here till you got back."

"Dawn, this is something for an adult to handle, not a couple of teenagers. Why didn't you just call me, or better yet, Rose's parents?"

"I wanted to, I really did. But Sylvie says Rose's dad was the one who kicked her out in the first place. He sounds like a major-league asshole, Mom. Sylvie called him, and he said he doesn't care what Rose does. He says she's acting like a spoiled little bitch, just like her mother. Sylvie told me he used to beat Rose's mother, and her too, probably. Oh, and now her mom is dead. No wonder the poor kid doesn't want to go home."

"What about Sylvie's mother? Does she know what's going on?"

"We called her, as soon as we got Rose back here. She's been working the night shift, so she asked us to keep Rose here until she got up. She said you should call her when you got home."

Great. If there's one person in the world who talks more than Sylvie, it's her mother, Greta. I need this? Yeah, like a *loch in kop*, a hole in the head.

"Dawn, I really wish you'd called me about this. If Rose really is thinking of hurting herself, she needs professional help."

"But you *are* a professional, Mom! You're a psychologist, you could talk to her. Couldn't you?"

I said nothing.

"Well, couldn't you?"

I drew a deep breath. "Listen, honey. I used to be a psychologist. Then some things happened at the hospital, and I decided to leave. That's when I started doing astrology for a living. You remember that, right?"

"Sure! But you still have all your training and stuff, don't you?"

"Rose needs more than what I can give her. She needs a safe place to stay, and people to watch over her to make sure she doesn't hurt herself. If she's cutting herself, she needs to be in a hospital, Dawn. Or a group home. Someplace safe."

"Well, what about Greg? He still works at the hospital, right? He'd come if you asked him to. The thing is, if we mention the hospital, Rose is going to really freak — she's only young, you know. Thirteen. She's really scared, Mom!"

"Dawn, you can't rescue the world," I started, but she cut in.

"I'm not trying to rescue the world, I'm trying to help one kid who doesn't have anyone else. You're the one who's always saying we have to look out for people less fortunate and all that. Have you changed your mind, or what?"

How does this kid always know exactly where to aim? My head started to throb. I rubbed a temple distractedly.

"Okay, okay. You're right. I'll call Greg and see if he can come. But if he says she needs to be hospitalized, she's going in. No ifs, ands or buts. Got it?"

"Got it. And Mom, I've been thinking. Rose shouldn't just be on the street, especially at this time of year. Do you think she could stay with us for a while? That is, if she doesn't have to go to the hospital?"

"I really don't think that would work. For one thing, we don't have the space —"

"But she can stay in my room," Dawn begged. "I'll sleep on the couch. Really, Mom, it'll be fine."

"I wasn't finished, Dawn. You can't just take kids off the street, as if they were stray kittens or something. If her parents can't or won't care for her, the Children's Aid has to be informed. They'll decide who's best suited to care for her. And given our circumstances, I don't think it's going to be us."

Dawn's face fell. "Mom, she's really in rough shape. She needs us."

"I know, honey, and I do feel for her. But it's not as simple as you'd like to think." I sat heavily on the bed, and pulled on my slippers. "How about this? She can stay here for tonight, and I'll talk to the Children's Aid in the morning. I think that's the best we can do, Dawn."

"Okay. I guess."

"Okay. Now come on — if we're going to start running a house for wayward street kids, we'd better get some supper on. Why don't you go start some pasta, and I'll see if I can reach Greg. And Greta, I suppose."

I called Greta first, keeping my voice low so Rose wouldn't overhear. This put me at a disadvantage with Sylvie's mother, though. To have any kind of conversation with her, you need to be assertive bordering on rude. A megaphone helps.

Greta picked up on the first ring.

"Katy! How are you? I was thinking about you when I saw that doctor — what was his name? — anyway, the one who was fooling around with the patients at the Royal, you know, who got arrested last fall — I heard they've stripped him of his license now, and he could be looking at a long jail term, the bastard. Didn't you work for him at one time? I thought I remembered that."

"Yes, but that's not why —" I began.

"No, you're calling about Rosie, the poor little thing. She's such a mess already, I don't know how she's going to deal with her mother's death, you know?" Greta's voice quavered, then righted itself. "It's a tragedy, we just couldn't believe it. My baby sister, gone, just like that! So sudden, and no warning at all. I guess you just can't tell about these things. You know, she took her medicine every day of her life, since she was a little kid, but you just can't tell with something like that. The doctors said they didn't understand why the stuff she was taking stopped working, but there you go, you just don't know when your time will come, do you?"

"Greta, what are you talking —"

I tried to break in, but it was like farting against thunder. She just rolled on.

"...Horrible, horrible, they said she was in one long seizure for hours, and then her brain just kind of stopped working or something. I don't understand all that medical stuff, but we never knew she could actually die from it — it was just this thing she had, you know? No one ever thought anything of it."

Greta paused to blow her nose, and I seized my chance.

"Greta, what are you talking about? Whose brain stopped working?"

She let out a shriek, and I nearly dropped the phone.

"Oh, my God," she wailed. "You didn't know? Oh, God, the poor thing, the poor little thing..."

"Greta, please! What are you talking about?"

"Well, this past weekend, Marion went to some fancy party, and I don't know what happened, maybe she drank too much or something, that's what the doctor said. She had some kind of epileptic seizure, just like she used to have when we were kids, but this time it went on too long, and she died. Just like that. And poor little Rose, that slug of a father of hers kicked her out on the street a couple of days ago – and now she's got no mother, either. They were always so close, you know, when she was a little girl. I don't know what happened between them, but it's a shame, it really is..."

"Wait a second!" My head was spinning. "Are you telling me that Marion is Rose's mother? Marion, the woman who died at Carmen's party on the weekend?" Despite myself, the image of the woman convulsing on the floor hit me forcefully, and I swallowed back my bile.

"Yes, exactly! At the party! Oh, you know her? Our poor little Marion..." Greta paused, her voice suddenly small. "Well, you must know the whole story, then – so awful, just awful. I just can't believe she's not coming back, you know? I keep expecting her...no, never mind, I don't want to be morbid." She seemed to be running out of steam.

"Greta, does Rose know her mother's dead?" I whispered, not wanting the girls in the living room to hear.

There was a longish silence. "I don't know. I told Sylvie last night when I found out, and told her to bring little Rosie back here today when I woke up. But Sylvie says Rose doesn't want to come, she's just sitting in a heap on the floor, so that's why I wanted you to phone me. You know, I just don't know what to do, Katy! It's not bad enough that I've got kids to feed and an ex who thinks court orders are a joke, and a job that's sapping the life out of me – now my baby sister is dead, and her daughter is living on the street! It's too much, it's just too much..." Her voice broke, and she blew her nose, thankfully aiming away from the phone receiver. Then she continued.

"Katy, you're much better at this sort of thing than I am. You could talk to her, help her through it, you know. I just can't bear it...just thinking about how close they were..." Greta's voice shot up several octaves, and she was crying again.

I waited for a decent interval, but when she hadn't stopped after five minutes or so, I intervened, as gently as I could. "Greta, I know this is hard on you, but I need to understand what you're asking me to do. I can't just go out to some kid I've never met before, and tell her her mother is dead, can I? Who's supposed to pick up the pieces afterward, Greta? This just isn't right. She should be with her family right now, with people who know her and love her. Especially if she's already suicidal to begin with —"

"Suicidal!" Greta gasped. "What? What do you mean? Who told you she was —"

I spoke slowly, as though to a young child. "Greta, Dawn told me that Rose was going to slash her wrists this morning. Isn't that why you let Sylvie go off looking for her?"

"Well, yes – but she's not suicidal, for God's sake! She just – she cuts herself, you know? It's some kind of fad thing, that's what Marion told me. She sent Rose to this kiddy psychiatrist last summer, and he told her not to get too exercised about it. Young kids, you know, they cut themselves up...I don't know, I think it's disgusting, but he said it would be okay, if Marion spent some extra time with her or something."

"Oh." That put a different face on it. Self-mutilation isn't pretty, but it's not life-threatening, either. "So...what now, Greta?"

"Well, I haven't had time to think much since...since I heard about Marion. It's just so hard, you know...my baby sister..."

More crying. I've never had a sibling, so I couldn't even begin to imagine what Greta must be feeling, but my main concern right now was for Rose. "Greta, please, we've got to think about this. Rose needs some stability right now, of all times..."

Greta's sobs eased off again. "Well, that's why I thought – I mean, if you're up to it, I wondered if you could do me a huge favour..."

I waited.

"Rosie is a good girl, really," Greta continued. "She puts on a tough act, but she's a sweetheart under it all. I'd take her myself, in a flash, but you know I've already got two teen-age kids in this tiny apartment, and it's not easy, with Billy eating me out of house and home already. And Joe, that's my ex, he hasn't paid a penny in support since he left, two years ago. So I was thinking, maybe Rose could stay with you for a few days, just until Marion's funeral is over, and we can work out something better for her."

"Well, actually, I'm not so sure that's a good idea," I began, but I was forgetting: Greta is a pro.

"But Katy, don't you see, it's the only solution?" she cut in. "She'll stay with you and Dawn for a little while, and afterward, we'll find her a good place to stay. Someplace where she'll be happy, poor thing. I know how good you are with kids — you just have a little talk with her, and I'm sure you'll be able to get her to listen to reason. Sure, she's a little wild, but you can handle that, with your professional experience, right? I have to say, even though Marion was my sister and I loved her to death — oh, my God, did I really say that? How awful, that was just awful — but you know, Marion really did spoil that child. Anything she wanted, she got, even when they really couldn't afford it, and she never made her do chores around the house, you know, you can't raise a child like that and then turn around and expect them to cope with reality like an adult, now can you? Rose just needs a little talking to, and I'm sure you can turn her right around in no time. With all your training, I'm sure you must be good at that," Greta finished brightly.

My head was reeling, as it usually does when I speak to Sylvie's mother for longer than about five seconds. Was I really allowing myself to be shanghaied into playing therapist and den mother to a depressed, sulky thirteen year old semi-orphan? As I hung up I silently cursed Greta, Dawn, Sylvie, Rose, and the horses they rode in on.

I dialled Greg's number next. As I'd expected, he was still at work, and Val, his secretary, answered for him.

"Sorry, Katy, he's with a patient now. And he's got a seven o'clock flight to catch — he's going to a meeting in Toronto."

"Okay, don't bother him." I fiddled with the phone cord. "This isn't all that urgent. But do you know when he's due back?"

"Tomorrow morning. He's got a couple of patients booked, but he's free at four. Should I get him to give you a call?"

"Sure. Thanks, Val. And if I don't talk to you before, have a good Christmas, okay?"

I hung up, a bit dispirited. Greg wasn't going to be able to rescue me from this one — I was on my own. I drew a deep breath, girded my loins (I've never known exactly what that means, but it sounds like the kind of thing to do before broaching her mother's death with a suicidal runaway) and returned to the living room.

Dawn stood in the kitchen stirring fresh pasta into a pot of boiling water. Sylvie was still sprawled in my armchair, and I jerked my head toward her, summoning her to the bedroom.

"Hi, Mrs. K.," she said, as I closed the door behind us. She stood uncertainly by the bed, until I gestured her to sit.

"Hey, Sylvie. Rough day, huh?"

She nodded, tears forming in her eyes. "The worst." She slumped forward, her knees nearly touching her chin, and began fiddling with my duvet cover, rubbing it back and forth between green-nailed fingers. I resisted the urge to stop her.

"Sylvie, I was just talking to your mom. She says you know about your aunt dying?"

"Uh-huh. She told me. Last night."

"And what does Rose know about it?"

Sylvie turned her head from me, eyes downcast. "Nothing. Mom wanted me to bring her home, but she wouldn't go. She thinks my mom's going to stick her in a home or something, I don't know. Sometimes I think Rose is kind of out of it, you know? My mom would never do something like that."

"I'm sure she wouldn't. So — what happened after Rose refused to go home with you?"

"Well, she kind of freaked out, you know? She was, like, clawing at me — see?" Sylvie pulled back her sleeve to show me the fingernail marks. "So Dawn and I thought we could just keep her here for a while. Dawn didn't think I should tell her about her mom, you know, 'cause it would just make her worse, but I didn't think it was right, her not knowing. So I tried..."

"You told her?"

"I tried to tell her, Mrs. K. Really. But she wouldn't listen to me. She started screaming and moaning, like a crazy person, and she said I was lying. Then she said she was going to cut herself if I didn't shut up, and she showed me the razor blade she uses. Like, she cuts her arms and stuff, y'know? It's freaky."

"Does she do that a lot?"

Sylvie nodded. "She used to bang her head, when she was little. Her dad told her to stop or he'd bang it for her. So she stopped, but then she started cutting herself. And burning, sometimes. With cigarettes, you know? She showed me, the first time, and I told my mom, and everyone freaked about it for a while, you know — they tried to send her to the Royal, but they said she wasn't fucked up — I mean, they said she wasn't sick enough. So she came home, and it seemed like she'd stopped doing it. But a few weeks ago, I saw she had these, like, bandage things on her arms. And I knew she'd started cutting again."

"Did she say why?"

Sylvie shook her head. "No. Just that it made her feel better to let the blood out. And she says it doesn't hurt. I just think it's weird, y'know?"

I closed my eyes for a moment. My head was throbbing. I drew a deep breath.

"Sylvie, has anyone talked to the Children's Aid about Rose? You know, about a group home or foster care or anything?"

"I'd be afraid to say anything about that," Sylvie said, lowering her voice to a whisper. "Rose'd think we were going to have her put away. She's got this major thing about being put away. You know, her dad did it to her mom, and then he tried to do it to her, too..."

"Her dad did what to her mom?"

"Had her put away!" A note of impatience crept into her voice. "You know — committed. Locked up. He sent her to the loony bin."

"He did? What for?"

Sylvie shrugged. "He's one sick puppy, if you ask me. He's always pulling shit – doing stuff like that. Rosie hates him."

"Okay, thanks, Sylvie. I'm going to go talk to Rose now."

"Good. That's what Mom said you'd do." Sylvie looked pleased. How come everyone seemed to assume I'd handle this?

Rose sat precisely where we'd left her, her head sunk into her knees. Was she even awake? I perched on the edge of the chair next to her, and leaned over to speak to the top of her head.

"Rose?"

No answer. She was so still that I watched for a few moments, to make sure she was breathing. She was.

"Rose, my name is Katy. I'm Dawn's mother. Could we talk for a minute?"

Silence.

"I have to tell — I mean, there's something we have to talk about. And I need to know that you can hear me. Can you?"

Did I detect a slight shift in her body? She might have moved her head, but I couldn't tell if she'd nodded or not.

"That's good." I was going to assume she'd acknowledged me. "Rose, Dawn's cooking supper. Are you hungry?"

Nothing.

"Well. Listen, I talked to your aunt just now, and we agreed that you can stay here for a while, if you want to. What do you think about that?"

A single brown eye peered out at me from behind a screen of over-processed blonde hair. Barbie-doll hair. The eye blinked. What did that mean?

I tried to looked sympathetic and helpful. My temples throbbed.

"Okay, at least we know you're in there." I grinned encouragingly.

The head lifted a little, and a second brown eye became visible. Eyeliner had been applied with a heavy hand, but it had melted long since, ringing her eyes with black goop.

"Leave me alone," came a raspy whisper.

I sat back, unsure of what to say next. Where, oh where was Greg when I needed him? And whose brilliant idea had it been to leave me in charge of this kid?

"Rose, I know things look bad right now," I started, sounding pretty lame even to my own ears. "But could you please let me try to help you?"

"Why?"

"Because you look like someone who needs help."

"I'm fine. Leave me alone."

"Well, if you're so fine, what are you doing here?"

As soon as the words left my mouth, I regretted them. Rose started to scramble to her feet, and I put a restraining hand on her shoulder.

"Let me go!" She screamed and thrashed away from me, wild-eyed. "Don't you touch me! Don't touch me!"

I pulled my hand away as though I'd been scalded. Rose was on her feet now, tripping and stumbling toward the front door.

"Rose! Stop!" I mustered all my adult authority, and hollered at the top of my lungs. It didn't stop her, but she slowed down, and turned to look at me, as though for the first time.

"What do you want from me?" She stood, poised for flight, one hand on the front doorknob.

"I just want to talk to you, Rose. Just to talk to you. It's been a hell of a day, hasn't it?"

Her face crumpled, and she leaned back against the door, averting her eyes from mine. I crossed the room and stood near her, not touching her.

Slowly, she slid her back down the door, landing in a heap on the floor. I crouched next to her. Tears formed in the corners of her eyes, and a hank of hair flopped into her face. Slowly, not wanting to frighten her, I reached out and stroked the hair away from her forehead. Rose grabbed my hand in her own small one. The grubby nails with their chipped black polish looked like a child's. A little kid, playing at being tough.

She began trembling and sobbing, grief rattling through her small frame in monstrous gusts. The news of her mother's death could wait. I sat with her on the floor, letting her grip my hand and weep silently.

✦

True to her word, Dawn sacrificed her own bed to Rose and spent the night on our too-short, too-lumpy couch. Rose wouldn't eat supper, but she did allow herself to be led to Dawn's bedroom, where she climbed into bed fully clothed. She lay passively, eyes shut, as I covered her with a duvet.

In the living room, Dawn was wriggling around on the couch, trying in vain to find a comfortable position to sleep. I sat on the edge of an overstuffed armchair and we spoke in hushed voices, so as not to disturb Rose.

"She's so skinny," Dawn said. "You can practically see through her."

"Well, how long has she been living on the street?"

"I don't know. Only a couple of days, I think — but Sylvie says she ran away from home a couple of times last fall. They found her staying in some church or something. The minister was friends with her mother, and sent her home."

"Seems like an odd place to run away to," I said, more to myself than to Dawn. "Most kids head downtown, I would have thought."

"Well, her family's big on religion. Not her dad so much, but her mom for sure. And Rose is only thirteen, so maybe the idea of living on her own downtown scared her too much. Sylvie says Rose's mother babied her all the time."

"What about her father?"

"He's a real asshole, Mom. A major-league jerk. He was the one who threw her out of the house — he told her to leave and not come back until she could start acting right. She's just a kid, you know! Goddamn moron — what does he think she's going to do, living on the street?"

"Dawn, how many times do I have to tell you to watch your swearing?" I sighed, and Dawn grinned, unrepentant.

"Sorry, Mom, I forgot. Well, anyway, he is. An ass- ... I mean, a jerk. She can't go back to him, that's for sure."

"You want to know something strange? Rose's mother was the woman I told you about, the one at the party. She died yesterday, in hospital. Carmen told me. Funny that I should be there for her death, and now this."

"The one who collapsed or whatever? Her?" Dawn's eyes bulged in disbelief. "That's just too weird, Mom."

"That's the one. She had epilepsy, and she had a

really big seizure. The oxygen supply to her brain got cut off. Carmen said she never woke up from the seizure."

"I knew she was dead, but I didn't know who she was. God, that's horrible."

"Sylvie said she tried to break it to Rose this afternoon, but she wouldn't listen. Threatened to cut herself, so Sylvie backed right off."

"Yeah, she told us she wanted to hurt herself, but we took turns watching her so she wouldn't."

A lump of pride formed in my throat, and I reached out and tousled Dawn's hair. "That's my girl," I said. "You know, I'm really proud of you for handling this. Even though you should have called me."

"Yeah, well." Dawn looked embarrassed, and changed the subject. "She can't go home now, that's for sure. We called her father this morning. What a loser. Sylvie told him Rose was thinking about cutting herself again, and he said to tell her to go ahead and do it. He didn't care. Sylvie says he was drinking or something — his voice was all blurry."

"Well, I'll speak with him tomorrow. Maybe I can catch him before he has a chance to get half corked. If it's as bad as all that, we're going to have to find a permanent place for Rose to live. She can't stay here forever."

Dawn's looked stricken.

"She's not a stray kitten, Dawn. And she self-mutilates. That's hard for anyone to handle — she needs professional help. I'm going to have to phone the Children's Aid."

"No, no, you can't do that! They'll put her in some kind of home or something, and she'll be just miserable ..."

"Hey, we're not talking about monsters, sweetie. If Rose has to be taken into care, the Children's Aid will try their best to find her something that works. There are group homes, but there are also families who can take teenagers with problems. Or they might ask Sylvie's mom or some other relative to help out. I'm just saying there should be some options for Rose. Poor kid, she's going to need all the help she can get."

"She could stay here for a while, though, couldn't she? She could move into my bedroom here, and I could stay upstairs at Dad's," Dawn volunteered.

"Sweetheart, I barely make enough to support the two of us now — how am I supposed to stretch that to cover another mouth?"

"I thought of that already," said my resourceful daughter. "One of the kids at school lives in a foster family, and she says the government or someone pays her foster parents to look after her. She says they actually make money off her. And we'd treat Rose better than Kim's fosters treat her, that's for sure."

She sounded so certain, so determined to make things work. I wanted to laugh, but tears prickled behind my eyes.

"Dawn, I don't want to make money looking after Rose. I just want to find her a place where she'll be reasonably happy. We can't fix her problems. She's lost her mother, and her father isn't going to be much help. We can't change that. All we can do is try to help her start over."

Dawn's shoulders slumped. "I guess."

I rubbed her back through her flannel nightgown. "It'll be okay, honey. You'll see."

That night I sat propped up in bed reading a Margaret Atwood novel. It was about a motherless girl with an uncaring father who drank the family into misery and left the kid to fend for herself. This was getting to be a theme.

5

TUESDAY, DECEMBER 14
Moon square Neptune, opposition Saturn ✦
Sun square Jupiter ✦
Mercury conjunct Pluto ✦
Mars trine Uranus ✦
Saturn square Neptune ✦

The early light that crept into my bedroom seemed abnormally luminous, and even with my eyes only half open, I knew that last night's snow had stuck. The world had that peculiar soft, muffled quality that comes with a fresh snowfall, and I knew that if I looked out our front window, I would see an unploughed street, buried sidewalks. I decided not to look.

Dawn had moved the cushions from the couch to the floor, creating an impromptu nest for herself. She still snored softly, only the top of her head visible amongst the blankets. I skirted around her and made for the kitchen, where the coffeemaker beckoned. She woke and mumbled something as my nightgown brushed past her.

"What, dear?" I asked, preoccupied with measuring coffee and pouring water.

"I said, how's Rose?"

"Don't know. She's not up yet."

"I'll go."

The apartment was still shaking off its nighttime chill, so Dawn wrapped herself in a blanket and gently nudged the door to her room.

"Rose? ... Rose?" Then, louder, "Mom! She's not here!"

I shook my head impatiently.

"Hang on, Dawn, I'll be right there. She's probably just in the bathroom or something."

I sighed and clicked the coffee machine into gear, then half ran to Rose's room. Dawn was practically vibrating with anxiety, so I put what I hoped was a calming motherly hand on her shoulder. The bed in her room was indeed empty, neatly made up with the duvet turned down and the pillows fluffed. No trace of Rose's presence remained.

"Where could she have gone? This is all my fault," Dawn moaned.

"Hey, let's not jump to conclusions," I tried to reassure her. "Maybe she just decided to go home. Or maybe she's gone to Sylvie's. Let's try not to panic, okay?"

"She wouldn't go home, Mom, she wouldn't! She told Sylvie she'd rather die than go back to her dad." Dawn sat on the edge of the bed, looking up at me miserably. "Oh, God, I know — I bet she overheard us talking about sending her to the Children's Aid last night. That's why she left! I just know it ..."

"Dawn, settle down. What time is it, anyway? I'm phoning Rose's father right now, I'm going to get this thing settled. What's his last name again? S- something ... Sherman?"

"Stanley, Phil Stanley. They live out on Paul Anka Drive, way out in the south end," said Dawn.

Yes, folks, there really is such a place in this city. There is also a Rich Little Drive and an Elvis Lives! Lane. Ottawa rocks, yeah.

I ran my finger down the list of Stanleys in the phone book. Phil Stanley on Paul Anka ... yes, here he was. I dialled the number, letting it ring about fifteen times. I was getting ready to hang up when someone picked up the receiver.

"H'llo?" said a dull voice that was not distinctly male or female.

"Hi, I'm looking for Phil Stanley."

"Yeah, Phil here," said the voice, stuporously.

I must have woken him up. Well, too damn bad. If my teenage daughter was roaming the streets cutting herself up with razor blades, do you think I'd be lying in bed sleeping off a bender? Damn straight I wouldn't.

"Mr. Stanley, this is Katy Klein. I'm calling about your daughter, Rose." I kept the moral outrage out of my voice, or at least I tried to.

"What about her?"

Deep breath, Katy. "She spent the night here yesterday, Mr. Stanley. She had no place to go, so I let her stay here with me and my daughter. But when we woke up, Rose had gone. I wanted to check and see if she'd come home, just to make sure she's safe."

Mr. Stanley was quiet for a moment. Foolishly, I assumed he was considering my words, perhaps castigating himself for his own parental negligence. Not.

"How the hell should I know where that little bitch is? She never tells me nothing. She takes off all the time, doesn't say where she's going or who with. I told her last time, you do it again, you don't come home, understand? Do it again, you're not my kid. Forget it. I've had it up the yingyang with her."

"Mr. Stanley, Rose needs your help. She's a child. And I understand she's just lost her mother. She's going to need you to help her, to give her understanding and love. Teenagers can be difficult, I know ..."

"Mind your own fucking business. What're you, some kind of fucking social worker? No one tells me how to raise my kid. If she even is my kid," he spat.

I didn't bother to touch that one. Clearly, I had caught Mr. Stanley on a bad day.

"So you're saying you wouldn't mind if I called the CAS – the Children's Aid Society – and reported Rose missing?"

Hey, between this charmer and John Keon, I was getting some great practice in keeping my legendary temper under control. I look at it as building up good karma. Mr. Stanley, however, did not seem to appreciate the effort I was making on his behalf.

"Phone whoever the fuck you want. Leave me out of it," he said, and hung up on me.

I turned to Dawn, who stood expectantly at my elbow.

"I see what you mean. Looks like this guy's a graduate of the Andrew Dice Clay Charm School," I said. "He doesn't want to know from Rose. Said we can call whoever we want about her — he's washed his hands."

"Asshole. So what do we do now?"

I didn't bother to correct her language this time. For one thing, it was hard to argue with her assessment.

"Well, for starters, you can go get ready for school."

I ignored her indignant glare, her mouth half opened to protest.

"And I'm calling someone at Children's Aid to see about Rose's options. After that, we'll see."

"Mom, why don't you let me go look for her? I could find her and bring her back here — I know she'd listen to me."

"She might, but you've already missed a day of school. And you've got an exam coming up, haven't you? No, I'll do the legwork today, Dawn. Why don't you call Sylvie's place and check with her? I wouldn't be surprised if Rose headed over there this morning, and we're getting all worked up over nothing."

I had just stepped out of the shower when Dawn reported on her call to Sylvie's place. No luck. Unwillingly, I caved in to the inevitable: I was going to have to try to find her. She'd spent the night here, so I supposed I had some responsibility for ensuring her safety. Not that I had the faintest idea where to look for runaway teenagers.

"What about the Rideau Centre?" Dawn offered.

"What about it?"

"Well, that's where Sylvie and I went to meet Rose in the first place. A lot of street kids hang around there, especially when the weather gets cold. She might have gone there."

The Rideau Centre is one of those huge downtown malls built during the hedonistic frenzy of the early eighties. It now occupies a fair chunk of prime real estate in Ottawa's core. The shopping mall, the Ottawa Congress Centre and a fancy-schmancy hotel were built simultaneously, destroying most of the west end of Rideau Street, which had been a charmingly eclectic, if somewhat run-down, bargain hunter's paradise. Now it is a combination traffic problem and flophouse for street people and kids like Rose.

Dawn was right. The odds were good that Rose would head for the mall, with its maze of corridors, back hallways and shops that provide warmth and relative safety for any number of Ottawa's homeless. That is, until the mall security guards catch up with them – then they are unceremoniously turfed out to freeze. Or broil, depending on the season.

"Okay, Dawn, I'll go have a look around before I head in for work," I said. "And I'll call someone at Youth Outreach, tell them to keep an eye out for her, okay?"

Dawn grudgingly accepted this compromise and went off to shower and dress. I sat down with my coffee. The CAS was not answering its phones yet, as it was only eight in the morning. When was Greg due back from Toronto? When we used to travel together for work, we'd usually catch the early flight back, arriving home by around eight-fifteen. I nursed my coffee, trying to concentrate on the morning paper, until quarter to nine, when he'd be back home.

Greg picked up on the first ring. His cats, Gemini and Ezekiel, yowled for their breakfast in the background. The twin red-point Siamese cats, dubbed by me the Evil Shredders of Doom, had become a focal point in Greg's life when his wife left him a few years ago to take up a torrid romance with her personal trainer. I personally do not think the cats have any redeeming qualities, though I have to say I prefer them to the former wife. Just an opinion.

"Glad you're home," I said. "Listen, I have a question for you."

"Shoot."

"Well, it's about a friend of Dawn's. She ran away from home yesterday, stayed the night with us, and this morning, she seems to have flown the coop. Her mother just died over the weekend — and that's a story and a half, too."

"Can you give me the *Reader's Digest* condensed version? I have to head to the office as soon as I finish my coffee," Greg said. I didn't take offense — Greg is the original workaholic.

I told him about Carmen's party, Marion's strange collapse and her death the next day. "The thing is, I'm not sure whether Rose really knows her mom is dead or not. Sylvie tried to talk about it, but Rose started screaming at her, threatening to cut herself if she didn't shut up. I think the poor kid's in shock — maybe a bit out of touch with reality. I tried to call the father this morning, but he was worse than useless."

"That sounds like a terrible scenario, Katy, but you know I don't do child and family psychiatry," Greg started.

"I know, I know, but I hoped you might know of someone over at the CAS who could help us out," I said. "I'm going out looking for Rose this morning, but I want to have something worked out for her. I can't just send her home, not with her father the way he is. Her aunt says she can't stay there, she's strapped as it is. And she can't stay with me forever."

"Mmm. I see what you mean. Hang on a sec, I'll get my pocket scheduler. That's where I keep my phone list these days."

His phone receiver clunked down on the table. The Shredders of Doom were obviously interested. I could hear little mewling and purring noises as they butted their heads into the receiver. They must have known it was me; they only make nice with people who can't stand them. I tried to send negative vibes through the phone wire, but they didn't take the hint.

Greg came back to the phone and I heard him making kootchie-kootchie noises with his kitties. Imagine, a grown man. Still, I guess everyone's entitled to their eccentricities.

"Here we go," he said presently. "I've got a Mrs. Walker listed here, Pearl Walker. She helped me out a few weeks ago with the kid of one of my patients. Old man was in the slammer, mom was long gone and the kid needed a place fast. Pearl got him a placement by the end of the day."

Since the forced resignation of the former Director of Forensic Psychiatry earlier in the fall, Greg has been acting as *de facto* director of the unit. Years ago, when I was a wet-behind-the-ears psychological intern in the unit, Greg had been my supervisor. Later, we developed a close and abiding friendship. Just to set the record straight, nary a stray sexual impulse has passed between us in all our years as colleagues and friends. Don't ask me why; it's one of those chemistry things. I'm a big believer in chemistry.

"Mrs. Walker?" I repeated, jotting the name on a legal pad. "That sounds great. Is it okay if I mention your name?"

"Oh, sure. She might not remember me, though."

"You underestimate your charms, my dear," I laughed. "Trust me, she'll remember you. Anyway, thanks." Another thought flitted through my mind. "Oh, and listen, I was wondering if you'd like to join us for supper tonight?"

"Sure, that sounds like fun," he said. "What should I bring?"

"Just your own sweet self," I said. "We're thinking of sitting down around six-thirty. I've asked my friend Carmen, as well. You remember Carmen, right?"

There was a pregnant pause. "Katy, stop trying to set us up, okay? It's not going to work."

"God, you're so paranoid. Why shouldn't I invite two of my closest friends for dinner? Just because both of you happen to be temporarily unattached, there's no reason to …"

"Quit while you're ahead, kid."

"Yeah, I guess," I admitted. "Sometimes you're no fun at all, Greg. See you tonight, okay?"

Mrs. Walker was not at her desk yet, presumably due to the foot and a half of snow clogging the city streets. It's bizarre: this city gets hit with a ridiculous amount of frozen precipitation, yet no one who lives here is ever prepared for a storm. Each year, the first major accumulation of white stuff sees all the drivers acting as if they're hot off the plane from Waikiki and have no idea what to do in this cold, slippery landscape. Drivers slam into telephone poles, skid off bridges and slide into one another, always with this look of complete surprise. What? Snow and ice require more cautious driving? Well, I'll be damned.

Maybe it's like women who forget the pain of childbirth immediately after they've been through the most excruciating labour. Oh, it wasn't so bad, they say, when only hours earlier they were screaming at someone to put them out of their misery. But forgetting about the pain of birth seems like an adaptive biological mechanism to me, one of those things that keeps us reproducing. Forgetting how to drive in winter is just plain stupid.

But I digress. I left a message for Mrs. Walker, asking her to call me at my office. Then I bundled myself up against the cold and hit the trail for the Rideau Centre. The sidewalks on Centretown's side streets had not been cleared yet; it was like slogging through wet cement.

Several drivers attempted to navigate the slippery streets in their summer tires, gunning engines and fishtailing wildly as they tried to accelerate, then slamming on the brakes and sailing blithely through intersections. And of course there were the ones who'd parked by the curb overnight and were now struggling to dig themselves out from under a bank of ploughed snow. Not to mention the pedestrians who had apparently forgotten that boots are de rigueur in winter weather. What to do but shake one's head?

I actually kind of like a fresh snowfall before the car exhaust and general city grime have a chance to foul the pristine whiteness. Clean like a newly bleached sheet, reflecting back and amplifying December's meagre allotment of sunlight.

On Elgin Street, the three-foot high banks of snow that now lined the road were already spattered with grey slush and exhaust fumes from passing traffic. My cheeks and nose were growing numb with the morning chill, so I pulled my turtleneck up to cover them and marched onward to the Rideau Centre.

The mall was just groaning to life as I entered. A few hopeful shoppers hung around waiting for the shops to open. Commuters strode purposefully, using the mall as a thoroughfare between the buses on the Mackenzie Bridge at one end and the infamous Rideau Bus Mall at the other.

A couple of enterprising coffee shops had opened early to take advantage of hapless caffeine addicts like myself. The sludge they sold was barely worthy of the name, but I sipped it anyway. It was dark, hot, and most important, a good daily source of caffeine.

I took a seat in the food court, where I had a clear view of Rideau Street. The mall's a big place, with lots of spots for an enterprising teenager to hide out. Given that, it made little sense for me to attempt to scout out all the possible hidey-holes. Better to wait for Rose to come to me. I am by no means a surveillance expert, but this seemed the most sensible plan.

There are less interesting ways to spend a morning than people-watching at the Rideau Centre. It was a school day, but a surprising number of teens milled about in clusters of four or five, chattering amongst themselves. There were also quite a few street people. Some conversed with invisible companions and dragged bundle-buggies full of grubby possessions; others were less conspicuous, staring at the floor, shoulders slumped forward. They weren't necessarily crazy, just poor. I found it hard to look at them.

Canned music permeated the mall, urging us all to have a merry Christmas and a happy New Year, to hark unto the herald angels and come all we faithful, not to mention decking the halls with boughs of holly. After the first dozen falalalalas, my head started to hurt and I thought longingly of industrial earplugs.

I nursed my ersatz coffee for over an hour, scanning the place for Rose's improbably blonde mop, watching for the brown leather jacket Dawn had described, but none of the kids I saw looked even vaguely familiar. I debated asking around, checking whether anyone had seen her, but decided against it. For one thing, if word got back that someone was looking for her, she might take greater pains to hide herself. Also, though I wasn't keen to admit it, some of the kids here made me nervous.

This is one of the cardinal signs of true middle age,

I think. At one time in my life, my primary goal was to strike fear into the hearts of the older generation. I wore the obligatory long hair of the sixties, even ironing and bleaching my unruly locks to mimic the dead-straight blondeness of Julie on "Mod Squad." I sported the mini-est of miniskirts, the widest of bell-bottoms, the most garish collection of love beads. I indeed wore flowers in my hair, leather thong bracelets on my ankles, tons of hammered silver on my grubby fingers and toes, and buttons declaring my commitment to peace, love and eternal grooviness. I even managed to get tickets to Woodstock, an event that profoundly influenced my youthful consciousness. (But if I'd known they were going to declare it a free concert halfway through, I wouldn't have bothered to pay up front. That still irks me.)

All of this is to say that I was young and idealistic once, too. Adults had looked at me in horror, which was the point. I preferred to interpret their dismay as recognition that it was my generation's turn at bat. They could see a new day coming, and it scared them to death, because now we'd be the ones making the rules. And those rules would be good ones, not middle class and bourgeois like the ones our parents lived by.

Yes, the times they were indeed a'changing, and now in the Rideau Centre they had changed so much that the prospect of approaching a Doc Marten-clad, green-haired, body-pierced, tattooed, hormonally-charged youth for information on one of her missing peers made me nervous. So I didn't do it.

Instead, I found a payphone and called Mrs. Walker again. This time she was in.

"Pearl Walker here," she said.

"Mrs. Walker, this is Katy Klein. Greg Chisholm gave me your name."

Her voice warmed perceptibly. "Of course, I remember Dr. Chisholm. How can I help you, Ms. Klein?"

"Please, call me Katy. I'm calling about a thirteen-year-old girl, Rose Stanley, a friend of my daughter's. She came to our house yesterday — she was threatening to self-mutilate, and apparently she's done that in the past. Her father had kicked her out of her home a couple of days ago, and her mother died over the weekend. I called her dad, but he showed no interest at all — he sounded like he'd been drinking. Anyway, this morning when we got up, Rose had left the apartment, and frankly, I'm very worried for her. I'm at the Rideau Centre now, trying to find her."

There was a long pause. "Have you spoken to Youth Outreach yet? Or Operation Go Home?" Pearl asked. "They're probably more appropriate. You see, if you were to report that this girl wasn't being cared for at home, I could just send someone around to check, and if things were bad enough, we might possibly be able to have her removed from the home. Especially if there's evidence of actual abuse or neglect. But since you don't actually know her whereabouts, my hands are tied."

"What about sending someone out to find her?"

"Katy, we don't operate like the dog pound, sending someone around with a truck and a net to catch kids. I wish we could haul in all the street kids in the city and get them decent care, but it doesn't work like that. For one thing, with all the budget cuts lately, we just don't have the personnel to go out looking for lost kids. We're strapped enough looking after the ones who are still living at home. And even then, believe you me, there are a lot we don't see until it's too late."

"I — I just don't know what to say. I assumed –"

"I know. Everyone assumes. But it takes money to keep kids safe, and people these days are more interested in tax cuts than child welfare. That's the grim truth."

I sucked my breath in through clenched teeth. This was going to be harder than I thought.

"Pearl, what if I do find her? Can you do something then?"

"Maybe. We'd need to interview her father, check out the home, that kind of thing, but we might be able to get a court order to remove the child from the home if everything checked out as you described it. But you need to have a child for us to place in care. Without that, we're stuck."

"Of course. I appreciate your advice."

"Not at all. I'm sorry I can't give you better news. Please let me know if you find her." Pearl sounded genuinely concerned. Everyone was genuinely concerned. And there was not a damn thing any of us could do.

I wasn't accomplishing much, standing around getting overheated in the oxygen-deprived mall. Pearl had mentioned Youth Outreach — didn't they have a centre a couple of blocks away? It felt good to emerge into the freezing air, to stride along the newly cleared sidewalks. There was a bite in the air, but not enough to make walking unpleasant. And it was quiet. Nary a Christmas carol to be heard.

The Youth Outreach Centre occupied a couple of floors on a corner of Rideau Street. The only occupants were two young women who sat chatting on a shabby couch. As I pushed open the heavy glass door, one of them butted out her cigarette and hopped up to greet me.

"Hi," I said, "are you the co-ordinator here?"

"No, I'm just a worker. Nancy," she introduced herself, holding out a hand.

She was much shorter than I, and a whole lot younger. Her hair was slicked back from her smiling face and she had the fresh, shiny look of the novice street worker.

"I'm Katy." I shook her extended hand. "I'm looking for a young girl named Rose. Someone suggested I check with you about her."

"Rose? We get a lot of kids in here, you know. Can you tell me what she looks like?"

"Young, about thirteen; dyed blonde hair, multiple eyebrow piercings, wide-legged corduroys, brown leather jacket. She's small, thin. That's all I know for sure. I only met her yesterday."

Nancy looked sideways, searching her mental memory banks. She called to the young woman who still slumped on the couch, smoking.

"Hey, Jamie, what was that kid's name, the one who said her father kicked her out the other night?"

Jamie, whose plump knuckles were tattooed with pentacles, considered the question, exhaling smoke slowly through her nose.

"Was it Rosie or something? She was really young," she said. Like Jamie wasn't just a child herself, I thought. But her words gave me a tingle of hope.

"When was this?" I prompted.

"Not last night ... no, it must have been the night before. Sunday," Nancy said. "She was super quiet, kept to herself, and one of the guys here went up to her, said she was cute, asked her her name. He didn't mean anything by it, most of the guys here look a lot tougher than they really are, but she told him to fuck off, started kicking at him. Completely freaked out, you know? We try to keep things cool here, so I took her into the office, talked to her for a while. She just cried. Didn't say much."

"Did she say where she was planning to stay?" I asked.

Nancy shook her head, and my hopes sagged. This was going nowhere. I was never going to find that damned kid.

"Look, Nancy, can I give you my phone number?" I asked. "I really want to make sure Rose gets off the streets. She's way too young for that kind of life."

Nancy didn't disagree. "Sure, write it down here, okay? I'll let everyone know to call you if she shows up."

I thanked her, and on an impulse, I pulled out my wallet and handed her my last twenty dollar bill. Nancy looked surprised and pleased. She tucked the bill into a drawer of her desk, and I left.

Out on the street again, I paused uncertainly. The morning was half over. I had made absolutely no headway, and my answering machine at work must be getting backed up by now. I didn't really want to give up my search for Rose, but despite those who claim Ottawa is a small town, it can seem pretty damned huge when you're looking for one young girl.

Not knowing what else to do, I started the long trudge back to my office. I chose the route that runs by the Rideau Canal, which in winter is transformed into the world's longest skating rink. I'm not making that up; it really is. But it was too early in the season to see skaters. The waterway had been mostly drained for winter, with only a couple of feet of partly frozen water remaining, edged with new snow. The Canal had an abandoned, bleak look. I knew this would improve once the weather got colder, but for right now, it was just plain depressing.

Last summer, a dead man had been fished out of the Canal's murky waters. My obsessive interest in his death had thrown Dawn, Greg and me into the path of his killer. That all seemed a very long time ago now. Dawn and I had spent a month at Greg's cottage trying to regain our equilibrium, and now I could look at the Canal without envisioning Adam's body bobbing amongst the weeds and garbage.

I was no longer searching for clues to a murder, though. Now, I was more interested in the living.

6

There was no doubt about it now: the heat in my office was definitely on. The place felt like a sauna, as the antiquated radiators clanked and rattled, radiating for all they were worth. Either John Keon was having his little joke, or the inspector had adjusted the furnace to the highest possible setting yesterday. Even the cold wind squeezing in around my makeshift patch on the window was not enough to render the office habitable.

I stripped off my anorak and heavy sweater, grabbed my chisel and set to work opening a stuck window. Fresh air, no matter how chilly, now seemed like an extremely good idea. One of these days I'm going to cave in and move to a decent office, I swore as the chisel slipped and gouged my thumb. Soon. A better office. Yes.

I wedged the window up a couple of inches, propping it open with a couple of thick astrology books, then checked my answering machine for messages.

Mornings are my busiest time. I have a number of regular clients who check in with me on a daily basis. Jim the money-manager had called to check out the stock markets. He's so cute — he always whispers into the phone, fearful of the censure of his colleagues, unaware that several of them also consult me. Mrs. O'Brien, another regular, had called for an update, as had Jerry.

Mirabile dictu, Jerry was no longer calling to get the low-down on another unsuitable relationship. Now, he and his girlfriend, Tammi, whom I had been advising for the past year, were looking for a good date to tie the knot. I was happy for them. Jerry never heeded my cautions, but Tammi seemed to have a good head on her tattooed shoulders.

The next message surprised me.

Beep. "Katy, I want to ... talk to you again, I guess. I forget what you called it, but I want to know more about my future. Call me when you get a chance. Uh, thanks. Oh, it's Diana. Sorry."

I raised my eyebrows at the answering machine — I really hadn't expected to hear from her again. Certainly not this quickly. I made a note to call her, and hit the "Play" button again.

Beep. "John Keon here. I hereby serve you with notice that our rental agreement is no longer in effect, as of December 31 of this year. You will be required to leave the premises as of that date. If you fail to comply, your belongings will be seized. So long, bitch." Click. Dial tone.

My stomach in knots, I played the message a second time, to be sure I hadn't misheard it. I shook my head impatiently, played it a third time. Maybe someone was playing some kind of ghastly prank? No, it was Keon all right. What did he think he was doing? I mean, we'd had our differences, but I always pay my rent on time, and I keep the place in good repair. If you overlook the small matter of the shattered window, which wasn't my fault. Damn him — what did he think he was doing?

Keon picked up on the first ring.

"John. What the hell do you mean, leaving me a message like that?"

"You heard me, all right. You're being evicted." He sounded amused at my outrage.

"What! Would you mind telling me why? I believe you require a reason to prematurely terminate a written contract, unless my lawyer is mistaken." This was a bluff, and he must have known it.

"Damage to the property. I saw the hole you put in that window. It's gonna cost me a fortune to repair. Plus, the city's outlawing the practice of fortune telling, and I don't want any damn lawbreakers renting property from me. And you, honey, are a fortune teller. So you're outta there."

I could just imagine the smirk on his shiny, overfed face. My fingers clenched the phone receiver so tightly that they began to go numb.

"What the hell are you talking about? There's no law against practising astrology! You can't do this, Keon. You have no right —"

"Hey, bitch, you don't like it, you call city hall. I'm not the one who makes the laws. But I'm gonna enforce this one." He laughed at his own joke.

Then, for the second time in as many days, he hung up on me.

I grabbed the phone book and began riffling the pages frantically, looking for the number of the city councillor for the Glebe. What the hell was her name? Thomas? Tompkins? Something like that. I was hyperventilating by the time I found the number.

"Yes, ma'am, I believe the councillor is supporting

that by-law amendment," a polite young woman informed me when I reached my ward representative's office.

"Well, I want to speak to her." I fought to keep my voice steady. "This is a matter of some concern to me. When will she be in?"

"She's at an executive meeting just now. I can have her call you this afternoon, if she has a moment."

"You do that. Tell her it's urgent."

My adrenaline levels abated not a whit as I hung up. This was the first I'd heard about any move to declare my occupation illegal, but I'd heard tales of it happening in other cities. Who or what was behind this? My livelihood was at risk here, and I'm self-employed — there's no safety net for out-of-work astrologers. I had a sickening vision of myself dragging a bundle buggy, my head low in defeat, just like the homeless people I'd seen this morning.

Who else might know about this by-law thing? Peter? Maybe. I reached my ex-husband at his desk.

"I haven't heard anything about it," he said, "but I'll look into it for you, if you want. Look, Katy, you know Keon's a pompous ass. He might just be yanking your chain, you know?"

"I thought that, too, at first. But then I phoned Janet Tompkins's office, and her assistant said she was supporting the by-law. It sounded like it's practically a done deal. Peter, they can't do this! I'll be out of work, and you know what the job market is like out there ..."

I am embarrassed to say that I started sniffling at this point.

"Hey, don't worry, okay? I'll check it out, I'm sure it's not so bad. And even if it is, we'll think of something. We might be divorced, but we're still family, remember?"

I blew my nose. Peter promised to call me in a couple of hours. Meanwhile, I had work to do, and I might as well keep doing it while it was still legal. I began to call my regular clients, dispensing wisdom over the phone, making appointments where necessary.

Diana was out when I called her. A man answered, his voice deep and soft. Like velvet, I thought. Probably her brother, Nigel.

"Hello. Would Diana be available?"

"Oh, I'm sorry, she's not in just at the moment. Could I tell her who's calling?"

This was trickier than it might seem. I like to maintain at least a semblance of confidentiality for my clients, as some of them aren't keen on having the whole world know they're seeing an astrologer.

"I'm Katy — a friend of hers. I wonder if you'd mind passing on a message?"

"Not at all, Katy. Let me just get a pencil, all right?"

He put the phone down for a moment, then returned.

"All right. Now, what did you say you were calling about?"

"Uh, I'm just returning Diana's call to me," I fumbled. "She has my number, I think." Idiot. Of course she has my number, she just called me, didn't she?

"You're Carmen's friend, aren't you?"

"Yes. Yes, I am. I think we met at her party, right?"

"Of course, of course. Right before —" He broke off with a slight cough.

"Yes, exactly. Right before Marion collapsed."

"What a tragedy," Nigel said. "A terrible thing. Carmen tells me the poor woman died. I was shocked, but I suppose we can't know what plans the Almighty has for us."

"Uh, no," I said. I wasn't touching that one. Fortunately, he changed tack quickly.

"Katy, I had no idea you knew my sister. Have you been ... friends a long time?" The pause was barely perceptible, but I caught it, and with it his inference.

"We haven't known one another very long," I said, deliberately vague. "We met the same night I met you. Well, nice chatting with you!"

"Yes, very nice indeed," he said. "Well, I'll be certain to give her your message. Bye, now." He hung up before I had a chance to say good-bye back.

I dropped the receiver back into its cradle. Talking to Nigel Farnsworth made a nice change from my recent chats with John Keon, I supposed, but there was something almost too ... too nice about him. That beautiful, resonant voice seemed to caress my ear long after I'd hung up the phone.

You're never satisfied, are you, Katy? I muttered, as I made a note to myself: *Re-check Diana's chart, transits, progressions; set appointment time.* I propped this helpful reminder up against the phone where I'd be sure to notice it.

I couldn't see that there was much else to do in the office at this point, with the exception of billing, which I loathe. I tossed a ballpoint pen idly into the air, considering my options. There was still the matter of Rose.

I had little hope of actually finding her, but I would despise myself, and worse, Dawn would never forgive me, if I stopped trying. Under a dusty stack of unsorted paper that I seriously planned to get around to someday (just not today), I located my Ottawa-Carleton Community Directory, a somewhat outdated listing of the agencies and services available in the region. The book is one of the few things I retain from my old life as a clinical psychologist. Each time I look at it I am reminded with a lurch of the way I left my so-called "promising career."

Six years ago, I walked in on my boss, Dr. Frank Curtis, as he fondled a heavily-sedated patient on the ward where I worked. I made the grave error of trying to confront Curtis myself, and he attacked me, too. So I packed up and left, just like that. Recently, I'd broken down and told Greg the story, and within a couple of months, Curtis had been driven from the hospital. But I have felt no desire to go back, even though Greg's asked me a couple of times to come in as a consultant.

I shook my shoulders and shrugged them up and down once or twice to squeeze out the residual memories. It didn't work, but it left me with marvellously tingling shoulder muscles.

As I ran my finger down the lists of agencies I'd relied on five years ago, I mentally counted off in my head: Dead. Gone. De-funded. Nope, that one folded too. I put in a few calls, but was mostly met with taped messages informing me that the agencies were operating on reduced hours, or had been eliminated altogether. Some of the phone numbers had already been reallocated. This was getting scary. Was there really nothing out there for Rose?

I closed the directory and sat with my elbows on my desk, pressing my palms into my throbbing forehead, where a doozie of a headache was revving up. Pearl Walker had said the Children's Aid couldn't do much until I found Rose. Ergo, I reasoned, my job was to find the kid. But how the hell was I going to do that? Rustle up a posse, head out with a bunch of cowpokes and haul her in? I was a little rusty on my lassoing skills.

The phone rang a couple of inches from my right arm, and I jumped about a foot, then grabbed it, happy for the interruption. Ruminative depressive episodes just aren't my style.

"Katy? Diana here."

"Wow, that was fast," I commented.

"What do you mean? I called you about two hours ago." She sounded annoyed.

"No, I mean you got back to me quickly. Your brother and I just hung up."

"You were talking to my brother? When was this?"

"Mmm ... maybe ten, fifteen minutes ago? Why?"

"You didn't tell him —"

"Don't worry. I don't tell anyone what I do. He remembered me from Saturday night, though. We did chat a bit, and he said he'd leave you a message."

"You chatted? What about?"

"Nothing much, Diana. Small talk. Listen, it's really not important. Now, did you want to set up some more time for us to meet?"

"Don't tell me what's important and what's not, all right?" She bristled, and I scowled into the receiver. "You don't know what it's like around here. He's constantly — no, never mind. I can't talk about it right now. Fine. Let's meet tomorrow. Two o'clock. But I can't stay long. I have to be back at work by three."

"Fine," I said, just this side of snapping at her myself. "Two o'clock it is."

Yeesh, I thought, hanging up. Living with Diana must be like taking up residence with a cactus — all thorns and spikes. How did Nigel stand it? He must have some pretty deep control issues indeed, if he'd invited her back for the sole purpose of running her life. I couldn't see where it would be worth it.

Still, Diana was a paying client, and this was a slow time of year for me. Besides, attending to my astrology practice felt like something I could control.

As opposed to searching for lost teenagers on the streets of Ottawa. Or getting rocks heaved through my window, or having my practice closed out from under me. Or being evicted. Stop it, I told myself sternly. Getting yourself into a state won't solve anything. Get out there and look for Rose; at least you'll be doing something.

Sighing, I pulled on a sweater, a fleece jacket and my anorak, hunted a few minutes for my gloves, which I finally located exactly where I had left them, in my knapsack. I laced on my boots, pausing momentarily to reflect on the amount of time Canadians waste putting on and taking off winter clothing. Another unfair disadvantage to living in the land of ice and snow.

I closed up the office and clattered down the rickety unlit stairs to Bank Street.

✦

The mid-afternoon air was still frosty, but the sky was crystalline and blindingly bright as I made my way north along Ottawa's main thoroughfare. Although it's one of Ottawa's primary arteries, Bank Street looks like the main street in any rural town in the province. Most of the buildings are brick, turn of the century, and no more than a couple of storeys high. Some have been sandblasted into renewed life, but most look scruffy and tired.

I had no plan, really, but I strode under the Queensway Bridge as though I knew exactly where I was going. The further north I walked, the more run-down each block became. From the upscale boutiques, cafes and specialty shops of the Glebe, I had entered Centretown's domain of pawnshops, greasy spoons, and adult video stores. There still remained the occasional health food shop or futon store, relics of a more prosperous time, but over the past ten years, all the money had been sucked out of the downtown core, and with it had gone the area's soul.

Now skinny, underdressed young women, shivering in tight jeans and vinyl boots, cigarettes clamped between high-gloss lips, wheeled sad-looking babies in cheap strollers that kept stalling in the snow, the plastic wheels clogging every few yards. I passed a woman yelling halfheartedly at her older kids: "Stop throwing snow at your sister. I mean it, Jason, stop it now! Krystle, if you don't cut it out, I'll give you something to cry about. Santa Claus won't come if you don't quit it. Quit it, did you hear me?"

Elderly women carried string-bags home from the local bargain store, having stocked up on out-of-date cat food and stale tea at rock-bottom prices. A middle-aged man in grimy, stained clothes urinated casually as he wandered across the street, pee running down into his sneakers. He seemed not to notice. No one else even looked at him.

Some kids were panhandling while others just hung out in amorphous clusters outside the video arcade, kicking at the snow and occasionally shoving one another. One, a bored-looking girl with multi-coloured hair pasted flat against her head with gel and bobby pins, watched me sidelong. She opened her mouth wide as I passed, waggling her pierced tongue.

Was that a challenge? A dare? Or was she just bored out of her mind?

I was hungry and getting cold, and I still hadn't seen Rose. In search of something that might pass for lunch, I entered the huge grocery store that dominates the corner of Bank and Somerset. The floor was slippery with grey slush, despite the pimpled kid dragging a mop across the linoleum.

"Joy to the world," sang the tinned music, "the Lord is come. Let earth receive her King." I hummed along despite myself. This stuff really is insidious. I was wandering around the produce department, searching for the last of the locally grown apples, when I saw Rose.

She was biting her lip, pausing for a moment to select a ripe Bartlett pear. She sucked her cheeks in as she concentrated on the task at hand. Glancing around quickly, she tucked the fruit inexpertly into her jacket pocket. As she tried to saunter away, I ducked around the display of Moroccan oranges, reaching her just as a young man with too-glossy hair and an official-looking uniform grabbed her by the shoulder.

Rose froze in her tracks. The security guard tightened his grip, unable to resist a triumphant grin at his own cleverness. He couldn't have been much older than she was, probably some high school drop-out taking the first job that'd make him feel like a real man, a somebody: the guy who gets to play grocery store cop and lord it over the other kids. For minimum wage, yet.

Rose's brown eyes flickered uncertainly between the guard and me.

"Get your hands off me, creep," she hissed.

"Going somewhere with that pear, miss?" the guard enquired, all faux politeness.

She wrenched her shoulder out of his grasp and stood facing both of us, her defiance betrayed by a trembling lip.

"Rose, give me the pear," I said. "I'll pay for it."

Silently, she handed me the fruit. I couldn't read her expression. The security guard puffed out his scrawny chest, making a show of his authority, reluctant to release his prisoner. He'd caught her fair and square, right in the middle of a felony, and now I was pulling his conquest out from under him.

"Ma'am, I'm going to have to turn this girl in," he began.

I turned my patented Katy Klein Death Stare on him and he took an uncertain step back, hooking his thumbs in his pants pockets. Given the choice between collaring the perp and facing down a large and irate middle-aged customer, I was willing to bet he'd cave.

"You aren't authorized to act until they walk out the door," I snarled. "Why don't you go on home and read up on the law? Anyway, my daughter here wouldn't shoplift — she was just picking up a pear for me. Right, honey?"

For the first time since we'd met, I got a small, tentative smile out of Rose. Taking her by the elbow, I guided her away from the security guard, into the frozen foods section. She kept her head bowed, as if expecting me to light into her now that we were alone.

"Rose, where have you been? I've been looking for you all day! We've been so worried."

All my worry burst out of me, and I hugged her to my chest. She remained stiff, so I released her quickly.

She looked up for an instant, her eyes flicking in surprise; then she turned her head from me and pretended to concentrate on a display of frozen fish and chips.

"Why don't you just leave me alone?" she whispered, low enough that I had to stoop to hear her. "I was stealing. It would have been my own fault. You should have let him arrest me."

"And then what? You spend the day at the cop shop, and they turn you out on the streets again?"

"I can look after myself."

"Yeah, I can tell. You're doing a hell of a job so far!" I snapped before I could stop myself. She flinched. "I'm sorry, Rose, really. Anyway, I butted in because that guy bugged me."

I was rewarded with another tiny smile.

"He was just doing his job. Happens all the time."

"Rose, we need to talk," I began.

"Look, Ms. Klein. I can take care of myself. You said yourself, you can't afford to keep me. And I'm not going to any foster home or whatever."

Ah. Dawn had been correct: Rose had overheard our discussion last night.

"Hey, could you just hang on a second? I know I said you can't stay with us permanently, but that didn't mean you had to leave today. Let's go back to my place and talk, all right?"

Rose looked at her feet. "I have to go now."

"I'll buy you lunch," I wheedled. "Come on, you look hungry."

"Whatever."

She let me lead her toward the cash, where I paid for her pear and a couple of sandwiches made from something that passed for whole wheat bread, with fillings I could not readily identify. Outside the store, I unwrapped our food. Had Dawn seen this dreck, she'd have had a cow.

"Eat up, Rose, you need it."

Yikes — now I was starting to sound like my own mother. *Ess, ess, kindeleh* — eat, eat, little one. Well, too bad. The kid looked like she could use a good meal. Obediently, she stood chewing on the sandwich, but she wouldn't meet my eyes.

"Rose, please. You can stay with us ..."

She shook her head stubbornly.

"I'm not some kind of a loser. You don't have to worry."

"I *am* worried. You need a place to stay. If you don't want to come to our place, then what about one of your aunts? They could put you up for a while, couldn't they?"

"Aunt Greta's too stressed out, and Aunt Nora wouldn't want me. Look, this is none of your business, okay? I have to go now, I've got things to do."

She turned as if to leave me. I grabbed her jacket sleeve, but she shrugged her shoulder angrily, jerking away.

"Rose! Please listen. You need a place to stay. I'm not, I mean I can't just let you take off like this."

She stalked away from me, her spine straight, head bent forward. I ran to catch up with her.

"What's the difference?" she spat, speeding up her pace. "If I'm staying with you, or at Sylvie's place, or on the street — nobody really wants me. What difference does it make? I might just as well be dead. At least then I'd be with my mother ..." Her voice shook.

So she'd heard Sylvie yesterday, after all. At least I wouldn't have to break the news to her.

"That's not a solution, and you know it. Come on

home. We'll figure something out. Come on, Rose, I'm getting out of breath here. You don't want to make this old lady have a heart attack, do you?"

"Whatever," she said again, but she slowed down and allowed me to lead her home.

We trudged wordlessly to my apartment building, our feet squeaking on the packed snow. Outside the building, I fumbled for my key.

"Okay! Now, there's food in the fridge, so just help yourself if you get hungry, all right? Make yourself comfortable — you can stay here till I'm home from work. Then we'll talk, okay?" My voice sounded artificially chirpy, but Rose didn't seem to notice. She made a noncommittal noise which could have been a yes.

"Can you promise you'll wait right here?" I asked.

"Fine," she whispered. She plunked herself down on the living room floor, scrunched up in the fetal position, head on knees, arms folded around the whole bundle. I scribbled my office number on a scrap of paper and set it on the floor beside her.

"If you need anything, I'll be at this number, okay?"

"Sure."

She sounded anything but, though she jammed the slip of paper into the pocket of her hideous wide-legged pants. Job number one would be to get her something better to wear. I suddenly realized I was assuming she'd be with us a while.

"Rose? We're going to figure something out. Don't worry."

I left, shutting the door carefully.

Back at the office, I dialled Greta's number again. This time, I decided, I'd take a more aggressive approach. So I dove right in, accelerating the speed of my words to fend off any interruptions. The trick, I found, was to talk without any punctuation, and not stop to breathe.

"Greta? It's Katy. Yeah, hi. listen, we need to talk about Rose. I called her father this morning and he isn't interested in having her home any time soon. She can't stay with us for very long, for one thing because I just can't afford it, but also, it's not right, not good for her. She needs a more permanent situation, a real family, and I can't give her that. I think you and your sister – Nora is it? – you should talk and decide which one of you can take care of her. She needs you and your family now, not strangers."

I paused, slightly giddy from lack of air. Greta had probably never allowed anyone to make such a long speech before.

"Uh, yeah." She sounded slightly stunned. "You're probably right. But you can look after her for a little while, right? Like we agreed? I'm really stressed out, Katy, and I'm doing all I can here — it's been so hard, losing my baby sister and all. I'll have to talk to Nora, but she's away until next week, in Acapulco ..."

I broke in again, ruthlessly taking advantage of Greta's momentary hesitation.

"Isn't she coming back for Marion's funeral? When exactly does she get back? Has she left you any number to reach her? I think this really qualifies as an emergency, don't you? Rose's father is pretty much a dead loss, so you're going to have to take up his slack. You're the only family that kid has left."

"There's not going to be a funeral." Greta's voice was tight. "Phil is insisting on a private service, just him and the minister. The bastard. So I'm trying to arrange a memorial service for a couple of weeks from now, so Nora can come, too. I called her, and she said no way was she cutting short her holiday if she didn't have to. She got one of those airfare deals, you know, holiday of a lifetime, she's always going off on one holiday of a lifetime or another, she doesn't have any responsibilities, and she sure can live it up, not like Marion and me, always having to think about kids ..."

Damn. She was starting to build up steam.

"Another thing, Greta ..."

I raised my own voice slightly, heading her off at the pass. Hey, I was getting the hang of this. Don't actually wait for her to stop talking — just dive on in, keep my voice loud and fast, and she'd concede to my superior firepower. Not for nothing had I been champion of the debating club in high school.

"Greta, this thing about Rose cutting herself. It's not just a fad, no matter what that shrink said last summer. She's going to need some professional help, and I think you should get started now, looking for someone who can treat her. I can tell you, the waiting lists are long, and she's going to need something soon."

"What do you mean, it's serious? I thought it was just a phase. Why would it be serious?"

"It's a symptom, Greta. A lot of kids do it, but it's usually because there's something seriously wrong at home. Has she had problems with her father for a long time?"

Greta snorted.

"Phil is an idiot. He treated my sister like dirt, and he's never been much of a father to Rose. It's always his way or the highway, that's how Phil operates. He got Marion pregnant when she was only seventeen, if you can believe it, and then he insisted on marrying her — but when the baby came, Phil was outta there. Not that he left them, but he spent all his free time down at the neighbourhood pub. Left Marion on her own with a little baby, and then blamed her when she got depressed. It's a wonder Marion and Phil stayed married as long as they did — I give all the credit to Marion on that one. She didn't want to raise her kid on welfare, you know? So she put up with his garbage."

"Sounds rough," I commented. "But now Rose has a worse problem than being on welfare. You're going to have to do something soon, unless you want to see her placed in foster care. With strangers."

I emphasized the last two words. Slather on the guilt. Greta sighed heavily.

"Okay. I'll try to get hold of Nora, and we'll talk it over. I've always been like a second mother to that poor girl, you know, just like I was to Marion after our parents died ..."

And she was off. I won't bore you with the entire speech, which went on for another twenty minutes, but the upshot was this: Phil was an insecure, jealous man, who'd made Marion's life a living hell, accusing her of infidelities and all manner of betrayals. But Greta never actually thought he'd believed everything he said about Marion. Greta thought he was just accusing his wife so she'd have to defend herself, and she'd have no energy left to fight him on other things. Not that she ever really fought back, especially after the times he had her hospitalized ... and so on.

I had other calls to make this afternoon, but I waited patiently, tapping a pencil on the edge of my desk. If I didn't hang up soon, they'd have to remove the receiver surgically from my ear. Finally, I decided to call a halt. She was in mid-volley, but I cut in.

"Okay, Greta. Well, look, it's been nice chatting

with you. Let's see what we can do about finding a place for Rose, though, okay? I can keep her a few days, but as soon as Nora gets back, I think we should all talk about a more permanent arrangement."

With that, I signed off, and went on to the next call on my agenda.

7

Councillor Tompkins was in her office when I called back to complain about the new anti-astrology by-law. Like all politicians, Janet Tompkins had mastered the newspeak vocabulary, and it took some time to get her to cut to the chase.

"The fact is, Councillor, I earn my living as an astrologer, and if this by-law is enacted, my livelihood will be cut off. Believe me, I plan to protest this."

"I certainly sympathize with your concern, Miss, uh, Klein," she said. "But you should realize that your, uh, practices — well, they do offend certain segments of the community, and we must be sensitive to the needs of all our constituents, mustn't we?"

"Pardon? Which segments of the community are we talking about here? What do you mean?" Despite the chilling breeze from the open window, a bead of sweat rolled off my forehead.

"Oh, well, now, I am really not in a position to name names, you understand. There are issues of confidentiality at stake. But I can tell you that this is not a personal vendetta against people like you, Mrs. Klein. As an elected representative, I must respond to the wishes of the majority ..."

Like hell, I thought. And I was getting tired of being referred to as "people like you."

"It's Ms." My voice was frosty. "Ms. Klein. Not Miss. Not Mrs. I pay taxes in this city, Councillor. I believe I have a right to know who is targeting my livelihood, don't you?"

She hemmed and hawed and squirmed around, but I got nothing further out of her. It was like trying to nail Jell-o to a wall; she kept slipping just beyond my grasp. I made some threatening noises about taking the city to court (which both she and I knew perfectly well I could never afford), but finally gave up. Maybe Peter would have better luck; I'd talk to him tomorrow. Wearily, I dropped the phone receiver into its cradle.

After the day's frustrations, working on a client's chart came as a welcome relief. I puttered away in silence for a couple of hours, until the dying light outside forced me to flick a couple of lamps on. By five, I was ready to leave.

Rose had actually stayed put, and was still on the floor, but now she was sprawled on her belly, propping her cheek in a palm as she played cards with Dawn. I even heard a smothered giggle from Rose as I unlaced my boots and hung up my anorak. Maybe this could work, after all. I couldn't see putting her up here permanently, but a few days might not hurt.

Trying not to disturb the girls, I slipped into the kitchen to start preparing supper. Greg and Carmen would be here in an hour or so. While they had to know me well enough by now not to expect cordon bleu, I wanted to serve something edible. Quickly, I ransacked my kitchen cupboards. I emerged triumphant, clutching my favourite cookbook and a can of artichokes.

Soon, a respectable artichoke and cheddar cheese puff sat browning in the oven, while I whisked plain yogurt into the cream of carrot soup that simmered on top of the stove. Nothing quite like a substantial soup during the dark nights of December. I'd have to forage for dessert, but at least we had the basics.

Carmen arrived first. As usual, she was breathless, but she was half an hour early — not like her at all.

"Oh, my God, what's that wonderful smell?" She tilted her head to one side, sniffing appreciatively. "Katy, you didn't go to any trouble, did you? Dawn, honey, careful with that coat — wouldn't want it getting all muddy from the floor. And who have we here?"

Rose put her cards down and glanced up at Carmen, then ducked her head again.

"Carmen, this is Rose, a friend of Dawn's. She's staying with us for a while. Rose, Carmen is one of my oldest friends."

"One of them? My dear, you and I go back to before the flood! Lovely to meet you, Rose." Carmen swished into the kitchen, where she gave the soup another stir before she tasted it. "Needs dill," she pronounced.

Obediently, I snipped a sprig of the herb from the window garden I'd started as a fall project. It was one of the many make-work endeavours I'd started since last summer, primarily to keep myself from thinking too hard about what had happened then. Sometimes it worked.

But if my goal was to avoid thinking about the past, Carmen seemed equally determined to stir things up. I know she doesn't do it to hurt me, but she has this uncanny ability to find and press my most sensitive points.

"So, heard from Brent lately?" she asked, oh-so-casually.

I kept chopping dill as a hot flush crept up my neck to my face. Brent had been my first lover back in university, and I'd lost him then, mostly through my own stubbornness. When he'd reappeared last summer, I had foolishly allowed myself to hope we could mend things and start over. It had not worked, for reasons too convoluted and painful to go into.

"Carmen, you just can't let it drop, can you? I told you, it's over."

"My dear, where there's life, there's hope. You two are perfect for each other — if you'd stop being so stubborn."

"That's not fair. There's no going back for either of us, and that's that. So give it up, okay?"

She shook her head sadly. "But he's so perfect for you. You love him, he loves you, he even gets along with Dawn. He didn't mean any harm, and you already said he tried to apologize. I just can't believe you'd be so unforgiving. You have to learn to accept that people make mistakes sometimes ..."

"This is none of your business, Carmen." I punched the buttons on the microwave with unnecessary force. "I really wish you'd stop talking about him. Just stop."

She arched an eyebrow at me. "So. You've tried every trick in the book to throw me at your friend Greg. I've told you, I don't find him attractive, but do you listen? No. And yet I'm not supposed to notice that you just threw out a guy who made you the happiest you've ever been? That hardly seems fair."

"Point taken. We'll have a nice meal tonight, and I'll stop pushing you and Greg at each other, no matter how perfectly I know you would suit each other. Except for your cat allergy," I added, in the spirit of fairness.

Actually, the thought of the Evil Shredders of Doom having a go at Carmen's picture-perfect apartment made the corners of my mouth twitch involuntarily.

"Thank you. And in any case, poor Greg would find himself superfluous, these days. Redundant."

There was a note of smugness in her voice.

"So — give! What's the story? You're going out with someone? Is it that Nigel guy? The one I met the other night?"

I suppose it was inevitable, as I have never known her to be without a man for longer than a few weeks, even in junior high. She's always been of the opinion that men make nice centrepieces at dinner parties and such; plus, they accessorize so well. A strapless evening gown just doesn't look right unless you've got a man on your arm.

Why am I being bitchy about my best friend's good fortune? All right, I'll be truthful: I don't necessarily have the greatest track record when it comes to my own love life. It's always been this way. Carmen attracts men like flies to honey, whereas I tend to scare them away. The ones I don't scare away, I dump, and then spend years wondering what the hell is wrong with me.

Carmen smiled a Mona Lisa, you'll-never-guess kind of smile.

"*Nu*?" I pressed.

"Let's just say we're at the exploratory stage. I don't want to jinx it, so my lips are sealed."

"Smirking doesn't become you, Carmen. So tell me about it, already! How did you meet him, what's his alimony situation? You know, just the essentials."

She paused demurely, looked down, opened her rosebud mouth, but whatever she was about to say was drowned out by the opening bars to "California Dreaming."

"What's *that*?" Carmen looked startled.

"The doorbell." I gritted my teeth. "Dawn chose it. It's one of those programmable monstrosities. Soon as I get some spare cash, it's history."

Greg stood in the hallway, clutching a bouquet of carnations and a bottle of German wine. Dawn had him by the hand by the time I got to the door and was dragging him in to meet Rose and Carmen.

"Dawn, take it easy," he laughingly protested. "At least let me get out of these boots. Katy, something smells amazing!"

I thanked him for the flowers and went off to find a vase. Dawn, meanwhile, relieved him of his overcoat, hanging it on a hook by the door.

When I came back, Greg and Carmen were still in the hallway chatting, but both looked relieved to see me.

"Katy, sweetie, can I help you set the table or something?" Carmen took me by the elbow, propelling me toward the kitchen. Greg cocked his eyebrows at me over her head, and I suppressed a grin. Okay, so maybe they wouldn't be so completely perfect for each other.

"Greg! Come on!" Dawn pulled him off to the living room.

In the kitchen, I handed Carmen a stack of dishes, and she began laying out the table, while I put last-minute touches on the food.

"So — you were going to tell all about your new love. What's the story?"

"I told you, I don't want to jinx it," Carmen said. "Katy, don't you have any cloth napkins? All I can find are these paper things."

"Sorry, the damask and lace are out at the cleaners. We'll have to do without. Trust me, it won't hurt the food." I plopped the soup tureen on the table and announced that supper was served.

Dawn and Greg trooped into the dining nook off the kitchen, oohing and aahing about the meal I'd prepared. Rose followed behind them, eyes downcast.

"Wow, Mom, this looks amazing!"

"Hey, you don't have to sound quite so shocked," I protested. "I do cook once in a while, you know."

"Yeah, sure, but not like Sabte. She makes a career out of it — you just do it when you're in the mood," Dawn teased.

"How are your parents, Katy?" Carmen asked. She's always had a soft spot for my mother, in particular. Carmen's own parents weren't what you'd call the nurturing kind, so as kids, we spent hours in Mama's kitchen, watching her work, dunking our *mandelbrot* in mugs of warm milk.

"Not too bad. I finally convinced them to go somewhere warm for the winter, so they took off for Arizona a week ago."

Dawn made a face. "I didn't want them to go, but Mom insisted. It's the first Hanukkah we've ever had without them. I know it's better for Zayde, after the stroke, but I wish they were here."

We crowded round the kitchenette table, five at a space meant for two, elbowing one another good-naturedly and trying not to spill soup into our neighbour's laps.

"So, Greg," Carmen said, "are you still working at

the hospital? That must be simply fascinating work. I understand there was some kind of scandal there recently? But I suppose it's all been fixed up now, right?"

"That's right. They're looking for a new chief, and I think the board is eyeing me for the job," Greg said offhandedly. "I've been filling in on a temporary basis, but I don't really think it's for me. I like straight clinical work much better than this juggling act. My secretary will tell you, paperwork isn't one of my strengths."

Carmen laughed. "Oh, I'm sure you're a great boss, Greg."

I watched them, fascinated. Had she not just finished telling me she wasn't interested in Greg? So how come she was doing the fluttering of eyelashes thing? I felt like I ought to be taking notes: *How to Relate to Men*. Greg seemed to respond to the treatment, too. He ducked his head modestly, and a tinge of colour crept up his neck.

Carmen turned to me. "Katy, you never did tell me the whole story about that horrible man at the hospital — what was his name, Curtis? The one who used to be your boss, right? Didn't I read something in the paper about him being thrown in jail for fooling around with some patients?"

"I — uh ..." I fumbled for words. Everyone looked at me, and my throat constricted suddenly.

"Katy? Are you okay?" Carmen leaned toward me.

"Fine," I said. "Just choking. Crumb." I stood up and went for a glass of water, buying some time.

Greg, bless him, picked up the conversational ball effortlessly.

"The papers got it right, Carmen. Curtis was messing around with his patients, he got caught, and the

Board asked him to resign. I understand he's been stripped of his license now. I wasn't sorry to see him go. He was a complete and utter bastard — but he had a talent for hanging onto our funding, and he did keep things running smoothly. Like Mussolini and the trains, I guess. Ever since the province started slashing away at the health system, it's been pretty desperate. The hospital is basically turning into a collection of fiefdoms, each department squabbling over what little money we can scavenge, everyone defending his own turf."

I had to hand it to Greg: he had casually moved the topic from Curtis, a subject he knew would pain me, to hospital politics. Go, Greg, go.

After we'd finished eating, the adults remained at the table a while, chatting and sipping the extremely fine wine Greg had brought. For all my two friends had resisted my matchmaking attempts, they seemed to be getting along fine, and it felt good to spend a cold night around a cozy table. Sociopathic landlords, religious nuts, eviction threats and even rocks through windows all faded into a mellow haze of wine and full tummies.

I was vaguely aware that Rose and Dawn were in the alcove with the computer, probably surfing the net or something. I had just dug out an ancient bottle of liqueur, probably last used a year or so ago, and was pouring thimble-sized servings, when Dawn touched my elbow.

"I don't think Rose is feeling well, Mom. Can you come?"

Sure enough, Rose clutched the edge of the computer table, looking as though she might fall over any second. Her face was grey, her eyes looked glassy, and there was a pale greenish tinge around her mouth. Poor thing, she was probably exhausted.

"You look worn out, Rose. Why don't you try and lie down for a while? It's been a long couple of days for you." I began to guide her toward Dawn's room.

"I'll be okay," she said, not meeting my eyes. "I think I just ate a bit too much."

I had never seen anyone faint before, and it kind of surprised me, the way her legs just seemed to lose their ability to support her. It wasn't at all the way it happens in the movies, where the heroine claps the back of her hand to her forehead before swooning elegantly into a conveniently placed chaise longue.

One second Rose swayed gently, and the next she was sprawled on the floor. Just like that. Live and learn.

8

Carmen and Greg leaped to their feet in unison, nearly upending the table in their stampede to assist Rose. I knelt over her, slapping her wrists. This, according to information gleaned from too many evenings spent watching movies, is the correct procedure for dealing with people who have fainted. Greg gently but firmly pushed me aside.

"Let me take a look. Don't worry," he murmured, checking Rose's pulse and peering under her eyelids. "It looks like a simple faint. Probably just fatigue and stress. Dawn, would you mind bringing me a pillow, please?"

Dawn dashed to her room. I grabbed the pillow from her and went to lift Rose's head, but Greg stopped me again.

"We need to elevate her feet till she comes round," he said. He lifted Rose's legs and propped them gently so they were a few inches above her head. Well, fine, Mr. Know-it-all.

Within a couple of minutes, Rose was struggling to sit up.

"What happened?" she kept asking.

"It's okay, you just fainted," Greg reassured her.

"Oh, my God ..." She stared at him. "You mean, like my mother?"

"Not like your mother at all," I said. "This is just from being too tired. Stress, you know. What your mother had was different. Don't worry about it."

She didn't look convinced, but she did agree to go lie down for a bit. We half-walked, half-carried Rose into the bedroom and settled her into Dawn's bed. She closed her eyes obediently when I suggested she try to get some sleep.

Back in the living room, Carmen raised her eyebrows at me. "What in heaven's name is going on with that girl? Shouldn't you phone her parents or something, to let them know she's sick?"

I shushed her, leading her into the kitchen where there was less chance we could be overheard. I wasn't about to repeat last night's error, letting Rose overhear us.

"Carmen, I thought you knew who she was," I whispered.

My friend frowned and shook her head. "No ... why? Should I?"

"She's Rose Stanley — Marion's daughter. I told you she was staying here."

"What! You most certainly did not!" Carmen stared at me, her eyes huge and dark. "Believe me, Katy, I'd have remembered!"

"I did too," I insisted, though now I wasn't so sure I had said anything. Well, who could blame me? The past few days had been a bit of a blur.

"What's going on?" Greg squeezed into the kitchen.

"I was just explaining to Carmen about Rose. Her mother died over the weekend, and her father won't take her back home. I'm trying to find her someplace to live."

Carmen leaned heavily against the counter. She looked stricken.

"Oh, my dear, that poor little thing." Her voice was thick and soft. "I had no idea!"

Carmen always has been sympathetic to children in distress, probably because of her own childhood. Her father was some kind of hotshot lawyer with the government, and her mother spent most of her time in bed with a bottle of gin for company. Carmen became a fixture at my house, particularly on her family's housekeeper's days off. Like I said, we were almost like sisters.

"What are you going to do with her?" she asked, dabbing at the corners of her eyes with a piece of paper towel. "Surely she can't stay here forever? I mean, I know things are tight for you, aren't they? I know you'll do your best for her, but ..."

"Rose is going to stay with us for a while," I said firmly. "At least until we can make alternate arrangements. I don't know how long that might be, but I'm sure we'll work something out."

"But what about her future? Kids need stability," Carmen objected. "You have to think about the future."

"No shit, Carmen. I've been working on it, believe me. I'm talking to her aunts, and we're working something out." I feigned confidence I was far from feeling. "Anyway, it's not your worry. I'm dealing with things."

"Katy Klein, don't you take that snippy tone with me!" Carmen reached for the Drambuie bottle. Her hand shook as she poured herself another measure. She threw back the burning liqueur in one gulp.

I sighed and started stacking dishes in the sink. "Then don't treat me like some kind of incompetent. You always —"

Greg interrupted us. "Ladies, please ..."

I closed my mouth on what I'd been about to say. "Sorry, Greg. You're right. Bickering isn't what Rose needs right now."

Dawn poked her head into the kitchen. It's a good thing she didn't try to join us, as she would not have fit. "Rose says she wants to talk to you, Mom. And she asked for a glass of water. Geez, guys, aren't you feeling a little claustrophobic in here?"

Rose looked tiny, almost lost amidst the duvet and pillows. Her pale cheeks were shiny with tears, her eyes puffy.

"Hey, Rose ..." I sat on the edge of the bed.

"Hey." She tried to smile a bit, but the effect was merely grotesque. More tears slid down the sides of her face, pooling in the hollows of her ears and in the bony indentation at the base of her neck. I pulled a handful of tissues from the box on Dawn's bedside table and handed them to her.

"Rose, look. Things might feel pretty bad right now, but they'll get better, don't worry. They'll be just fine."

Rose struggled upright, propping herself against the pillows. The tears stopped, and she looked soberly at me.

"Things aren't going to be fine ever again," she said. "My mother — she's dead, isn't she?"

I felt the grief of her words like a clenched fist in my chest. I nodded.

"I thought so. Sylvie told me, and I said she was a filthy liar, but deep down I knew she was telling the truth."

"She wasn't lying. Do you want to talk about it?"

She stared down at the duvet cover, spreading her fingers apart. Absently, she used her index finger to chip at the peeling nail polish from her thumb.

"I dunno. Probably not. She's gone — that's all there is to it, isn't it?"

"Sort of. But it's better if you can talk about how you feel about it."

"Yeah, yeah. That's what the social worker at the Royal told me, too. When they locked me up. Talk about it, she said, it'll make you feel better. Well, I talked and I talked and I talked, and then I went home and everything was exactly the same as it was when they stuck me in the hospital. Talking didn't change anything."

I couldn't argue with that. "Well, if you want to talk to me, you know where I am."

"Yeah. Well." Suddenly, the greenish tinge around her mouth deepened, and Rose threw back the covers. Holding her mouth, she ran for the bathroom, stumbling in her haste. I heard the sounds of her vomiting. The toilet flushed, and shortly she reappeared, looking even more haggard.

"Fuck," she said. "I hate it when that happens. I hate puking."

"Been doing it a lot?" Suddenly the pit of my stomach felt like a lump of lead. I didn't want her to answer. I was afraid I already knew what she was going to say.

She nodded. "Just this past month or so. It's gross."

"Oh," I said. I couldn't think of a more intelligent response. Just, "oh."

She crawled back into bed, pulling the covers up until they nearly buried her head. I sat for a couple of minutes, trying to think of something to say, but my brain was a numb blank. Finally, I told her to try to get some sleep, and I left, pulling the bedroom door shut behind me.

Carmen, Greg and Dawn had moved back to the living room, and they all looked up as I emerged from the bedroom.

"What was that all about?" Greg whispered. "I thought I heard her throwing up?"

"I think she might be pregnant." As I said it, I knew there was no doubt. Intuitive flashes of insight are not really my forte, but every cell in my being told me this was a certainty.

"Mom, is that even possible?" Dawn was appalled. "She's younger that I am! I mean, I know it's possible, but -"

I flopped down into my favourite spot on the couch, rubbing my temples to make them stop throbbing.

"So who could the father be?" Greg whispered. "Does she have a boyfriend?"

Dawn shrugged. "Sylvie never said anything one way or the other. But Rose doesn't say much about herself — she could be going out with someone and just not tell anyone."

"She's way too young for this," Greg said. "And she looks anaemic already. She's going to need a lot of support if she decides to go through with this."

"What about an abortion?" Carmen said, looking a little green around the gills herself.

"I doubt it," Dawn said. "She goes to some religious school or something, and Sylvie says Rose's church won't even let people use birth control or anything. It's all about God's will, or something. I don't get it."

"Come on," Carmen said. "Aren't we putting the cart before the horse, here? We don't even know for sure that she's ... well, you know."

"I know," I said. "In my gut. But you're right, we're going to have to get her to a doctor for a test. And a check-up. She doesn't look all that healthy to me."

"So what do we do now?" Dawn asked.

"I guess we'll have to inform her father at some point," I said, "but I don't want to be the one to do it. Greta needs to know, too, I suppose, but I've already talked to her twice in the past two days, and I'm all Greta'd out at the moment. It'll just have to wait until morning."

"Poor little girl, all alone," Carmen said to no one in particular.

She sounded a little fuzzy, and I wondered exactly how much of my liqueur she'd consumed. Tears rolled unchecked down her cheeks, carving channels through her carefully-applied make-up.

"How did her mother die? Does anyone know?" Greg asked.

"Good question," I said. "At Carmen's party last weekend, Marion just collapsed on the floor in an epileptic seizure. Went into status epilepticus, right out of the blue. And only about half an hour after she'd taken her meds, too."

Greg frowned. "That shouldn't happen, not in a well-controlled case. It sounds really weird."

I looked at him curiously. "What do you mean?"

"Well, epilepsy itself is like an electrical storm in the brain. If a person's taking their meds regularly, and they have good seizure control, they shouldn't even have a single seizure, let alone an uninterrupted string of them."

"So what happened to Rose's mother?" Dawn looked puzzled.

"Well, I'm pretty sure the only cause would be drug non-compliance. Did she have a history of this kind of thing?"

I shook my head. "Non-compliance? Greg, I told you, I watched her take her meds, not half an hour before she started seizing. And I'm absolutely certain her sister told me the epilepsy was well-controlled. This is really weird ..."

"It's all my fault," Carmen wailed. "If I hadn't had that damned party ..."

"Don't be foolish," I snapped, more quickly than I'd intended. "How could it possibly be your fault?"

Carmen said nothing, but she wiped her nose on her sleeve and glared at me blearily.

"You don't understand. How could you? It wasn't your party."

"Mom — you said her husband was pulling at her, right?" Dawn intervened.

I nodded. "It took a couple of guys to pull him off."

"And Rose told Sylvie that her dad used to beat on her mother all the time. He hated her. So what if he did something to her? Put a drug in her drink, or something? I bet you anything he killed her."

Okay, it wasn't one of those Agatha Christie moments when someone announces the name of the murderer, but Dawn's words dropped like hot coals. We sat transfixed, none of us wanting to touch them. There was much uncomfortable shifting and hemming and hawing. At last, Carmen broke the silence.

"Come along, now, Dawn. If Rose's father really had killed Marion, wouldn't someone have noticed by now?"

She sounded like a chiding schoolmarm repri-
manding a student. It would have been more convinc-
ing if her words hadn't sounded so out of focus. I made
a mental note not to let her drive home.

Dawn's cheeks flushed, and I could see impending
signs of a don't-patronize-me-just-because-I'm-young
tantrum on the horizon. Dawn does not care to be
talked down to.

"Dawn could be right, for all we know," I defended
my daughter. "Rose's father is a mean-mouthed
troglodyte who doesn't give a shit about his daughter.
Maybe he did do something to his wife. We just don't
know."

"You're right, we don't," Greg pitched in.

He was doing his patented Voice of Reason thing.
I'd heard him use this tone in a psychiatric group, when
Joey was threatening to inflict physical harm on
Ahmed should the latter refuse to withdraw his recent
comment on Joey's mother's sexual proclivities. It
worked in group; it worked here. Everyone stood down.

But a sullen bunch we were. Carmen cracked first.
Brightly, she exclaimed, "Well, my dears, it's been
a ... remarkable evening. I really hate to be the one to
leave first, but," and here she yawned eloquently, two
manicured fingertips delicately shading the perfect O
of her mouth, "I've got a lot of work to do tomorrow.
Must turn in early. Katy, thank you so much for everything."

Carmen goes out of her way to detour around any
kind of unpleasantness, and the evening's events must
have driven her conflict-meter right off the scale. I
can't say I blame her. She grew up in a house where
even minor disagreements meant ducking to avoid the
flying gin bottles.

I called a taxi, then accompanied my friend to the front vestibule and handed her the silk-lined fuchsia wool coat Dawn had deposited carefully on my bed. That coat would have cost me two months' pay, I thought irrelevantly.

"I'm sorry the evening ended like this — we'll have to go to a movie together soon." I tried to smooth things over. "Give me a call, okay?"

Carmen shrugged the exquisitely cut coat over her equally tasteful suit, lost her balance for a moment, then steadied herself and smiled beatifically at me.

"Of course, of course. Couldn't be helped. Not your fault. You do live such an ... interesting life."

Whatever in hell that was supposed to mean. She hugged me and promised to call later in the week.

"Oh," she said, turning in the doorway on her way down the steps, "did Diana Farnsworth ever get in touch with you?"

"Yes. Yes, she did. Sorry, I meant to thank you for the referral. How'd you convince her to come to me?"

Carmen smiled her lazy cat smile.

"Ve haf our vays," she said. "Tell you all about it next time. Anyway, must dash. I'll call you."

She tottered out the front door, and I watched her descend the steps and slip into the taxi. People like Carmen can be extraordinarily irritating, I have always thought. What right has she to hog all the social ease, the elegance, the truly stunning coats that I'd give my eyeteeth for? She makes mere mortals like me feel boorish, frumpy and socially retarded. Even half-looped, Carmen made a graceful exit. I'd probably have thrown up on my shoes or something.

I frequently ask myself how two such radically different women have managed to tolerate, let alone love one another, for close on forty years. All I can think is that the shared investment at some point grew too great to throw away. Even our arguments have a flavour of familiarity that keeps us on speaking terms. That's friendship, I guess. Or something.

In the living room, Dawn and Greg sat murmuring together. Remembering Rose's panic at overhearing us last night, I quietly peeked into Dawn's room. The little lump under the duvet had not shifted, and I could hear Rose's faint, even breathing as I closed the door softly.

"What now, gang?" I kept my voice low.

"Dawn was saying we should go have a chat with Rose's father," Greg said. "I don't think that's a bad idea, under the circumstances. I'm not so sure about the theory that he killed his wife, but I think he needs to take a bit more responsibility for his daughter."

"Isn't it Pearl Walker's job to interview this guy?" I countered. "When I talked to him this morning, he wasn't any too friendly, and I don't think he's going to be thrilled to hear from us."

"But Mom," Dawn said, "this Mrs. Walker isn't going to come out and ask him if he murdered Rose's mother, is she?"

"Probably not," I admitted, "but what are we supposed to do? Show up at his house and say, 'Hey, buster, you have a responsibility to look after your teenaged daughter, who incidentally is pregnant, and by the way, did you happen to kill your wife? Just asking.' I don't think it would be productive. Besides, that's not the point here. The point is, what's going to happen to Rose?"

"But Mom, don't you even care? What about Rose's mother? We have to find out —"

"We don't have to find out anything, Dawn.

Marion died, and that's sad, but if there's any evidence her death wasn't accidental, well, that's why we have a police force. I'm sure they've already looked into it. Our job is to find a home for Rose."

"You never would have said that before last summer," Dawn grumbled.

"Maybe not, but I learn from my mistakes. And I say we leave this alone. Catching Adam's killer was a once in a lifetime experience, Dawn, not something I'd care to make into a habit."

"Your mother's right, Dawn," Greg said. "We nearly got ourselves killed. I think we need to focus on the task at hand here."

Dawn scowled ferociously at us; we ignored her.

"Well, when the social worker goes out to see Rose's dad, we should go with her," she pronounced. "What if she needs some backup? We know what's been going on better than anyone else ..."

I laughed. I can't imagine where this kid gets her persistence. "Honey, after last summer, I hung up my tights and cape. For one thing, we don't know if or when Mrs. Walker is going to go see Phil. And secondly, Pearl is an experienced social worker. If she feels she needs backup, she can take another worker, or even a police officer, along with her."

"But ..."

"But nothing. I spent almost all day today hunting Rose down, and I'm not about to get myself into another *kasheh* on her behalf. I've got enough problems in my own life. Plus, I'm not going to stick my nose in and then have to back away again — she doesn't need us adding to her troubles."

"You're right. Absolutely." Greg stood up and stretched. "I have to get going, ladies. But Dawn, you should listen to your mother. I think she knows what she's talking about, here."

As he adjusted his cashmere scarf and tucked it into his Burberry, he added, "By the way, you are going to call Pearl in the morning, aren't you?"

"Sure. I'll call her first thing and let her know about the new situation. She said this morning that if I could find Rose, the system could rev into gear. I'll talk to Greta, too. She needs to know about the possibility of pregnancy. I don't see that it's up to us to decide what Rose should do, but she's too young and underfed to even think about having a child. Maybe Greta can have a word with her. Or several, knowing Greta." I grinned.

"Okay," Greg said. "And I'll see if I can track down Bill James. He's a neurologist, a decent guy. This business about Marion just keeling over for no reason doesn't sit well with me. I'll call you if I find anything, okay?"

We hugged briefly, and he stepped out into the night.

I spent the next hour scrubbing plates, pots and pans, losing myself in the repetitive mindlessness of soapy water and clattering dishes. Although I was still certain I'd been right to insist on a policy of non-intervention as far as Rose was concerned, I wasn't at all sure that the system would really help the girl.

9

WEDNESDAY, DECEMBER 15
Moon square Uranus ✦
Sun square Jupiter ✦
Mercury conjunct Uranus ✦
Venus square Mars ✦
Saturn square Neptune ✦

It was past midnight by the time I fell into bed, and it seemed only a few minutes had elapsed when I was wakened by the shrill summons of my bedside phone.

"Um. Hello?" I croaked, squinting at the red glow of the clock radio.

Seven-thirty. That would be morning, I supposed, though my room's semi-darkness gave no clue one way or the other.

"Ms. Klein?"

The voice on the other end sounded official, and for a moment I was confused. Had I been summoned to the principal's office again? Why? Oh, right. Another late slip. This time, I'd probably have a detention ... damn. Unfair.

"Hello?"

The voice again. Male. Middle-aged, perhaps. Something familiar about it dragged me upward to the surface of consciousness, and I tried my best to concentrate. I think it would be fair to say I'm not at my best before sunrise.

"Yes?"

"Ms. Klein, this is Detective Steve Benjamin, Ottawa police. I wanted to catch you before you left for the office today."

Wait a second. Detective Steve Benjamin. I know this guy. Wasn't he the cop I met last summer? Right. We'd barely been on speaking terms the last time I saw him.

"Benjamin," I managed. "What do you want? I didn't ask for a wake-up call."

I immediately regretted the harshness of my words. Well, what does he expect, calling before the sun is even up? Did this count as harassing witnesses? Whoa, girl. No paranoid fantasies before your first cup of coffee.

"I wanted to catch you before you left for work. I need to ask you to come down to the station as soon as possible," Benjamin was saying when I tuned back in.

"I don't ... I mean, why? Is something wrong?"

"I think it might be best if you came in. There's something we need to discuss. When can I expect you?"

I sat on the edge of the bed, searching in the dark for my slippers while I tried to sort out what in God's name Detective Steve Benjamin could possibly want with me at this unholy hour.

"I suppose I could drop by on my way to work. If I have to. But I really wish you'd tell me ..."

"That's just fine." He was irritatingly bland. "So I'll see you in an hour or so. You know your way to the department."

He hung up, and I let my eyes close again. Unfortunately, this allowed an image of Detective Steve Benjamin to float through my consciousness. Large and shaggy, he was a by-the-book cop, slow and methodical. And he didn't like me. Oh, he'd never come right out and said it, but he didn't have to. His very posture, the way he pulled back ever so slightly when I talked to him — it all spoke volumes.

So I can't say I was overcome with delight to be wakened by his call. I could think of no reason he'd want to see me, other than possibly to clear up some details about last summer's escapades. If that were the case, couldn't he have waited till a decent hour?

I grumbled my way through my first coffee, then showered and washed my hair. I'd like to say my mood improved as I slid into the rhythm of the day, but it would not be true. In fact, by the time I towelled my hair dry, I was in a foul temper. It wasn't as if I didn't have enough on my mind, without Mr. Officious Cop waking me out of a sound sleep to demand a command performance. He was going to get a piece of my mind, I can tell you.

Dawn and Rose were still asleep when I left the apartment, so I scribbled a note to let them know of my whereabouts, and crept out as quietly as I could. More snow had fallen overnight, and the walk to the police station took twice as long as it needed to. Passing cars still had their headlights on in the early morning gloom, and few pedestrians shared the sidewalk with me.

I was not in a particularly friendly frame of mind by the time the receptionist at the front desk greeted me. It didn't help that she knew me by name. I don't happen to believe that being on a first-name basis with staff at the local police station is a mark of status. Without a word, I stabbed at the elevator button, not caring that I had tramped slush and road salt onto the lobby's shiny tile floors.

At Benjamin's desk in the Major Crimes division, I stood for a moment watching him fill in a form. Then I cleared my throat to alert him to my presence. He lifted his massive head slowly, nodding perfunctorily.

"Ms. Klein, nice to see you again."

He gestured to one of the vinyl chairs in his screened-off cubicle. I sat, my boots dripping the last of their accumulated slush.

"I really don't understand why you need to see me now," I said. "I thought you'd finished taking my statements already. I thought I didn't have to do anything else except show up in court. That is, assuming they ever get around to scheduling the bloody trial. What else do you need from me?"

"This isn't about the Cosgrove case," Benjamin said.

"What do you mean?" I shook my head impatiently. "Why else would you call me?"

"Ms. Klein, do you know a Reverend Nigel Farnsworth?"

I squinted at him stupidly. "Um, yes. Sort of. We've met, anyway. And talked on the phone once. Why?"

"Exactly how well do you know him?"

"I told you. We've met. Actually, I only met him last week, at a party. Benjamin, what's this all about? Why did you drag me out of a sound sleep to answer questions about some guy I barely know?"

"Nigel Farnsworth was found this morning in his home. He's dead."

I blinked rapidly a few times. "Wait a sec. Are we talking about the same guy? Sort of a small-time televangelist? Deep voice? Black hair? Good-looking? He seemed fine when I talked to him yesterday. What did he die of?"

"He was stabbed."

"Benjamin, you're not ... I mean, why do I need to know about this?"

Benjamin just looked at me, his face an irritating blank.

"Oh, now come on!" I protested. "You don't think I had anything to do with his death, do you?"

Benjamin said nothing, but studied my face. I felt myself flush. With anger and outraged indignation. Not guilt. Because after all, I had nothing to feel guilty about.

"Get real! What could I possibly have to do with it?"

"I was hoping you could tell me."

A wave of dizziness swept over me, and I sat back heavily, resting my head against the burnt orange room divider. "Why? Why me?"

"There's some evidence ..."

"Wait. Just tell me one thing. Am I under arrest here?"

"No. No, you're not under arrest. If I'd wanted to arrest you, I wouldn't have phoned you like that. We're just having a friendly chat."

"This by you is a friendly chat?" I wanted to scream at him, but I kept my voice as calm as I could. "You're practically accusing me of killing some guy I hardly even know. What in the world would make you think I had anything to do with his death?"

"Well, your name and phone number were in Mr. Farnsworth's pocket when he died. In his handwriting."

"So? That's stupid! So if he'd had his plumber's card in his hand, you'd have called the poor schmuck out of his warm bed and hauled him down here to interrogate him? Lots of people have my name and phone number, Benjamin! Although —" I paused.

He waited, his eyebrows raised. "Although?"

"Well, it's a tiny bit odd. Not a big deal. I did talk to him yesterday, just to leave a message for his sister. But when I talked to her, she said he'd never given it to her. But he sounded so nice on the phone. Friendly. I don't know why he wouldn't have told her I called."

Benjamin wrote something down. "You know his sister?"

"Sure, Diana. I met her at the same party where I met him."

"And you were phoning her? Why?"

"It's really none of your –" I started, then corrected myself. In point of fact, it was his business. "She's a client of mine," I finished. I'm sure I sounded petty and resentful.

"A client? You mean in your, uh, astrology business?" I watched him closely, but I couldn't discern even the faintest evidence of a smirk.

I nodded. "I saw her once. Monday. She called yesterday to arrange a follow-up appointment, and I called her back. Nigel answered, but he didn't give her the message. That's all there is to it. Can I sign a witness statement and go to work now? I have to earn a living, you know."

Benjamin gave me a look, then wrote something in his notebook. Probably "unco-operative witness." I told you he doesn't like me.

"Ms. Klein, I'll be sure to let you know when I'm done. Now. Did Diana Farnsworth tell you anything about her relationship with her brother?"

"A little," I said. "She told me her brother was a real

nudnik, nosy as they come, and very high energy. Oh, excuse me. A *nudnik* is kind of like a pessimistic busy-body — a nosy person who never has a good word to say about anything."

"I know what a *nudnik* is, Ms. Klein. My parents spoke Yiddish in our home," Benjamin said, obviously enjoying my astonishment. He actually allowed something resembling a smile to flit across his saturnine features.

"Sorry, I ... I mean, you don't seem ..."

What do I say here? Geez, you don't look Jewish? Well, he didn't. In fact, I would have said Irish or maybe Scandinavian. All that red hair. I tried to picture him wearing a yarmulke, but the image eluded me. Well, so much for my acute powers of observation. I flushed, and said nothing.

"Forget it." He brushed aside my embarrassment. "Have you spoken to Ms. Farnsworth since her last appointment with you?"

"Yes. She called me back, shortly after I spoke to her brother. She sounded angry that he hadn't given her my message."

"What did she say?"

"I can't really recall," I said, and that was true. "Something about ... I think I told her it was no big deal, and she said yes it was. That was it."

"Well, if you should happen to hear from her again, I'd appreciate knowing about it."

"But — she lives with him. Wasn't she there when the cops ... when you found the body?"

Benjamin shook his massive head. "I can't discuss Ms. Farnsworth's possible involvement in the case. But we haven't interviewed her yet."

"You're saying she's ... uh, on the lam?" Next thing

you know, I'd be asking if she was packing heat. This police thing is contagious.

"It's possible she is avoiding contact with the authorities, yes. But we aren't making any assumptions at the moment. If you see her, get her to call me."

"Yeah, right. But this is weird ... two in the same week."

"What? What do you mean?" He glanced at me sharply.

"Nothing. It's probably just coincidence. In fact, it has to be."

"Ms. Klein ..." There was a warning edge in his voice.

"Sorry. It's just that I know someone else who died this week — someone who went to Farnsworth's church."

"Exactly how did this, uh, person die?" Benjamin picked up his pencil again.

"She had a massive epileptic seizure. She was a known epileptic, and that's not unknown. But the thing is, I saw her take her meds not half an hour before she collapsed. So it's just odd, that's all. Not in the same league with a stabbing, of course."

"What was her name?"

I gave him Marion's name, rank and serial number, and he wrote them down dutifully. "Okay, Ms. Klein, I think that's it for today. Be sure and let me know if you think of anything else, okay?"

I resisted the urge to snap to attention and salute. "Is that all? You don't need me for anything else?"

"I'll let you know. But if you think of anything, no matter how trivial, please call me. You have my number, right?"

I nodded and began to suit up for the hike to work. Benjamin handed me my gloves, which had dropped to the avocado-green carpeting, some decorator's idea of a soothing colour, no doubt. Or maybe it just hides coffee and puke stains well. I rose to leave, and Benjamin accompanied me to the elevator.

"Don't forget — anything at all," he repeated. "And thanks for coming in, Katy."

✦

Trudging through the slush on my way to the office, I pondered deeply. Nigel Farnsworth was dead — stabbed, Benjamin said. And Diana was missing. The obvious conclusion was that her temper had finally got the best of her. She'd been afraid of that, hadn't she? I read somewhere that stabbings often take place during the course of domestic disputes. Well, Nigel and Diana had been a domestic dispute just waiting to happen. And maybe my phone call had triggered them. I shivered, though I was dressed warmly enough for the chill outdoors.

Despite his official obfuscating, Benjamin had obviously reached the same conclusion. I mulled over my last meeting with Diana, probing for clues. She'd said something about not being free until her brother was dead, hadn't she? Or was I embroidering? I'd have to check my notes.

I stamped my feet on the landing outside my office, shook snow off my shoulders. I turned the key in the lock, and nothing happened. That is, the key turned, but the deadbolt did not click back. The damn lock was broken. Keon would be thrilled to hear from me again.

It was only then that I noticed the splintered door-frame. I gave the door a push and it swung loosely on a broken hinge. Stepping into the room, I let out an involuntary yelp.

The place had been trashed. My futon had been ripped open, and tufts of cotton batting spilled out onto the surrounding floor. Baskets of files lay overturned, several years worth of notes littering the office. My posters, my precious posters of planets and stars, all ripped off the walls, crumpled and tossed into the shambles. The astrolabe my father had given me was bent and broken.

I couldn't look at this. Gulping back tears of rage, I ran downstairs to the bakery and pounded my fists against the door, ignoring the pain. Presently Joanie answered, brushing floury hands on her apron. She was just taking the morning's first batch out of the ovens.

"I need — I have to use your phone," I choked. "Someone broke into my office." Tears streamed down my face and I wiped at them with my bruised fists. Joanie took in the situation wordlessly and led me to the phone behind the counter. I called the police first. Then Greg. Don't ask me why, but in a real crisis, he's the one I turn to first. I guess it's his innate steadiness. I could use a little steadiness just now. Greg was out on rounds, but his secretary promised to have him call me as soon as he got back.

Joanie poured me a fennel tea and gave me a fresh steaming apple cinnamon muffin. She offered a sympathetic hug, and I didn't even mind getting flour on my black turtleneck. The tea smelled vile, but I sipped it politely. It was hot, and it was a distraction from the destruction above. Finally, I trudged back upstairs to await the cops. It was only then that I noticed: someone had spray-painted a large red cross on the inside of the door. And a Star of David, with an X through it. Bitter gall rose in the back of my throat and my eyes watered with the effort of not throwing up.

Nothing in my life could have prepared me for this kind of wanton, random destruction and hatred. My heart ached as I surveyed the room that used to be my refuge. I wondered if this was a tiny inkling of what my mother had felt as a young teen when her family and neighbours had found themselves easy targets for the Nazis who had overrun her native Poland.

The place was freezing, too. In one still-functioning corner of my mind, it occurred to me that I would have to get on Keon's case again. Not that it mattered now. I wouldn't be able to accomplish much work here for a while.

The police constable arrived, the same guy I'd met yesterday. He did a double take when he came in, but he was very sweet about it all, took down the details, asked if anything was missing. Missing? I hadn't thought about that. But if anything was gone, how would I know it?

"Kids," he said. "They probably came in here looking for stuff they could sell. You know, computer equipment and whatnot. Happens all the time in the Glebe."

"So what — they found out I had nothing, so they tore the place apart?"

"Pretty much. I see three or four of these a month, you know. Not likely to happen again — but I'd get a better lock on that door, just in case. And you should try not to touch anything. I'll get them to send someone over to print the place for you."

"Print? Oh, you mean fingerprint. Do they have to?"

"Yep. If you want to find out who did it, they do.

Makes a bit of a mess, but it looks like you'll have some housecleaning to do anyway." The cop chuckled at his own feeble joke. I didn't.

I waited until the cop had gone before I sat down amongst the ruins and sobbed. Then, defying his orders, I rummaged halfheartedly through the mess for an hour or so, stacking things in piles and trying to salvage some of my posters. What was the point of fingerprinting this mess? They'd never find the culprits, I thought. I bet the fingerprinting guy wouldn't even bother showing, for something like this. After all, no one died.

The phone was ringing, somewhere under a pile of paper and cotton futon innards, and I dug around until I found it. It was Greg. I gulped out what had happened.

"Oh God," he said. "Wait. I'll be right over."

"No. There's no point, now. Nothing you can do."

"But –"

"No, really. I just needed to hear a friendly voice. It's just such a …" I searched for the right word. "Such a violation. Brutal."

"Oh, Katy. This is the last thing you need. You make sure and let me know if you need anything, okay? You're not always as tough as you think you are."

"Sure. Thanks. The only thing I can think of now is some paint. I need to get rid of the decorations on the door. I can't imagine working here with that staring me in the face."

"Why don't you let me take care of that?" he offered. "I can come by tonight and do the job, you won't even have to see it when you come in tomorrow."

"Would you?" Somehow, this brightened my spirits considerably.

"Sure. Just leave the key with Joanie downstairs."

"You won't need a key, trust me. Not unless Keon gets a fire under him and fixes the hinges. Which ain't too bloody likely."

After I'd hung up, I set to cleaning with renewed vigour. I hauled the futon downstairs and deposited it in the dumpster in the back alley. If I couldn't re-file all my notes, at least I could stack them in piles by year and shove them back into their respective baskets, which weren't damaged at all. Somehow that felt like a gift — something left intact.

I rewound the answering machine tape and jotted down the messages, half my mind occupied with the task of choosing a new futon. Maybe I'd go for a brighter pattern this time. Wasn't there a sale on at the shop in Centretown? I'd have to check it out at lunchtime.

"You have ignored our warnings, Jezebel."

The answering machine message jolted me to attention. My heart skidded to a standstill. The voice was rich and resonant, the words menacing.

"You unrepentantly practise your Satanic arts. You have refused our offers of salvation. Now it comes down to it: repent or die. We will tolerate no further abominations in the eyes of the Lord." Click.

For an irrational moment, I feared my answering machine had developed a life of its own: the Case of the Possessed Answering Machine. Fumbling, I switched it off. My fingers trembled as I dialled the police station once more. This time I went straight to Detective Benjamin.

"Listen to this," I said when I finally had him on the line.

I played back the message, though I wanted to put my hands over my ears to shut it out. Hearing it once had been bad enough. Benjamin was quiet on the other end of the line.

When the message was done, he said, "Can you think of any reason why someone would leave you a message like that?"

"Because they're a major league nutbar? How the hell should I know?" My voice squeaked, and I coughed to cover up my panic.

"Okay, listen. I need that tape. Could you bring it over to the station for me?"

"Well, the thing is, I'm kind of busy here. I forgot to tell you, when I got in this morning, the place had been torn apart. Completely trashed. And the door was ripped off its hinges, and anti-Semitic stuff spray-painted on it –"

"What?" I could almost see the big man half-rise from his seat. "Why the hell didn't you call?"

"I *did* call." What did he think I was, the village idiot? "An officer was here. Constable McGillivray. He left about an hour ago. Anyway, the vandalism I could handle, sort of. It's this ... this message that's bothering me. I'm starting to feel like someone's after me, Benjamin, and I don't see any cops outside my door to stop them."

"Okay, okay, I get it. You're scared, and that's natural. Who handled the B and E call, again?"

I gave him the officer's badge number, and he sounded mollified.

"Okay. I'll give him a call. And if you could drop that tape off to me when you go home, I'd appreciate it." He was trying his best to be pleasant; I imagined the effort it must be costing him.

"Sure thing. Do you think you can actually catch this maniac? It's not a nice feeling, knowing someone's on the loose who wants me dead. In fact, it's damn scary, Benjamin."

"Well, whoever it is, they've just graduated from making harassing phone calls to uttering death threats. That makes it my business. As to whether we can put our finger on who's doing it, let's just say there's a good chance of it."

"It must be the same person who trashed my office, though, right? I mean, it's pretty obvious ..."

"Could be. That's not really your concern, though, is it? I thought you learned your lesson last summer about butting into police business?" There was a smile in his voice.

I laughed. "You'd think so, wouldn't you?" Suddenly, I was struck between the eyes by a realization. "Oh, shit. Oh, shit, I am such an idiot. I can't believe it!"

"What?" Benjamin sounded alarmed, as well he might.

"Fingerprints. Clues. All that stuff. I've already started cleaning my office. I've probably made it impossible for you to find anything useful." That's what you get for defying a police officer's direct orders, Katy Klein. The small, reproving voice in the back of my head was getting on my nerves.

Benjamin sucked in his breath, and let it out in a long, slow whistle. "Yep, I'd say that was a bit of a blunder, all right. A bit of a blunder."

"So — what should I do now?"

"Look, just leave everything the way it is for now, okay? I'll have a crew come over in about two hours, and they'll have a look around. See if anything's salvageable. Just don't touch anything else."

"I won't."

"And Katy?"

"What?"

"It's not really your fault. The beat cop should have called us in. The cross and the X-ed out *mogen David* should have alerted him that this is more than a simple B and E. Okay?"

"It doesn't make me feel less stupid, but thanks."

We hung up on surprisingly good terms. I turned to the increasingly pressing matter of getting some warm air into this meat locker. Keon's voicemail was on, so I left him a message.

"John. This is Katy Klein. Remember, the tenant you're trying to evict on no grounds whatsoever? Two things: one is that someone just broke in here, and I'm going to need a new lock on the door. In fact, I'll probably need a new door. And two, the heat is off again, and if you can't get over here and turn it on, I'm afraid I'll have to call the city inspectors again. Which will be billed to you at the rate of fifty dollars a shot. So you might want to consider keeping the furnace on, save yourself a bit of money. Just a thought. You're welcome."

Put that in your pipe and smoke it, you little *putz*. Greg would say I was sublimating my anger, turning my rage at the vandals toward a safer target. Maybe so, but I didn't care.

An hour later, I could stand it no longer. I yanked on my boots and jacket and headed down the street to Java De-Lux, the neighbourhood latté bar. Here, I intended to indulge my caffeine addiction in a relatively warm environment while attempting to ignore the shrieks and squawks of the intensely cerebral acid jazz that the café's owners inflict daily on their customers.

Normally, I would have ordered my cappuccino to go. Instead I perched on a metal low-backed stool at a tiny café table, thumbing through a magazine quiz on how to keep your man happy in bed. Hah. How about how to find someone you'd even want within a hundred feet of your bed?

As if to underscore my already foul mood, some idiot jostled my table, sloshing frothy coffee onto my clean anorak. I gritted my teeth and looked up. It was John Keon, swaggering in front of me with his beady little capitalist eyes narrowed to slits in his overfed face.

"You left me a message," he said.

"Whoa, can't put anything past you, John."

His face reddened. Not an attractive look. "I already told you, the furnace is on. You got nothing to complain about. By the way, I stuck your eviction notice on the door. I notice you damaged the lock and the frame. Guess you can give me a cheque for that before you leave."

"I told you, John, someone broke into my office. Not my responsibility. As I understand it, landlords are supposed to keep their property in good repair."

"Yeah, sure. But I have only your word for it that someone broke in, right?"

He leaned toward me and I pulled back involuntarily to avoid a mouthful of his leather jacket. I could have bitten him, but pigs aren't kosher.

Slowly, I pushed back my stool and rose to my full height of five feet, ten inches, a couple of inches taller than Keon. Expressionless, I took a step toward him, and he stepped back involuntarily. He looked alarmed at this sudden turn of events. I stared at him impassively, saying not a word. Just call me the Terminator.

He edged sideways, his body was at a slight angle to mine. I stepped forward again, squaring off against him once more. He kept moving backward at an angle, and I kept countering him, neither of us saying a word, for a full minute. We were making a series of slow circles around the small café, and the few customers in the place stared at our strange dance of aggression.

Finally, Keon backed up against the dessert counter and could go no further. His eyes darted from side to side, looking for an escape route.

"I want the heat turned on, John."

"It is on, b–" He caught himself and moistened his upper lip with a pink tongue. John liked to do his name-calling where there were no witnesses.

At that moment, Joanie, the purple-haired baker from Fruits of the Earth, came into the café. She looked irate. Her lip-ring trembled with rage, her floury fists were parked on her slight hips.

"John, our oven just stopped working. Have you paid the gas bill?"

All eyes in Java De-Lux turned to Keon. The morning coffee break crowd were getting their money's worth today; this was better than Jerry Springer. Keon ran a nervous hand over his sparse hair.

"Yeah, sure. I always pay my bills."

"So if I were to call the gas company, they'd say there was no problem, right?" I made a move toward the payphone in the back of the café.

"I'll call them," he said, sweat beading on his forehead. "Don't you girls worry about it. Just some mix-up. It's all taken care of." He slid past me, toward the door.

"Sure, John," I called after him. "Just let us know when the building will be habitable again, okay? Wouldn't want to have to call the inspectors ... again."

As the door swung shut behind our landlord,

Joanie and I looked at one another and giggled uncontrollably.

"*Don't you girls worry about it,*" Joanie intoned pompously. "It's really not all that funny, though. No gas means we don't get all our stock baked today, so we'll probably lose about five hundred dollars. And you can't possibly work up there in your office. It must be like a deep-freeze. Did the police tell you anything, by the way? Do they know who did it?"

"Not really. I'm trying not to think about it. God, it did my heart good to see Keon beetle off like that. Why don't you let me get you some tea while we wait? May as well enjoy our time off."

So we sipped our drinks of choice, then wandered back to our building, where a van from the gas company was parked. Inside Fruits of the Earth, a very polite young man was re-lighting the pilot flame on the huge oven. He assured us that the furnace was now on, though with the building's decrepit heating system, it would take a while for my office to warm up.

"Better make sure Keon pays you in cash," I said.

"We always do, ma'am. He's one of our regulars." The guy grinned broadly.

On my way back upstairs, I realized I hadn't made any of the calls I'd planned for this morning. To be fair, it's not every day I get a wake-up call from the police, followed by having my office trashed, but that didn't make Rose's plight any less urgent. I booked an appointment for her with my doctor, a soft-spoken woman who wouldn't spook the kid too much. Then I called Pearl Walker at the Children's Aid.

I explained the New, Revised Rose Situation, and Pearl promised to open a file that very day and initiate an investigation into Rose's home life. There was one small caveat, however: the investigation could take several months.

"Several months?" I squeaked. "Why so long?"

"Katy, we're operating under severe budgetary constraints. As long as we can't pay enough workers to cover the waterfront, kids will keep falling through the cracks, and the cracks are going to keep getting wider. It's the basic economic equation: we get what we pay for."

Indeed. So I really hadn't accomplished much — Rose needed a place to live now, not in a few months. Frustration seemed to be the motif for the week, I decided, as I rifled through stacks of disorganized client notes, searching for my session with Diana. It was nowhere to be found, but neither were any of my current client files. Irritated, I flung down a stack of papers. They fanned out across the floor, and I just sat there and looked at them. Then I remembered — I wasn't supposed to be touching anything. I buried my head in my hands and moaned. It was not turning out to be a good day.

10

It took a couple of hours for heat to start clanking and hissing its way through the antiquated radiators, but gradually I was able to take off my anorak, then my gloves. Ah, luxury. I sat in a corner of my office, waiting for the police evidence crew to arrive. There was nothing to do but stare at the chaos around me. It was almost a relief when the phone rang.

"Katy? It's Greg. Just wanted to see how you were doing."

"Not great. I can't touch anything till the cops get here, and once I do, it's going to take me forever to get this place functional again. I guess that means you shouldn't come to paint the door until tomorrow night, if that's okay with you. Oh — and I had an early morning phone call from our friend Detective Benjamin. Seems that a guy I met at Carmen's party was stabbed to death. And his sister, whom I also know, has disappeared. Oh, plus I had a showdown with my sleazy landlord. It's been a hell of a day, Greg. How about a scrip for some tranquillizers?"

He laughed. "Sounds godawful. But you don't need tranquillizers — you need a vacation. What did Benjamin want from you?"

"Well, I think he wanted to accuse me of murder, but I convinced him I was clean. It was that Farnsworth guy — you know, the one I told you about? I think Carmen had a bit of a thing for him ... oh, shit!"

"What?"

"Well, I don't know if she knows he's dead. I should call her. She's going to hit the roof — first Marion, now this guy."

"Yikes. Well, speaking of Marion, you'll never believe who I ran into at Grand Rounds today."

"Enlighten me."

"Remember I mentioned Bill James, the neurologist? I was going to check with him about the way Marion died."

"So what did he say?"

"Well, to start with, Marion was his patient."

I made a noise of astonishment, something between a snort and a gasp. "You're kidding! So did he know how she died?"

"Well, it's basically what you already know. Saturday night he was on call, and who does he see in full seizure but his perfect patient, the one who's never given him any trouble. Of course they tried to pump her full of Valium, to arrest the seizure, but obviously they couldn't feed it in fast enough."

"You mean there was a chance they could have stopped it?"

"Oh, sure. If they'd got to her sooner. But by the time Marion got to the hospital, she was just too far gone. Her body temperature had already started skyrocketing, and her brain basically fried."

If I miss a dose, my brain fries. Isn't that what Marion had said to me at the party?

"That's what she told me, too," I said. "But I don't

understand. Greta told me her sister's epilepsy was well-controlled, and I saw her take her meds. Green-and-yellow pills, right?"

"Right. Bill couldn't figure it out either. He said Marion had a history of non-compliance when she was first diagnosed, back when she was a kid. After she had Rose, though, she was fine, no problem at all. There were a couple of breakthrough seizures while they adjusted her dosage, but that was it."

"But this makes no sense. Could the drugs have just stopped working for some reason? Or could she have accidentally skipped a dose or two? Because I'm absolutely positive I saw her take her meds, Greg."

"To go into status like that, she'd have had to miss at least two doses, according to Bill. She was a brittle epileptic — needed the drug on a regular basis, around the clock. Every four hours."

"Weird." I shook my head, unable to fathom it.

"Well, her pills were in her purse when they brought her in, and according to the pharmacy records, she was right on target — the correct number of pills in the case. She had one of those little cases with compartments for each dose, so she could make sure she'd taken the right amount. There was an autopsy, but it didn't show much — her blood levels were all wonky because of the drugs they'd pumped into her, trying to save her life."

"They checked the pills? Dilantin can't ... you know, go bad? Lose its effectiveness?"

"Sure, any drug can do that. But there's nothing to indicate anyone checked the pills for active medication. That's a good point."

"I wonder if they still have them?"

"Doubt it. No one but you actually saw Marion

take the meds. Bill says her death was officially chalked up to non-compliance. Death by misadventure. They probably just chucked the rest of the pills."

"So we'll never know, then."

"Doesn't look like it. I guess the only thing we can do now is make sure Rose is taken care of."

"Hah." I told Greg about my conversation with Pearl Walker, and he groaned at the news that it could take months to process her case.

"So what are you going to do?"

"Good question. I'll have to meet Greta and her sister, I guess, and try to find the poor kid somewhere to live in the interim, at least while Pearl gets things in motion."

"Let me know if I can do anything, okay?"

I assured him that I would, and hung up. The sky was a deep greyish purple by quarter to five, and I could see no point hanging around the office any longer. Joanie would be downstairs till nine, and she'd let the cops in if they ever got there. I might as well head out and drop the answering machine tape off at Benjamin's desk.

Of course, by the time I left my office, the indoor temperature was just about perfect — a comfortable 20 degrees Celsius. By tomorrow, the place would be sub-Saharan. Maybe this eviction thing was all for the best.

Outside, the mercury had taken a nosedive and the air practically crackled, it was so cold. By the time I reached the police station, my chin was numb and I couldn't feel the tips of my fingers. Plus, the day's accumulation of slush had frozen to slick ice, and I fell three or four times along the way, hurting my hip and my knee. This day had been a disaster from start to finish.

Bruised, frozen, my eyes and nose streaming from the cold, I staggered into the dazzling light of the main lobby, emitting a steady flow of cuss words in your choice of English and Yiddish. I'm sure I was an impressive sight.

Benjamin was not at his desk when I arrived. I hovered uncertainly near his cubicle, close to tears of fatigue and frustration, until another officer, this one in uniform, let me know that Detective Benjamin had been called out, but that he was expected back any minute, and was I Ms. Klein? The detective had been expecting me, and he'd asked if I could possibly wait for his return. Would I like a cup of coffee? Sorry, but all they had was non-dairy creamer, would that be okay?

Sighing, I began the slow process of removing my outdoor layers, and by the time I'd stripped down to my cotton turtleneck and handknitted sweater, Benjamin popped his shaggy head round the corner. His hair looked like he'd been engaging in hand-to-hand combat with a weed-whacker. Just once, I'd like to get that man a decent haircut. I'd do it for free, a gesture of charity. A public service.

He apologized for keeping me waiting, and I handed over the tape. One might almost have thought we were developing a good working relationship.

"So — what happened to your office? McGillivray tells me it was a bit of a mess. Did the team get there before you left?"

I shrugged. "Nope. And McGillivray is right about the mess. But he chalked it up to neighbourhood kids, out scrounging for computer equipment to sell. I'm not so sure. I get these phone calls all the time, you know, I don't usually think anything about them.

They're just nutcases who think I practise black magic or something. No one's ever done anything like this to me before."

"And do you?" He grinned, transforming from a scruffy-looking dog into ... well, at least Cro-Magnon Man. In fact, he looked almost likeable. "Practise black magic, that is?"

"I'm not even going to dignify that with an answer. Did McGillivray tell you someone heaved a rock through my window a couple of days ago?"

"He did. You think it was the same people? Religious nuts?"

"I don't know. I assume so. It's not like I have a lot of enemies. Oh, except my landlord."

Benjamin nodded. "What's his name?"

"Keon. John Keon. Look, I'm not trying to tell you your business, but do you really think a landlord would vandalize his own property? No matter how much he dislikes me –"

"No telling," Benjamin grunted. "I'll get it checked out."

"Thanks. Maybe you could get him to keep the furnace turned on, while you're at it."

"Sure thing. We aim to please. Listen, I'm off work in a couple of minutes. It's nasty walking out there — you want a lift home?"

"Oh, great! My neighbours would love to see me being dropped off in a police car. They already look at me funny after you guys came around last summer, with all the sirens and lights and what-not." I meant it as a joke, but it didn't come out the way I'd intended.

Benjamin flushed, and looked hurt. "I do drive my own vehicle after hours. Obviously. But of course, if you don't want to be seen with me, I understand."

"Oh, God, I'm sorry. I didn't mean — I mean, thank you for your kind offer; a ride would be very nice."

I tried to sound like Carmen: gracious, on top of things, unrattled. He drove me home in a perfectly respectable-looking black Taurus, no flashing light or siren in sight, and we were silent the whole way. I'd had a long day, and apparently Benjamin didn't engage in small talk.

"Well, I'll see you around," he said awkwardly, as I scrambled out of the car, directly into a frozen snowbank.

I turned to look at him, but I couldn't read the expression on his face. So I just thanked him for the ride and let the car door swing shut.

The apartment was quiet for a change. I flopped into an armchair for a few minutes, basking in the unaccustomed silence. Dawn and Rose had gone to Sylvie's, according to the scrawled note on the counter. I curled up on the couch for a while, resting my head and trying to motivate myself to get up and make supper.

Eventually, with Wilson Pickett strutting and wailing in the background, I began to throw some food together. I was just discovering the limitations of trying to dance to "In the Midnight Hour" while chopping onions, when Peter, my ex-husband, let himself in, ostensibly to borrow a cup of flour.

"Nice try, honeybun," I said, not missing a beat as I gyrated over to the sink. Dancing to the Wicked Pickett while making supper is about as close as I get to aerobic exercise. "When's the last time you made anything involving flour? That's way out of your league. Weren't you the one who managed to burn eggs while attempting to boil them?"

"You wound me," he sniffed. "It just so happens

that I am teaching myself the finer points of making bread, and the recipe I chose calls for a cup more flour than I have on hand. Whole wheat, if you've got it. Seriously, I bought one of those breadmaker things, the kind where you pour all the stuff in and leave it on overnight. It's great — you wake up with a nice fresh loaf of bread, hot out of the oven."

"Please pardon me for doubting you." I clattered through the oven drawer in search of a frying pan. "But you have to admit, you've been making yourself scarce lately. And now you just happen to turn up, asking for flour, yet? I figured you were butting your little news-hound nose in again."

"Why? Is there something I should be nosy about? Don't tell me: Brent's back."

He held my ex-lover's name at arm's length, like a particularly malodorous dead fish. I pursed my lips in irritation.

"Why does everyone assume I'd be willing to take up with Brent again, even if he did ask me, which he hasn't, not that it's any of your business. No, I figured you'd want to know about the kid who's staying with us. In fact, I'm surprised you didn't come down earlier."

"Wrong-o. Dawn already told me all about it. She says you think Rose might be pregnant, too."

"Oh. You knew. Well then, you must be here to enquire as to why Detective Steve Benjamin gave me a lift home, right?"

"Nope. How come you were talking to Benjamin? I thought the trial wasn't scheduled till spring."

"Oh, don't ask. Some guy died yesterday in mysterious circumstances, clutching my name and phone number in his hot little hand. Well, cold little hand, actually. Since he was dead. Benjamin assumed the worst."

"What guy? And why did he have your phone number?"

"Nigel Farnsworth. I met him at Carmen's party last week. He's a minister. With a television show. And a sister who hates him. I don't know much more than that. Peter, it's been a day from hell."

Peter whistled. "No kidding. What happened? Sit down and tell Petey all about it."

"Well, you know I get calls now and then from religious types, right? Well, I got a doozy today. Called me a Jezebel and said I deserved to die. And they trashed my office."

"What?" Peter's voice rose a couple of octaves. "Someone trashed your office? Shit, Katy, I wish you'd let me know! When —"

"This morning. I knew you were at work, and I didn't want to bother you. Anyway, I called the police. And Greg's painting over the door tomorrow, bless him."

"Hey, I can help you put things back together. I've got some time over the weekend." He put an arm around my shoulder, and I didn't push him away.

Then, his news-gathering instincts leapt to the fore. "So — about this Farnsworth guy. Do the cops know who killed him?"

I shook my head. "Apparently his sister is missing, but I can't believe she'd do a thing like that. I mean, she's a bit on the prickly side, and she said she hates him, but she was adamant that she totally abhors violence. Although she did wonder ..."

"Wait a sec!" Peter had stopped listening. "You know the victim's sister? Katy, what's going on here? Tell me the whole story, from start to finish."

So I did. I told him about my first meeting with

Nigel and Diana, at Carmen's party, and about Diana's visit to my office. I told him about Carmen's obvious infatuation with the preacher, and about her having referred Diana to me. And I told him about Diana's anger and frustration with Nigel, and her question about how long he might be around to make her life miserable.

"You realize this doesn't sound good for her, right?" Peter leaned against the counter, his eyes hooded in thought. "Two days after she spills her guts about how much she hates the guy, he shows up dead? And you say she admitted to having a temper. I dunno ..."

"I'm sure she didn't mean anything by it. She struck me as someone with high principles, even if she's a bit hard to get along with. She'll turn up soon, you'll see. Maybe she spent the night with a friend, or something. She might not even know Nigel is dead. We don't know."

"Well, did you tell Benjamin about her wishing he'd die?"

I turned away from Peter.

"Katy ... you didn't, did you?"

"It didn't seem important."

"Why are you protecting her? Come on, Katy — if she said she wanted him dead, don't you think that's something the police should know?"

I sighed. "I don't know. Maybe. I didn't get the feeling she was planning to bump him off, though. More just that she wished she could be free of him for a while. The impression I got was that she's always lived in his shadow, and he's pretty hard on her. A sibling thing, I think."

"You mean, like Cain and Abel?"

"Very funny, Peter. Ha, ha. Anyway, what good does it do for the cops to know she hated Nigel, if she's disappeared? Benjamin said they haven't been able to track her down yet ..."

I stopped pushing onions around with a spatula for a moment, and stared into space. A thought had leaped unbidden into my mind. Peter knew the look.

"What? What is it? Come on, Katy, tell."

"Nothing really. I just thought — Carmen referred Diana to me. That means they're friends, right? I just wonder if maybe Carmen knows anything about this? Like maybe even where Diana is?"

"Can't hurt to ask. Want me to watch the onions while you call?"

This was his extremely delicate way of indicating that he wanted me to call *now*. Peter is very good at his job — he can smell the beginnings of a story at fifty paces.

"I don't trust you not to let supper burn. No, it'll wait a few minutes. It's only a possibility that Carmen knows anything, not a certainty."

Peter stood tapping his fingers against the countertop. I finished sautéing the onions at my own leisurely pace, added them to the brown rice along with some beans, eggs, cheese and other good stuff approved by Dawn for human consumption. Then I popped the whole thing into the oven. The whole procedure took at least ten minutes, and by the time I had finished, Peter had graduated to kicking lightly at the baseboards, his long body practically vibrating with curiosity. He has always been a bit hyperactive.

Finally, with exaggerated care, I dialled Carmen's number. The phone rang several times, and I was just about to give up when my friend answered.

" ... Yes?" She sounded distinctly out of breath.

"Sorry, I didn't mean to pull you away from your Stairmaster," I said. "It's just that something's come up that I wanted to check with you. Got a minute?"

"Not really." Her voice was frosty.

Whoa. The last time I'd heard her sound like this, we'd been in our early twenties, and she was refusing to speak to me because I'd rejected her advice and ended my relationship with Brent. The first time around, that is.

"What is it? Have I done something to make you mad?"

My mind raced, checking off possibilities. I thought we'd parted on good terms last night. Had I missed something, some subtle nuance that a more sensitive person would have noticed immediately?

"Sorry, Katy. No, it's not you." She sounded a little friendlier, but tension laced her voice. "It's just ... I've had a hard day at the office. You know. Didn't mean to take it out on you."

"Oh, well, I won't keep you then. I was just wondering if you'd spoken with Diana Farnsworth recently."

There was a long pause. "Diana? No. I haven't. Why do you ask?"

I am not known for my discretion and tact, but Carmen sounded as though the least little thing would send her screaming for her stash of Valium and vintage wine right about now. So I decided the news about Nigel Farnsworth could wait.

"No reason. I was expecting to see her this afternoon for an appointment, and she never showed. That's all. Don't worry about it, it's nothing to do with you. Listen, go have a hot bath, okay? You sound like you could use something to unwind."

"You're absolutely right. I'll do that. Bye."

"You didn't push her very hard." Peter sounded aggrieved.

"She was practically on the edge of a nervous breakdown."

"So? When is Carmen not like that?"

"Come on, Peter. You know how she can be sometimes. She said work was awful today, and I didn't want to make things worse for her."

"But Katy, this could be really important. You could have nudged her just a bit."

"Look. I know you're not overly fond of Carmen, but she's my oldest friend. I didn't want to upset her."

Or reactivate her tendency to seek solace in wine and prescription chemicals. I didn't say this, though. Peter judges Carmen harshly enough as it is.

They have never liked one another. Peter is desperately uncomfortable around women who flutter their eyelashes at men; Carmen, for her part, is acutely aware that her legendary prowess as a seductress cuts absolutely no ice with my ex-husband. As for me, I just try to keep the two of them apart.

"Listen, forget about Carmen, okay? It was a long shot anyway. Want to stay for supper?"

He accepted enthusiastically. Peter might be expanding his culinary horizons by learning how to use an automatic breadmaker, but he never turns down home cooking, even mine.

Dawn and Rose burst through the front door in a giggling, chattering mass, their cheeks pink from the cold. Their jackets were covered in snow; the remains of a snowball clung to the side of Dawn's knitted cap. To look at them, you'd think Rose hadn't a care in the world. It was a nice illusion. I hadn't thought I'd ever see her this relaxed. Obviously, Dawn's natural good humour was rubbing off on her.

Then she saw us, and the wall went up again. The laughter drained from her eyes, and she turned to take her outdoor clothing off. Dawn didn't seem to notice, though she is usually pretty perceptive about nuances. Peter gave me a questioning look, and I shook my head.

"Later," I mouthed. He nodded understanding.

During supper, Rose said not a word to anyone, but she did have a second helping of the rice dish I'd slaved over in the kitchen. I was not vain enough to attribute this to my finger-lickin' good cooking. More likely the appetite of youth, or possibly even pregnancy, which I didn't really want to think about right now. Whatever the cause, I was happy to spoon more casserole onto her plate. Sometimes there is more of my mother in me than I care to admit.

At the end of the meal, she pushed her chair away and began to scuttle off to the adult-free confines of Dawn's room.

"Rose, before you go ..." I said, and she froze in her tracks.

Dawn took this as her cue to clear the table, and she enlisted Peter's help. I followed Rose into the living room and gestured for her to take a seat. She said nothing, but shook her head.

"Rose, I just want to talk about, well, you know. Your future. Is that okay with you?"

She shrugged. "What future?"

"Well, I've been doing some asking around, and it might be possible for someone I know, a social worker, to get you removed from your father's care. That doesn't mean you can't visit him if you don't want to –"

"I don't." She looked directly at me for the first time that evening. "He doesn't give a shit about me. I never want to see him again."

"Oh." I paused a moment to digest this. "Well, that's up to you, of course. But as I was saying, the social worker said we'd need to find you a more permanent living arrangement. You know Dawn and I are happy to have you here, but this place isn't really big enough for three people. I was thinking, maybe one of your aunts could look after you, once we get things straightened around. How does that sound to you?"

She studied her chewed fingernails. "Yeah, whatever. I guess."

"Rose, listen. I'm honestly not trying to push you out the door, but I want you to have a stable home. It's important, at your age, especially, and in your ..."

I stopped myself. Rose said nothing, just kept twisting at a button on her shirt. Carefully, she removed several imaginary pieces of lint from the shirtsleeves. When she looked at me again, the colour had disappeared from her cheeks.

"Whatever. Sylvie's mom says the same thing. So I guess they'll want to stick me in some group home or something, right? Isn't that where they put the kids no one wants?"

"Come on, you know that's not true ..."

"What? That no one wants me? Right, sure. Name someone."

"Rose, I'd keep you here if I could. I would. I want what's best for you —"

"Everyone wants what's best for me," she spat. "How many times have I heard that one? But no one wants to actually do anything about it."

"That's not true! Anyway, what about your Aunt

Nora? Is that her name?"

"She and my mom hated each other. She wouldn't want me."

"We don't know that."

"I know it. She's a selfish bitch, that's what my mom always said. I'm not going there."

"Okay, okay. Look, I'm not going to allow anyone to put you anywhere you don't want to go. But we have to find something better than this for you. Do you understand that?"

Rose nodded silently.

"Can I go now? I want to lie down."

"Sure," I said.

She slipped past me into Dawn's room, just as Peter emerged from the kitchen, clutching a dishrag.

"Everything okay?" he whispered.

I shook my head and whispered back, "I'll tell you later."

Suddenly, someone rapped on the front door. I stomped to the foyer, ready to growl at some poor kid selling chocolate bars for a field trip to Paris, or ski passes for Mont Tremblant, or whatever.

Through the peephole, I saw a middle-aged man shifting from foot to foot in the front hallway. Stoop-shouldered, a sparse beard, as though he'd randomly grafted wisps of underarm hair onto his chin. He looked familiar; I'd seen him before. But where? I frowned.

I pulled the door open a couple of inches, and spoke around the chain.

"Yes? Can I help you?"

"Are you Katy?" He peered down at me through thick glasses that were quickly fogging up in the warmth of the hall.

"Yes. How can I help you?"

"I'm here about my daughter. You've got her here."

Phil. Of course. Last time I'd seen him, he'd been wearing that rented tux, and he'd been screaming at Marion as she lay dying.

"Rose. My daughter. She's here, isn't she?" he repeated.

"My, if it isn't Phil Stanley." I spoke quietly, hoping Rose wouldn't hear. "Nice of you to drop by. Geez, your daughter's only been away from home for — what? The better part of a week?"

My sarcasm was lost on him. Like a broken record, he said, "You got my girl in there. I want to see her."

"I think it's a bit late for that, Mr. Stanley. Maybe you should have thought about that when I called you the other morning. Now, I'm afraid I'm very busy. Good-bye."

I tried to slam the door closed, but he quickly jammed a sneaker-clad foot into the gap. This was not going well.

"I got a right to see my daughter," Phil Stanley said, a muscle twitching in his cheek. "I want to see Rose."

I stared at him wordlessly.

"Where is she?"

"Mr. Stanley, I should inform you that you have been reported to the Children's Aid Society as an unfit parent," I said, in my most official voice. "I really don't think it would be in Rose's best interest to see you at this time. She has asked to have no further contact with you. Now please remove your foot from my door-way before I call the police and have you arrested for trespass. Which I will do, I assure you."

Peter came out into the hallway and stood behind

me.

"What's the problem here, Katy?"

"Mr. Stanley here doesn't want to leave. Peter, would you go call the police for me, please?"

"You heard what she said, Mr. Stanley. I think you should go."

Phil Stanley looked from one of us to the other, uncertainty creasing his brow.

"I'll take my foot out," he said finally, "but I want to see my daughter. You people got no right keeping her from me."

"Now, that's odd," I said. "Yesterday morning, you told me you didn't care what happened to her. Didn't you tell me she could go wherever she wanted?"

Stanley looked at the floor sheepishly, flushing. "Lookit. Sometimes I say things I don't mean. You just caught me at a bad time yesterday, that's all. My wife just died, you know. I've been a bit upset. Rosie's my kid, and I'm going to take her home with me, the way a good dad should."

"Good dads don't get half-cut and tell their kids they don't want them," I snapped. "Good dads don't let their thirteen-year-old daughters hit the street, without even bothering to check and see if they're safe. Good dads don't —"

Unexpectedly, just as I was hitting my oratory stride, Peter cut in.

"Katy, why don't you and I and Mr. Stanley here go up to my place. We can discuss this like civilized people."

Before I could marshall my objections, my ex-husband was shepherding me out of my apartment, into the hallway. I gritted my teeth, trying to contain my fury.

This was just like Peter, he's always doing things like this. I was the one busting my ass to help Rose, not him. And now he just waltzes in and announces we'll all go upstairs and chat over tea with Phil Stanley? This was the final insult, the last damned straw.

"Peter!" I hissed. "What the hell do you think you're doing?"

"Trust me," he murmured, taking me by the elbow. I shook him off, but he renewed his grip, and finally I allowed him to escort me upstairs, with Phil Stanley trailing along behind us.

11

Peter and I sat facing Phil Stanley, who hunched awkwardly into one of the matching leather loveseats. Despite the man's height, there was something small about him. Not that he was skinny, exactly, but he held himself as though guarding against an expected blow.

"Mr. Stanley," Peter said, "I have to say, your visit comes as a bit of a shock to us."

Stanley sucked on his crooked front teeth. I realized what he reminded me of: a ferret. A cornered ferret who refused to meet our eyes.

"Look," he said. "I know you people don't think much of me. That don't matter. All I want is to get my Rosie and go on home. Girl that age belongs at home. With her family."

"Maybe," Peter said. "But before we make any decisions about that, don't you think we should consider what's in Rose's best interest? She told us she doesn't even want to speak with you."

Stanley bristled. "It's no one else's damn business. You got no right sticking your nose into our private family business. A father's got rights, you know. I want my girl back, and I'm not leaving here without her."

"Rose says you used to beat her mother. Is that

true?" Peter leaned forward, his elbows on his knees, chin cradled in his right hand. This was his Perry Mason shtick — I'd seen it before.

"It makes no difference if I did or if I didn't. What happens behind closed doors in a family doesn't go past those doors. Now where the hell have you put my daughter? We're going home." Stanley's pale fingers dug into the fabric of his green twill pants.

Peter wasn't finished, though. "You know, it can be very psychologically damaging to a child, witnessing violence in the family. So of course, we felt obligated to tell the Children's Aid worker — we couldn't just let something like that go, you understand. I expect you'll have heard from Mrs. Walker by now?"

"Fuck you!" Stanley screamed. "I told that bitch to mind her own fucking business, get her stupid do-gooder nose out of my life, and my kid's life too! You don't know nothing about me or that fucking stupid cow I was married to. You don't know what it's like, living with a woman who makes herself sick on purpose, just to get attention! And you wanna know how I know that? Do you?"

He jabbed a finger in Peter's direction.

"Well, I'll fucking well tell you! That stupid slut, you know I had to have her put away at the mental a coupla times, and you know what the doctor there said to me? He said she's an 'immature manipulator,' those're his exact words. 'Immature manipulator.' And man, did she ever manipulate me. Thought she had me tied around her little finger, didn't she? She musta thought I was fucking stupid, or something, that I wasn't gonna notice her whoring around right under my nose. How'd you like to live with that kind of bullshit, mister? How would you like it?"

Phil Stanley's ferret-like face was contorted with rage, and he thrust his head within inches of Peter's nose as he spat out his last words.

Peter looked taken aback at the tirade he had unleashed.

"Mr. Stanley ... Mr. Stanley," he kept repeating. "You have to understand, we're looking out for Rose's best interests here. Her welfare has to be our priority."

Stanley looked as if he wanted to spit on Peter's hand-knotted Persian carpet, but then he thought better of it. That was probably a wise decision; it takes a lot to incite Peter to violence, but that would have done it.

"That's all I want." Stanley's voice diminished from a roar to a wheedle. "All I want's for Rosie to be happy. Marion always said she was my personal emotional punching bag — maybe she was right. I'm not afraid to say I made some mistakes, okay? But I see my chance now to do right by Rosie, and I want her to come home so we can start over. Can you see what I'm saying?"

Somehow, this self-abasing whine was even harder to bear than Phil Stanley's rage.

Peter tried to negotiate. "Listen. Things are up in the air right now. The Children's Aid has been called in, and once they've been called, they can't be stopped. So why don't you just go with it for a while? Co-operate with them, work with them on trying to be a good father. If you're serious, they can help you. But if you really care about your daughter, you've got to let her stay away for a while longer. She's not ready to go anywhere yet."

Stanley leaped to his feet, knocking over a carved Indian coffee table.

"That's it!" He bared his scissored front teeth. "I'm

calling the cops. I'm going right home and calling the cops, and then you'll see who you're calling a bad father. I'll have you both up on kidnapping charges, that's what I'll do. They're gonna lock you both up and throw away the key, that's what! You fucking do-good-ers, think you know everything. You think a guy like me don't know his own rights. You assholes know noth-ing!"

He gave the upturned table a savage kick, turned with as much dignity as he could muster, and limped out of the apartment. I hoped he'd broken a toe — on him it looked good.

Peter and I followed him to the landing. Stanley banged fruitlessly on the locked door of my apart-ment. Then he tried the handle, with no better results. I hoped the girls would have the sense to stay inside. Stanley kicked my door with his good foot, turned, and left in a whoosh of frigid air, the heavy oak door slam-ming shut behind him.

Back downstairs, I found Dawn and Rose huddled together on the couch, close as Siamese twins. Dawn's arm was wrapped protectively around the younger girl, whose usually pale face was positively ghost-like.

"Is he gone?" Rose whispered. She was shaking.

I nodded. "He can't do anything to you, Rose, don't worry. We've already notified the Children's Aid, and they'll have to investigate the situation before he can even think about having you come back home. If he sets foot in this apartment again, I'll have the cops on him before he knows what hit him."

"I never want to see him again. That bastard!" She glanced my way, as though expecting a reprimand.

"Hey, you won't hear any objection from me," I grinned, and she rewarded me with a tiny smile.

Rose crossed and uncrossed her legs, studying the pattern in my carpet — what she could see of it, under the piles of magazines and papers that littered the floor. She opened her mouth as though to speak, then closed it again. Finally she spoke.

"I wanted to ask you something," she mumbled. I leaned forward, straining to hear. "You were there when it — when my mom, uh, when she died?"

"Sort of. I was there when she had the first seizure. She died later, in the hospital."

"What happened?"

Peter, Dawn and I looked at one another.

"It's okay. I can handle it. I want to know."

I cleared my throat. "Well, I didn't see how it started. I was talking to someone else at the time, but suddenly someone shouted, and I could hear a man ... your father, yelling something. By the time I got to your mother, she was lying on the floor, having a seizure."

"Then what?"

"Rose, are you sure ... ?"

"I need to know. She's my mother."

"Well, your dad ... he was yanking at her. Yelling at her, and I think he might have slapped her face. Maybe he was trying to snap her out of it, or something?"

Rose shook her head. "He always did that. He thought she was just putting it on, any time she got sick. He thought if he hit her enough, she'd smarten up."

"Did she have seizures often, Rose?"

"Hardly ever. Only a couple of times that I remember, and I was really young. She took her medicine religiously. Like, she had this little alarm thingy built into her watch, and when it went off, she'd practically run for her purse and take her pill. I used to tease her about taking her meds, you know, like she was a psycho or something ..." Rose's eyes filled with tears.

I put my hand on hers, and squeezed it. "Honey, I'm so sorry."

"It's just not fair! Why her? Why my mother? She was always good, she never did anything wrong in her life! And she loved me! She's the only person who ever did." She sobbed loudly, all the week's grief and rage pouring out of her. For the first time since I'd met her, I saw Rose for what she was: a young teen, scared and grief-stricken.

Useless words of comfort stuck in my throat. Nothing could help Rose now; there was little to do but wait till her wails died down to muffled sobs, ending with whimpering noises like a beaten puppy.

Afterward, Dawn and I half carried the girl to bed, where she obediently curled up under the duvet. I sat with her, stroking her back, while Dawn soaked a washcloth and bathed her swollen face. Her eyes closed, and she seemed to sleep, though she jerked and twitched every few minutes.

Later, Peter, Dawn and I sat quietly in the living room.

"I just can't begin to imagine," Dawn whispered. "Mom, how much can someone take, before she just completely cracks up? I mean, I'm really worried about her."

I shook my head. "Everyone handles trauma differently. She might have more resilience than we know. We just have to hope it'll work out."

"That Stanley guy was a real piece of work," Peter remarked. "I wasn't so sure about keeping Rose here, till I saw him with my own eyes."

"No kidding. I just kept thinking, 'I wonder how Marion and Rose ever managed to live with this jerk.' By the way, Fischer, I owe you an apology."

"For what?"

"I was furious when you herded us upstairs — doing your usual thing of taking charge without consulting me — but I admit you were right. There. I'm not saying it again, so enjoy it while you can."

Peter laughed. "Thanks. I thought it would be safer to haul him upstairs, where he wouldn't have a chance to catch sight of Rose. Plus, to be honest, I wanted to hear his side of things. Not that I didn't believe Rose, but ..."

"I know, Dad," said Dawn. "It's a journalist thing, right? Always interview the other party. Balanced and accurate reporting ..."

He poked at her playfully, and she squealed and jumped away. "Come on, kid, let's do your mother a favour and finish up those dishes."

I curled into a corner of the couch, cradling my head in the crook of my elbow. I needed some thinking time. It wasn't really my business, but Marion's death was just wrong. I hadn't imagined her taking her meds. Something was not right. And then, only a few days later, the minister Marion worked for was stabbed to death — how coincidental was that?

Were the two deaths related, or just a horrible coincidence? I closed my eyes. Phil Stanley's ferret-like face came into focus. Could Dawn be right — could he have lost his temper and done something to Marion? He said he'd had her committed, years ago. Why? Well, if it had happened in Ottawa, there was only one place he could have sent her for a long term-stay — the Royal Ottawa, my alma mater, and Greg's current employer.

"Katy! I just picked up the paint for the door — hope the colour's okay," Greg said when I reached him.

"Hey, whatever colour it is, it'll be an improvement over what's there now. Thanks. Listen, we had an interesting visitor this evening. Have you got a minute?"

I told him about Stanley, and I could almost hear the wheels turning in my friend's head.

"You're right," he said. "If Rose is right that her mother was fanatical about taking her meds on time, the seizure shouldn't have happened, unless she was taking something that counteracted her Dilantin."

"Like, someone slipped her a mickey?"

Greg laughed. "Maybe. But I wouldn't stake my life on it. Besides, why would anyone want to kill her? She sounds pretty inoffensive, if you ask me."

"Well, what if ..." My mind whirred and clicked. "What if Phil Stanley found out she was playing around with someone on the side. Wait — Carmen told me she was planning on leaving the jerk. Maybe she told him, and he decided to do her in."

"Possible. But you can't go accusing him on that evidence, Katy. The most you can do is let the police know, and I don't think they'll be eager to open a case on someone who died of apparently natural causes."

"But Greg, I saw her take that pill. I'd swear to it. And Phil is such a shit — the more I think about it, the more I think he must have had something to do with it."

"Last time I checked, being a shit still wasn't against the law, dear."

"Okay, okay. But Greg, can you do me a big favour? I mean, aside from painting my door, which I appreciate very much?"

"Shoot."

"Well, Phil said he stuck Marion in a psychiatric hospital. I want to know why."

"You know this is none of your business, right?"

I sighed. "Yeah, yeah. I know that. But something is nagging at me, and I can't seem to let it go. Could you look into it for me, pretty please?"

"Oh, fine. I can do a global search of the hospital system, I guess. Shouldn't take too long."

"Terrific, thanks. Those were the bad old days, eh, when you could get someone committed against her will? On the other hand, with Phil waiting at home, maybe a stint in the Royal would have felt like a trip to Club Med to poor Marion."

We laughed, and he agreed to call me the next day. I had no sooner hung up the phone than it rang again.

"Hello?"

"Katy, this is Steve Benjamin again. We've just had a call from a very irate gentleman, a Mr. Phil Stanley."

"And what did Mr. Stanley have to say for himself?" A thin film of sweat broke out on my palms.

But Benjamin sounded surprisingly casual. "Well actually, he's accusing you of kidnapping his daughter. Now just hold on, okay?" He anticipated my torrent of protestations. "He hasn't actually come down to the station and laid charges yet, he said he was planning to come in. I'm just calling to let you know what he's saying, okay?"

"Sure. Great. So I'm about to be charged with kidnapping."

"As this girl's father, he does have a legal right to take custody, Katy. You know that, don't you?"

"Yeah, I know that," I said slowly. "But did Mr. Stanley tell you exactly what happened here tonight?"

"Well now, that's exactly why I called." I could almost hear the grin in Benjamin's voice. "Knowing you, I figured there'd be more to this than meets the eye."

"*Oy*, have I got a story for you!" I told him about Phil Stanley's visit.

"So you've already called the Children's Aid on Mr. Stanley?" Benjamin asked, when I'd finished.

"That's right. Does that make any difference to the kidnapping charges?"

"It might. If you can make the case that you removed the child from the home for her own safety, it might look better. Though you don't qualify as a child welfare organization, officially."

"Look, I didn't remove anyone from anywhere. Rose was on the streets, and my daughter asked if she could come and stay with us for a few days, that's all. When I asked Mr. Stanley if that was okay by him, he said, and I quote, 'She can stay wherever the hell she wants'. Only tonight, he changes his tiny little mind, and now I'm keeping him from his daughter. Frankly, this is really starting to piss me off, Benjamin."

"Hey, take it easy. I'm not even on duty right now, okay? You're not under arrest or anything — I'm at home, and when I called in for messages I heard this guy Stanley had called. I'm trying to do you the favour of warning you about it, that's all. I realize you're in a tight spot, but don't shoot the messenger, okay?"

"Uh, yeah," I said awkwardly. "Thank you. I guess. I mean, I've never been charged with anything in my life before — I just got a little carried away with the concept."

"Look, don't worry too much about it. My guess is that Stanley might sleep it off. I've seen this kind of guy before — they get themselves all worked up, figure the world owes them something, they're being hard done by, and all the rest of it. So they make all kinds of threats, try to throw their weight around a bit, until they realize they might have to answer a few questions themselves — at which point they drop the whole thing. You shouldn't get yourself into a state about it. But you might want to make sure your bases are covered. Talk to the aunts, get the kid's story substantiated, light a fire under the Children's Aid, you know."

I thanked him for the advice. On reflection, I could see that he might be right on target. Stanley was a little creep whose nose was out of joint. Tonight's performance had been the posturing of someone fundamentally powerless, who'd be damned if he'd admit it.

I hung up slowly. Unpleasant as it was to hear about Stanley's plans to have me thrown in the slammer, it did give me the impetus I needed to call the dreaded Greta once more. Sylvie picked up on the first ring, and I asked to speak to her mother.

"Sorry, Mrs. K., she's not home right now. She had to go out to the airport to pick up my aunt," Sylvie said.

Why does that kid always insist on calling me "Mrs."? I must have told her a thousand times ... Then it dawned on me.

"Your aunt? You mean Nora?"

"Yeah, she's on her way back from her holidays. Do you want Mom to call you back when she gets in?"

"Perfect. That'd be perfect, Sylvie. Thanks."

Somehow, the news that Nora was back in town felt encouraging. It was getting more and more urgent to find a home for Rose. She needed a family, people who could really care for her. There were practical considerations, too: for instance, she hadn't been to school in who knew how long.

So when Greta called back an hour later, I suggested that she and Nora and I meet for breakfast the next day. I wanted this situation fixed, and fast.

"Sure, we can go for breakfast," Greta prattled on. "Where do you want to meet? Sydney's? No, that place is overpriced, unless you just go for the coffee, which I grant you is good there, they put cardamom or something in it, yummy — but who can have nothing but coffee for breakfast? Not me, that's for sure. I was always raised to believe that old saying about breakfast being the most important meal of the day, I think it really sets a tone for the day, don't you? Gives you the energy to get out there and get moving, you know?"

Exercising my verbal muscle, I rammed my way through Greta's barrage.

"Greta, I agree completely. Why don't we meet at Bert's Diner on Elgin? It's close to your place, and not too expensive. How about eight tomorrow? Would that be okay?"

"Eight will be fine. I have to be at my office by nine, you know, and I think Nora has a couple more days off work —"

Greta covered the receiver with her hand, and I could hear her consulting briefly with her sister.

She came back to me: "Nora says eight is fine, too. You won't believe how good she looks, Katy! Healthy, tanned — I think we should all go gallivanting off to Mexico in the winter, don't you? Not that I think she abandoned her family in the middle of a crisis or anything, I'm not saying that, she deserved the break as much as anyone, but the timing could have been better, couldn't it? Still, that's not Nora's fault, or anyone's, really, when you come right down to it …"

I tuned out at this point. All I could hope was that the vaunted Nora was not as talkative as her sister. Two of them would be unbearable. Finally, I excused myself with as much politeness as I could muster; it felt like I'd been on the phone much longer than half an hour. If there is a hell, it's full of *yentas* like Greta.

Peter had settled at the other end of the couch to wait out Greta's attack of verbal diarrhea, and Dawn sat on the floor, leaning back against his legs as they watched the late news. The volume was turned down to a barely audible murmur. I glanced at the television as I hung up the phone, and a familiar face flashed across the screen. I sat bolt upright.

"Turn it up!" I barked. Peter obliged, with a questioning look.

There on the screen, in close-up, was a photograph of my client, Diana Farnsworth. It was impossible to mistake that angular model's face, the intelligent dark blue eyes and cropped hair.

"... have issued a warrant for the arrest of Diana Farnsworth, for the stabbing death of her brother, the Reverend Nigel Farnsworth. Ms. Farnsworth disappeared last night from the home she shared with her brother. Now, here's our correspondent, Allison Richards, with an update."

Cut to a fur-clad blonde woman, standing outside a nondescript bungalow in a snow-covered field.

"Thanks, Jim. I'm here at the Serenity Haven Alcohol and Drug Treatment Centre in Leitrim, the last known whereabouts of Diana Farnsworth, now accused of stabbing her brother, the minister who founded the centre. Diana has held the position of Director here for three months now, and staff here are very upset at the news that she's wanted by the law. We haven't been able to get anyone to consent to an inter-view, but I was told by a confidential source that Diana and her brother had a long history of conflict. In fact, there is an unconfirmed report that Diana had threat-ened to kill her brother in an argument here a few weeks ago. Certainly, the staff out here are pretty shak-en up at Nigel Farnsworth's death."

Bile rose in the back of my throat, and I clicked the TV off.

"She didn't do it," I said, to no one in particular. "I just feel it — she's not the type."

"Katy, everyone's capable of murder, if you push them hard enough," Peter said. "Even you."

"I don't care. She didn't do it." I clung stubbornly to that fragment of belief, and Peter, recognizing the set of my jaw, backed off.

"She's a real person, not a sound bite," I said. "But in two minutes of TV coverage, they've tried and con-victed her!"

"Maybe you're right — maybe there's some other explanation," Peter said. "But whatever it is, we just don't know who killed Nigel. And we're not likely to find out."

Dawn looked completely befuddled. "What are you guys talking about? Do you know that woman, Mom?"

I explained the story to her. "But I really don't think she could have killed anyone. She asked me how long her brother might live, and I told her I couldn't say, which is true. But it doesn't mean she actually killed him — she said herself, she's totally non-violent. She's outspoken, all right, but I just can't see her killing any-one."

"You don't know the circumstances," Peter said.

"Maybe it was a spur of the moment thing. I've interviewed plenty of killers who never thought they were capable of murder. Surprised the hell out of everyone, including themselves."

"Peter, I just don't believe it, okay? Could we drop the subject, please?"

He started to say something, thought better of it, and subsided into silence.

A headache was creeping up the back of my neck, stealing across my scalp and boring a permanent home in my temples. I didn't want to talk any more. Not about Diana, not about Nigel Farnsworth, not about Rose, not about goddamned Phil Stanley. I eased my head back against the needlepoint cushion Dawn had given me for my birthday. Even with my eyes closed, pain pulsed through my skull.

"Listen guys," I said. "Sorry to be a party pooper, but I'm going to bed. Make sure you lock up on the way out, would you, Peter?"

In my bedroom, I fumbled out of my clothing, tossed the whole lot on the floor, and lowered myself gingerly into bed. There ought to be laws against days like this. Weeks like this, in fact.

12

Though my alarm clock alleged that it was seven a.m., the darkness outside told a different story. It felt too early, but Dawn was up and about, brushing her teeth, flushing the toilet. I groaned and rolled over, swaddling myself in the duvet. Damn, I hate winter.

In the half light, inchoate thought fragments drifted through my brain. Gradually, one buzzed in for a landing and I remembered what day it was. I was supposed to meet Nora and Greta this morning. At eight. Grudgingly, I unwrapped myself and sat up, rubbing my eyes. Normally I wouldn't have suggested a meeting at this time of day, but Phil's surprise visit last night had added an edge of urgency to an already difficult situation. I guess you could say I was motivated.

Damp from the shower, I yanked on the first pair of jeans that came to hand, and rummaged around in my drawers for a more or less clean T-shirt. It was almost impossible to tell what I was reaching for, but I was in no hurry to expose my eyes to the glare of electric illumination.

Dawn was in the kitchen, pouring yoghurt over a bowl of granola. I explained my morning's errand while I ground the French roasted beans my system so desperately craved.

"Dawn, Rose hasn't mentioned the possibility that she might be pregnant, has she?" I switched on the coffee machine, which responded with a satisfying gurgle.

"Nope. I just can't tell what's going on in her head sometimes. She told me a bit about her father, how he used to beat up on her and her mom. One time, Rose had to throw herself between her parents to keep him from using a baseball bat on Marion. But she says it all in this dead voice, like a zombie. It's like she's telling me about something she read in the paper."

I snorted. I should be keeping notes on this, for Pearl Walker.

"Anything else?"

"Well, she's talking a bit more about her mother the last day or so. But she hasn't said anything to me about the pregnancy, or going back to school, or anything."

"Well, she's going to have to face up to reality at some point. I don't know if that scrawny little body can support a baby to term. You can practically see through her as it is."

"I know. But whenever I try to talk about anything important, Rose just shuts down. It's like I'm talking to a wall."

"Well, it's not your job to be her therapist, okay?

Once we get her living arrangements settled, I'm going to call every kiddy shrink in town, if that's what it takes to get her into counselling. A home, some stability, some counselling — I think that's the best we can do for her."

I kissed Dawn's cheek and pulled on my fleece jacket, then my anorak and boots. As I had expected, the vestiges of last night's headache had disappeared as my blood caffeine level rose, and the brisk walk to Elgin Street woke me up even more.

Snow had sprinkled over yesterday's ice, and the tree-lined side streets had a lovely frosted sparkle to them. However, the walking was treacherous, as slick ice lurked unseen under the snow. Still, the air was fresh and clean, and the grungy snowbanks were hidden beneath a layer of flakes that glinted in the sun.

The diner was one of the newer establishments on the Elgin Strip, Ottawa's answer to Big City Life. Elgin Street is the place where those Ottawans who think of themselves as young and trendy go to see and be seen. Its restaurants are the closest thing we have to the self-consciously hip dining establishments of Toronto or Montreal. Of course the latest fads in eating can take a couple of years to wend their way into the consciousness of this city, but that doesn't bother us: better safe than sorry, we say here.

Greta and Nora had already arrived and were sipping coffee as I stamped the snow off my boots and removed my anorak. While I'd never met Nora, I would have instantly pegged her as Greta's sister: the same stocky build, the same wavy auburn hair, the same olive-coloured eyes, the same pugnacious jaw, constantly in motion. Nora was perhaps ten pounds lighter than her sister, and her skin was tanned the colour of walnut.

Greta saw me first and stood to greet me, throwing her arms around my neck with an exuberance our casual acquaintance did not warrant. Her sister extended a more reserved hand.

"Nice to meet you, Nora," I said. "It's too bad it has to be under such difficult circumstances. I'm very sorry about your sister's death."

Nora nodded and murmured her acceptance of my condolences.

"So — Greta's told you about Rose's situation, has she?" Knowing how verbose Greta could be, and suspecting Nora might be her match in that department, I figured it was best to get down to business right away.

Nora pursed her lips impatiently. "We both told her, didn't we, Greta? I mean, we both told Marion not to marry that man. I knew from the beginning he'd be trouble, we all said so. Marion was quiet, you know, and you always thought you were getting through to her, but she was stubborn as a brick. Just like that kid of hers. Apple doesn't fall far, I always say. Anyway, she went right ahead and married Phil, wouldn't listen to any of us, just set her mind and went ahead and did it. And of course, now, just as I told her a million times ..."

Greta took up the banner. "Exactly. Now Marion's gone, and look at Phil! Useless. Sits around drinking and feeling sorry for himself, can't lift a finger to help himself, just hangs around watching TV and moaning about how everyone's done him wrong. He wouldn't even let us bury our sister properly — did I tell you that, Katy? Said it was a waste of money, even though I offered to help him pay for the casket and make food for the wake and everything. I've always known he was a bastard ..."

I was going to have to use a crowbar to get a word

in edgewise here. I raised my voice to be heard above the restaurant's clatter. "Actually, I'm less concerned about Phil than I am about Rose. She's in pretty rough shape right now, she needs a place to live. That's why I asked to meet with the both of you."

I described my talk with Pearl Walker, Phil's visit to my place last night, and his threat to have me charged with kidnapping. Finally, I told them my suspicions about Rose's pregnancy. When I finished, I expected a deluge of questions from the sisters. Instead, they sat in stunned, perhaps unprecedented, silence. Nora lit a cigarette and stared over my shoulder, exhaling smoke through her nose.

"Are you sure?" Greta spoke first. "And how is it possible that she doesn't know? Do you know who the father is?"

"No. Dawn says Rose never talks about having a boyfriend, but she doesn't talk much about anything. As for being sure, I've booked her an appointment with my doctor, but she can't get in to see her until next Wednesday. We'll know for sure then. But she's got all the symptoms."

Greta nodded and looked at her sister.

Nora cut right to the chase: "I expect the reason you wanted to see me was to ask if I could take her in, right? Well, I can tell you right now, I don't have room for a pregnant kid with a screw loose. She's exactly like her mother, and I want no part of it. You know how Marion was, Greta, though no one wants to talk about it — well, I'm telling you here and now, I'm not getting sucked in this time."

"Nora! How can you say such a thing? She's our sister's child, for God's sake!" Greta slammed a fist on the table, nearly tipping our coffees into our laps. Several patrons turned to stare, but Greta was oblivious. Her eyes were bulging, her cheeks flushed. "Katy's been good enough to look after her since Marion died, and I thought — dammit, Nora, you're the one with the high-paying job, the big house, the fancy car — you're the one who can afford to go gallivanting off to Mexico, leaving the rest of us up here to pick up the pieces! Oh, sure, just leave everything to Greta. As usual. But then I guess I shouldn't be surprised — you've always been spoiled, haven't you? Mom and Dad just let you get away with murder, gave you whatever your little heart desired, and now look at you! You can't even lift a finger to help your own flesh and blood! I just can't believe it ..."

Nora exhaled another stream of smoke and lifted her coffee mug to her lips. Then she set it down with a clatter. Her lips were clenched in a straight line.

"Are you quite finished, Greta? Good. Now let me tell you something. Just because you and Marion hooked up with losers who left you with a bunch of brats to raise, there's no reason on earth that I should have to get involved. Marion made a royal mess of what passed for her life, and it's not my job to fix that. I warned her about Phil, and to be quite honest, I thought it served her right when he had her put away. She pulled her 'poor Marion' stunt once too often, that's all. I say she got what she deserved, and I'll be damned if I'm taking on her kid just to make everyone feel better."

Greta stared at Nora. "How dare you?" She spoke in a whisper. "How dare you speak that way about our sister? You selfish bitch, you have no right to talk about Marion that way! As if you've never made any mistakes in your life — I could mention another girl who got pregnant a little before her time, couldn't I?"

But before she could say any more, Nora dashed the remains of her coffee in Greta's face. Then she grabbed her coat and bulldozed her way out of the restaurant.

Oy vey, had I opened up a hornet's nest.

Fortunately, we were able to sponge most of Nora's tepid coffee from Greta's sweater with paper napkins purloined from the next table. Greta shook with rage.

"Is she always like that?" I handed Greta a tissue.

"Sometimes she's worse." Greta laughed abruptly. "I don't even know why I bothered letting you meet her. She's the oldest, you know, and she always had an attitude about us. How stupid could I be, even thinking she'd lift a finger to help Rose. Nora looks out for Nora, and that's the way it's always been ..."

I listened with only half an ear to Greta's long list of grievances against her sister. The fact was, nothing had been resolved about Rose. We were right back where we'd started. I took a gulp of coffee and leaned across the table toward Greta.

"Listen. It's time to talk about your niece. Rose is suffering, and I can't keep her forever. Especially if her father is planning to charge me with kidnapping. We need to figure out what to do, in the short term at least."

Greta stared at me, tears welling up. "I know that. Do you think I haven't been torturing myself, thinking about it? I just don't know what to do, can you understand that? I work full-time, and I can barely squeeze by with Sylvie and Billy — they're eating me out of house and home, and they both need new winter clothes, and Christmas is coming up, and I have no idea how I can get through this month, let alone the next few years ... and then to add another kid, one who's having a baby, of all things. I just don't know what to do, Katy, I really don't!"

Oh, God. Awkwardly, I patted her hand.

"Greta, I know what it's like to be a single parent, believe me. And it's no picnic being short of money, either. But we can't just send Rose back to her father, can we? She'll run away again and keep right on running, and next thing we know she'll be living on the streets, on drugs or something. Or worse."

Greta said nothing, but her lower lip trembled dangerously. The waiter, who had been observing our conversation with avid interest, stopped by at that point to refill our coffee cups.

"Okay. We can't let her live with Phil anymore," Greta conceded, when the man had gone, "but I honestly don't know what else to do. So what now?"

Good question. I had no brilliant ideas either, but I wasn't willing to admit defeat yet.

"Look, I've spoken with a woman at the Children's Aid, a Mrs. Walker," I said. "I think it might help if you talk to her about all this. Maybe the two of you can work something out."

I scribbled Pearl's number on the back of one of my business cards and pushed it across the table. Then I signalled for the bill, paid and hugged Greta goodbye. I'm not normally quite so touchy-feely, especially with Greta, who really gets on my nerves. But it can't be pleasant to be related to someone who goes around throwing perfectly good coffee at you in public places. The walk to my office wasn't a long one, but it was slippery, and I was preoccupied. I walked slowly and carefully, mentally rehashing my meeting with Rose's aunts.

Growing up without siblings, I've always nursed the fantasy that if I had a sister, we'd be chums, lending each other clothes for the Big Date, supporting one another when the chips were down, that sort of thing. The reality of sisterly love took some getting used to.

And we'd resolved absolutely nothing. What to do now? Everyone seemed to think I would just somehow glue it all together like Humpty Dumpty's shell. And yet, what alternatives were there? I felt cornered, trapped into a role I couldn't play.

The police had been and gone from my office: I could tell by the muddy bootprints that traipsed across the hardwood floors. That, plus the neatly printed note from Sergeant McGillivray, taped to what remained of my door frame. "Thanks for your co-operation," it read. "Couldn't find any clear prints. Call Detective Benjamin if you have any concerns or questions."

Right. Benjamin. Just who I needed to talk to right about now. Not.

Just as I was unlacing my boots, the delivery person from the futon store puffed up the stairs. I helped the guy wrestle the heavy cotton-filled mattress up the narrow staircase, and we manoeuvred it into place. I signed for it, hoping my bank balance would bear the strain.

The light on my answering machine blinked happily at me. Oh, that's right, I remember now — I have a business to run. I rewound the tape and settled in at my newly reconstituted desk, anxious to get moving on some billable work. The call was not from a client, though. It was Carmen, and she sounded not at all well.

"Katy ... It's me. Uh. It's ... I'm ... yeah. It's around

five a.m., and I didn't sleep much last night (giggle). I wanted to talk to you about ... uh, no, wait, I'd rather talk in person, okay? Can I come over today? (Long silence) I mean, if I won't be interrupting anything. Call me." Click.

I frowned, replayed the garbled message once more. This was a Carmen I hadn't heard in months. If she had been touchy and snappish last night, this morning she sounded, well, hammered. She'd been back at the bottle again. Damn, damn, damn. I thought she'd dealt with all that — she'd sworn her hard-drinking days were behind her.

I dialled her number, but the machine was on. Ditto at her office number. I left messages at both places, urging her to call as soon as she could. If she was sliding back into the clutches of alcohol, maybe I could pull her back, arrest the process before it went any further. Someone slap me, my saviour complex is showing.

The second message on my machine was from Greg, asking me out for lunch. I called his secretary to let her know I'd be happy to dine with Greg at the restaurant of his choosing.

There were no further messages so I devoted the morning to a chart I'd been putting off for nearly a week. One of the services I provide is a written report, usually in the range of twenty to thirty pages, analyzing an individual's birthchart. I don't get these requests often, as they take more time and effort than in-person sessions, which makes them more expensive. Some people like them better, though, and they make great gifts. With the holidays approaching, I had a few to complete. I put a fresh disk in my laptop, tacked the printed chart to the corkboard in front of me and set to work.

I was engrossed in a particularly tricky stellium — Mars, Saturn and Mercury in Pisces in the eighth house — when the phone's shrill ring summoned me back to earth. Glancing quickly at the clock on my desk, I was shocked. The morning had slipped away already.

"I can meet you in an hour," Greg said.

"Great. I could use a boost. And I'm buying, okay? I want to thank you for the paint job."

"Hey, no problem. I think you'll be interested in what I've dug up about Marion Stanley." He sounded pleased with himself. "But it has to wait until lunch time, I've got a patient who needs a quick meds check right now. Want to try out the new pub?"

We agreed to meet at the faux English pub that had just opened down the street. Apparently just hanging out in a dank and ill-lit bar, chugging brewskis and listening to a tinny jukebox has been replaced by a more civilized drinking form: the micro-brewery, in which one is expected to savour the beer or ale or stout or whatever, as if one were a wine connoisseur. You know: "A nutty head, with a vibrant aftertaste of peaches," or some such thing. It sounded kind of intimidating, but maybe the place would be dark and no one would notice if I ordered a Labatt's Blue.

I arrived only a few minutes late. Greg was already there, his reading glasses perched on his longish nose. Never one to waste a moment in idleness, he was filling in hospital forms as he waited for me.

I stood at his elbow and cleared my throat. Startled, he pushed his paperwork unceremoniously into his briefcase.

"Hi! I figured I had a few more minutes before you got here."

"Sure — rub it in. It's not my fault I'm time-impaired. So, Watson, what's new on the Marion Stanley beat?" I plopped down across from him.

"Well, it looks like Phil was telling the truth about Marion spending some time in a psychiatric institution. I talked to Bill James, and he confirmed it. The first time was in her late teens — she married really young, and it was a pretty big adjustment ..."

"I'd classify being married to Phil as more than a 'big adjustment'. More like 'grounds for suicide,'" I said.

"Yeah, well, she never tried that. But she did try cutting back on her meds a few times, and Bill thinks it was her way of forcing Phil to stop bullying her — he couldn't very well torment someone in the middle of a seizure, could he?"

"Well, he wasn't doing a bad job at Carmen's party. He was yanking her arm out of its socket while she was puking and shitting herself and spasming on the floor."

"I know. Apparently some young resident got the bright idea of telling Phil his wife was just trying to get him to be nicer to her. Might as well wave a red flag in front of a bull."

"So that's what he meant."

"What do you mean?"

"He told us some doctor called Marion an 'immature manipulator' — like he thought that was a diagnosis, or something. When all she wanted was for him to treat her like a human being."

"Well, Bill has seen her for years, and he doesn't have much of an opinion of our Phil. He liked Marion, though. And when he saw her at her last check-up, he said she looked great — 'radiant' was the word he used. Better than he'd ever seen her."

"When was this?"

"About a month ago, I think. He asked her what was new in her life, and apparently she didn't want to tell him at first, but finally he got it out of her — she said she was in love."

"Yeah," I said slowly. "That ties in. She told Carmen a week or so ago that she was planning to dump Phil. I thought it was because Phil had threatened to turf Rose out of the house, but maybe she was planning to leave before that happened. I wonder if her new boyfriend even knows she's dead?"

"That would be awful, wouldn't it? I wouldn't want to be the one to tell him."

I stared into my beer for several minutes, watching the tiny bubbles rise through the light amber liquid and burst on the surface. Some neo-Celtic band sawed away in the background, a strathspey or reel or something, underlaid with hip-hop rhythms. Odd, but interesting.

Finally, I raised my eyes and met Greg's.

"Greg, here's the thing. There's something fishy about Marion's death. I saw her take that pill, and next thing you know, she's doing the backstroke on the floor. And what you're telling me makes it even worse. She was a young woman, she had a lot to live for. She was about to get out of her marriage to Phil, she was in love, she had a daughter to look after — why would she mess that up by cutting back on her meds? Even if she tried that a long time ago, why do it now? There's no reason for it."

Greg nodded. "I'm with you so far."

"Plus, her meds worked perfectly well for a dozen years or so. They don't just suddenly stop working, do they?"

"Nope."

"So what the hell happened?" I slapped my hand down on the table; a couple of diners shot me brief, puzzled glances.

"All I can think is that someone tampered with her medication. Or maybe fed her something that would conflict with them."

"But why? Only one person would have a motivation to do that. Our buddy Phil. He was about to lose his personal maid service and punching bag, right?"

Greg nodded. "And he's got a definite dog-in-the-manger streak — you saw that when he arrived on your doorstep looking for Rose. He didn't want her, but he sure as hell didn't want you to have her, either. Maybe he figured out that she was going to leave, and decided to make it a bit harder for her."

Our server arrived, bearing lunch. In true pub tradition, this place offered a passable ploughman's lunch of cheese, pickled onions, crusty bread and various relishes. My hunger surprised me, and Greg and I ate in companionable silence.

Finally, I brushed the crumbs off my front and said thoughtfully, "I wonder if anyone at Marion's church would have any clue about what happened to her? Her sisters told me she's heavily involved in the church. Of course, if she told her minister, we're out of luck — he's dead now, too. But maybe someone else there might know something."

"It's a possibility," Greg acknowledged. "But Katy, what are you trying to accomplish here? The woman is dead. That's the reality. You can't bring her back, no matter how much you want to make it all better for Rose."

I said nothing for a minute. On the surface of it, he

was right. "It just sticks in my craw, Greg. I just know Phil is mixed up in this somehow, and he's getting off scot-free. I need something to take to Steve Benjamin, something that'll convince him to have a chat with Phil. At this point, I don't even know if Marion's death is being treated as suspicious."

"Katy, you're like a pit bull with a really juicy steak bone. I guess there can't be much harm in poking around a bit, except that Phil might take exception."

I grimaced. "Oh, yeah, I'm really worried about what Phil thinks. He's such a scary dude, man."

"Don't laugh — sometimes those weedy-looking ones are stronger than they look."

Greg drove me the few blocks back to my office, so I was only about five minutes late for my next client. Fortunately, Marlene is a regular, and she knows to wait for me. I found her sitting patiently at the head of the stairs, and for an hour, all distractions disappeared from my consciousness as I threw myself into my work.

As I saw her to the door, though, I was hit with a wave of almost overwhelming sleepiness. Perhaps it was the lone beer I'd consumed at lunch, or maybe my brain was just short-circuiting. Too much information, not enough places to store it all. I couldn't afford a cat-nap — I had phone calls to make, charts to complete, a living to make. I needed coffee.

Throwing on my boots and anorak, I dashed out for a quick cup, and was back in my office within five minutes, clutching an ultra-large dark-roasted African blend. Not better than sex, perhaps, but a close second, in my book. I sat down with my laptop and fiddled around a bit with the chart I was supposed to have completed this morning, but my heart wasn't in it. I just kept thinking about Marion's short life and strange death.

There had to be some kind of pattern, some thread leading to the centre of the maze. What was missing? I had no real sense of Marion as a person. When I knew who she was, maybe I'd be closer to knowing how she died. Maybe.

I dialled Greta's number rapidly, and before she could snow me in with verbiage, I extracted her sister's birth data from her.

"But why do you need to know that?" she asked. "Are you filling out some forms or something? Is this something about Rose? I mean, what —"

I ignored her. "Thanks, Greta, I appreciate your help!" I chirped, dropping the receiver into its cradle. Rude, yet effective.

I stared at Marion's chart intently for a few minutes, then swung into action. I started jotting notes on the laptop, hammering at the keyboard in my haste to get it all down. Gradually, a picture of Marion began to emerge; fuzzy around the edges, but a real person.

Marion, like me, had a Libra Sun, but there all resemblance ended. Her Sun was in tight conjunction with both Saturn and Neptune: to get the love and attention she needed, Marion had denied her real self in some way. She'd played the part of the obedient "good girl," hoping to win approval. There was fearfulness here, too, and a feeling of entrapment.

Self-doubt and a glamorizing of others, particularly older men, who would seem to her to offer the answers she needed. This could tie in with her religious quest — God as the ultimate father-figure?

Her Jupiter was retrograde. Funny, I'd just seen a retrograde Jupiter — where was it? Oh, right. In Diana

Farnsworth's chart. Retrograde planets stand out wherever they are found, but Marion's was spectacular, linked to the Ascendant, the Midheaven and six planets. A regular Jupiter-fest.

I sat back and closed my eyes, allowing myself to free-associate. That retrograde Jupiter was one of the keys to her chart. Jupiter, king of the gods, ruler of Mount Olympus, unfaithful husband and frequent rapist — obsessed with control. I couldn't see Marion herself as a control freak; she seemed more the type to fall victim to a latter-day Jupiter, someone who would demand absolute loyalty from her. Like Phil, perhaps?

Astrologically, Jupiter rules expansion, philosophy, religion, higher education. Religion. Now there was something. Marion had reshaped her life around her church, her faith in something greater than herself.

Okay, so Jupiter has something to do with her religious beliefs; but why retrograde? Retrograde planets are the places in the chart that function autonomously, ignoring the conventions and inhibitions that keep most of us on the straight and narrow. They're the places where we might break out of our conventional lives. So in some way, Marion's religious beliefs might have conflicted with her traditional, good-girl image. That didn't sound right, though. Wouldn't her church have encouraged her to be an obedient wife and mother? I thought that was one of the points of traditional religions.

I chewed on the tip of my pencil, a bad habit I developed in kindergarten and have never quite outgrown. So maybe Marion hadn't been the milk-toast she appeared to be. After all, she'd had an affair and made the decision to leave Phil, and that must have taken some gumption.

The phone interrupted my ruminations: I answered distractedly.

"Katy? This is Steve. Steve Benjamin." As though I might have forgotten who he was.

I frowned. "Um, yeah. Hi. What can I do for you?"

"Listen," he said, as though it was the most natural thing in the world to just call me up for a mid-afternoon chat, "I was thinking about what you said yesterday. About Diana Farnsworth."

"What about her?"

He ignored the brusqueness of my response. "Well, I'd like to know what you two talked about."

I opened my mouth to reply, then shut it again. "I can't tell you that. It's confidential"

"Katy, client privilege doesn't extend to astrologers. You know that."

Damn. He had me. "Well, she didn't say anything you'd need to know about, I can tell you that."

"Why don't you let me decide that? Now, can you give me a rundown of what you two discussed?"

I sighed deeply. "Fine. Just a minute while I find the file."

I got up and rummaged around the office for a few minutes, making an audible show of opening and slamming drawers. Then I picked up the phone again.

"Sorry. I can't find it. I guess when this place got trashed ..."

"Katy, why are doing this? You're a smart lady. You can remember the conversation if you try. Now, did Diana tell you anything about her brother?"

"Yeah, she did. She said he was an upstanding and much-loved member of the community who founded a whole bunch of places like rehab centres, schools and stuff like that. She said he had buckets of energy and creativity, and she wished she could be more like him."

"Did she mention any ... conflict with him?"

"She said he was a bit controlling, but she didn't say anything specific, no."

"Why do I get the feeling you're holding something back?"

"Well, what do you want me to do? Tell you she planned to kill her brother? That didn't happen."

"But ... ?"

Oh, all right. I made an exasperated noise through my nose. "Fine, Benjamin, have it your way. She did ask me if there was any chance her brother would be ... getting out of her life soon. Just hypothetically. Because she wanted some peace and quiet, and she felt like he was constantly trying to butt in on her life. But there's no way she would have helped him along, I'd swear to it. I told her I didn't know, and that was the end of it. She was okay with that. All right? Are you satisfied?"

"Sure, sure. But you know, saying something like that a day before her brother winds up dead, it looks kind of bad for her, don't you think?"

I snorted. "Yeah, well, you should hear some of the things I say about you. You can't arrest someone for thinking evil thoughts, Benjamin."

He sounded irritated. "Look, Katy, I'm just doing my job. I'd appreciate some co-operation here, okay?"

"Detective Benjamin," I sighed, "I really can't say more than I've already said. I don't know what you want from me."

"Well, for one thing, you said you didn't think she could have killed her brother. Can you tell me more about that?"

"Look. I'm not psychic, okay? I'm an astrologer. I

can't say for absolute certain what anyone would do, if they were pushed to an extreme. Even when I was a psychologist, I couldn't have told you that. But I'm telling you the truth. I don't think Diana did it. She's a prickly person, a bit defensive maybe, but she is a very strong Christian. She lives for her faith, and she's one of those oddballs who actually seems to take the Ten Commandments seriously. Why are you asking me this stuff, anyway?"

"Because," Benjamin said slowly, "because for some reason I can't really fathom, I trust your judgment. Because I'm trying to figure out, if Diana didn't do it, who did? That's my job, you know."

"Well, it's a bit late for that, isn't it? There's already a warrant out for her arrest, according to the news last night. So you guys must think there's enough evidence to haul her in, right?"

Benjamin made a noise. "It's not an arrest warrant — we're just looking for her, want to ask her a few questions. The TV stations, as usual, go ahead and say whatever they want. Anything for a story."

"That's actually a relief to me," I said. "Probably the one positive thing I've heard all day. Look, you'll have to excuse me, okay? I've got work piled up waiting for me."

Which was a blatant lie, but I was getting less and less comfortable with this conversation. I didn't understand our sudden buddy-buddy status — why was he discussing this case with me? I am not the world's most sensitive person, and I have been known to overlook the subtleties in some situations, but I was beginning to get the drift here: Detective Benjamin was ... interested. In me.

Oy vey is mir.

13

It wasn't until close to five-thirty that I realized I still hadn't heard from Carmen. She'd left that garbled message, and I'd meant to try her again later, but it had completely slipped my mind. Some friend I am.

After I'd packed up for the walk home, I gave her a call back. Her answering machine picked up again, but I know from long experience that when Carmen's in rough shape, she screens her calls. Better for business that way. Doesn't drive away clients.

"Carmen, it's me. Sorry I didn't catch up with you earlier. I guess I'll stop by your place on my way home. If you're not there yet, I'll wait."

Carmen lives in the Glebe, in a second floor walk-up on First Avenue. It was a bit of a detour for me, but the more I thought about this morning's message, the more worried I got. I didn't want to stand by and watch my friend slide down that slope again. If I got there around six, I'd catch her coming from work and we could talk before she had time to pour herself a little drinkie. Maybe I'd even talk her out of it.

Time for Dr. Klein to make a house call.

The avenues in the Glebe are wide, well-kept streets lined with towering oaks and maples. The houses are solid brick, inhabited by well-educated people who wear Birkenstocks, drive Volvos, and send their breast-fed children to Montessori schools. Those residents without children own Dalmatians and Jack Russell terriers; those with kids have golden retrievers and Labradors. They make you take cultural literacy tests before you qualify to buy a house in the Glebe. If you fail, they ship you off to the Alta Vista gulag.

Carmen knows the names of all the architectural styles along her street: Queen Anne Revival, Gothic Revival, Arts and Crafts. I can't tell one from the other, so I take her word for it. To me, they all look like nice places to live. I like peeking into living room windows as I walk along, checking out the lifestyles of the well-to-do, scouting amongst the charming and discriminating for the truly tasteless.

Tonight, as well as Bartlett prints and wall hangings from Africa, I spotted a framed, life-sized poster of a sulking Michael Corleone, in glorious living colour. I giggled softly to myself. I wondered whether the Culture Police were aware of this blatant transgression?

The house Carmen lived in had once been a single family home, built in the 1930s by a local contractor named Younghusband, whose Glebe dwellings are much prized for their solid, unpretentious workmanship. Someone had subdivided the house into three spacious apartments, one on top of the other, but otherwise most of the original detailing was intact, a factor that ranked high in Carmen's estimation.

The heavy oak door at the main entrance was surrounded by the original stained glass panels; they glowed softly like beacons in the winter night, the light beckoning me indoors.

I kicked the snow off my boots, climbed two flights of stairs, and knocked tentatively on Carmen's door. At first there was no response, so I knocked again, this time more forcefully. I heard a scuffling sound, then the chain pulled back and Carmen opened the door a crack. I saw only an eye and a strand of unwashed hair, and I was uncomfortably reminded of Mr. Rochester's wife in *Jane Eyre*.

"Yes?"

I could scarcely hear her, but the word wafted toward me on a thick cloud of alcohol and cigarette smoke. Instinctively, I recoiled, and the door started to close.

"Carmen, it's me." I pushed my face closer so she could see me. "Can I come in?"

Instead of answering, she closed the door in my face. I stood irresolute on the landing, wondering if Carmen had it in mind never to speak to me again. And if so, why? What had I done?

More important, what should I do now? I didn't want to dangle about here like a fool, knocking on the door of someone who obviously didn't want to talk to me ...

Just as I had decided, with heavy finality, to leave, the door opened again. With a broad gesture, Carmen beckoned me inside. She was unsteady on her feet and clutched the door handle for balance.

The stench of old wine and stale cigarette smoke was overpowering. Inside the dark vestibule, I turned to her. "Carmen, you look like hell. Are you okay? What's going on?"

She reached for a chain above her and pulled the hall light on. Her hair hung limp, uncombed. Her eyes stared out, dull and lifeless, and there were purple rings around them, whether from sleeplessness, alcohol or prolonged crying, I couldn't tell. Probably a combination of the three.

"No," she slurred, "I'm not okay. Not at all."

Then she laughed loudly, a harsh croak that ended as abruptly as it had begun. She turned away from me unsteadily. I followed her into the living room. The coffee table, a gorgeous antique from Kashmir, was littered with crumpled, lipstick-smeared tissues, and four empty wine bottles, accompanied by one half-full glass and one empty, stood in a neat row.

The TV remote was stuck sideways into the half-full glass. Carefully I fished it out, dried it with a tissue and replaced it on the wall unit.

"Carmen, are you going to tell me what's going on here? You haven't done this for a long time — things must be pretty bad, huh?"

"I know," she said dully. "I'm really drunk. Really, really drunk. Hammered, in fact."

In the past she would have taken a swing at me for daring to point out her inebriated state; at least this time she was acknowledging there was a problem. Maybe it wasn't too late to get some sense out of her.

"Come on, I'll make you a nice cup of tea." I bustled off to the kitchen in full *yiddishe mama* mode. "You just sit, relax. It won't take long. You'll feel better, you'll see."

She straggled after me, rubbing at her bleary eyes with her fists. I could see she'd chewed most of the red lacquer off her nails. Bad sign. She paid a fortune for those nails.

"Katy, I'm so tired." Her whine sounded exactly like an overwrought three-year-old's.

"I know, honey. Here, let's get some nice mint tea

into you. It'll settle your stomach."

I spooned some honey into the hot liquid and stirred it noisily with a demitasse spoon, the only implement that came to hand. "There. Now, let's go sit down, and you can tell me all about it, okay?"

Obediently, Carmen sat, her tea untouched, hands on her knees. Occasionally, she listed dangerously, but she kept pulling herself upright, trying to retain some shreds of dignity. She stared at her tea, avoiding my eyes. Or perhaps she was just having trouble focusing.

"Katy? What would you do if someone you cared about did something wrong?"

"How wrong?"

"Really wrong. Maybe they thought it was for a good reason, but it was really wrong. Really wrong."

"And how much do you care about this person?"

She looked above my head at an embroidered wall hanging she'd picked up in Algeria. Carmen is the only person I know who just happens to pick things up in places like Algeria.

"A lot. Like, you care so much, you never thought you'd ever care for another human being this much. Someone who's like a brother to you. Or a sister. Or a sister-and-brother all rolled together ..." She threw her head back in a giggle, and the sudden motion was enough to tip her over sideways along the couch. She lay there a while as the giggles turned to small sobs.

I sighed. "Carmen, why don't you begin at the beginning? Someone you care about has done something wrong. That's a start. Go from there, okay?"

"Okay," she whispered, and struggled back upright. "I met someone a while ago, and there was something between us the second we looked at each other. We started seeing one another, then later on we both realized it was getting more serious than that. Really serious," she said earnestly, looking at me as if for confirmation. I nodded.

"Go on," I said.

"You know, I wasn't really looking for another relationship, but this — was different from anything I'd ever felt for anyone else. Total caring. Total commitment. I felt so ... loved."

She reached for another handful of tissues and blew her nose. Her hand drifted toward the half-full wine glass, but I handed her the tea in its place, and she lifted it unsteadily to her lips. Hot tea spilled down her shirt but she didn't bother to wipe it up. She grimaced at the minty steam, then took a small sip.

"But it started to go all wrong — it turned out there was ... a third party. Someone interfering, you know? In our way. Always watching. I'd known about it, known it might come up, but somehow I just underestimated things. It just kept getting worse and worse. Getting in our way. Always there, looking over our shoulders, reminding us ... and then I — then, it happened."

"It?" I asked. "What, exactly?"

"Things got out of control. You know."

She looked at me, drunkenly sincere. "No one meant for things to go that far, I promise, Katy. No one meant it. It was all just a ... a misunderstanding. A big mistake. A really, really big ..."

"Carmen, what happened? You can tell me." I tried to nudge her back on track. Then I remembered — she might not know yet about Nigel Farnsworth's death. Maybe she was agonizing about a relationship that didn't even exist anymore. I opened my mouth, then closed it again. If she didn't know, my telling her wasn't going to make things here any better. She'd just spin further out of control, mixing grief in with whatever else was going on.

"Ah-ah-ah!" she said, shaking a finger at me and winking. Unfortunately, her co-ordination wasn't great, and the wink came across as more of a grimace. "Secrets. Can't tell you, Katy. Better that you don't know."

"Come on, you'll feel better if you tell me. You know you will."

"I don't want to talk about this any more," she wailed suddenly, throwing herself sideways onto the couch and covering her face with her hands.

I am usually a fairly reasonable person, but this was getting to me. The semidarkness, the smell of expensive wine going sour, the miasma of smoke hanging in the close apartment, Carmen's weeping and snuffling, talking in riddles and now collapsing in histrionics. It was starting to piss me off.

"Look, Carmen. Either tell me what's going on here, or I'm leaving. I've got people waiting for me. I can't hang around here all night waiting for you to sober up. Shit or get off the pot, okay?"

She raised her face from the couch.

"Fine!" she said thickly. "Go. I don't need you. I can handle this myself. You think you know someone, think you can depend on them ... Oh, fuck it. Just go."

She flopped back down, the picture of despair.

So I went. I made it nearly halfway home, pumped with righteous anger and a feeling of having been mis-used. Who the hell did she think she was, making a Hollywood production out of another one of her failed relationships, sucking me into looking after her while she went off on a drinking binge? Again. Like I hadn't bailed her out of enough drunks, listened to her ramble on incoherently about one catastrophe or another, crawled out of bed to drive her home from enough bars at three in the morning. Time to look after yourself, Carmen.

And then, of course, the inevitable guilt set in. I kicked myself upside down and sideways the rest of the way home for not being more patient, more understanding, a better friend. I should know Carmen by now, know she never does anything by half measures. She doesn't drink to make my life miserable; she does it to numb her own pain.

But what did she want from me? This back-and-forth bullshit was quite simply crazymaking — icy cold one second, begging for help the next, falling to pieces, pushing me away — okay, fine, I could accept that she was in some kind of crisis, but I couldn't for the life of me guess what she wanted. From me or anyone else.

At home, Peter was waiting for me.

Knowing his feelings about Carmen, I maintained a discreet silence about my visit. Carmen had been maid of honour at our wedding, and right up to the taking of the vows, she had kept trying to convince me I could do better than a struggling rookie reporter whose left-leaning political ideals would keep him from ever being taken seriously by the neo-conservatives who control the media in this country. For his part, Peter found Carmen pretentious, overdramatic and condescending.

All of which is true, but she has a good heart and a generosity of spirit that Peter ignores. When he starts bad-mouthing Carmen, I feel obligated to defend her, a task I really didn't feel up to this particular evening. So I said nothing.

That turned out to be just fine, because Peter was

off on a tangent unrelated to Carmen's renewed love affair with the bottle.

Before I'd even struggled out of my wet boots, he pounced.

"Hey! You know that guy who died last night?"

"What guy? You mean Nigel Farnsworth?"

Who hadn't died last night at all, but I wasn't in the mood for nit-picking. I really was tired: usually, I consider a healthy round of picking nits good for the soul.

"That's the one. Well, I was at my desk this afternoon, when Larry brings me this envelope, literally a plain brown envelope, just like something out of Woodward and Bernstein — and you'll never guess what was in it."

"Golly, you're right, I'll never guess, Peter. Maybe you'll have to tell me."

Ignoring my sarcasm, he pulled out a sheet of paper and waved it in front of me. Someone had been watching way too many detective movies. Words had been carefully snipped from magazines and newspapers, and glued into place to form a crazy-quilt message:

DEAD MINISTER NOT WHAT HE APPEARED TO BE. ASK THOSE WHO KNEW HIM. POLICE ARE ON THE WRONG TRACK: MOTIVE IS THE KEY.

I handed it back to him. "God, how enthralling. Whatever do you think it means?"

"Aw, come on, Katy, don't be that way. Don't you think it could be from Nigel's killer? Or someone who knows who that is? You said yourself you didn't think the sister could have killed him. I thought you'd be excited to see this! They're saying the cops are on the wrong track, aren't they?"

"Well, it's not exactly informative. It doesn't say he

was dipping into the collection plate, or shooting heroin in the vestry, or laundering Columbian drug money, does it?"

"No," Peter said impatiently, "but it does say that all we have to do is ask — and I figure, what have we got to lose? If we ask and come up with nothing, we're no further behind, but if someone divulges he had secret offshore holdings in Bermuda or something, we not only have a good story, but something to give to the police, right? Get your friend Diana off the hook?"

"Sorry, Peter, I guess I'm just worn out. You're right. You should probably check into it. Besides, how often do you actually get a plain brown envelope with a cryptic note inside? That in itself must have made your day."

"I was thinking you might want to come with me." Peter sounded like he was offering me a gift I couldn't turn down.

"What for?" I pushed past him into the kitchen and opened the fridge, hoping to find something to make for supper.

He followed me like an eager puppy. "Normally I'd just make a few phone calls, see if there's anything to it, but no one's answering at Farnsworth's church, and his home number has been cut off. I thought we could take a run out to the church, see if anyone is around."

"I don't know, Peter. It's been a hell of a week. And besides, how do you know this isn't just some kind of nasty joke?"

"I don't!" Peter looked indignant. "I'm not a complete fool, Katy. I know it might be nothing. But I thought you'd at least want to check it out with me."

"Hey, I hung up my detective hat after last summer. I'm strictly civilian these days."

"Hah. So I guess it doesn't matter to you if poor Diana gets framed for something she didn't do?"

"That's not fair. Of course I care. But I don't see ..."

Peter shrugged. "Well, it's okay by me. You'd probably get in the way anyhow."

"Hey! I would not! Fine, I'll go. But not tonight — I'm too tired. Plus I'm hungry. Aren't you?"

"Aren't you forgetting something?" Peter asked, half teasing.

"What? ... Oh, God, it's the first night, isn't it?"

Tears of fatigue and frustration, held back all day, now started to spill down my cheeks. It was Hanukkah. I'd completely forgotten: I had no latkes made, no damn matches to light the menorah, no candles to put in it, and worst of all, no present for Dawn. In all the week's crises, I hadn't even thought to make time for our family ritual. What was happening to me?

Peter handed me a tissue from his pocket, and I blew my nose noisily.

"Listen," he said. "It's not too late. Dawn's over at Sylvie's with Rose, and the car is more or less running today. I even put gas in it. We can dash out, grab a little something for the girls, get some candles, and pick up some latkes at the bagel shop, okay?"

It was seven-thirty by the time we returned, and Dawn was waiting impatiently for us. Rose was sprawled on the couch watching "The Simpsons," but she did tilt her head toward us as we came through the door.

"Where have you been?" Dawn demanded. "I thought tonight was the first night? Did you remember that we needed candles? And I couldn't find any potatoes! Aren't you going to make latkes?"

Laughing, Peter and I presented her with her gift,

a new sound card for her computer; she'd been asking for one for months now. For Rose, I'd picked out a polar fleece hat with matching mitts and a scarf. Neutral, yet practical. And, I hoped, not too tragically unhip. Then of course there was the Hanukkah *gelt*, the gold foil-covered chocolate coins that Dawn has loved since she was a little girl.

Dawn dug out the *dreydls* and she and Peter cleared a space on the floor and started a game of penny-ante gambling. Rose watched out of the corner of her eye. Eventually, when her show was over, she turned the TV off and came to watch.

"What's this all about, anyway?" she asked no one in particular.

Dawn explained the holiday to her, and Rose actually seemed interested. "So it's kind of like the Jewish Christmas? What do you do at Christmas?"

"We don't celebrate Christmas, Rose. It's not a substitute for Christmas — it's a whole other holiday," Dawn said.

"So ... you're Jewish? I think you're the first Jewish people I've ever met."

"And we don't have fangs," Peter joked. Rose didn't smile.

"Tell me, Rose," I said, "what do you know about the Jews?"

"Well, they told us in Sunday school that Jesus couldn't come back until all the Jews were living back in Israel — and they said you were ... I mean, that the Jewish people were too stubborn and greedy to go back on their own, that we'd have to ..." She stopped, embarrassed.

"It's okay, Rose. I've heard worse. Was this the church you and your mother went to?"

She nodded.

"Well, it's just ignorance that makes people say things like that. Like the people who threw the stone through my office window and trashed the place. It's hateful, but sometimes people are afraid of things they can't understand."

"Someone threw a rock through your window? Why, because you're Jewish?"

I forgot, Rose didn't know what I did for a living, unless Dawn had told her. "No, I think it's because I'm an astrologer."

The girl's eyes widened. "Oh. Like — a fortuneteller? That's what you do?" Guess Dawn hadn't mentioned it.

"Not fortunetelling, no. I look at the placement of the planets at the time people were born, and try to help them understand themselves. Why?"

"Well, I always thought –" She stopped herself.

"What?" Dawn prodded her. "What did you think?"

"Well, that astrologers were, like, Satanists or something. That's what they told us."

Dawn started to giggle. "Mom? A Satanist? Doubt it! She hasn't sacrificed a goat in years!"

We all chuckled, and I went to find the box of matches I'd just purchased.

Something about lighting the Hanukkah menorah, the special nine-branched candelabra signifying the flame that reconsecrated the temple after Antiochus and the Greeks had defiled it, always brings a lump to my throat.

It's kind of ironic, really. I've never been able to summon up faith in any kind of god — how could any deity worth his or her salt have let my mother lose her childhood, her innocence, her faith, her family, in

Hitler's death camps? But I also cannot go a year without performing this small ceremony. Maybe it's something to do with reclaiming a kernel of good out of destruction and chaos. It keeps me connected to something larger.

We stood, all four of us, around my small kitchen table. Peter lit the *shammas,* the single candle that lights all the others, and passed it to Dawn, who used it to ignite the lone first candle. Each night we would repeat the ritual, adding another candle, until the menorah was full — eight lights plus the taller *shammas,* a small beacon in the darkest part of the winter. As we set the flames aglow, we sang the blessing: *"Baruch atah adonai elo haanu melach ha olam ..."*

Rose stood in silence, reading along with the words Dawn had written out for her, Hebrew lettering transcribed into English. The blessing complete, we hugged one another and sat down for supper: latkes, traditional potato pancakes fried in oil, served with applesauce and sour cream.

Okay, so they were store-bought, not made by my Polish mother, who'd slave all day grating potatoes, covering them with water to keep them white, mixing them with eggs and matzoh meal, hovering over the hot frying pan to keep the production line coming in a steady stream to the dining room, where the rest of us sat, devouring them as fast as she could turn them out. But it's the thought that counts.

We sat talking until the candles flickered and died. I sent a silent thought to my parents, who'd be lighting their own candles in the desert heat. I'd call them later this evening, just to check in.

Something had been salvaged from the day, after all.

14

I was up and making coffee the next morning before I remembered Peter and I were scheduled to check out the New Morning Christian Life Church. I couldn't see much sense in schlepping all the way out to the west end on a Friday morning when I had work to do — but I supposed it wouldn't do any harm to case the joint. And it would keep Peter happy.

Peter was at my door early, all shaved and showered, bright-eyed and ready to go. I was still sitting in my disreputable-looking terry bathrobe, my hair flat on one side from having slept on it, drinking my first coffee of the day.

"Hey, you're not even showered yet!"

I shot him a baleful look. "No guff."

"Come on, let's go! Here, I'll get you some cereal."

"Sit down, Peter. Have a coffee. And stop dancing

around — you're giving me a headache."

How long has this man known me? Should he not have twigged by now that I don't do mornings?

Peter helped himself to coffee but stood bouncing from one foot to the other, like a dog waiting to be taken for a walk. My ex-husband is a Sagittarius with an Aries Moon, brimming with fire and eager energy. He can't help being this way, but to those of us who require several hours to come to life in the morning, his jump-out-of-bed-and-embrace-the-day approach can be a major pain in the ass.

There was no point in stalling, though, because he'd just continue ricocheting around like buckshot in a tin shed. Better to empty my cup, have a brisk shower and run a cursory comb through my hair. Maybe I could close my eyes for a few moments on the drive to Nepean.

Dawn was whizzing one of her tofu creations in the blender when I came back to the kitchen, towel-drying my hair.

"Hey, Mom. Dad told me where you're going. Can I come with you guys? It sounds interesting," she said.

"Definitely not." I located my nearly empty cup and drained it. "For one thing, it's a school day. And we're only going out to look at some church. You wouldn't be interested."

The lower lip came out, and Peter snorted. "See? This is what comes of trying to go over my head, young lady."

Dawn gave him a mutinous glare, but he ignored her.

"Hey, besides, if you come with us, Rose will want to come too. We wouldn't exactly be incognito then, would we?" I kissed Dawn on the top of her head and went off to find something to wear.

Ten years ago, Peter bought the Flaming Deathtrap secondhand from one of his editors. Despite the handfuls of money he's since thrown into its repair and rehabilitation, F.D. has never run any better, or any worse. It wheezes along at its own pace, making alarming noises that never amount to anything, its body a tribute to the miracles of modern welding techniques, its exhaust system threatening imminent collapse.

We exited at the west end of the Queensway, and found ourselves in suburban Nepean. In contrast to the elder statesmen of Centretown and the Glebe, the houses out here had been born in the heady days of the fifties and sixties, when land was cheap and bungalows and split-levels were all the rage. Apparently there had been a run on fieldstone and vinyl siding at the time, as well as cedar hedges; nary a yard was to be seen without them.

This glorious winter morning the sky was a deep crystalline blue, the sun low in the southeast, glinting off windows and snow, throwing long winter shadows across quiet streets.

When I first saw the New Morning Christian Life Church, I thought someone had plunked a very large piece of origami at the crest of a small hill. The building was all odd jutting angles, topped with a plain wooden cross that loomed forward over the main entrance. Clearly a relic of the heady days of sixties architecture.

The church's parking lot had not yet been ploughed. A number of cars lined the street, and we found a parking space a long suburban block from the church.

"I still don't know why we're here," I complained. "I'm sure there won't be anyone around."

"Look, when we're done, I'll take you for coffee, okay? Now stop griping."

"Yeah, yeah. And then maybe I'll even be able to get some work done."

"Let's just take a peek," Peter said. "I bet there's a janitor or someone around. They're going to have to clear the parking lot and get the sanctuary ready for services on Sunday."

Reluctantly I climbed out of the car, finding myself knee-deep in a snowbank. Gripping the side of the car, I manoeuvred step by step through the snow, cursing as my boot sank even deeper and I lost my balance. My glasses fogged up with my curses.

By the time I had waded out to the road, Peter was already halfway to the church. A path had been trampled to the building's door. Flushed and breathless, I caught up with Peter at the side door of the church. He rang the buzzer.

I may be an astrologer, but I'm no psychic, so my reaction surprised me as much as it did my ex-husband.

"Peter, don't!"

Fear caught at my breath and made my heart pound. I wanted to yank Peter's hand away, pull him back down the path, push him into the safety of the car, drive far away from here.

"Why? Katy, cut it out!"

"Peter, this is wrong. We shouldn't be here. Let's just go, okay?"

"Listen, why don't you go wait in the car? I'll just be a minute."

"No, I'll be okay. I just don't think we should ..."

Footsteps approached from inside the building and the door opened. A solidly built woman of late middle age looked expectantly at us, arms folded across her substantial bosom. In the background, voices were raised in song; we must have interrupted choir practice.

The woman looked us up and down, her face stony.

"This church is closed. Services are at ten on Sunday. Come on back then." She started to close the door.

"No, wait," Peter said. "We're not here for services. We came to talk to you."

"Me?" She looked suspicious. "Why on earth would you want to talk to me?"

"Well, you're the caretaker, aren't you? We just wanted to have a few words with you, about ... the building, the architecture ... we're writing a story ..."

Peter was thinking on his feet here, grasping for excuses. The woman's face darkened.

"You're with the newspaper, aren't you? Can't you just let the poor man rest in peace? I don't have time to waste talking to you. I got work to do."

She did shut the door this time. There was a click as she turned the deadbolt.

"Well, we tried." Peter kicked a piece of snow ahead of him as we trudged away from the church.

"Yup. Now we get to go for coffee, right? You promised ..."

"First we'll just have a look-see at the school," Peter said, dashing my fragile hopes to smithereens.

"What school?"

"Katy, weren't you listening? The New Morning School. Reverend Farnsworth was on the founding board, and he's the director. Or was, at least," Peter amended.

"Oh, fine. Where is it?"

"Over there. Past the playground."

The school was not nearly as flamboyant in its structure as the church. It was a small, flat-roofed building of clay-coloured brick, tucked into a corner of the church property. The main entrance was unlocked, and we wandered into the main foyer without encountering any resistance.

My nostrils were assailed by the odour of chalk dust, wet woollen mittens hung to dry, gym sneakers and discarded sandwiches. The smells evoked memories of sitting in cramped rows, laboriously pencilling letters into smudged scribblers while secretly wishing to run outdoors and hurl snowballs at my childhood friends.

The foyer was lined with ten framed portraits of the inaugural board members, arranged around a five-foot-high cross carved of unvarnished cedar, below which an engraved copper plaque read, "And God so loved the world that He sent His only begotten Son, that those who believed in Him would not perish, but have Everlasting Life."

Next to this splendiferous display, the faded eight-by-ten of a young Queen Elizabeth II in her coronation regalia looked pretty insignificant.

I stood gazing at the portraits.

"Look, Peter, here's Nigel Farnsworth," I murmured, pointing to a tall man with raven-coloured hair and blue eyes that glinted from a chiselled face.

"Wow, he's a looker. He's got charisma written all over him, doesn't he?" Peter said. "Come on, let's go take a look around."

We climbed the short staircase to the office. Glancing through the pebbled glass in the door, I could discern several people inside, and sure enough, before we could pass, a short blonde woman wearing a black suit and reeking of Chanel No. 5 bustled out to greet us.

"Welcome, welcome! You must be here for the vigil. Now don't be shy, everyone else is in a state of shock too — of course we're all just devastated, but who among us knows the true will of God? We must assume our loss is all part of the Plan, mustn't we?"

Peter and I looked at one another, then back at her. We nodded in silent unison, and the woman took each of us by an arm, leading us down the main corridor.

"We're all meeting in the main gymnasium today — it's the only place big enough. It's very crowded, but we should be able to find you a seat. Now, what grade did you say your child was in?"

Fortunately Peter was quick on his feet.

"Oh, grade six," he lied easily. "Did you know the Reverend well? I just can't believe it. So tragic."

The woman shook her head, and her chin-length bleached-blonde hair fell disarmingly over her left eye. She brushed it back and smiled confidentially at Peter. "We really don't know much." She lowered her voice to a whisper. "But apparently the police are still looking for Diana. His sister, you know. I never knew her — she wasn't involved in the school at all. Such a shame, but you know," she lowered her voice even further, "I've heard rumours that she was ... unnatural. You know. A three-dollar bill."

"His sister?" I put in disingenuously, taking my cue from Peter. "You mean she was a lesbian? My, my. Shocking."

"Yes, terrible. Such a waste. Of course, those are only rumours, mind you. But you can see why the

police would want to question her. I just can't understand what would make a woman that way, wanting to
be like a man. Who could not like being a woman?" She
twinkled up at Peter through thickly mascaraed lashes.
"No offense, of course."

I sensed Peter's instinctive recoil, but he rallied
quickly.

"Oh, none taken. Did you know the Reverend
well?" he asked again.

"Oh, yes. All of us who knew him loved him,"
Blonde Lady confided. "But he was a very busy man.
Running the church, keeping tabs on the school here,
doing his pastoral counselling, working with those
unfortunate drug people. And of course, the television
show. But the school was very important to him. The
children, you know."

She dabbed at her eyes. Something was rolling
around in the back of my brain, and it took me a
moment to get hold of it.

"I had this friend who used to work in the church
office," I said. "Maybe you would have known her? She
spoke very highly of Reverend Farnsworth. Her name
was Marion ... Marion Stanley?"

Blonde Church Lady stiffened and glanced sharply
at me; then her face resumed its previous perkiness.

"Oh, yes, poor Marion. Tragic, wasn't it?"

"Terrible. Did you know her well?"

Church Lady gave me another hard look. "Not
many people knew Marion *well*, now did they?"

"Oh, I don't know," I said sweetly. "We were quite
close, but I suppose she could be ..."

I pretended to grope for words, trying to describe
my unfortunate deceased friend. Blonde Lady
watched me struggle, her face a mask of polite piety.

"Oh, well," I finished lamely, "she was certainly a very devoted mother. Her daughter and ours are very close."

"Yes, I suppose so," said Blonde Lady, turning away. "And of course, Reverend Nigel relied on her totally. In the office, I mean. She was very efficient. Well, I must get back. Bye now!"

She threw these last words over her shoulder as she practically sprinted toward the office, her high heels click-click-clicking on the polished linoleum.

"What in hell was all that?" Peter asked me, sotto voce.

"I'll tell you later. Just checking out a hunch."

Clearly, Blonde Lady felt Marion had been too close to the late Reverend Farnsworth. So exactly how close were we talking, here? This would bear further investigation.

The gymnasium smelled strongly of burning wax and wet boots. Despite the room's size, it was heated to a sauna-like level. Not surprising, given that the front of the stage was covered with perhaps a hundred candles of various shapes and sizes. Every few minutes another mourner would rise, walk with bowed head to the front of the hall, light a candle from one of those already burning and place their own among the others. Aside from this, the gym was dead quiet. Only the occasional sniffle broke the thick hush.

Suddenly claustrophobic, I fought an urge to break and run for the nearest fire exit. Irrational, Katy. Get a grip. You have as much right to be here as anyone. These people are here to mourn their minister, not lynch astrologers. Or Jews. Or Jewish astrologers. I battled with my instincts, finally herding them into a small corner of my brain, where they sulked uneasily.

Peter and I settled into our seats at the back of the gym and tried to look inconspicuous. This was not easy — in sharp contrast to most of the people here, I was wearing jeans and a somewhat tatty sweater under my anorak. My clothes were clean, but they didn't compare to some of the get-ups I observed around me.

The woman to my right, who I guessed was about my own age, wore a vivid pink long-sleeved dress with a deep V-neck that accentuated her cleavage; the effect was dramatized by an exaggerated shawl collar. The dress fabric was stiff; each time she shifted in her seat, it made a noise like sandpaper. The woman kept fishing tissues out of her handbag, blowing her nose in delicate little sniffs. Her face was swollen with tears.

Pink to a funeral? I don't go to funerals that often; perhaps the dress code has evolved in recent years. Katy Klein, fashion critic to the stars.

I was sweating profusely and my lungs screamed for fresh air. No one here was saying a word, incriminating or otherwise, about the dearly departed. Why exactly were we here again? I looked meaningfully at Peter, cocking my head toward the door, but he just smiled and folded his hands in his lap.

I cleared my throat a couple of times, until the woman in front of me turned and gave me a hard stare. Fine, I will maintain a decorous silence. My resolution lasted about a minute; then I nudged the woman in pink.

"Could you tell me where the ladies' room is?" I whispered. "I'm feeling a little faint."

To prove the point, I let my eyes roll upward slightly; then I clutched at her arm. That did the trick.

"Oh, my, of course. Come with me." She stood in a

rustle of pink, and led me carefully past our seatmates.

I smirked at Peter as I squished past him; he raised his eyebrows but said nothing. Out in the hallway, I leaned against the wall for a second, breathing in the cool chalk-laden air. My companion supported me as best she could, though I towered over her. Slowly we walked back down the corridor toward the girls' washroom. Pink Dress hovered apprehensively as I bent double over a child-level sink and splashed my face with tepid water.

"Oh, thank you," I said. "That feels so much better."

"Are you sure you're all right?" Pink Dress asked. "Maybe we should sit down for a few minutes."

"No, no," I protested weakly, but I allowed her to guide me toward the open door of an empty classroom.

We sat at a round table, on miniature chairs. My knees were up around my chest somewhere.

"I'm so sorry to pull you away from the vigil like that," I said. "But it was very close in there, didn't you find?"

"I really didn't notice it. I was thinking more about our loss. That poor, poor man."

Her eyes filled with tears. She dabbed at them with yet another tissue; she must be carrying a whole boxful in that purse.

"Oh, yes, our loss," I echoed. "A terrible thing. Were you close to the Reverend?"

"He was such a wonderful person," Pink Dress said. "It was a privilege to know him. So kind, so giving ..."

"Oh, definitely." I tried to encourage her. "I've been wondering how we'll even carry on, now that he's ... been taken from us."

I turned my head away from her and pretended to wipe away a tear. Sometimes I hate myself.

"I can't imagine how the school will go on," Pink Dress said. "He was like the glue that kept us all working together, doing the Lord's work."

"Of course, we'll all miss him," I echoed. "So ... do you think his sister really did it, like the police said?"

"I don't know." She studied her hands. "I ... I know Diana wasn't popular with some of the ... the more militant members, but I liked her. She helped my husband a lot, you know. Out at the rehab centre. Our family owes her a great deal."

"Well, that's what I was thinking. I mean, she's such an ethical person herself, I just couldn't see her ... doing that," I said. "I think the police have it all wrong."

"Oh, do you?" Pink Dress brightened. "That's such a relief. I thought I was the only one. Now, if I were the police, I'd be talking to that Phil Stanley character. Marion Stanley's husband, you know. Seems to me, he's the logical person to look at."

"What makes you say so?"

"Well, everyone knew ... I mean ..." She flushed, fumbling for words, suddenly anxious.

"You mean, about Marion? And the Reverend?"

"Well, yes! Exactly! It was pretty much common knowledge."

So Marion and Nigel *had* been an item.

"I never really knew Marion. What was she like?"

"Oh, sweet to look at. Butter wouldn't melt in her mouth. Always rushing around the church office, getting this or that for Reverend Nigel, you know. Those big brown eyes — and the way she dressed sometimes! She was a big girl, but she'd wear these dresses that showed off her — well, I'm not a person to judge, but really! I'm sure that's why —"

"You mean," I lowered my voice to a conspiratorial whisper, "you mean she seduced him? Oh, my!"

Pink Dress nodded emphatically, her eyes round. "I can't imagine it any other way. Reverend Nigel never had time for — that sort of thing, before. He was always so busy with his other projects. Then, suddenly, he didn't seem to have as much time for us, once Marion was working full-time in his office. It's almost as if someone put her there to keep him from his real work."

"And his real work was ..." I prompted her.

"Well, leading the war against Satan, of course!"

"The war against Satan?"

"Well, it's so important, isn't it? Of course, I don't know anything about it, really, just what I've heard. From my husband, and a couple of others. And I shouldn't really be talking about it ..." She fiddled with the sleeve of her dress, flattening the material and rubbing it with a manicured nail.

"Well, we're all in it together, though, aren't we?" I offered.

"Yes, of course, but there are some things that Reverend Nigel told me it's best to keep quiet. Like the Soldiers, you know. Talking about them freely could be dangerous for them."

"Right," I said, not having a clue what she was talking about. "But the Soldiers ... they're so —" I groped for words, and as I'd hoped, Pink Dress supplied one.

"Brave! Of course they are! But they have to be, don't they. I only wonder how they'll carry on, now that ..."

"Now that Reverend Nigel is gone, you mean?"

She nodded, her eyes full of tears again. "He had such great hopes for all of us," she sniffed. "He said the forces of good were starting to win. There will be laws, laws preventing the Satanists from practising anywhere in the city. Then it'll be provincewide, then the whole country. It's only a matter of time."

"The Satanists? Oh, you mean the fortunetellers and so on?"

She nodded, just as Blonde Lady, our original tour guide, popped her vivacious head around the corner. She did not look delighted to see me in conversation with Pink Dress.

"Shelley!" she remonstrated sharply.

Pink Dress jumped guiltily, a child caught with her hand in the cookie jar.

"Oh, Carol, hi," she said weakly. "This lady and I — what did you say your name was?"

"Shelley, shouldn't you be back with the others?" Carol's tone brooked no protest.

As Shelley left, Carol narrowed her eyes at me.

"Mrs. Klein, I believe you should leave now."

"I — but — how do you know my name?" I stammered.

She ignored me. "Your kind are not welcome here. If you don't leave now, I'll have you and your husband escorted from the premises. This is a private vigil. Now get out."

She certainly did sound like she meant business. I headed quickly for the nearest exit, and just as the door swung shut behind me, I saw Peter approaching around a corner. We made tracks for the Flaming Deathtrap.

In the car, I said nothing until we were safely under way.

"How did they figure out who we were?" I asked.

Peter shook his head. "I don't know. After you left the gym, I sat there for ten or fifteen minutes. I thought you'd be back, and we could go find someone to interview. Then that blonde woman marched up to me and asked me to step outside. She had a couple of young guys, clean-cut and very large, waiting for me in the hallway. They asked me to leave, and I didn't think I had much choice."

"The Soldiers."

"The what?" Peter shot me a sideways glance. "Katy, are you all right?"

"That woman in the pink dress, her name was Shelley, she told me about a group she called the Soldiers. She was a bit vague about them, but it seems they do the Lord's work, ridding the world of Satanists and so on."

"What, you mean like vigilantes, or something?"

"I wouldn't be surprised if they were the ones who trashed my office," I interrupted. "Of course, I can't prove anything."

"No, but from what Rose said last night, it doesn't sound all that far-fetched. Some of the stuff they were teaching her was pretty far out."

"Another thing: Shelley said Nigel Farnsworth was behind that ridiculous by-law. You know, the one that's supposed to put me out of business?"

Peter looked thoughtful. "This guy really got around. I think this bears further investigation, don't you?"

"Hey, hold on a sec," I protested. "I already told you, my detecting days are but a faint memory, and I plan to keep it that way. If you want to check out the Reverend, you do it under your own steam, thank you very much."

"Even though he might have trashed your office, threatened to have you killed and pressed for laws to put you out of business?" Peter asked. "And that blonde woman nearly jumped out of her skin when you mentioned Marion. I'd be willing to bet he was boinking her on the side. Maybe he even killed her, Katy."

"Peter, you know I hate that expression. But even if Marion and Farnsworth were having some kind of torrid romance, it doesn't prove anything. Why would he kill her? And why would he die shortly afterward?"

"Well, okay then, what about Phil Stanley? He had the motive, if his wife was about to leave him for her minister. I could see him poisoning her, then stabbing Nigel in a jealous rage, couldn't you?"

"Peter, stop it. I'm not getting involved. I told you, I had my fill last summer."

"Well, it's your loss, sugar. I'll do it on my own then."

I said nothing, pressing my lips together in a firm line. He wasn't roping me in. No sir.

15

We clanked most of the way home in silence. Okay, not in silence exactly: a peculiar grinding noise was audible above the tinny music emanating from what passed for the F.D.'s stereo speakers.

"So what are you going to do?" I conceded finally.

Peter had the grace not to smirk. "I'll talk to my police contact, see what she knows about these Soldier guys. You might not be the first person they've attacked. Maybe you should call Councillor Tompkins again, drop a hint that you know about Farnsworth's church putting on pressure to outlaw astrology. That might shake a few things loose."

I shrugged wearily. "I suppose it's as good a place to start as any. Tompkins wasn't much help when I spoke to her before. But maybe if she knows we know the real source of the by-law amendment, she'll think twice about supporting it. Separation of church and state, and all that. Make a good news story, wouldn't it?"

Peter nodded. "There's no law against churches lobbying for political change, but this reeks of influence-peddling. An amendment like that should have generated quite a discussion, but no one even heard about it. Doesn't look good."

Peter pulled up in front of our building. It's trickier than one might think to parallel park against a snowbank, with one side of the car a foot higher than the other, but he negotiated the F.D. masterfully, killing the engine with a flourish.

"And what about the sex angle?" he continued. "Your friend in the pink dress implied Marion Stanley was romantically involved with the Reverend, didn't she? I wonder if Rose knows ..." His eyes got that glazed look of a newshound on a fresh scent.

"Peter Fischer! Absolutely not. You're not saying anything whatsoever about this to Rose. She's got enough to worry about, without you dragging up a bunch of groundless gossip about her mother."

"Katy, I would never do that!" Peter looked outraged. "I want what's best for her, too, you know. I was just thinking of letting her know we attended the vigil, and seeing what comes up. I don't see what harm that could do."

"Then you don't see very much at all, do you? Let's just say Shelley was right, and Marion was having a torrid affair with Nigel. First of all, do you think Marion would have shared it with her teenage daughter? And even if Rose knew somehow, it would hurt her to hear about it from you. It's a stupid idea, Peter. Give it up."

"Fine, fine. So we're basically no further ahead. I'd kind of hoped ..."

"Well, there's always the Phil angle."

"True," Peter acknowledged. "Why don't you give your buddy Steve Benjamin a call, see what he thinks?"

My face grew hot at the reference to the detective.

"Knock it off, Peter. He's not my buddy. But yes, I believe I will give him a call. Meanwhile, I'm going to grab a bite before I go back to the office. Care to join me?"

But Peter had other fish to fry. Inside, he dashed upstairs, eager to dig up more dirt about the Soldiers. I hung up my outdoor gear and started searching for edibles in my kitchen cupboard. It was past lunchtime, as my stomach informed me self-righteously. I was just sitting down to a very nice midday meal of extra old cheddar cheese melted on two halves of a fresh sesame seed bagel, when Dawn came bursting into the apartment, breathless and pale.

"Mom — Mom, you've got to come outside! It's Rose, she's sick."

Dawn yanked on my arm, pulling me to my feet before I could protest. Dawn doesn't panic readily, and my heart started thudding in response.

"Wha'isit?" My mouthful of bagel suddenly tasted like toasted sawdust.

"I don't know what's wrong, I don't know!" She threw my boots toward me.

I swallowed with some difficulty. "Wait a second, Dawn. Where is Rose? Maybe I should call an ambulance?"

"There's no time! She's lying on the sidewalk, down by the corner — we need to get her inside. There's blood everywhere—"

I paused long enough to call 911 and give them Rose's location. I threw on my anorak, stuffed my feet into my boots without bothering to lace them up, and Dawn and I raced to the end of the block.

An elderly couple, out for their afternoon walk, had paused on the street corner next to Rose and were staring down at her uncertainly. They seemed very relieved to see me.

Rose lay crumpled on the sidewalk, her head propped on Dawn's folded jacket. She was deathly pale, that greenish tinge was back around her mouth, and her eyelids barely fluttered. Her baggy jeans looked dark and wet. Blood feathered out onto the ice, as though someone had spilled a tin of red paint across her narrow hips.

I took off my anorak and wrapped it around her shoulders for warmth. Then I took her limp wrist and felt around for a pulse; eventually I located something like a vague heartbeat. Recalling from my high school first aid course that you're not supposed to move people who have collapsed, I knelt on the icy walk next to her, grasping her small cold hand.

"Dawn, go back to the apartment and bring a blanket," I ordered. She dashed off, eager to do something, anything.

As we tucked the woollen blanket around Rose, I heard a siren in the distance. The ambulance howled to a standstill, lights flashing, and the attendants took charge quickly and efficiently, loading Rose onto a stretcher and strapping a blood pressure cuff around her skinny upper arm. One of the women turned to me.

"You're her mother?"

"Aunt," I blurted without thinking. "Sort of."

Well, that was more or less true. And it gave me standing to accompany Rose to the hospital. Dawn remained behind, with instructions to phone Greta and meet us at the Children's Hospital. For once, she didn't argue.

I'd never been inside an ambulance before, and the siren's shriek was deafening, as we careened through Centretown, across the river to the hospital on Smyth Road. Cars pulled over to let us pass. When they didn't move quickly enough, I swore at them: get out of the way, you moron, don't you know an ambulance when you see one? I didn't notice right away that I was crying.

At one point the attendant turned to me. "I'm getting a pulse here, but it's kind of fluttery. Does she have any history of this kind of collapse?"

I nodded, thinking of her sudden faint in my living room, only a couple of days before. "She might be pregnant."

She looked at me, eyebrows raised. "How old is this kid?"

"Thirteen."

Strapped onto the stretcher, bare arm extended, Rose didn't look a day over eleven. Her hair splayed out, a straw-coloured halo; her eyelashes lay long and dark on her still-plump cheeks. Her lips were bluish against her blanched skin.

We pulled into the breezeway outside Emergency. Rose was unloaded and pushed through the automatic doors. A crowd of nurses converged on her still form, and I drew back, letting them do their work. Eventually, someone directed me toward the parents' waiting room. A few minutes later a resident, who looked to my aging eyes not much older than Dawn, summoned me to the examining room.

"Your daughter is having a spontaneous abortion," he said. "She seems to have lost a great deal of blood. Were you aware of her condition?"

Despite myself, I cringed at his palpable judgment. Bad mother, his voice said. Letting your kid run wild, get pregnant — how can you be so irresponsible?

"I'm not her mother. And you know nothing whatsoever about this child's history. I'll thank you to keep your moralizing to yourself."

The resident, a Dr. Fred Thorsten, looked taken aback. "Okay, why don't you tell me what you can about Rose? The more we know, the better we can help her. Mrs ... uh ..."

"Klein. Katy Klein. Rose has been staying with us for the past couple of days. She's thirteen years old. Her mother died a week ago. Her father is a drunk with a nasty temper, and he doesn't want her around. We only discovered a few days ago that she might be pregnant. She had no idea about it, as far as I know. We don't know who the father is. I was going to take her to my own doctor next week to confirm the pregnancy."

Fred Thorsten scribbled in Rose's file. Without looking up, he asked, "Do you know how far along the pregnancy was?"

I shook my head. "No idea."

Thorsten sighed. "Okay. We're going to do some tests on Rose. We need to do an ultrasound, check her hemoglobin, stuff like that. Can you sign as her guardian?"

He thrust the form toward me, and I signed, holding my breath that I wasn't doing anything illegal. An orderly came in to wheel Rose's gurney away, and I wandered back down the hall to the parents' area, where a big-screen television was broadcasting "The Lion King" to an empty room.

Greta and Dawn arrived half an hour later, and I brought them up to speed.

Greta, ever the diplomat, said, "Well, I have to say it's kind of a relief that she's losing the pregnancy. How could that poor little thing ever look after a kid? She's only a baby herself, you know. Did they say how she was doing? When can we see her?"

She continued to pepper me with questions, not bothering to pause for answers, until Dawn cut in.

"Want a drink, Mom?"

Raiding my wallet for quarters, she wandered off to the juice machine down the hall. Greta kept up her interrogation. I tried to focus on the Disney version of life on the savannah. The colours were very pretty, the tunes catchy.

Eventually, Greta noticed that I wasn't bothering to answer her, and she subsided into a sulky silence. The three of us sat nursing tins of orange juice until Fred Thorsten came back. I introduced him to Greta, who was uncharacteristically silent.

"She's in pretty rough shape," Thorsten told us. "She's lost a lot of blood, and it looks like she might have been around fourteen weeks or so along. That's late for a spontaneous abortion, and it increases the risk to the mother. She's expelled some fetal material, as well as part of the placenta. We're just waiting now to see if she can expel the rest on her own. She's conscious, but pretty groggy. I'm not sure she knows what's happening to her. Can you sign here to authorize a blood transfusion, please?"

Blood transfusion. Doesn't that increase her risk of AIDS? How clean is our blood supply now, anyway? I'd stopped paying attention some time ago, and now my mind reverberated with questions.

"I don't think I should sign them — Greta, could you do it? You're her aunt, at least."

Greta signed the forms without a word and shoved them back toward Thorsten.

We crowded into the observation unit, an open ward with nine beds, decorated with cartoon characters. Plastic toys, the kind fast-food places give small children with their burgers and fries, hung by threads from the ceiling. Something to look at when you're flat on your back, I suppose.

But Rose wasn't looking at much. Her eyes were closed, and as we arranged ourselves around her bed, she barely stirred. Her skin, pale already, was waxy now, and I had to look hard to see her little chest rising and falling under the flannelette sheet that covered her. I picked up her hand, giving it a gentle squeeze. Greta stayed at the foot of the bed, silent and uncomfortable, shifting from one foot to the other.

"Rose, honey?" I asked.

Her eyes opened slightly, though she did not move her head.

"Rose, do you know where you are?"

"No ..." she whispered. Her eyelashes flickered and rested on her cheeks.

"You're in the hospital. Don't worry, okay? You're going to be fine, you're just a bit weak right now."

"Too much blood. Blood everywhere ..." She struggled briefly, as though she would sit up. I put a hand on her shoulder and stopped her easily.

"That's right, you lost some blood and then you fell," I said. "Dawn ran for help. We brought you here a couple of hours ago. Look, don't try to talk right now. You need to rest."

We sat in silence, listening to the bustle of sick children in the hall outside. In the observation unit itself were four little kids with asthma, a girl with a dislocated elbow, a teen who'd been spending a restful day under the Mackenzie King Bridge sniffing glue from a plastic bag. This I overheard from the social worker who conferred with a nurse.

Most of the kids were pretty quiet, except for one

little girl who objected fiercely as her parents tried to persuade her to use the inhaler mask. She screamed and thrashed, trying to pull the hissing plastic thing from her face. There wasn't much to do here, except sip hospital coffee from cardboard cups and thumb through out-of-date magazines.

Nurses drifted in and out, checking Rose's pulse, removing the empty bag of blood dripping into her arm and replacing it with another, shooing us away and drawing the bedside curtains while they changed her blood-soaked padding. Dr. Thorsten came by every half hour or so. At one point I saw him in the glassed-in nursing station, shaking his head as he and the head nurse looked at a clipboard. I hoped it was not Rose's.

He emerged from the station looking solemn, and I willed him to go visit some other bed. But no, he was coming toward us. I held my breath, awaiting the verdict.

"Rose is a very sick little girl," he began.

Dawn let out an involuntary whimper. I pulled her toward me, and she sat heavily on my lap. She weighed more than I remembered.

Thorsten went on. "She's losing blood faster than we can get it into her — the site where the placenta was attached is bleeding very heavily, and unless we do an emergency dilatation and curettage, to clean out the uterus, she's going to keep losing too much blood. I'd originally hoped she'd pass the placenta on her own, in which case we could give her a drug to help the blood vessels dilate. But we need to get her upstairs now and do the D&C before things get any worse. Do you understand?"

I nodded. "Greta, you really ought to sign for her, I

think. And maybe you should go call Phil. Whatever he is, he's still her father."

Obediently, Greta reached for the forms and scrawled her name without even looking. She walked stiffly to the public phone in the hall. When she returned, Rose had already been wheeled upstairs. By the time Phil arrived an hour later, all beer-blustering and demanding to be led to Rose's side, his daughter had expired on the operating table.

While Fred Thorsten took Phil into a private room to break the news of his daughter's death, I grabbed Dawn's chilled hand and led her to the hospital's front entrance, where I flagged a cab. The darkness outside surprised me — had we been here that long?

At home, we slumped at the kitchen table, watching the flickering second-night candles burn down. I had not wanted to light them, and my voice choked and strangled around the words of the blessing, but Dawn had insisted. I kept envisioning Rose's face last night, her eyes wide at the unfamiliar Hebrew.

As the candles finally extinguished themselves in tiny streams of smoke, I tried to improvise a silent Kaddish, the Jewish prayer for the dead. I could only remember a smattering of the words, and I couldn't recall the order, but I think I got the message across.

If anyone was listening, which I doubt.

16

SATURDAY, DECEMBER 18
Moon square Jupiter ✦
Sun square Jupiter ✦
Mercury conjunct Pluto ✦
Venus square Mars ✦
Saturn square Neptune ✦

I didn't sleep much that night. When I did, I dreamed of flickering candles and dead white faces. When I finally woke fully, I struggled to recall exactly what had happened the day before. Rose occupied a numb place in my heart; it hurt too much to feel. I wanted to cry, to mourn her properly, but all I could do was lie in bed watching her last hours replay on an endless feedback loop in my head.

Had she known what was happening? More to the point, could I have done things differently, read the stars more closely to avert disaster? I have heard it said that it's possible to extract meaning and wisdom from tragedy. I guess that only works for those more mature and evolved than I am, because I wasn't getting a damn thing. All I could think was, a child died. A child died, for no reason, and I couldn't keep it from happening, even though I was right there.

I got up and made coffee, checked on Dawn, who was sleeping on the couch as though her own bed were still occupied by Rose. She stirred and moaned, then sat up as I walked past her into the kitchen.

"Last night really happened, didn't it?" she asked.

I nodded. "I'm afraid so. Are you okay?"

"My head hurts."

"Mine too. I think it'll take a while for it to really sink in."

Not really tasting my coffee, I tried to remember what I was supposed to be doing right now. I was going to have to paint by numbers for the next little while — perform my life by rote.

I called Peter first. Dawn had phoned him from the hospital, so he knew about Rose's collapse. Now he simply said, "I'll be right down," and hung up the phone. Within seconds, we were hugging and crying together.

"I'm so glad I didn't ask her about Nigel Farnsworth," Peter said, after we'd used up nearly half a box of tissues.

Dawn, who had wandered into the kitchen to find some breakfast, eyed him curiously.

"Who's that, Dad?"

Peter explained.

"So he was the minister of her church?" Dawn asked.

Peter nodded. "Founder and minister. Why? Did she say something to you about it?"

"Just that when she ran away from home a few months ago, that's where she stayed. She said he let her stay with him for a couple of days, but then she got kind of freaked out and called her mom."

I frowned. "Why would he let her stay at all? Seems like an odd thing to do."

"She told him her father was beating her mom up, and he felt sorry for her, she said. And he knows her family really well — maybe he thought he could protect her?"

"Well, couldn't he have called the Children's Aid, like I've been doing?" I wondered. "It doesn't really make sense, letting her stay in the church. Where would she sleep?"

"In his office, she said. On a couch. But she said it was creepy — there were always people around, having meetings and stuff."

"Dawn," Peter said, "did Rose mention anything like 'the Soldiers'?"

Dawn looked up from her whole-grain toast. "I don't know. Maybe. I think so. Rose is — she was kind of odd that way. She'd mention something, and if you asked her about it, she'd act like she hadn't heard you. But I think she might have mentioned something about soldiers. Soldiers for God, or something like that."

"See?" Peter turned to me. "I told you. I think this bears further investigation. Especially with all the stuff that's happened to you — rock throwing and death threats and office vandalism. How do we know the same thing hasn't happened to other people the Soldiers don't like?"

"I wish you'd keep away from it," I said.

"How about some breakfast?" he offered.

"You're changing the subject."

He raised an eyebrow at me and dug around in the cupboard for some cereal. There wasn't much point in arguing with him — he'd do what he liked, whether I wanted him to or not. So I let him make me some oat-meal, which I ate with lots of brown sugar. Usually this would have cheered me up somewhat, but not today.

It was close to eleven before I remembered: I'd intended to call Steve Benjamin about yesterday's vigil at the school. No point in phoning on a Saturday morning, though. He'd be off-duty, probably at home in his jammies, tending his pet snake or something. I tried to imagine Detective Benjamin in his leisure hours. The visualization was not a success.

Well, I didn't much feel like chatting anyway, so I decided to leave a message on his voice mail. If he was interested enough, he could call me back. I dialled, and was taken off guard when Benjamin picked up on the first ring.

"Oh, uh, hi — I didn't expect you to be there," I stammered.

"You always call people when you think they're not in?"

"No, I — that is, I thought of something and I fig-ured I'd just leave you a message while it occurred to me."

"Oh? What did you remember? Something about your interview with Diana Farnsworth?"

"Nothing. I mean it's not something I recalled, it's more like something I did. I went out to Reverend Farnsworth's school yesterday. I thought I should tell you about it."

Benjamin drew a deep, patient breath, expelled it slowly. Oh, how could I forget — he doesn't like it when civilians go poking around on so-called police business.

"Well, I didn't see *you* there! It's not my fault you guys didn't think to go out there. So do you want to hear about it, or not?"

"Okay," he sighed. "What happened?"

"Well, they were holding a candlelight vigil for Reverend Nigel in the school gym. So I went in and got talking to this woman who was really broken up about the minister's death."

I recapped the story about Shelley, the Soldiers and their war on Satanism, and her allegation that Marion had been involved in improprieties with the minister.

"And then," I wrapped up, "this woman Carol poked her head back into the room and identified me by name. She said they didn't like my kind, and I should get out before she had her thugs turf me out. I took off in a hurry, I can tell you."

"Did you get the names of the people you spoke with?"

"Just first names. I wasn't walking around with a clipboard or anything. I just went because ..." My voice trailed off.

"Yes?"

"Ah, well, because my ex-husband, you know, Peter Fischer, the journalist? I think you met him last summer. He wanted to take a look around and I agreed to go with him. Kind of for moral support, you know. It was a spur-of-the moment thing."

"I see." Benjamin's voice was glacial. "You decided to mount your own private investigation of a homicide, without notifying the police, so that your ex-husband could write an article for the paper and screw up the official police investigation that is already proceeding? And then you interview two women, discover that the murder victim may or may not have been engaging in sexual impropriety. And you fail to obtain the full names of these two witnesses. Who will now know to keep their mouths shut, should they be interviewed by actual police investigators, thus further fouling up the case and making my job about fifty times as difficult as it needs to be. Thanks for letting me know. I appreciate it."

"Well, if you're going to be that way about it, I just won't bother telling you anything. I called you as a courtesy, you know. I didn't have to. If you don't like what I have to say, I can forget your number."

"Katy ..."

But I wasn't listening. I was on a roll now. "I don't owe you a thing, Detective Benjamin, so why don't you just take the poker out of your ass? It'll improve your disposition. Might even make you fit for human company, although somehow I doubt it!"

I slammed the phone down. I realized I'd forgotten to tell him about the anonymous tip that had set us off in the first place, but I didn't care. He was being a jerk.

Within a minute the phone started ringing, and I stared at it, my ugly mood growing darker by the second. Finally, on the eighth ring, I picked up.

"Katy," Benjamin said. "I don't want to fight with you. I understand you phoned in the information because you wanted to help. I do appreciate it, okay?"

"Okay."

"It's just that ..."

"No, really, it's okay. I guess we did kind of overstep. I honestly didn't think it would go that far. I just thought we'd take a quick peek at the buildings, see if anyone was hanging around, and come straight back."

"Yeah. Fine. So you say the vigil was being held at the school?"

"That's right. Actually, that's kind of odd, isn't it? I mean, there were about two hundred people crammed into that gym, all sweating like pigs. Wouldn't the church have held more?"

"Probably," he said. "Who did you see at the church?"

"Some lady, a caretaker by the looks of it. Why?"

"Did you see anyone else?"

"No," I said slowly. "I didn't see anyone, but I heard people singing. You know, that hymn — 'Onward Christian soldiers, marching as to war' — that one."

"Are you sure?"

"Sure I'm sure. Why? What difference does it make what they were singing? What's going on, Benjamin?"

"Nothing you need to know about. We're looking into a few things out there, that's all."

"Fine, don't tell me. But I think I know someone who might have had a motive to kill Farnsworth, if you're interested."

"What? Who?"

"Phil Stanley. Marion's husband."

"Interesting. What makes him your prime suspect?"

"Well, what if someone like Phil Stanley were to get wind of his wife playing around with the minister? I wouldn't put it past him to get all fired up and kill both of them. I still think her death was suspicious — maybe he poisoned her or something."

"Okay, I'll talk to him. Anything else?"

"No ... oh! I almost forgot. The reason we went out there in the first place."

"And that would be?"

"Well, Peter got this anonymous note. You know, the way they look on TV — little letters cut out of magazines and pasted on a piece of paper. It said to ask around at the church if we wanted to find Farnsworth's killer."

"And has your husband –"

"Ex-husband."

"Right, sorry. Has he turned this note in to the police yet?"

"Um. I don't know. Is he supposed to?"

There was a long silence.

"Yes, Katy, he's supposed to. It's evidence in a major crime. If he withholds it, that's a criminal offense. Get him to call me, would you?"

"Sure." I wasn't at all certain Peter would be thrilled about this development, but there was nothing for it now.

"Okay, so is that it? Did you have anything else you wanted to get off your chest?"

"Uh, no. No, I don't think so."

"Good. I mean –" He cleared his throat. "Listen, Katy, I was just thinking — maybe you and I, uh, well, would you like to have a coffee with me sometime? I know I've been a bit abrupt with you, so I'd understand if you said no ..."

"Sure," I said too quickly, my voice rising to a Minnie Mouse-like squeak. "That would be nice. Sometime. Well, gotta go."

I sat for a while, scowling into my coffee cup. If there was one thing I did not need, it was a new love interest. No, that's not true. I was lonely sometimes, but my encounter with Brent last summer had left me pretty bruised.

Besides, Steve Benjamin was not my type. I just couldn't imagine him and me, me and him ... I shook my head impatiently. Maybe I was jumping the gun. Maybe he was just being polite. You know, buttering up the witness? I see that on television all the time. There was this one show where the key witness in a murder case was a major airhead with a huge crush on one of the cops, and you could see that he was playing on her feelings to get all he could out of her, and then he just dumped her when the case was solved. Well, Detective Steve Benjamin would have another think coming, if he thought I'd fall for that one.

I picked up the phone and dialled. I'd tell him exactly where he could get off. When I opened my mouth, though, something completely different came out.

"There's one more thing I wanted to tell you."

"What's that?"

Half talking, half crying, I told him the story of Rose's collapse, her trip to the hospital and her death. I poured out my grief, my helplessness in the face of Rose's pain. Somehow, I felt Benjamin would understand.

He listened sympathetically, making supportive clucking sounds in all the right places.

"What about her father? Is Phil blaming you?"

"I don't know. Probably. Last I heard, he was planning to charge me with kidnapping his daughter. Now he'll probably up it to murder. Somehow, I just can't find it in me to care."

Benjamin promised to check the police computer to see if I was on Canada's Most Wanted list yet. He told me not to worry.

"I'm sure Phil's going to blame me for Rose's death," I said. "I blame myself, so why wouldn't he?"

"Whoa, hold on a second. You blame yourself? How could a young girl's miscarriage possibly be your fault? You did all the right things. There's nothing anyone could have done, Katy."

"I don't know. Maybe I should have insisted that

the doctor see her the day after I figured out she was pregnant? Maybe I should have made sure she ate extra? Maybe I should have let her come to live with us? I just don't know." Hot tears streamed down my cheeks, pooling in the hollow at the base of my neck.

"Come on, Katy, you can't take responsibility for everything bad that happens in the world," he chided me gently.

It wasn't enough, but the words made a small dent, and I was grateful.

17

Sigmund Freud he wasn't, but I took some solace in Benjamin's words. At least one person in the world thought I had done right by Rose. For some time after I'd hung up, I sat at the kitchen table, watching dust motes dance in the wintry light.

Eventually, Dawn joined me.

"Honey, we need to talk," I said.

She nodded.

"Can you tell me what happened yesterday?"

Dawn frowned, as though remembering an event in the distant past. She swallowed hard, then spoke slowly, her speech punctuated by long silences.

"We were on our way downtown. Rose was all happy. She said she'd wondered if she was pregnant, because she'd missed a couple of periods, but now she knew everything was okay — she'd started her period after all. We were horsing around, and then Rose said she had a stomachache, so I said we should go home. I thought it might have been the latkes from last night. We both really pigged out, you know. Anyway, we started for home, and by the time we got to the corner, she was leaning on my shoulder. She said she felt awful — crampy, and she was sweating, but cold.

"Then she fell down on the sidewalk. At first, I thought she'd just slipped on the ice, but when I tried to get her back onto her feet, it was like she was made of rubber — I couldn't get her to move. Then I saw her jeans were soaked with blood, and I put my jacket under her head and ran for you."

Dawn's face, normally so animated and rosy, was grey.

"I should have phoned for an ambulance as soon as she said she felt sick, but I honestly thought it was nothing important, Mom." She sniffled, and I reached for her hand. "I didn't ... I didn't know it could be that bad ..."

"Oh, honey." I gave her hand a squeeze. "We're all feeling awful, but it wasn't really anyone's fault. We tried to help Rose — she was in a rough spot. But no one could have done anything differently. It just happened."

Dawn nodded. "I know that, but I wanted so much to make things all right for her. I feel like we had a chance, and we blew it."

Later that afternoon, I called Greta. She was as subdued as she had been yesterday at Rose's bedside.

"How did Phil react?" I asked.

"Bad. He came out of that room blubbering, reeking of booze, and I think he would have tried to hit me if that resident hadn't been there," Greta said. "For all I don't have the time of day for Phil, I have to say I did feel a little sorry for him. First Marion, now Rose. It's a lot for anyone to take." Greta's voice wavered, and I felt a sudden wash of shame.

"How are you doing, Greta?"

She sighed heavily. "I don't know, Katy. I guess I wish I'd taken more of a hand in looking after Rosie. I was putting myself first, and that wasn't right. Don't get me wrong, I think you did a great job, and believe me I appreciate it, but she was part of our family. I guess I was just kind of mad at Marion for dying like that and sticking me with the responsibility. I don't know."

Welcome to the League of Guilt-ridden Women.

"Hey, you had other things to worry about. We all wanted to help Rose, but where was her father when she needed him?"

"I guess you're right. But I can't help wondering how things might have turned out if I'd gone over there sooner, brought her home a few months ago ... when she asked me to."

"Rose asked you to take her home?"

This I hadn't heard before.

"Yes. Last time she ran away from home. She called me from the church, where she'd been staying with that Reverend Whatshisname — the one Marion was so sweet on. You know, the one who was murdered. I thought she was just being ... what's the word? Hysterical? Like Marion used to get sometimes. I thought she was just trying to get attention. I turned my back on her then, and look what happened ..."

Greta's sniffles turned to gulping sobs. I said nothing, waiting for the storm to abate. Gradually, she collected herself, blew her nose.

"Greta, did Rose tell you why she wanted to leave home?" I asked.

"Not exactly. She said she couldn't live with Phil, he was always screaming at her. And she said Marion didn't love her anymore. Of course, that's just plain silly. And she said she didn't like the church anymore, she just wanted to get away and start over again."

"Did she say why she didn't like the church?"

Silence.

"Greta?"

"I thought she was lying," Greta mumbled.

"Lying? About what? What did she say to you?"

"She said — she said someone had been touching her. You know — in a sexual way. She said she was scared. She wanted me to take her in. I told her to go back home, where her parents could look after her."

"Did she say who was touching her? Her father?"

"No, not him. She said — but Katy, she's so much like Marion, I'm sure she was just saying things to get a rise out of me, to get me to take her in."

"Who was touching her, Greta?"

"That minister. So she said."

"So she tried to reach out to you, knowing her mother was infatuated with Nigel Farnsworth and might not believe her, and you turned her away?"

"But Katy, I swear, I didn't know!"

"Well, now you do know." I hung up on her.

I paced the room, resisting the urge to kick furniture. It was all very well to hang up on Greta, but that wouldn't avenge Rose's death. There isn't any such thing as avenging a death, I realized. There is only honouring a life. Quick, someone write that down.

I poured myself another cup of high-test coffee, the stuff I reserve for emergencies. It didn't help; I put it down after a few sips.

Emptying my cup into the sink, I rinsed it out and left it on the drain board. This was no good. There had to be something I could do, some place I could put all this nervous energy. Rose was dead. And Nigel was dead, too. There was nothing more to be done. No one to call to account.

Then I remembered: I was supposed to call Janet

Tompkins, the city councillor, about the stupid by-law that was about to shut down my business. It was a Sunday, but that was all to the good. I could bypass the usual secretarial runaround and ambush the councillor. She'd never even know what hit her. It would be a place to put some of my cooped-up anger, where it might actually be of some use.

Somewhere around here was a *Glebe Report* ... here it was. And right there under her monthly ad and mug shot was Ms. Tompkins's home phone number. I stabbed the numbers into the telephone and waited while it rang. After five rings someone picked up.

"Yeah?" said a male voice.

"Could I please speak to Janet Tompkins?"

"What do you want?"

"I'm a constituent of hers, calling on city business."

The man dropped the phone. I winced as it clattered in my ear.

"Hello?"

Tompkins sounded wary. Maybe she had a Call Display phone. Or maybe I was imagining things. The week's events had me on edge.

"This is Katy Klein, Janet. We spoke earlier in the week, about the by-law against fortunetelling. Perhaps you remember?"

"Mrs. Klein, this is not something I wish to discuss with you right now. You are reaching me at my home, you know. This may not be your sabbath, but it is mine. Perhaps we could arrange a time to speak during regular business hours?"

"Or perhaps you'd like an opportunity to explain your connection with Nigel Farnsworth and the Soldiers? How much did they offer to pay you for your support?" I was fishing, trying to provoke a reaction. I succeeded beyond my wildest dreams.

"What's that you said?" Tompkins hissed. "What are you talking about? You can't prove —" She caught herself up short.

"I think you know."

"I refuse to discuss this with you."

"I don't think you want to be too hasty about that, Janet. You could be making a mistake." Geez, I sounded like someone from a bad movie.

"What do you mean? This is ridiculous! I'm hanging up right this minute!" The quaver in her voice betrayed her.

"Tell you what. Meet me in half an hour. At the coffee shop at the corner of Lisgar and Bank. We can chat, just us girls. And I won't tell anyone about the Soldiers. At least not just yet."

I hung up without waiting for her answer. This was more like it: I was acting instead of agonizing. I hummed tunelessly as I tried to force my wayward hair into some kind of order and skimmed through my wardrobe for something suitable to wear. Jeans and a sweatshirt felt just too *outré*; but my little strapless number was at the cleaners. Finally I settled on a pair of soft black pants and a white turtleneck, topped with a teal green unstructured jacket. Dignified, yet not too formal. I even hunted down a tube of lipstick and some partly dried-out mascara.

At the coffee shop, I chose a booth, feeling it would offer us some privacy. I ordered a decaf. The last thing I needed was more caffeine zinging around my overloaded nervous system. Then I sat back and waited for Janet Tompkins. She showed up right on time, a tall, slim woman with dark brown hair that curled past her shoulders in tight ringlets. She looked young for a city councillor, but only her plastic surgeon knew for sure.

The consummate hostess, I smiled and invited her to sit down.

"Why do you want to meet me?" she demanded. We hadn't even had time to exchange pleasantries about the weather.

"Now, I'm glad you asked that, Janet. You see, I'm a bit concerned that you're planning to support a by-law that would make it impossible for me to earn a living. I do have a child to support, you know, and I feel it's important for city councillors to support local small business initiatives."

"I've told you, I'm responding to the needs of my constituents. You're only one person —"

"And you're just following orders, right?"

"What the hell is that supposed to mean?" She leaned toward me, her eyes narrowed.

"Oh, give me a break, Janet. Nigel Farnsworth told you to put astrologers out of business, and you jumped to attention, right? Problem is, now he's dead. But his vigilante group is still around, and I think you're up to your eyeballs with them. Right?"

She looked around the restaurant. A film of perspiration formed on her perky nose and unlined forehead.

"You don't know what you're talking about. You should keep your mouth shut — you could get hurt."

"I already have been hurt. Rocks through my window, death threats ... this is serious stuff, Janet. And the police have already been notified. They're gathering evidence as we speak. You know, if I were an up-and-coming young city politician, I don't think I'd be too quick to affiliate myself with a group like the Soldiers."

"What? Who have you been talking to? What do you want me to say?"

"Well, why don't we just get down to brass tacks: how much pressure Farnsworth was putting on you to lobby your fellow councillors, and what he threatened you with if you didn't see things his way. And you could tell me why the Soldiers saw fit to trash my office, too. That would be a good start."

"Who told you all this?"

Her face was chalky under her make-up.

I smiled my most irritatingly bland smile. "That would be telling. And I'm really more interested in resolving this unpleasant situation. I'm pretty certain your constituents would be shocked, just shocked, to know their elected representative was so deeply involved with a bunch of loony religious vigilantes. Even in this political climate, it wouldn't help your chances for re-election. Or for moving out into provincial politics — which I've heard you're planning to do, right?"

"Are you trying to blackmail me?" she whispered.

I studied my fingernails, then flicked an imaginary piece of lint off my jacket. "Janet, really. Would I do that to you? I thought we should keep this between us. Just us girls. I'm just trying to give you a bit of advice, that's all."

Strangely, Janet Tompkins did not relax. "What, then? What are you going to do?"

"Well, how about this? You call your friends on city council, let them know you've had second thoughts about all the poor starving astrologers. You really don't want to see them out on the streets or clogging up the welfare rolls, right? You could frame it as supporting small businesses, local economic development, you know the rhetoric. Once I know you've done that, we'll just call it a day, shall we? I won't even bring up the financial side of things."

"What are you talking about?" She really was a little dense. Or she thought I was.

"Oh, you know," I said. "The money that helped put you in office. The money Farnsworth's organization gave you, that you just kind of overlooked when you made out your election expense forms. I'm sure it was very handy for Reverend Nigel to have his very own elected councillor. It must have made things so much easier for him."

She stared at me for several minutes. I gave her a high-wattage smile, basking in her anxiety. My face started to hurt, but it paid off. Tompkins nodded.

"Fine. I'll do it. And this ... this gossip you've told me, it'll stay between us?" Her voice was tight.

"Count on it," I said.

All in all, I felt it had been a productive meeting.

18

I stopped to pick up provisions at the Herb and Spice. By the time I got home, the sky was almost completely dark. As I fumbled in my pocket for the key, a figure moved toward me from the shadows in the dimly lit hall. My grocery bags crashed to the floor, and my heart scudded to a standstill.

"Katy?" someone whispered.

"Shit!" I started breathing again. "Carmen! What the hell are you doing here? You nearly gave me a heart attack!"

She still looked like death warmed over, though she had covered her hair with a passably clean silk scarf. Her eyes were red-rimmed and nearly swollen shut, her hands trembled, but I couldn't smell anything stronger than coffee on her breath. Which was a good thing, as I wasn't sure I wanted to deal with Carmen on one of her benders just now.

She averted her eyes from mine. "Sorry I startled you. I need to talk to you. If that's okay."

"Of course, of course, come on in," I said, a hand on her too-thin shoulders. "Have you been eating? I can feel your bones, Carmen."

She shook her head. "I've been a bit upset. But I'm

getting better. I haven't had a drink all day."

"Hey, good. That's really good. Maybe you should think about going back to your AA meetings."

Inside my apartment, I took Carmen's leather bomber jacket from her and hung it up. It reeked of stale sweat and cigarettes. Behind me I heard something drop, and Carmen muttered a curse. Make-up, pills, tissues, loose change littered the hallway. I knelt to help her scoop up the contents of her oversized handbag, but she pushed me away with a rueful smile.

"I'll get it. Sorry, I'm kind of a mess right now."

"Carmen, I want to say I'm sorry about what happened the other day," I said. "You needed me to be supportive, and I've just been feeling awful about how I –"

She interrupted me. "I was acting like a nutcase. Don't worry about it. I'd had some bad news, a bit of a shock, really, and I got back into the wine, which I knew even then was just plain stupid, but I did it anyway. By the time you got there, I couldn't even see straight. So I can't blame you for losing your temper with me. I deserved it."

I laughed and hugged her. "Okay, so we're both sorry. Do you want to tell me what was upsetting you?"

"Katy, I do want to, believe me, but there are some things that I just can't talk about yet. Too painful," Carmen said. "I came today for two reasons — to apologize to you about the other day, and to ask if you could do me a favour. Oh, God, I just realized how that must sound. I'm not just apologizing so you'll help me out, okay?"

She put her hand on my arm, entreating me to understand.

"Hey, it's okay. You're my oldest friend, Carmen.

What do you need? You know I'll do anything I can."

"Damn, this is awkward," she muttered. Then, to me, "You remember you told me you were supposed to meet with Diana Farnsworth a few days ago? You were going to discuss her future, that kind of thing?"

I nodded. How likely was I to have forgotten that?

"Well, something has happened — I don't know how to ..." Carmen turned her head away from me and fished for a tissue in her purse. "It's terrible. Her brother — Nigel —"

I leaned toward her. "Carmen, it's okay. I know. It was on the news. He died, and the police are looking for Diana for questioning, right?"

She nodded. "It's so ridiculous. Anyone who knows her would tell you, she couldn't have killed her brother. I can't understand why they're even interested in speaking with her. But I've been encouraging her to go talk to them, get this whole disgusting mess sorted out."

My heart gave a hard thud against my chest. "Carmen, are you saying you've spoken with Diana since the murder? She's wanted for questioning in a murder case, for God's sake! If the police knew you'd heard from her, they'd be all over you like a rash. In fact, I'm not sure you aren't doing something illegal by not getting in touch with them right away."

"Sure, I know the police are looking for her. I saw it on the news. The thing is, she's scared. Really scared, Katy. It's so obvious that the cops are just looking for a scapegoat for Nigel's death. You don't really think she killed him, do you?"

"No. Of course not. But that's just my opinion. And if the cops are looking for her, isn't it better for her just to turn herself in, answer their questions and clear herself?"

"No! If she does that, they'll just lock her up. We've been over and over this, she and I. She knows she couldn't have killed him, but her memories of that night are kind of hazy. You know, I think she must have been in shock or something. So she took off, and next thing you know, she was at my place, just freaking out. It was unbelievable — she's always so cool, but by the time I saw her, she was a wreck. An absolute wreck."

"Carmen, was this the day I came to your place?"

She nodded. "She showed up that morning, and I didn't know what to do. I called you, and then I thought the better of it. I didn't want you to get in any trouble, you know?"

"Well, this is definitely trouble. Is she still at your place?"

"No. She's in hiding."

"You've got to convince her to go to the cops, Carmen. If she doesn't go, it's going to look really bad for her."

"Oh, come on!" Carmen snorted. "They're not looking for the truth. They just want someone to blame, and she's the most likely candidate! How can I send her right into the lion's den?"

"There might be other suspects, you know. What about Phil Stanley? Marion's husband? What if he found out Marion and Nigel were like this —" I held up two crossed fingers, "— and lost it? I already told the police about that, and they're looking into it. So it's not a sure thing that they'd arrest Diana."

"How did you know about Nigel and Marion?" Carmen looked stunned.

I shook my head. "It doesn't matter. But the point is, not all the evidence points in Diana's direction. You have to tell her to turn herself in, Carmen."

"She didn't even tell me where she was. She was calling from a payphone — it said so on my call display. You know, you really must have made an impression on her, and she doesn't impress easily. She said she wanted to talk to you again, that you'd helped her last week, and she thought you might be able to give her some ideas about what she should do now. She told me she trusts you, that you shoot from the hip, and she likes that. Your advice might help her decide how to handle things. She needs us, Katy. Can you help her or not?"

Carmen tried to smile engagingly as the words tumbled out, but with her red-rimmed eyes and soggy, booze-soaked face, the effect was more grotesque than appealing. I stared past her at the cross-stitch sampler on the wall.

"Carmen, tell me something honestly, okay? In your heart of hearts, do you think Diana had anything to do with her brother's death?"

"What do you think?" Carmen threw my question back at me.

"I hope not. No, I don't think she could have done it, but you seem to know her better than I do."

"Yes, I do know her pretty well. She liked the way you cut right to the core when you did her chart. She said you struck her as very insightful. I guess that's why she wants to talk to you now. She's scared, Katy. Will you at least talk to her? No one has to know, if that's what you're worried about."

"Okay," I sighed. "I'll check things out, and she can call me tomorrow. But I don't want to know where she is, or how to get hold of her. The less I know, the better. Tell her to phone me. Okay?"

"Great! This will mean a lot to her." Carmen

hugged me with sloppy enthusiasm.

It reminded me of times when my mother's friend's Pekingese dog would drape itself across my shoulders, drooling. I resisted the urge to shove Carmen away.

This was giving me a very bad feeling. Granted, Carmen hadn't told me Diana's whereabouts, and in fact maybe she didn't know. But the situation didn't feel right. Still, Carmen is my oldest friend, I chided myself. She deserves my help when she asks for it. It's not like I'm aiding and abetting a criminal, or something. Because she's not a criminal if she didn't do it — she's just trying to protect herself. Plus, maybe I can actually do something useful for someone. For a change.

Ah. That's the ticket. I'd felt so damned helpless all week, watching events swirl around me in their own chaotic rhythm, and now here was a chance to intervene, to do something that could make a difference to someone. If I couldn't rescue Rose, by God, I'd rescue Diana.

All she wanted was a bit of reassurance that this phase of her life would pass. Maybe she didn't understand that her continued absence was only making the cops more anxious to find her. Perhaps I could talk her into coming forward, maybe even accompany her to visit Steve Benjamin, and we could get this whole ugly thing cleared away. Yeah. That didn't sound so bad.

Carmen declined my offer of tea. Grabbing her jacket, she slung it over her shoulder, gave me a peck on the cheek and thanked me again. It was only after the door had swung shut behind her that I realized: I hadn't even told her about Rose. Maybe that was for the best, though. No point in disturbing her fragile sobriety.

The apartment once again felt hollow, silent without Rose's presence. She wasn't coming back, and the realization slammed into my gut again like a bag of wet sand. This was going to be harder than I'd thought.

Not knowing what else to do, I sat at Dawn's computer, a much fancier and faster machine than my valiant laptop. I set to work on the transits and progressions to Diana's birthchart. Once I had started, I realized this was exactly what I'd needed: I fell into the task hungrily and was soon drawn completely into the orderly, predictable yet constantly shifting realm of planets and signs, houses and angles. It's mesmerizing, this work.

First, I checked out the positions of today's planets in relation to Diana's birthchart. I started with the outermost planets — Pluto, Neptune, Uranus, Saturn and Jupiter — that would mark the broad directions in her life.

Right away, I noted a heavy transit: Pluto opposed Diana's Moon, with no sign of letting up soon. Here was her burning frustration, her sense of being smothered and stifled. There was obsession here: she was being forced to face her own demons. Had her brother's death brought relief, or had it intensified her guilt? If the stars knew, they weren't saying.

I closed Diana's file and rolled my chair back from the desk. What if I was wrong about Diana? What if she really had lost it and murdered Nigel? She'd admitted to a fierce temper — in fact, she'd told me she feared the consequences if it ever got the better of her. I had assumed her faith and integrity would keep her safe, but could I be certain of that? For the first time, I could imagine her killing Nigel Farnsworth, and it scared me.

Just after I'd shut down the computer, Peter bustled in to update me on his investigation into the Soldiers.

"I talked to my police contact, then went through all the keywords in the paper's archives," he said, "and it turns out there've been a number of episodes involving religious vigilantes. No one had tied them to any one group, until now."

He started to read from the articles he'd collected.

"There's been vandalism at the Jewish and Muslim cemeteries; they've trashed the offices of three other fortunetellers in the past year, and there's one account of a beating — a palm reader, leaving the teashop where she was working on a Saturday afternoon, was mugged and left lying on a side street. She said her attackers were young, didn't take anything, said nothing to her. But there was a cross spray-painted in red on the sidewalk a few feet from her head."

"Like the cross on my office door," I said. "How long has all this been going on?"

"The earliest confirmed incident was, let's see, about ten years ago."

"So it's not like a sudden rash — just strategic strikes, with breaks in between? That would help them keep a low profile, I guess. Is that why no one put it together?"

"Probably. Their main targets are people they call Satanists. Oh, and I found a reference to the shooting outside that abortion clinic, you remember?"

I did indeed. Two escorts had been shot while accompanying a woman into the newly opened clinic, about three years ago. One of the escorts had died, the other had lost a kidney. The attackers had never been caught, but there were rumours at the time that some U.S.-style religious vigilantes had been imported north to spearhead a campaign of anti-abortion violence. Then the issue seemed to fade from the spotlight, replaced by the next flavour-of-the-month news item.

"Okay, so is there anything connecting the Soldiers with Nigel Farnsworth?"

This, to my mind, was the key question.

"Well, here's the interesting part," Peter said. "According to witnesses at the abortion clinic shooting, two men and a woman were involved. One of the guys, a James Adamson, was identified, but he's never been found. He started his life of crime as a teenage runaway, then did a stint at a drug rehab centre out in Leitrim, and seemed to have gone straight, until the abortion clinic shooting. He was the getaway driver. I'm still looking into the connection with Farnsworth, but I have the feeling I'm getting close."

"Drug rehab centre? Which one?"

"Um, let's see. I have it here somewhere. Serenity Haven? Yeah, that's it."

"Bingo," I said. "That's the place where Diana Farnsworth was director — her brother founded it."

Peter jumped up and grabbed my shoulders, planting a large wet kiss on my forehead. "Katy Klein, you are a genius! This is amazing!"

"What are you going to do with all this, Peter? Do you think there's enough here for a story, or what?"

"There are a few things to check out, and there's probably stuff I haven't even touched, but I talked to my editor, and he's saying I should run with what I've got. Apparently Legal has no problems, it's really just a rehash of some old stories, stringing them together into a pattern, mentioning the Soldier connection, throwing in some anonymous comment from 'police sources'. But it's still big news, especially in a town like Ottawa. And knowing about Serenity Haven is a bonus — it'll give the story a current angle. Murdered minister was leader of vigilante cult — I can see it now!"

He was practically foaming at the mouth, so eager was he to skedaddle off to his keyboard and start bashing out the sordid details. Peter on the tail of a Big Story is a sight to behold, all jumpy energy and eyes bulging with barely repressed glee. Static electricity jolts out of him in all directions, and I've found it's best just to keep out of his way.

"Okay," I said. "You get to it, and I'll deal with feeding our child."

Peter bounded upstairs, leaving Dawn and me to kindle the third night Hanukkah candles. We sang a subdued blessing and sat down to a light dinner.

Over omelettes with multi-grain toast, Dawn turned the conversation back to Rose.

"I guess there'll be a funeral?" she asked. "Did Sylvie's mother tell you anything about it?"

"Actually, no," I admitted. "I've been trying not to think about it."

"I know. It's like ... well, sometimes I think she's still here. I have to keep reminding myself that she's not."

"I'll have to call Greta tonight and see what's happening," I said. "I suspect if there's going to be any kind of funeral it'll be pretty simple. I can't see Phil springing for a big affair."

Dawn shook her head. "I can't imagine having a father like that, Mom," she confided. "I saw him for just a minute at the hospital yesterday, and he wasn't crying over Rose or anything — he was just standing there arguing with the nurse about whether he should be charged for the ambulance ride."

After supper, Dawn wandered off to the computer, where she could be counted on to occupy herself till I pried her away at bedtime. I settled into a corner of the couch with my sewing basket and my latest needlepoint project. After a few stitches, though, I dropped the canvas into my lap.

I picked up the phone and called Greta. She didn't sound thrilled to hear from me, but I guess that was natural, given our last conversation.

"Listen, maybe I was out of line," I admitted. "I didn't mean to imply that Rose's death was all your fault."

Greta sighed. "It's okay. It's nothing I haven't thought about sixty zillion times myself. You were right. I should have paid more attention. Should have listened to her."

"Hey, I've been beating myself up, too. So — when's the funeral?"

"Well, we're in luck this time." She laughed bitterly. "At least Phil has agreed to spring for a proper funeral. A short, cheap one, at the funeral home, and he's having her cremated, but at least we can go to say good-bye." Her voice shook on the last few words.

Again I was trapped in yesterday's endless moment, watching as the life trickled out of Rose, her delicate little soul disengaging from her body, leaving no trace behind. I swayed back and forth, trying to dislodge the image that obscured my vision, but it wouldn't shake loose, no matter how much I willed it away.

In the bathroom, I found a half-empty bottle of Xanax, prescribed by Greg last summer, when I had felt like my head would explode if I thought for one more second about Adam and Brent and what had almost happened to all of us.

Filling a plastic cup with tepid water, I swallowed a double dose of the tranquillizer, then went to bed and prayed for oblivion.

19

MONDAY, DECEMBER 20
Moon conjunct Sun ✦
Sun square Jupiter ✦
Mercury conjunct Pluto ✦
Venus square Mars ✦
Saturn square Neptune ✦

Funerals suck. The careful solemnity of hired men who stand around in suits, waiting to assist in disposing of the earthly remains of the deceased; the tastefully arranged flowers; the mourners who stare at the ground, shuffling awkwardly as they try to think of comforting things to say to the family — it all gets to me.

Rose's funeral was a modest enterprise, attended by her cousins and Greta, Dawn and Peter and myself, and of course her father, Phil, in a state of inebriation he must have cultivated all weekend. He was vertical, but just barely, his spindly frame swaying alarmingly as we stood to sing and sat to listen to inanities about Rose being in a better place. Though I suppose she couldn't very well have been in a worse place.

Peter, Dawn and I sat near the back of the chapel, not wanting to intrude on Dawn's closer family. I mouthed the words to a couple of unfamiliar hymns, but somehow this formal farewell to Rose felt devoid of meaning. We kept our distance from Phil Stanley, but he had clearly not forgotten me.

After the pitifully brief eulogy, delivered haltingly by a clergyman of indifferent denomination who had never met Rose, Stanley's stares across the small chapel grew more penetrating. When we stood to leave, he lurched among his wife's relatives, navigating unsteadily toward us.

He was now clean-shaven, perhaps in deference to the occasion, but he had done the job carelessly. Several nicks, staunched with tiny flicks of toilet paper, were visible along his jawline. This is what comes of shaving while drunk.

The suit he wore might have dated back to the early seventies, a flat brown number made of 100 percent pure polyester, topstitched in black thread. The sleeves and legs were too short, and he had not managed to find matching socks to wear to his daughter's funeral.

"You've got a lot of damn nerve, showing up here." His reedy voice rose above the murmur of conversation surrounding us. "I should have you all arrested — letting my little girl die like that!"

Well, with an opener like that, who could blame everyone in the room for turning to stare? Encouraged by his audience, he pushed closer to me. Every instinct urged me to step back, if only to avoid keeling over from the fumes.

Instead, though, I recalled my game of chicken with John Keon at Java De-Lux. I threw my shoulders back, fixed Stanley with an icy stare, and angled my not insubstantial body toward him. He stopped, baffled.

Stanley hesitated, stepped sideways, averted his stare. I pursued my advantage.

"What exactly do you mean, I let her die?" My voice was frostily polite. "As I recall, you were at home getting soused when Rose needed you most. Where were *you* while your daughter was dying, Mr. Stanley? I believe everyone here knows exactly how much concern you expressed about her safety and well-being. I don't think you're in a position to throw stones."

There was a cautioning hand on my shoulder, but I shook it off and bore down on Phil Stanley, who swayed as he backed away. I was seriously considering taking a pop at the guy — and my right fist clenched at the ready.

The hand on my shoulder came back, more forcefully this time, and I whirled round to tell Peter to mind his own damn business — only it was Dawn. She looked mortified as she clutched at me.

"Mom. Please. Let's go," she whispered.

Instantly, my rage crumpled into shame. I stumbled out of the room after Dawn and Peter, my cheeks aflame, stomach twisting.

Outside, the sharp chill of the last few days had given way to damp fog. The sky was a leaden grey, dripping rain that had transformed the snow along the cheesier end of Somerset Street to slush and melting muck. The drizzle was okay with me, though, as it blended in with my own tears of humiliation. If my mascara ran, I could always blame the weather.

Peter, Dawn and I walked in silence for a few blocks, Dawn tucking a consoling arm into mine.

"I know how you felt, Mom," she said presently. "I wanted to smash him in the face, too. I wanted to scream at him. But it just didn't seem right."

"I know," I said. "I was completely inappropriate, and I'm really sorry I embarrassed both of you. I let him bring me down to his level."

Dawn gave a short laugh. "Don't worry, you'll never be on that jerk's level, Mom."

I do so love my daughter. Peter, who had maintained a discreet silence during this exchange, chimed in.

"Katy, you reacted out of your love and grief for Rose, that's all. Maybe what you did wasn't in the funeral etiquette guidebook, but it was a natural response. Besides, I enjoyed the look on that schmuck's face when he thought you were about to punch his lights out. So do you want to go home for some coffee before we all have to head back to the salt mines?"

I puttered around the kitchen, making fresh coffee. Peter detoured upstairs to change from his one dark suit and silk tie into his regular working garb: jeans and a sweatshirt.

"Mom?" Dawn summoned me from the front hall. "What's this?"

"What?"

I set the mugs down on the table and joined her under the hall light. She held a small green-and-yellow capsule between her fingertips. It was imprinted on the green end with the name of a pharmaceutical company; at the other end, it said "100."

I frowned and shook my head. "No idea, honey. Obviously it's some kind of medicine, but it's not mine. Where did you get it?"

Then I recalled Carmen's visit the day before, the spilled handbag, hastily restuffed.

"Oh. I think I might know who it belongs to. Carmen was here yesterday; she must have missed it when she dropped her purse."

"Looks like an antibiotic or something," Dawn said. "Do you think she'll need it back?"

I shrugged. "Give it to me, I'll give it to her this afternoon when I see her," I said, tucking it into my pocket.

The three of us sat at the kitchen table, Peter and I indulging our mutual coffee addiction while Dawn virtuously sipped chamomile tea. Peter had finished his piece on Farnsworth and the Soldiers, a great journalistic coup, by all accounts.

"Not that there's much competition for investigative stories in this town," he admitted, "but there's a chance the wire service'll pick it up. This kind of thing, religious nuts who take things to the level of violence, it's big right now. The story could go national."

Ottawa is home to two papers: the *Telegraph* and the *Star*. The *Star* belongs to a chain of tabloids renowned for shrieking ten-thousand-point headlines, editorial policies somewhat to the right of Atilla the Hun, and the notorious Page Three Starlight Girls, full-page close-ups of simpering co-eds who are obviously too poor to afford much in the way of clothing.

The *Telegraph* used to provide a limping alternative to the *Star*'s right-wing ravings, until the newspaper chain of which the *Telegraph* is a part came under the control of a certain John Baldwin. Baldwin now controls a majority of the country's newspapers, and protests regularly that this won't affect the public's right to unbiased reporting. Sure, I'm convinced.

So there are no longer any true newspapers in this city. On the other hand, cancelling my subscription to the newly reconstructed *Telegraph* has saved me a few bucks a week. You win some, you lose some.

Peter, who covertly agrees with my gloomy assessment, has nevertheless struggled to retain his position as a reporter at the *Telegraph*. I can't say I blame him. Though we are constantly being told the economy is "in recovery," it's still a real feat just to hang onto a job, never mind go off in search of a new one, especially when you're in your forties and have devoted half your life to a single newspaper.

I used to sneer at my elders' obsession with security. Now I wouldn't mind some myself, if anyone happened to offer it. Thinking of jobs and security and such reminded me: my office beckoned. I finished off my coffee in a single gulp.

"Well, guys, nice taking a break with you," I said, stretching and pulling on my anorak. "Time to go earn my keep."

Dawn, who was supposed to be studying for tomorrow's French exam, took herself to her room. She claimed she was studying, but when I peeked in on her just before I left, she was lying on her bed, staring at the ceiling. Her French text lay unopened beside her.

"Honey?"

"I can't do it, Mom. I can't concentrate. And I don't know how I'm supposed to just pretend everything's back to normal now."

"I know," I said. "I don't get it either. And I hate those clichés, like 'life must go on.' But I don't know what else to do."

Dawn rolled over, her back to me. "Neither do I."

I blew her a kiss and shut the door.

Fate had decided to cut me a break. My office was warm for the second working day in a row, which was a good thing, as I had three appointments booked for this afternoon.

Absently, I peeled and ate three mandarin oranges in rapid succession as I returned calls, made notes for my afternoon meetings and prepared bills I hoped would be paid promptly enough to keep Dawn and me fed for another month. I was a model of brisk, competent efficiency, until I squirted myself in the eye with orange juice.

Washing the stinging juice out my eye, I was bent almost double over the tiny bathroom sink when someone banged at the office door. I jerked upright and cracked the back of my head on the pine shelf above the sink. A plant tipped and fell from the shelf, dirt showering down my neck and back, causing me to say several impolite words.

So I was squinting from the orange juice, swiping ineffectually at my dirty neck with a damp tissue, and applying pressure to the goose egg on the back of my skull when I opened the door. Just hope it isn't Keon, I muttered under my breath.

On the darkened landing, Steve Benjamin looked wary and ill at ease. His initial discomfort changed to a frankly puzzled look as I greeted him, dirt smeared on my neck, my free hand glued to the back of my throbbing head.

"Um ... if I'm interrupting something, I can leave," he said.

"Not at all. I was just — no, never mind, it's too complicated. But I promise, it's not some obscure astrological ritual. Would you like to come in?"

I am not a small person, but Steve Benjamin's

shaggy physique seemed to take up a disproportionate amount of space in my office. He scanned the walls, absorbing what was left of my eccentric decorating style. At my invitation, he sat on the new futon, his bulky frame awkward in the unaccustomed low seat that forced him to sit with his knees up around his ears. I perched at the other end of the couch, waiting for him to introduce the purpose of his visit.

"Sorry to barge in like this," he said. "I just thought ... you know, I was in the neighbourhood, so ..."

I decided to put him out of his misery. "It's okay, really. I don't think you've ever seen my office, huh?"

"I was checking out some ... some tips in the area, and I remembered you said you were up here. Nice place."

He tried to smile, but it came out more as a grimace. Perspiration gleamed on his forehead.

"Thanks. So is this a social visit?"

Benjamin avoided my gaze and stared fixedly at the brass model of an astrolabe my father had given me when I was ten.

"Social visit? Yeah, I guess so," he laughed uncomfortably. "I wanted to see, you know, what you do here. I don't know anything about this astrology stuff, except what I see in the papers. If you're Sagittarius, wear purple today and be assertive with your boss. You know the kind of thing."

I grimaced. Newspaper astrologers are one of my pet peeves. Not that I need to go looking for pet peeves — they seem to find me. I can't understand it, but I guess it's just my lot in life: Katy Klein, Peeve Magnet.

"There's a lot more to astrology than what you see in the paper," I explained. "Those little blurbs just talk about your Sun sign — but that's just one point in the chart. By and large, the newspaper forecasts can't tell you anything much; they're way too general. The work I do involves all the planets, the Sun and Moon, and a bunch of points having to do with the position of the solar system relative to the earth. It's a lot more complicated, but also more interesting."

I stopped myself. What in hell was I doing, delivering a lecture on the practice of astrology to a detective from the Major Crimes division?

"Yeah, well, I'm sure it is. Interesting, I mean."

He shifted in his seat and I heard the wooden futon frame creak alarmingly. Maybe I should have offered him a cushion on the floor, but that would have been just plain cruel. Still, I couldn't afford to replace the couch again, should it collapse under Benjamin's weight.

"Actually," I said, "I'm glad you dropped by. There's something I wanted to check with you."

"Shoot."

"Well, it's about that Soldiers group. My ex, you know, Peter Fischer? Well, he did some digging around about them, his story will be in tomorrow's *Telegraph*. I'm pretty sure they're the ones who threatened me and trashed my office. Do you know anything about them?"

Benjamin shook his head. "Probably not much more than you. They keep their heads down, and so far we haven't had much luck tracking them. We got a positive identification on one of them, but that was a while ago, and he's nowhere to be found these days. Since then, nothing has really come up. What makes you think they're the ones who trashed your place?"

"I don't know it for sure, but I do know that they were putting pressure on Janet Tompkins, the city councillor, to put astrologers out of business. It's not a huge leap from that to trashing my office, is it?"

"I'll definitely look into it," Benjamin said, pulling out his omnipresent notebook and jotting something in it. "Try and stay clear of that lot, would you? Someone's liable to get hurt."

I nodded. "I'll try. So, how's the investigation into Nigel Farnsworth's death going?"

Benjamin looked at his hands.

"Not bad," he said after a pause. "I hate to be a pessimist, you being her friend and all, but there's really only one suspect at the moment."

"You mean Diana?"

"I'm not really supposed to talk to you about this, but yeah. I'm sure she had her reasons. You know, her brother physically attacked her a couple of times — she called 911, but when we got there, she wouldn't press charges. So I'm figuring, maybe he took a swing at her again, and she just lost it. Happens all the time." He looked apologetic.

"It's okay. I have to admit it might not be outside the realm of possibility that Diana did it. But what about Phil Stanley? He had a motive, too. I told you his wife was fooling around with Nigel, right?"

"Yeah, but he checks out for that night. He worked late, and there's a couple of witnesses to back him up."

"So I guess it does kind of point to Diana now, huh?"

"You think so?"

I laughed. "Hey, you're the one who's supposed to know, not me! Besides, I've already told you: all I can give you is my opinion. I'm not one of those psychics who can hold the victim's sock and visualize the killer, okay?"

"No, I didn't figure you for that type," Benjamin said. "There's one other thing you might want to know, by the way. You were right that Nigel Farnsworth was messing around with Marion. Turns out he was video-taping the whole thing. And I mean everything. We found a stash of tapes in his study, very neat, all labelled by date and name and so on. Kind of sick, if you ask me."

"You're kidding," I said. "Huh — well, he liked being on TV, that's for sure. Though when I met him, he seemed like such a nice guy."

"Don't they all?" Benjamin asked. Then he picked up the crumpled remains of my astrolabe and turned it over in his hands a couple of times. I could swear he was blushing.

"Listen, this is kind of hard for me," he said. "I did-n't really come here to talk about the Farnsworth case. It's more ... I wanted to see you, you know. I thought maybe you and me ... you know, maybe we could go out somewhere. You know?"

Now that it was out in the open, it didn't sound so bad. What if I did, say, go out for an evening with Steve Benjamin? Aside from the fact that it would seriously annoy my daughter, who felt Benjamin talked down to her, would a date with the cop be such a terrible thing? I opened my mouth to answer, then closed it, opened it again.

Benjamin looked at his shoes.

"I've embarrassed you," he said. "I'm sorry. I got my signals crossed. I should go." His face coloured up even more, until even his ears were crimson.

"No, no, it's not that," I said hastily. "You didn't embarrass me. It's just ... Well, the last few months have been kind of rough on me. That thing last summer, now Marion and Rose. Not to mention the religious nuts. I hadn't been thinking in terms of going out at all, so you just kind of surprised me. But sure, that sounds very nice. Thank you."

"Really?" Benjamin grinned widely.

"Sure." I stood up, and he followed. "I'll let you choose the time — I think your schedule's less predictable than mine."

"Friday night?" he asked hopefully. "I'm off that night. We could go to Mama Teresa's, they've got a good lasagna. You don't keep kosher, do you? I know one of the owners, they'll make it up special for us."

Funny, I kind of had Benjamin figured as a meat and potatoes fellow. Lasagna, by comparison, sounded like an exotic culinary adventure.

"Sounds great," I said. "I don't want to be rude, but I'm expecting a client in five minutes, and I think he'd be surprised to find the cops here. If you know what I mean."

Benjamin laughed, and I held the door open for him. As he brushed past me, he kissed me lightly on the forehead. Watching Benjamin lumber down the narrow stairs, I decided I must have lost my already tenuous grip on my mind.

I shoved Steve Benjamin resolutely out of my consciousness for the next three hours as I met with clients and delved into the mysteries of their charts. Just as I was saying good-bye to the last one, a very nice woman who wanted help relating to her teenaged son, Carmen came clattering up the staircase.

She looked almost normal today, one of her pink Chanel-type suits with big black buttons visible under that fabulous fuchsia wool coat, the skirt fashionably short to accent her legs. Her hair had been washed and styled, and I had to look closely to see the traces of red around the rims of her eyes. Somehow, seeing Carmen almost back to her old self made me feel better, too.

"Hey, astrologer-lady," she called out gaily, "want to come and have a decaf latté with me?"

"Have you ever known me to turn down an offer of coffee?" I laughed. "But I'm not going for any wimpy decaf. Give me the real thing, or give me death."

So off we went, arm in arm, to Java De-Lux. School was out by now and the place fairly reeked of teen spirit: kids dressed in polyester and platforms, smoking their little brains out and tying up the courtesy phone to discuss what Jennifer had said to Brad in chemistry class.

Carmen and I squished into a corner table, unsuccessfully ducking the smoke that permeated the establishment.

"So, toots, are you ready to talk?" I teased her gently.

She pulled a face and waved my question away. "Hey, it was a passing thing, okay? I was just blowing things out of proportion. You know me."

"I hate to sound like a *yenta*, but you were in pretty rough shape there for a while. As I recall, you promised to fill me in. Now would be a good time."

Too much, too soon, as it turned out. Carmen's eyes filled up again, and she searched in her handbag for a tissue.

"Okay, okay," I backed off. "It was stupid and insensitive of me to push. But I've been specializing in stupid and insensitive lately. Let's forget I asked, and we'll just have a nice chat about the weather."

Carmen laughed halfheartedly. "Sorry. It's still just a bit too close to the surface. I promise, I'll tell you when I can."

"Sure, sweetie. No problem. You know I'll be there when you want to talk. Anyway, to change the subject completely, have you heard from Diana again?"

"Actually, yes," Carmen said, watching one of the kids at the next table. "She wanted me to tell you that she's got some things to do, so she's going to call you tomorrow."

"Okay, fine. But Carmen, do you think it's possible she actually did kill her brother? Maybe without meaning to? You know, what if she lost her temper and just lashed out without thinking first?"

"How should I know?" she retorted sharply. Then she reined in her annoyance and said, more gently, "I wasn't there, and I don't know what happened, Katy. I just know she's out there, and she's scared. What makes you ask?"

"Nothing, really. Except that I could see how something like that might have happened. The more I learn about Nigel Farnsworth, the more I think Diana could have been provoked into bumping him off."

"What do you mean?"

"I mean, there's videotaped evidence that he was screwing around with Marion. Plus, I suspect he was behind a group of wackos who run around shooting people who disagree with their religious views. And he was trying to push through a city by-law amendment to outlaw the practice of astrology. I don't want to speak ill of someone you cared about ..."

"It's fine. I know most of what you're saying." Carmen's voice was cold. Had I offended her?

"Oh. It must have come as a shock —"

"It did. But I'm over it. What's this about city by-laws, though?"

I told her about my office, and my discussion with

Janet Tompkins. Carmen's eyes widened.

"How did you figure he had a hold over the city councillor?"

"Just putting two and two together. But when I hinted at it, she hit the deck, so I knew I was right. There's something else, too." I lowered my voice, and Carmen leaned forward to hear me. "You know Rose? The girl you met at my place the other night?"

Carmen nodded. "Marion's daughter."

"Right. Well, apparently she told her aunt that Nigel Farnsworth had been sexually abusing her. Last time she ran away, she went to the church for shelter, and he took her in. Next thing you know, she's pregnant. And now, she's dead."

Carmen looked at me wide-eyed. Beneath her rouge, the colour had drained from her face.

"Katy, you can't be serious! Dead? How can that be? Who killed her?"

"She died of natural causes, more or less. She had a miscarriage, and she was so frail to begin with, the bleeding basically finished her off."

Carmen said nothing, but her hands shook as she lifted her coffee to her lips. Finally, she looked straight at me. "Why didn't you tell me this before?"

"I didn't think you were in any condition," I said. "It happened while you were — well, you know. You were a bit out of it."

"Oh."

"Carmen, there's nothing anyone could have done to prevent this. You know I don't believe in God, but if I did, I'd say this qualifies as one of His acts."

She nodded. "Well, do keep me informed." She drained her cup and wiped her lips daintily before reapplying her lipstick. "I have to meet a client a couple of blocks away. Sorry, Katy. I have to run."

She pushed away from the table and drew her coat around her shoulders. I reached into my pocket for my gloves. As I did so, I felt the capsule Dawn had found in our front hallway.

"By the way," I said, dropping the pill on the table, "is this one of yours?"

Carmen raised her eyebrows. "No, I don't think so. At least, I don't recognize it. Where did you get it?"

"Dawn picked it up in our hallway, and I wondered if it might have fallen out of your purse yesterday. No big deal, I just thought if it was an antibiotic or something, you'd need it back."

I reached for the pill, but Carmen picked it up first.

"Now that you mention it," she said, "it might be one of the antibiotics I've been taking. For a bladder infection. I'd forgotten — I usually keep them at home, but yesterday I had the bottle in my purse so I could take one at the right time. While I was out, you know. I've been so forgetful lately."

She flashed one of her astonishing, brilliant smiles. "Thanks, Katy. I know I've been a pain lately, but it's great to be back among the living."

With that, she kissed my cheek and hurried away in a blaze of fuchsia wool.

20

Peter's story on the Soldiers hit the newsstands the next day and all hell broke loose. First thing in the morning, the paper started getting phone calls, threatening every known form of retribution, legal and illegal, should Peter not immediately withdraw the story. Now, many people think newspapers steer clear of this kind of controversy as much as possible, but in fact the truth lies in the opposite direction. Big stories like this provoke contention, and attention, negative or positive, sells papers, which after all is the point of the whole enterprise. Sell papers, get exposure for your advertisers, get more ads, make money. A neat equation.

So, far from worrying about the hostile reaction, Peter was delighted, and his editor was pleased, and I'm sure if anyone had consulted John Baldwin, he'd have been rubbing his grubby little hands together in capitalistic glee.

"I can't believe the calls I've had this morning," Peter enthused at me over the phone. "The Vancouver affiliate picked the story up, and they want to run with it. This could make a big difference in my career."

I listened politely, but my mind wasn't really on the Soldiers this morning. I was worried about Diana. I wanted to know she was safe, but more and more, I was wondering about her guilt. How had I let Carmen shanghai me into acting as advisor to a murder suspect? As Peter yammered away about his grand journalistic coup, I doodled absently on a scrap of paper at the kitchen table.

Eventually, he noticed my lack of enthusiasm. "What's up? You sound like you're off in outer space."

"Sorry. It's just that so much has happened in the last few days. I'm kind of muddled about it all. And you caught me on my way to the office."

"Well, you could show a little more enthusiasm. This is a big thing for me, you know."

"I said I was sorry, Peter. I have to go now." I hate it when Peter pouts at me. We hung up on a discordant note, and I hurried to the office, determined to focus on the day's work.

I smelled it several blocks away: something like burning tar, an acrid smoky haze that assaulted my nostrils, made my eyes tear up. In the frigid air, the smoke hung motionless. The closer I got to my office, the thicker the haze. A couple of blocks away, I got a sick feeling in my stomach, and I sped up to a jog, then a sprint. My heart pumped furiously and my breath came in gasps as I stopped in front of the charred hole where my office building had once been.

It looked as though the fire engines had been in place for a while before I arrived. The building that had formerly housed both Fruits of the Earth Bakery and Star-Dynamic Astrological Counselling was little more than a smoking mass of ice and blackened wood. Firefighters still sprayed great gusts of water over the shambles, and now and then as the water hit a hot spot, a billow of steam would hiss up, then subside.

Traffic had been rerouted around the block, but a crowd of locals had gathered outside the black and yellow ribbons declaring this an emergency area. I stood and gawked with the rest of them.

Joanie, the baker, was wrapped in something resembling a multi-coloured woollen blanket that complemented today's hair colour: electric blue. She looked blankly at the remains of the bakery. When I tapped her elbow gently, she jumped.

"What in God's name happened here?" I had to raise my voice to be heard above the fire engines.

"I don't know. I came in early to get the first bread started." She didn't look at me; her eyes seemed riveted to the place where our building had been. "I'd just set the dough to rise when there was this loud bang, like someone dropping a big load of books or something. I thought it came from upstairs, and I went out to see if you needed help. But when I got to the foot of the stairs, there was all this smoke billowing down, so I just ran and called for help."

I squinted at the building as though it would be possible to discern anything in the smoking debris.

"You're saying something went boom in my office? And then the whole place went up in smoke?"

I'd heard her words, but they had detoured on

their way to my cerebral cortex. The information wasn't going in.

She shrugged, dispirited. "Yeah. Just like that. Keon should be here soon, too. I gave the cops his number."

Oh, terrific. Just the man I wanted to see, as I watched five years of my life hiss and steam into vapour this crisp winter morning. I hadn't the heart for it today. I picked up my briefcase, patted Joanie encouragingly on the shoulder and walked back home.

My steps felt mechanical. I knew I'd probably hear from the police at some point, but that could wait. For now, I just wanted to be alone.

At home, I called the phone company, had them reroute my office calls to my home number. At Dawn's insistence, I keep back-up files for all my clients on the home computer, so I supposed all was not lost. I could still work. For what it was worth.

Almost reflexively, I called Greg at his office.

He sounded anxious. "God, Katy, are you okay? I just heard about the fire on the radio, I wasn't sure if that was your building. They said the fire was preceded by an explosion, and my first thought was that whoever trashed your office the other day ..."

"I'm okay. Just barely. I'm not even sure why I called you — I just wanted to hear a friendly voice –"

Greg offered to come right over, but I put him off. Just hearing him on the phone was enough for now. An oasis of normality in a sea of insanity.

I tried not to think of my office, burning, burning. I picked up the phone again and dialled Benjamin.

"They burned me out."

He made me repeat myself several times before he seemed to get the gist of what I was saying.

"Don't move, I'll be right there," he said.

I sat down heavily, feeling like one of those people whose mobile home has just been whisked away by a tornado. Stunned, I guess the word would be.

Benjamin visited in his official capacity this time, no mention of dinners or dates or any such foolishness. He had his notepad and pencil at the ready, and I told him what I knew of the fire. He took down Joanie's name, and Keon's, and said he'd let me know if he found anything.

"It was the Soldiers," I said. "They did it. Peter wrote a story about them. They knew we were getting too close. They burned down my office." As I said the words, I realized that I sounded like one of the paranoid schizophrenics I used to treat. Well, sometimes paranoia just means having all the facts.

"You could be right," said Benjamin. "I'll check into it. Meanwhile, I'd keep my head down if I were you. These guys mean business; you don't want to go getting hurt. Probably the newspaper article set them off, so you might want to warn that ex of yours, too. I'll have someone patrol this street for a few days, make sure nothing happens here, okay?"

"Sure." I closed my eyes and rested my head against the back of the couch. I thought briefly of the small gun I had bought several years ago, after I'd been assaulted at the hospital. I wondered if I could remember how to work it. I'd have to find the ammunition, first.

After Benjamin left, I went outside and did a quick tour of the apartment building. No one suspicious seemed to be lurking anyplace nearby, so I went back in, just in time to hear the answering machine click on.

"Hi, Katy. It's me, Diana. Carmen said you might

be willing to talk to me. I'd appreciate that, if it's still okay with you. Could you please call and let me know?"

She left a number, someplace out of town. I stood in the vestibule, snow melting into a puddle at my feet, paralysed with uncertainty.

What if talking to Diana made me some kind of accomplice or accessory or something? Maybe I should check with Benjamin first? I played with the idea, but in the end I rejected it. I claim not to read people's minds, but I could predict how he'd respond to this: let the police handle it. He'd want to send out a bunch of cops, surround the place, take the perp by storm — I watch enough television to know how this kind of thing works.

Why couldn't I just do it myself? Meet the woman, check out my suspicions, advise her kindly but firmly to turn herself over to the cops, even accompany her to Benjamin's office myself. Wouldn't he be impressed if I turned up with his primary suspect?

Yes, the more I thought about it, the more I felt confident I could do this. I have a doctorate in psychology, for God's sake. I worked with people in trouble with the law for years. It's not like I'm some kind of snot-nosed amateur, blundering around putting my foot in things.

I called the number Diana had left, and she picked up on the first ring, greeting me by name. I guess she wasn't giving her number out to just anyone, these days.

"I thought you might not want to get involved. Carmen said you didn't want to." She didn't sound accusing, just resigned.

"I'm still not so sure this is a good idea," I admitted.

"Well, thanks for taking a chance on me. I didn't do it, you know."

"Uh-huh. I wouldn't talk to you if I seriously thought you had."

"Can I meet you at your office?"

I was seized with an urge to laugh hysterically, but I fought it off. "I don't have an office anymore. It got burned down. By a militant group called the Soldiers. You might know of them."

There was a small gasp, followed by a long silence.

"You know about these guys?" I asked.

"I can't discuss them over the phone. Shit. I had no idea. Listen, where can we meet?"

"I'm no good at this hole and corner stuff. Why don't you name a place?"

"Okay, how about the greenhouse in the Bank of Canada building?"

In the middle of winter, the ground floor greenhouse of this otherwise unremarkable highrise could pass for a tropical parkland. It's quiet, except for the soothing trickle of water, and it smells of earth and summer and life. I used to take Dawn there when she was little, and she'd shed her boots and snowsuit and dash around delightedly, free of winter for a few heady moments. It seemed as good a place as any to meet Diana. We agreed to meet at two.

Just before two o'clock I found a quiet corner near a giant schefflera, shielded from passers-by. There weren't many people here, mid-afternoon on a weekday. I cased the joint, checking for places where a listener might lurk, and when I was satisfied, I settled on a wooden bench and allowed myself to tune out the world for the first time in a week.

Diana didn't look nearly as bad as I'd anticipated.

Granted, she had dyed her short black hair a very unbecoming shade of burgundy, and she wore Jackie O sunglasses that covered most of her face.

"Have a seat," I said. "The shades are a nice touch."

She gave a thin smile. "Thanks. I've never been on the run before."

Diana pulled an envelope from her pants pocket and handed it to me. I raised a curious eyebrow.

"Your fee," she explained. "I didn't pay you for our last meeting, and I've added some for this one. Take it while you can. I don't know when I'll have access to cash again."

"Thanks. You didn't have to —"

"Yes, I did. I don't go back on my commitments."

I pocketed the envelope. "So what do you know about these Soldier people?"

That's me — no beating around the bush, get right to the point. Diana folded her hands in her lap.

"Thugs. Ignorant, narrow-minded thugs. Nigel didn't start the group, but he didn't put a stop to them, either. When his church broke away from the larger church, there were some zealots who wanted to take the word of the Lord to the street. Fine, as far as it goes, but it got out of hand."

"How long have you known about them?"

"A couple of months. When I found out, I confronted Nigel. He tried to tell me he couldn't control them, that they were a power unto themselves, but I didn't buy it. He was a very charismatic leader — they would have listened if he'd tried to put a stop to their nonsense. I started screaming at him, and he struck me."

"You didn't report the Soldiers to the police?"

"I was going to — but I was afraid. They're very organized, you know. There are more of them than I know about, and I thought if I went to the police without being able to name every last one of them, they'd hunt me down. They don't think all that highly of lesbians, either, you know." She gave me a wry grin.

"I don't doubt it."

"There's a database," Diana explained. "They keep lists of people they don't like; they're very thorough. I know it sounds like a paranoid fantasy, but they make it their business to collect information on people. Pictures, family histories, that kind of thing. They're a scary bunch."

"So how did they decide on me?"

"I don't know. Maybe they saw me go into your office that day? That could have set them off."

That made sense. The first rock had come through my window right after Diana had left.

We sat quietly for a few moments. The greenery around us was silent, except for the trickle of water. I spoke first.

"I was looking at your chart before I came over here, you know, and I was thinking about Jupiter."

Diana looked blank.

"It's a funny thing, you having such a strong Jupiterian influence in your chart. Did you know that Diana was the name of one of Jupiter's daughters?"

"I think I remember something about that. From grade school."

"The Huntress. The independent one. The one who sticks up for people in need, who always champions the underdog."

Her smile was tight. "I guess that'd be me, all right."

"Well, I was also thinking about Jupiter himself. He's got this great reputation as a benefic planet, you know. He represents growth, expansion, fortune — all the good stuff. But he's got a shadow side, too. He's the king of the gods, but he abuses his power. He stands for religion, but religion can become a tool for hurting others. Jupiter figured that because he was the ruler of Olympus, he had a right to get his needs met any way he chose. He used to transform himself into all sorts of shapes and come down to earth and rape women, you know. Ever hear of Leda and the swan?"

"What are you trying to tell me?"

"Just that things aren't always what they seem."

"That's kind of what I'm afraid of, Katy. That things aren't the way they seem. It takes a lot for me to admit this, but I'm scared. You struck me as a calm, rational person. Someone who will tell me the truth. I don't have too many of those in my life right now."

"I'm not sure what I can really do for you. I did work up your transits and progressions, but I don't know how much good that's going to do you, right now."

"I'm not sure, either. You think I killed my brother, don't you?"

"I'm not sure," I admitted. "Can you tell me what happened?"

"I don't know. Honestly, that's the truth. I was out late that night, working at the Centre, catching up on some paperwork. I came back at around one in the morning. I sat on the couch for a while, reading some papers from work, trying to wind down a bit. The house was dark, so I figured Nigel must be asleep. It was a relief — he usually waits up for me, checking to see where I've been."

"But —"

"Hang on, I'm coming to it. I was trying to read, but I was really wound up. I was thinking about what you and I had talked about. I knew I needed to make some big changes in my life, and I wasn't sure if I had the courage to do it. So I prayed for a while, and then I must have fallen asleep on the couch. When I woke up, I'd been having a really awful dream ... Nigel was pushing me, over and over, and I couldn't do anything about it, and he was just laughing, this deep, scary laugh. It was horrible."

Diana gave a small shiver and pushed the sunglasses up her nose. "The dream must have woken me up. I just couldn't get my heart to stop pounding. I was cold, and I got up and started pacing around the living room. Finally, I thought I'd get myself a cup of hot milk and go to bed, so I went into the kitchen. When I first turned on the light, I felt like I was still dreaming. The blood was everywhere. Along the counter, on the floor, splattered against the window, on the wall. And Nigel was lying there, looking up at me ..." Diana's voice trailed off. She was shaking.

"So he was already dead? You didn't kill him, did you? Why didn't you just tell the police that?"

"Well, I wasn't sure," she said slowly. "Whoever killed Nigel had stuck a knife in him. Over and over. He was bleeding everywhere. When I saw him, I thought —"

"What? You didn't —"

"Katy, I thought maybe I'd done it. Like, it was part of my dream, and I'd stabbed him without knowing it. Or maybe I'd had some kind of episode — you know, like an amnesic spell or something."

"Oh, come on! That only happens in movies.

Diana, you know you wouldn't do something like that."

"I'm not so sure. I'd just had that dream. And God knows I wanted ..." She stopped herself.

"You wanted him dead?"

She nodded.

"Diana, wanting him dead doesn't make you guilty. Think about it. If you'd really stabbed Nigel to death, you'd have blood all over your clothes. Did you check for blood?"

She shook her head. "I didn't think about anything. I just called 911 and got out of there."

"Not the brightest move," I said.

She flushed. "Don't you think I know that? I panicked. I was terrified, I didn't know what had happened, just that he was dead, and there was blood everywhere. It wasn't until later that I realized I would be a suspect. But you're right — afterward, when I checked my clothing, there was nothing. There was a bit on my fingers, but I think I must have touched the kitchen wall. When I saw Nigel, I felt like I was going to faint, and I grabbed the wall. Which means I probably left bloody fingerprints, you see?"

"You might have, but that doesn't mean you did it."

"I know. But then I heard on the radio that they were going to arrest me. I knew they must have found the fingerprints, and I just couldn't go back. First I went to Carmen's place. I figured she knew me well enough to know I couldn't have done it, and I was right. She believed me right away. But I couldn't stay there permanently. So I got in my car, and just drove around until I found a place to hide."

"But Diana, don't you see that running just makes it worse? It makes you look like the obvious suspect."

"You don't understand." Diana's gaze caught mine, and held it. "It's not just the cops I'm afraid of. It's the Soldiers. If the police are putting it out that I killed Nigel, don't you think the Soldiers know about it too? And if they catch up with me, jail will be a moot point. I'll be dead."

I said nothing for several minutes. I believed her, but I didn't know how I'd sell her story to Steve Benjamin.

"Diana, do you have a lawyer?"

"No. I've never needed one."

"Well, you're going to need one now. A good one. And you need to turn yourself in, before this gets any worse."

She snorted. "Worse? How can it get worse? My brother is dead, and I don't think I killed him, but I can't swear to it. I've got both the cops and a bunch of goons on my tail. And dammit, I don't want go to prison! I'm scared, you know?"

"Look, you can either decide to tell the police the truth, or you can wait until they figure it out for themselves. Either way, the truth will come out. Your prints won't be on that knife, for one thing. And what about your faith? Don't you think God will take care of you?"

She looked away from me. "I hope He will, but I keep having doubts. Katy, when I saw Nigel lying on the floor, I felt faint, I felt sick to my stomach, but I didn't feel sad. Don't you see? I was happy — I'm glad he's gone!" Tears trickled from under the dark glasses. "That's why I think maybe I had something to do with it — I just can't seem to feel sad about it. Do you think that's a sign?"

"It must have been a relief that he was gone," I said.

"Yes! And I'm so afraid ... Katy, I'm afraid God won't forgive me for feeling this way. I want to forgive Nigel, I really do. I'm obligated to, in fact. And if I were a truly good Christian, I'd be able to do it. But I can't. I just can't."

"So you're afraid God's going to desert you, because you've sinned?"

She nodded. "I keep thinking this must be His punishment. That I'll go to jail not for killing my brother, but for wanting him dead."

"I don't know how to argue with that, Diana. You're beating yourself up for a feeling you can't help. I don't know how this is going to end, but I really do think you should turn yourself in. I know a cop, he's a good guy. He'd see to it that you're treated fairly."

Diana grimaced. Then she looked contemplative for a minute. "Okay, I'll think about it."

I put a hand on hers. "Good. You'll do fine."

"Look, I need to do a few things, get some stuff in order before I go to the police, but I promise you, I will go. Today or tomorrow at the latest."

A wave of relief rushed through me. "I'm glad. I really think it's for the best, Diana. And please, please let me know if there's anything I can do for you, okay? You should know you have friends in all this."

"Thanks. I think I'm going to need all the friends I can get."

"One more thing, Diana. My ex-husband, Peter Fischer, got an anonymous tip, telling him to check out your brother. That came from you, right?"

She looked puzzled. "No, I never sent anything. To tell you the truth, until you just said it, I had no idea you even knew Peter Fischer. He's that journalist, right? With the *Telegraph?*"

I nodded. If Diana hadn't sent the tip, who had? But I had little time to ponder, for Diana was standing to leave.

"I really appreciate everything you've done," she said. "You've helped make things clear in my mind. Thanks, Katy."

With that, she left. I sat in the greenhouse a while longer, thoughts and emotions whirling around inside my head. I hoped I'd done right by Diana. Half an hour or so passed, and then I found a payphone and dug around in my pocket for a quarter.

"Detective Benjamin's desk, please. Hi, Benjamin. I'm at the Bank of Canada building. Diana Farnsworth was here. Yeah, she just left. She's going to turn herself in, she promised. Today or tomorrow. Yeah, I can be there in half an hour. Sure. Bye."

21

Benjamin was at his desk when I got there, and he greeted me in a detached, just-the-facts-ma'am voice.

"Can you tell me how you just happened to meet Diana Farnsworth? Start at the beginning."

"Well, she called me. At home. She wanted to meet me, and I thought if I went, I could persuade her to turn herself in. Which I did," I finished proudly.

"And where is she now? I didn't see her come in with you." There was an acid undertone in Benjamin's voice.

"Well, no. She said she had some things to do, but she promised ..."

"Katy, I just can't believe this!" He exploded. "Can you tell me exactly why you didn't call me as soon as you heard from Ms. Farnsworth? Instead of trying to freelance it — again? After I've warned you to stop, God knows how many times?"

"Well, I thought she'd be scared if the cops showed up. I thought she'd run away again. Plus, she trusts me. I didn't want to let her down. Geez, Benjamin, give me a break!"

"No, *you* give *me* a break! I could arrest you right here and now for obstruction of justice, you know!"

I extended my arms, wrists up. "Go for it. Cuff me. I try to help you, and this is the thanks I get! She'll be in, you'll see. She's a truthful person, Benjamin. Plus, I happen to know she didn't kill her brother."

Benjamin gave an exasperated sigh. "I'm not arresting you, Katy. Not yet. She's got twenty-four hours to get her ass in here, you understand? And what makes you think she's innocent?"

"She told me so, and I believe her. She said she found Nigel in the kitchen when she got home, and she panicked. She was afraid she'd be a suspect, and she was right, wasn't she?"

"Well, she's not making things any easier for herself, taking off like this. And Katy, you should know something. I've seen guys standing over their wives, holding knives or guns or whatever, look me in the eye and swear they didn't kill them. It's S.O.P. — standard operating procedure. Killers never admit their guilt."

"Diana's not like that."

"Yeah, right."

"She's an honourable person. She'll keep her word. Listen, I want you to do me a favour, okay?"

He grunted, and I took this as assent.

"When she does come in, can you please try to be decent to her? She's been through a lot."

"She'll get the same respect any suspect gets," he said in his official cop voice.

"Well, I'm sorry, but that doesn't really reassure me." The words escaped before I had a chance to edit them.

Benjamin sat up very straight and fixed me with the Cop Death Glare. "I don't appreciate a civilian trying to tell me how to do my job. What gives you the right to come in here throwing around shit like that —"

I cut him off. "I'm not telling you how to do any-thing. I just want to make sure this woman gets a little compassion, that's all. She trusts me, and I want to make sure I haven't pushed her into a worse situation than she's already in. Is that too much to ask?"

"I already said we'll treat her the same as anyone. We don't use rubber hoses and spotlights, you know. She's a murder suspect. It's my job to make sure she gets apprehended, brought before the courts, and tried for that crime. The courts will decide whether she's telling the truth. If you don't like that, Katy, maybe you shouldn't have come in here and told me all about it."

"It's 'Ms. Klein' to you." Rage clogged my throat. I jumped up and left before he could respond.

I stomped home in a blind rage, mentally eviscer-ating Detective Steve Benjamin all the way. I should have known — I never should have told him anything. I was just trying to do him a favour, and look where it got me. Lectures and threats!

Gradually the storm died down, and all I was left with was bone weariness. It was around six when I finally caved in.

I discarded one item of clothing after another on my way to the bathroom, where I ran a hot bath, poured in some sandalwood oil, and immersed myself up to the chin in the old claw-footed tub. As I lay there, fragrant steam billowing upward, warmth seeping into my flesh, random thoughts idly wandered through my overstressed brain. It wasn't until I finally heaved myself upright, stepped out of the tub in a waterlogged haze and wrapped myself in a gigantic bath towel that a stray theory hit me with a thud: Diana and Carmen were lovers.

I don't know where the thought originated, but the instant I thought it, I knew it to be true. When I was in grade seven, my science teacher, Mr. Plourde, had instructed us in the scientific method. First you develop an hypothesis, he would say, and then you see how many of the known facts fit that hypothesis. I tried it out, and it worked.

Hadn't Carmen hinted at a new love interest when she'd been at my place for supper? And she'd been coy about it — maybe she was only now realizing her attraction to other women? Maybe she was worried about how I'd react to her coming out of the closet. Then there was her devastation the day after Nigel Farnsworth died. She'd said someone she cared about had done something terribly wrong — she must have believed that Diana had killed her brother. And hadn't she told me some garbled story about someone interfering in her relationship? Of course: Diana had said the same thing.

And Carmen and Diana were still in touch — as they would be, if they were lovers. Diana would have needed a friend right after the murder, wouldn't she? A friend who could help her hide, protect her, run interference for her. She'd chosen Carmen. I couldn't imagine any other interpretation.

But I was flummoxed. I'd never known Carmen to be anything but determinedly heterosexual in her romantic affairs. This was going to take some mental adjustment on my part. The thought of my petite, ultra-feminine friend with the austere, angular Diana brought an involuntary smile to my face. They'd make a cute, if improbable, couple. Still, I told myself, I don't live inside Carmen's head — how could I know what turns her on?

Curled up in my flannelette jammies, I flicked through a few TV channels. People in their twenties trying to pretend they were high school kids; the news in French; two men debating the merits of beer as a food group; a local cable production of "Hair;" a show on how to tile one's bathroom. Could someone remind me again why I need nine hundred cable channels? I put the remote control down.

With a mental harrumph, I sank back into the couch cushions. My eye alighted on the telephone, beckoning temptingly at my elbow. Eventually discretion gave way to nosiness, and I called Carmen. She sounded surprised to hear from me.

"Hey, kid, I think I've finally put my finger on what's been eating you lately," I said jauntily. "I'm just surprised I didn't think of it sooner."

"What do you mean?" She sounded cautious.

I couldn't help but be delighted with my own ingenuity. "I was sitting in the tub a while ago, and it all fell into place. I realized what was going on between you and Diana, and suddenly everything made sense. I know this must be really rough on you, but I want you to know I totally support you, Carmen."

"You do?"

"Well of course. You're my best friend. I realize it must be incredibly hard on the two of you now, not knowing where all this is heading. It can't be fun."

Carmen said nothing, and I wondered briefly whether she might have hung up. Listening closely, though, I could hear her breath, shallow and rapid.

"Katy, I ... how did you figure all this out?"

Her voice was even higher than normal, and quavering. Of course, this must present a multitude of issues for Carmen. One of the huge worries in her life has always been "What will the neighbours say?" Her usual style might be a circumspect encounter with a married man, or a behind-the-scenes romp with a senior politician. She had to know that an affair with Diana would set tongues a-wagging.

"It was just common sense, really," I said modestly. "And of course when I thought back about some of the things you said to me the other night, it all just crashed into place. I realized I'd been overlooking what was right in front of my nose. Don't forget, I've known you a long time."

"Uh ... yeah. Yes, you have," she said. "So what are you going to do now?"

"What do you mean? There's nothing for me to do. I imagine Diana must have told you what we talked about today ..."

"You met Diana today?"

I couldn't read my friend's voice. "She didn't tell you? Oh, I guess she must have figured you had other things on your mind. Well, she called and we met downtown, and she promised to turn herself in to the cops. As soon as she deals with a few loose ends, she said. Don't worry, I'm sure she'll do the right thing. She's a very principled, self-disciplined person. You know, in spite of all this, I think you're lucky to have found her."

Carmen did not seem to be listening.

"Katy, wait. Hang on a second. You're saying Diana told you what happened, told you everything?"

"Yep. And I believe her, totally. The cops will, too, when she goes in."

"And now she's going to turn herself in," Carmen said slowly.

"That's right. I really do think it's for the best."

I had to cover my free ear to hear Carmen.

"I ... I didn't think she'd actually do that," she said, then paused and blew her nose. "She said she wasn't going to ... she promised she'd just lie low, and then, when some time had passed ..."

"Carmen, look," I said. "If you and she just left town or whatever, you'd both have to worry about this forever. I know it's painful now, but don't you think it'll be better to get the truth out, so you can get on with your lives? It's easy for me to say, I know, but I really think it's best this way."

I felt Carmen's abrupt intake of breath. Now I wished I'd waited until we could meet face to face and discuss it properly. Sometimes I could kick myself.

Carmen's voice was soft. "You know nothing at all about this. You think you know what's best for me, for Diana, but you don't. You persuaded her to turn herself in, didn't you?"

"Well, I —"

"It's just the kind of stupid, misguided thing you'd do, Katy Klein. I'll thank you to keep your damn nose out of my business from now on. In fact, I don't want you anywhere near me again, ever. Just leave me the hell alone!"

I jumped as the phone cracked down. I stared at the receiver in my hand for a few seconds and fought the impulse to immediately call her back. I tried to reassure myself: Carmen has always had an explosive temper, and she's terribly overwrought right now. Who could blame her for panicking a bit? She'll come round eventually. I've been the target of her wrath before, and even lived to tell the tale. I'm sure I'll survive this little tempest, too.

As for my own role in persuading Diana to turn

herself in, I felt no regret: I had only encouraged her in the direction she already knew to be right. I'd done nothing wrong.

It's a good thing the apartment was empty, because now I was pacing around the place muttering, trying to convince myself things would turn out just fine. Then I caught myself up short, smacked myself on the forehead. Shit! I'd forgotten the most important point.

If Diana turned herself in, the police would find out about Carmen's role in helping her hide out. In the eyes of the courts, that would make Carmen a criminal — hadn't Benjamin threatened me with a charge of obstructing justice, or some such thing? God, I can be dense sometimes.

I never should have called Carmen. Not for nothing do I get accused of leaping before I look. It's what makes me such a lousy chess player. I sat down and absently picked up my needlepoint, though I didn't get far. My fingers weren't co-operating this evening. They felt numb and cold, and eventually I gave up.

Peter and Dawn trooped into the apartment an hour later, stuffed to the brim with pizza from the parlour a few blocks away. Peter was still in a celebratory mood, hyped with the success of his story, and I did not feel much like discussing my latest major faux pas, so I kept silent.

"You won't believe the fallout from the story," Peter grinned. "Enough to make it worthwhile to do a follow-up piece, just on the reaction alone. I've even got the go-ahead from Ben."

Ben was his editor, a young pup barely out of J-school, greatly adored by *Telegraph* management, probably because of his youthful enthusiasm, combined with a certain wet-behind-the-ears malleability. He exemplified the *Telegraph*'s unspoken creed: keep it light, bright and tight, with an eagle eye on the bottom line. Peter both envies and despises Ben, but today that was less important than the adrenaline surge that comes with riding the crest of a fast-breaking story.

"Great, Peter! I'm really pleased for you. Want some hot chocolate?"

"Sounds good. No, don't get up, I'll get it ..."

He started toward the kitchen, but I stopped him. "Peter, it's times like this when I'm glad we're just friends, not spouses. Could you just this once take off your wet, slushy boots before you go traipsing into the kitchen?"

He gave me a look and kicked his boots off before heading into the kitchen. Of course, the boots were nowhere near the plastic boot tray, and they were still dripping salt and slush all over my hardwood floor. Sighing, I bent to pick them up, when a gleam of colour caught my eye.

Exasperated, I picked another of Carmen's antibiotic capsules from the gap between two floorboards. This capsule looked funny: there seemed to be a gap at one end, not enough powdered medication inside the two halves of the capsule. Defective.

I stared at the thing for a moment, then tucked it into my needlework bag. In her current state of mind, Carmen probably wouldn't appreciate my retrieving her stupid pill.

Shifting mental gears rapidly, I told Dawn and Peter about my day. Peter was appalled that I had not immediately called him about my building's untimely demise, but it's not like I'd had lots of time to think, is it? I related my meeting with Diana, and Peter and Dawn were both deeply impressed.

"If she contacts you again, do you think you might be able to persuade her to speak to me?" Peter asked.

"Peter, I know that gleam in your eye. I think Diana might have more on her mind than helping Ben sell papers."

"Katy, that's not fair! You know I don't think like that. But her story could break some things wide open — it would be a public service ..."

"Yeah, right. Well, she might want to talk to you, at that. But she's got to get through the cops first. I'm just hoping they won't stick her in the slammer."

"Mom, did you tell the police you'd seen her?" Dawn asked.

"Of course," I said, though I did not mention my little tiff with Benjamin. "I'm a responsible citizen, you know. Carmen's pretty pissed at me, but I still think I did the right thing."

Then I told them of my brilliant stroke of intuition about Carmen's new relationship, and related the conversation I'd just had with my best friend. Peter looked dubious.

"Carmen? You mean hyper-feminine, teeny-weeny batting-the-eyelashes whenever there's a Y-chromosome within fifty feet Carmen? Pardon my insensitivity, but I'm having a hard time envisioning her with another woman," he said. "Or am I just being heterosexist here? Really, Katy, she's the last person I'd expect ..."

"Look, Carmen was taught to behave a certain way. It's not her fault, Peter." I jumped in defensively with a treatise on the socialization of women and the power imbalance between the sexes, a knee-jerk response to Peter's overly harsh judgment. We always do this. He says tomayto, I say tomahto.

"You may not like her, but she's a decent person underneath. You don't have any right to judge how she comes across, and her appearance has nothing to do with her sexual orientation. And she's been there for me over the years, you know. She's been a good friend. You have to give her that."

"Maybe so," Peter conceded, "but I still can't see her with another woman. She just doesn't seem the type."

"Do you have any idea how homophobic you sound?" I blistered. "That's the equivalent of 'Funny, you don't look Jewish,' Peter. I can't believe you'd say such a thing. Gays and lesbians make up almost 10 percent of the population, and they're getting a little tired of the view from the closet, so you'd better get used to it, buddy!"

"Whoa, whoa," he said, holding up his hands. "I wasn't being homophobic — I was being Carmen-phobic. I know you care about her, but she makes my teeth itch. Anyway, let's talk about something nicer. Look, we saved you some pizza — and it's got anchovies!"

I had to laugh at his earnest attempt at peacemaking, and my rage dispelled instantly.

"Thanks." I took the proffered box. "It's cold, but I'll go zap it in the microwave."

Half an hour after Peter had left, I heard him moving around upstairs, getting ready for bed. Even after five years of living separately, I could envision his every move: off with the shoes, the shirt draped carefully over the back of the chair, pants hung on a hook by the door, padding off to the bathroom to floss. His nighttime ritual is like clockwork. So I was surprised when he called a few minutes later, asking for Dawn.

"What's up, Dad?" she asked. "No, I didn't touch it. Really! Look, I know you don't like me playing around with the VCR, and I'm telling you, I didn't touch it. No, I have no idea. Dad, don't just automatically blame me. Maybe you forgot to label them properly or something. Fine."

She rolled her eyes eloquently as she hung up.

"He thinks I was up there today playing around with his stupid VCR. You know how he tapes all that *Star Trek* stuff off the TV, and keeps it in the cabinet? Well, he found some unlabelled tapes lying next to the machine, and now he's going berserk about it, saying I've screwed up his stupid system. Like I'd even dare to touch it! I hate it when he starts blaming me for things I didn't even do."

I shook my head. "Sorry, honey, you'll have to settle it with Dad."

I make it a policy never to get involved in disputes between Dawn and her father. Let them deal with it themselves, I say. I was just packing away my needlepoint, checking the locks on the doors and generally going through my own ritual preparations for a good night's sleep, when someone rapped quietly but insistently at the front door.

Peering through the peephole, I saw an oddly foreshortened Peter, rocking back and forth on his heels, something he does only when seriously perturbed. He tiptoed into the apartment when I opened the door, and peered around the corner into the living room.

"Where's Dawn?"

"In bed. Look, if it's about your videos, can't it wait till morning?" I asked.

He shook his head vigorously. "No, no. I mean, it's

about the videos, but I don't want her to see what I've got. Can you come upstairs for a few minutes? It's important."

"Peter, I was just on my way to bed," I started to protest, but he grabbed my arm urgently.

"It's an emergency, Katy. I need you to see something."

Peter is normally a fairly stable person, but once in a while he goes bananas, getting all bent out of shape over some minor incident that anyone else would just shrug off. Might as well humour him tonight, or I'd never get any rest.

I climbed the stairs, yearning for the cozy comfort of my own bed. Did I not have enough stress in my life as it was, without my ex-husband going all twitchy on me? He should have more consideration for my needs. Let him deal with his own damn neuroses about his stupid "Star Trek" collection. I'm not the one who gets all worked up about keeping things in exact order, each episode labelled and colour-coded by season.

Peter went immediately to the huge entertainment centre that lines an entire wall of his apartment. It's a guy thing, he once informed me loftily. Or maybe it's just that none of the women I know can afford such toys.

He popped a tape into the video machine, pressed the play button. At first it was hard to see anything, there was a lot of greyish white static, and the picture rolled vertiginously. I squinted, wondering just what he was trying to demonstrate to me.

"Hang on, here it comes," he said.

The picture wobbled, the camera obviously hand-held, and there was a dark shadow obscuring the top right-hand corner. Someone's shadow? No, it was a jacket. Whoever made this film, they'd done it on the sly. A hidden camera.

The camera panned a large room, pausing to take in the faces of a bunch of men. One of them was tall, raven-haired, his clean-cut good looks visible even in choppy black-and-white film. Nigel Farnsworth. He stood, one hand on the back of another man's chair, listening and nodding as the seated man spoke. The words, like the picture, were hard to make out, but I caught fragments:

" ... need to rid the city of this pestilence ... Lord's work ... we warned them, but they wouldn't listen."

"Is this what I think it is?" I whispered.

Peter nodded. "A meeting. The Soldiers. And several of them are identifiable."

"Where did you get this?"

"That's why I called Dawn — it was sitting next to my video machine when I came up here. At first I thought she'd been watching one of my "Star Trek" tapes, and I was annoyed. I didn't believe her when she said she hadn't done it, but she wouldn't admit to anything, so I hung up. I was really pissed. The tape wasn't labelled, so I started playing it, trying to figure out where in the collection she'd taken it from. And then this."

"You have to take this to Benjamin. It's evidence. Like that anonymous letter — you did take that in, didn't you?"

"Yeah. But what I want to know is, how the hell did this get here? And why? My door was locked when I came in, and nothing else was touched."

"Diana." She must have done it. This must have been what she'd meant when she'd spoken of putting things in order.

"Okay, fine, say it was Diana. How did she get in? And why?"

I scanned the apartment, blinking to clear my head.

"I don't know, exactly. Have you checked the windows?"

"No, I came straight downstairs as soon as I realized what I was seeing."

He inspected the apartment, running from one casement to another, and stopped in the bedroom, calling out to me.

"Katy, take a look at this."

Peter's bedroom window opens onto a fire escape at the back of the building. The ladder stops six feet short of the ground, but a determined burglar could have grabbed the bottom rung and clambered up. The screen on the window itself had been neatly cut away, the window jimmied open. There were gouge marks on the wood, as if someone had pried it up with a chisel or some other sharp tool. Diana had clearly known what she was doing.

"Okay, so Diana broke in to leave me a little present. What I still don't get is why."

"She told me she would," I said. "Not in so many words, but she said she had some things to attend to before she turned herself in. As for why — well, isn't it obvious? She wants everyone to know exactly what Nigel and the Soldiers were up to."

"Fine. So why not just turn up at the police station with the videos in hand?"

"I'm not sure. Maybe she thought that if the videos were taken as evidence, they'd be locked into the court system for months, maybe even years."

"Right, whereas if she brought them straight to me, I'd make them public."

"Exactly!" I said. "You'd already shown your stuff, taking on that story about the Soldiers — she must have figured she could trust you."

Yes, that made a certain amount of sense. Of course, the problem now was that the tapes would have to be turned in to the police. But I supposed Peter could make copies before handing them over.

We sat in his living room several hours longer, until fatigue overwhelmed me. It must have been past three in the morning by the time I went back downstairs. Too much information crowded into my head, and I felt jittery, on edge. When I did finally fall into a light sleep, I kept jolting awake.

I phoned Peter once more, and he trotted obligingly downstairs, climbed into my bed, and held me until we both collapsed into blessed unconsciousness.

He's good that way.

22

Sunrise came and went without my knowledge or consent. It must have been eleven when I awoke, missing Peter's comforting warmth and bulk next to me. It took me a few moments to realize what had wakened me. I thumped the top of my clock-radio, hoping to quell the intermittent jangle that had intruded into my sleep. My well-placed fist didn't stop the noise — the phone kept ringing.

Groggily, I picked it up.

"Katy? It's me, Steve."

Steve who? Oh, right. Benjamin. I'm not speaking to you, Benjamin, I thought, though I was damned if I could recall why just at that moment. Never mind.

"Yes?"

"I'm sorry to bother you at home, but I need to speak to you. Don't worry, it's police business, not personal," he added.

"What the hell did I do now?"

I honestly couldn't think of any breach of the law I'd committed recently.

"This is serious, Katy. Can you meet me here in, say, forty-five minutes?"

I was too disoriented to press for further details, so I agreed unenthusiastically to yet another trek to the Ottawa Police station. Maybe they should just offer me a desk there. Save me travel time.

Then I remembered Carmen's anger at me. This improved my mood even further. I was feeling pretty darn surly when I approached Benjamin's desk forty minutes later.

He was scribbling furiously in his notebook when I arrived, but he put it to one side and stood politely to greet me. If he was thinking of the snit I'd been in yesterday, it didn't show. Rather, I read the kind of cultivated calmness and concern that police officers must be taught at cop school. I frowned. What was this all about?

"Have a seat," he said. "Listen, I'm sorry to have to keep asking you down here, but there's been a bit of a problem come up. It's about Diana Farnsworth."

"What? She didn't show up?"

"No, she didn't."

"Well, she didn't tell me an exact time, Benjamin — but she did promise me she would ..."

"Katy, Diana was found this morning, out south of the city, around Leitrim. In a field, by a farmer. His dog found her. She's dead."

Wham. Right in the gut. It's not fair when someone does that to you, just up and wallops you with no warning. Diana cannot be dead — I just spoke with her yesterday, and I'm sure she wasn't dead then. Not happy, exactly, but definitely not dead.

I must have sat there for some time with my mouth opening and closing like a beached codfish, because next thing I know, Benjamin was crouched by my chair, tilting my head back, offering me sips of water from a paper cup. The water was extremely cold on my parched lips. It sluiced down my throat so quickly I gagged.

Then I shook my head and looked more clearly at Benjamin, who was sitting back on his heels, looking unhappy.

"What ... do they know what happened?"

"She was shot. Looks like a .38, but I'm waiting for the report from ballistics. She was face-down, the bullet hit her from behind, in the skull. She probably never felt a thing, Katy."

This was meant to comfort me, I suppose.

"No ... I guess she wouldn't."

A bullet in the skull. Once I'd gone with some friends to a farm in the Eastern Townships of Quebec, and I'd seen a farmer casually exterminate a fox who'd wandered, delirious with rabies, into the yard. The animal had jumped with the impact, then flopped back down to earth, its cranium shattered, brain fragments splashed across the snow. Blood had continued to pump through the severed veins in its neck, like a little fountain.

From a distance, I heard Benjamin repeating my name over and over.

"It's okay," I said. "I'll be okay. I just need a few minutes."

"I didn't want to tell you over the phone," Benjamin said. "I'm sorry it came as such a shock. I have to ask you some questions, but if you want some time ..."

"No, no. Go ahead."

"Are you sure?"

I nodded.

"Okay. First, I need to know your whereabouts last night."

"I guess that shouldn't surprise me." I rubbed my temples, which had suddenly started throbbing. "I was at home."

"Any witnesses who could bear that out?"

"Uh, yeah. Peter. I was with Peter. Oh, and Dawn, of course. Benjamin, this is stupid. You know I couldn't have killed Diana."

"I still have to do it by the book, Katy."

"Yeah, okay. I guess."

"Are you aware of anyone who might have had a grievance against Diana?"

"I ... I don't know. I hardly knew the woman," I faltered. "Are you sure it's her?"

"We're sure. We had the janitor from her brother's church come in, and she identified the body. Katy, try to stay with me here, okay? I want you to think about anything you remember, any little thing you might have forgotten to tell me about Diana. It could be very important."

"Well, there's this one thing. I did talk to someone else about Diana turning herself in, and this person was pretty peeved. But I can't imagine her actually killing anyone. It just doesn't scan."

"Whoa, wait a second!" Benjamin held up a hand. "Go back to the beginning, would you? Who is this person, and why did you tell them about Diana?"

"Carmen. My best friend, Carmen Capricci. I've known her since we were little kids. I was lying in the bathtub the other night, when it just kind of occurred to me: Carmen and Diana were ... uh ... well, you know. Together."

"You're saying you think they were lovers?"

I nodded. "So I think Carmen might have been hiding Diana after Nigel's death — because Diana really didn't do it, you know? But when I told Carmen that I'd convinced Diana to come and see you, she hit the roof."

"And you think this is because ... ?"

"Because it might get Carmen in trouble. For hiding Diana in the first place, you see? Don't you call that obstructing justice or withholding evidence or something?"

Benjamin scribbled something on a pad of paper. "Okay. What's this lady's address, Katy?"

I gave it to him, feeling like a traitor.

"Oh, and there's something else I have to tell you, Benjamin."

"Shoot."

Oh, poor choice of words. Nevertheless, I told him about Peter's discovery of the video tapes of Nigel and the Soldiers.

"You witnessed these videos?"

"Of course," I said. "I'm sure Diana must have put them there. She knows — she knew Peter and I used to be married. And that he's a reporter. I guess she thought he'd make them public."

Before I had finished speaking, Benjamin was on the phone, barking orders to an underling. Next thing I knew, he had Ben, Peter's editor, on the line. I couldn't hear Ben's side of the conversation, but Benjamin sounded like he meant business. He demanded that the videos be turned over as evidence in a criminal investigation. If I'd been Ben the Wunderkind, I'd have saluted and snapped to attention.

Finally, Benjamin hung up and turned to me.

"I don't want to make problems for your ex," he said, "but if he doesn't hand the tapes over in the next half hour or so, I'm going to have to issue a warrant for withholding evidence. Just so you know."

I shrugged. Hey, what's one more legal entanglement? Besides, if I knew Peter, he'd have made copies of the tapes before the sun was up this morning.

"Is there anything else you need me for?" I asked.

"Oh, maybe just one more thing. I wanted to apologize about yesterday."

"What about yesterday?" I tried to remember, but the last several days were such a jumble in my brain, I couldn't recall what had happened.

"I was a bit harsh with you about Diana. I could have handled it better."

"Don't worry about it. We've both been under a lot of pressure." I tried to smile, but the corners of my mouth kept tugging downward. I needed to get out of here before I burst into overwrought tears.

"I can't apologize properly here," Benjamin said. "Are we still on for Friday night? I can pick you up around seven."

"Sure," I said. "Seven."

Then, coward that I am, I turned tail and fled.

I needed to think. As I ploughed my way through the grey-brown half-frozen gruel along Elgin Street, I tried to force my aching brain to co-operate. Come on, Katy, let's look at the facts.

Diana was dead. Shot in the back of the head with a .38. Had she chickened out, decided not to turn herself in to the police after all? Well, even if she had, it's not like she could have shot herself in the back of the skull. Who had a motive to kill Diana?

Suddenly I stopped walking. It was one of those smack in the forehead moments — how could I have been so stupid? Where was my brain? I'd been standing there talking to Benjamin, totally ignoring the most obvious answer.

"The Soldiers," I said aloud, ignoring a woman who gave me a funny look. What a dolt I was! Hadn't Diana been terrified that they'd find her? And now, her worst nightmare had come true.

I wheeled about and started back toward the police station, jogging this time.

Benjamin wasn't at his desk when I got there. Another cop, a young guy with a shock of blond hair, ambled over.

"Can I help you, ma'am?"

"Benjamin — Detective Benjamin," I gasped, out of breath from the unaccustomed exercise. I really need to get in better shape.

"He's gone out to interview someone. Should be back in an hour or so."

I cursed silently. "Would he be taking his own car?"

Blond Cop nodded. "Probably."

"Thanks!" I turned around and flew down the staircase to the parking lot, trying to recall Benjamin's car. A Chev? No, a Ford. A black Taurus. There it was, over there — he was just backing out of his space.

"Benjamin! Wait!" I waved frantically, and he stopped and rolled down the window.

"Katy? What's up?"

I shook my head, too breathless to talk right away.

"Never mind," he said. "Hop in, and I'll give you a lift. Where are you going?"

"It's just ..." I breathed deeply. "I think I know who killed Diana."

"Who?" He gave me a sharp look.

"Well, you and I and Carmen are the only people who know she didn't kill Nigel, right?"

"I don't know that, but yeah, I guess I could take it as a starting point."

"So as far as the Soldiers know, she killed their leader! And she told me herself that she was terrified of them. That was one of the reasons she'd gone into hiding — she was afraid of being hunted down."

"So you think they offed her? An execution?"

"Exactly! Hey, Carmen hung around that church a lot, when she was redecorating it. I wonder if she'd have seen any evidence of the Soldiers? She could probably identify some of them, or something, don't you think?"

"I'll ask her that," Benjamin said.

"I just hope she's in a condition to answer. Carmen's got a bit of a drinking problem, and it gets worse when she's under stress. Which she has been lately, with Diana and all."

Benjamin said nothing.

"Listen, Benjamin, I was just thinking ..."

"Sounds ominous."

I looked sideways at him. No trace of a grin. "Yeah, very funny. Well, what if I go with you to see Carmen? She knows me, she might feel more comfortable talking with me there."

"Thought you said you just had a big fight?"

"We did. But we have big fights all the time. It doesn't mean we don't love one another. Come on, please? Just this once? I won't get in the way, I promise."

"Katy ..."

"Pleeeeeease?" I tried to bat my eyelashes at him,

but I think the effect was more comical than persuasive.

"All right. Listen, you can come in, but you keep quiet until I tell you, okay? I don't want you jumping in and screwing things up for me."

"Well, thanks for the vote of confidence. But I'll behave. Promise."

We pulled up outside Carmen's place and jumped out of the car just like they do in cop shows, except that usually the guys in cop shows don't land in slushy snowbanks. Inside, Benjamin rapped lightly on Carmen's apartment door. No answer. He knocked more loudly. Still nothing. He turned to me.

"Do you know any of her neighbours, anyone who could tell us if she's been around?"

"Let me try," I said. I rapped on Carmen's door, calling her name. No reply. Without saying a word, I fished through my purse and found the key to the apartment. I was inserting it into the deadbolt when Benjamin stopped me, a hand on my arm.

"You can't do that," he whispered. "I need a warrant to enter the premises."

"Benjamin, I'm her friend. We've had one another's keys for twenty years now, and I'm going into my best friend's apartment to make sure she's okay. You don't have to come with me if there's some cop ethic that prevents you. It's up to you."

He didn't put up an argument. I twisted the key in the lock and felt the bolt click back. Holding my breath, I pushed the door slowly inward, cautiously peering into the apartment as I did so. No sound, no light greeted me.

"Carmen?" I whispered into the dimness. "Carmen, honey, it's me. Katy. Are you in there?"

No answer. I reached for the string to the overhead

light and pulled it. Light flooded the hallway. There was no sign of Carmen.

"Carmen, I just want to talk, okay?" My words echoed around the apartment in faint mockery. Standing there, I could see the familiar outlines of Carmen's living room, darkened by tasteful Roman shades. Nothing moved, and I expelled my breath. I hadn't realized I'd been holding it.

I pulled the shades up, allowing a shaft of sunlight to illuminate the apartment. The place was cleaner than it had been on my last visit, wine glasses rinsed out and replaced, bottles carefully stacked in the recycling box. I checked the bedroom, the walk-in closet, the bathroom — Carmen was definitely not here.

Now I felt a little silly. She was probably at work. I could just imagine her giving me shit for this latest incursion into her private life.

"We'd better go," I said. "She's not here."

Benjamin seemed to have overcome his inhibitions about entering the premises without a warrant, for he was now rummaging enthusiastically through the small kitchen.

"Come on, Benjamin, we'd better get out of here," I said again, but he didn't follow me.

"Katy, you said Carmen had a drinking problem?" He sounded distracted.

I snorted. "Do bears shit in the woods? Yeah, she's always had a tendency to hit the bottle when the going gets rough. I wouldn't say she's a chronic alcoholic, though — it's more like she goes through periodic crises, then cleans up her act. I've seen it a dozen times or more since I've known her."

"Well, it looks like she decided to do something about it," Benjamin said. "Have a peek."

He pointed to a photocopied brochure that was pinned to the bulletin board next to the phone in the kitchen.

"*Does your drinking control your life?*" it asked. "*Are you looking for the inner peace no bottle can give you?*" And so on, the usual stuff touted by alcohol and drug recovery programs. Let go and let God, that sort of thing. I opened the brochure and skimmed its contents. It advertised a treatment centre on the outskirts of Ottawa, one of those twenty-eight day spin-dry places. Addicts can get some counselling, attend some groups, try to get a grip on their lives — and then they go back to real life, and some of them actually do manage to stay clean and sober. Others don't.

"Have you heard of this place?" Benjamin asked me. "Serenity Haven. There's no address on the brochure."

"It's the place where Diana worked," I said. "Nigel started it, and Diana has been the director there for the past three months."

I picked up the phone and dialled the number on the brochure. After about six rings, a machine picked up, and Diana's voice announced, "You've reached Serenity Haven Treatment Centre. The Centre is closed until further notice. We can't answer the phone now, but your call is important to us ..."

"That's weird ..." I murmured. I hung up.

"What?" Benjamin raised a shaggy eyebrow.

"The phone message. It's Diana's voice, saying the Centre is closed. But it didn't close until after Nigel died. I'm sure that's what they said on the news. So how could she have changed the message, if she was on the run?"

"So that's where she was hiding." Benjamin fished

his notebook out of an inside pocket of his tweed jacket and scribbled something in pencil.

"I thought you guys already looked there?"

"We did. She must have gone back after we'd left.
Whoever killed her must have figured out where she
was hiding."

I leaned back against the doorframe. "But no one
knew she was there ..."

"Hang on a sec," Benjamin said, fumbling at his
belt. "My beeper's going off." He checked the number
on the tiny screen, picked up the phone again, and
dialled.

"Benjamin here ... yeah ... no problem. Sure, you
should check that out. Yeah. Well, it looks like she was
staying out there. Uh-huh. Okay, well it'll keep till I get
there. Give me twenty minutes. Right." He hung up.

"Listen, I have to go out to the scene," Benjamin
said. "Should I drop you at your office?"

I swallowed hard, not really up to explaining that I
no longer had an office. "Do you mind if I tag along for
now? I won't get in the way, promise. I'll just sit in the
car and do my nails, or something."

The truth was, I didn't want to be alone. If the
Soldiers knew where Diana was staying, they might
have seen her meeting with me yesterday. That did not
bode well for my future well-being and happiness.

Benjamin and I said nothing as we drove from
Carmen's apartment to Bank Street. The car edged
slowly south through the late morning traffic, past the
familiar shops of the Glebe. I closed my eyes when we
passed the blackened hole where my office used to be.
If Benjamin noticed it, he made no comment. Over the
canal into Ottawa South we went, past Billings Bridge,
under the railway tracks, and on out past the fast food

joints, discount stores and used car lots at the south end of Bank Street.

Finally there were only snowy fields lined with gigantic rolls of hay, covered with tarps and capped with snow that glinted against the pale sky. This was a good place for a rehab centre. Not much chance of the clientele sneaking off to the nearest pub for a wee nip — there was nothing out here but fields and woods.

We pulled in behind two police cars parked on the shoulder along a narrow road. Beyond them, the snow was trampled flat, as investigators measured and took pictures and did whatever it is they do at the scene of a murder.

Benjamin gestured to me to stay put as he got out to chat with a uniformed officer who stood guard by a rickety wooden gate.

I sat obediently. Whatever might be out in that field, I didn't want to see it. Presently, Benjamin returned to the car and pointed down the road.

"The treatment centre is down that way. No one's there — the scene crew has already checked it out."

"Would you mind if we had a quick peek at it any-way?" I wanted to see this place. He didn't question me, just gunned the car into action. The fields gave way to scrubby woods, second-growth poplar and alder.

No sign advertised the presence of the treatment centre. At first glance, I thought we were approaching one of those pre-fab bungalows, the type that's just a step shy of a mobile home. Bland, mushroom-coloured vinyl panelling on the outside, small win-dows high up under the eaves, cast concrete steps leading to an unprepossessing entrance.

Benjamin stopped the car and I got out. No one

had shovelled the walkway here, though the drive had been ploughed perhaps a couple of days ago. They probably had a farmer come in and do it after each snowfall. Footprints trampled the walk to the front door. The police had already checked the place out after Nigel died.

Benjamin joined me as I walked through the carport and round to the back of the house. The snow here was undisturbed. I knelt in front of a basement window and peered in: the room was large, lined with bookshelves. Stacking chairs were neatly placed along the far wall and a wide-screen television stood on a table at one end. A meeting room.

The window itself was smallish, probably too low and narrow to accommodate me. I returned to the front of the house, which looked no more promising. The door was solid, deadbolted, and I have no lock-picking skills to speak of. Besides, Benjamin probably would have drawn the line at allowing me to break and enter. Not that there'd be anything to see inside, anyway.

We walked back to the car and I got in, but left the door open. I sat with my back to Benjamin, staring at the house, my legs dangling outside the vehicle.

"Benjamin, did the officer back there tell you where Diana was when she —"

He nodded. "Yeah. Her tracks started at the edge of the road, about a hundred metres from the end of this driveway. She went about halfway into the field down the road, then the bullet caught her. She was running."

I had not wanted to know that.

"Any sign of the killer?"

"The prints were pretty small, close together. A short person, likely female. They stop about ten feet behind the victim. Afterward, the killer turned and walked away. The tracks stop at the road."

"I think the killer is still somewhere around here," I said.

Benjamin gave me a humour-this-poor-woman-she's-clearly-losing-it look. I ignored him.

"Okay," I said. "Let's go get some coffee. Whoever it is, they're not going to show their faces with us sitting here in the car." Turning, I pulled my legs into the car and slammed the door.

"Katy, I don't know if you've noticed this," Benjamin said, "but I am a police officer in the middle of a major crime investigation. Contrary to popular belief, cops don't all spend their time hanging around doughnut shops, swilling coffee and trading gossip while gorging on fried pastries. I've got work to do."

"Fine," I said. "You can just leave me here. I want to take another look around. I'll catch up with you down the road when I'm done."

"Like hell you will." Then his curiosity got the better of him. "What are you planning to do, anyway?"

"I'm not altogether sure, to be honest. I just have a feeling."

"Well, you're the psychic," he said.

"How many times do I have to tell you? I'm an astrologer, not a psychic. Anyway, you don't have to be a psychic to have a hunch, and I have a hunch that there's more here than meets the eye."

"Take my word for it, Katy, the killer hightailed it out of here as soon as the deed was done. And besides, if they are here, it seems a little on the dumb side for you to hang around waiting for them, don't you think?" Now he was being condescending. I hate that.

"If it's who I think it is, she won't kill me. Not in a

million years." I didn't realize until the words were out of my mouth that I knew who'd killed Diana.

"Have it your way," he said. "In my considered opinion, gained in the past God-knows-how-many years on this police force, the person who killed your friend is long gone. Look, I've got to get back to the crime scene. D'you want me to drop you off at the coffee shop down the road, or would you rather wait in the car? I won't be long."

"I'll just hang around here," I said, and got out of the car.

"Katy, don't be stupid. There's no one here. Get back in the car."

"Is that an order, Detective?"

"Fine, suit yourself," he growled. "I'll be about half an hour. Do up your jacket, you'll freeze out here."

I did not deign to answer him. I stalked to the woodpile at the far end of the carport, cleared myself a space and sat down. The car pulled away, and suddenly it seemed very silent in this place. No birds, no crickets, just the leaden winter hush. Although it was still early afternoon, the sun was low in the southwestern sky, casting long shadows. I wrapped my arms around myself, trying to keep warm.

I'd hopped out of the car on impulse, in part because I was annoyed with Benjamin for telling me not to, but now I began to doubt my own judgment. What if the killer really was here? What would I do?

Years ago, when such things were popular, I went to an ashram to learn to meditate. Now, sitting on this woodpile, with splinters of pine and birch digging uncomfortably into my derrière, I tried to recall the technique. I figured it would help me pass the time. Focusing my gaze on an oil spot a few feet away, I concentrated on emptying my mind, letting my thoughts drift ... Suddenly one drifting thought snagged on my consciousness, and I sat bolt upright, electricity zipping along my spine.

The pills. In my distress over the events of the last eighteen hours, I'd forgotten the damned pills. Now I knew, without any doubt, what they meant. And I knew why I'd felt so strongly about staying here at the treatment centre.

What in hell was I thinking, sitting here unprotected? I leaped to my feet and started to jog down the driveway toward the road. The crime scene wasn't that far from this place. Even in my pathetic physical condition, I could jog there in, say, ten minutes.

I was close to the road when I heard the click behind me. I spun around, my breath trapped in my chest.

Carmen stood watching me, her face expressionless. In her small gloved hands, she held a ridiculously large gun, which she was aiming directly at my abdomen.

23

"Carmen ..." I said. Still wordless, she pointed the gun a bit higher, at my head.

"Carmen, please, you don't want to do this," I tried again. "Can't we talk?"

She stood stone-faced, with her feet braced apart.

"I have to kill you now, Katy. I don't want to, but I don't have any choice. I told you to keep the hell away from me, didn't I?"

Her voice was toneless. I didn't have any answer for her. Yes, she had told me to back off, but has anyone ever known me to heed well-meant advice?

Carmen nodded toward the treatment centre.

"Get over there, into the carport. I don't want to do this out in the open."

This cannot be happening, I thought dully. I trudged back along the driveway, Carmen following a few feet behind.

"Carmen, please. Talk to me. Tell me how it happened — did you really mean to kill Marion, or did you just miscalculate?"

I thought I heard Carmen's step falter behind me for a nanosecond, but her voice was low and level when she answered.

"Of course not. I had no idea she'd actually die. She was supposed to get sick, that's all. Anyway, what does it matter now?"

Good question. Especially if I was to be next on the list, knowing the truth wasn't going to do me much good, was it?

"I know you didn't mean to kill her, Carmen. And you don't want to kill me, either. Come on, put the gun down, and we can talk. We'll figure something out."

"Shut up. It's over, Katy. There's nothing to talk about any more."

"Carmen, come on. I know you. You're not the kind of person who can just kill someone in cold blood, you know you're not. You fiddled with Marion's pills, maybe substituted flour or something in a few of her Dilantin capsules, but you didn't really want to hurt her, right? Just get her out of the way for a while, isn't that how it happened?"

Although the evil-looking revolver was still directed at my head, I thought I saw irresolution in my friend's face.

"Nigel and I had something truly special, but that stupid woman Marion was always there," she said. "He said he didn't really love her, but he wouldn't just tell her to forget about him. He didn't have the guts. She had too much on him. So I figured if she had one of her fits at my party, made a big mess of herself, he'd see her a bit differently. He'd see how weak and silly she really was. That he had nothing to fear from her. I didn't know it would kill her — how could I have known?"

"But ... what kind of hold could someone like Marion have on Nigel?"

"Don't be an idiot," Carmen snarled, her eyes darting fire. "What the hell do you think? Rose. Marion knew about Nigel and her daughter, but she pretended not to, so she could keep Nigel on a string, stay at the top of his list. Just like my own fucking mother did to me. If you want to keep your place in line, you've got to make a few sacrifices, right? That was all that mattered, for either of them. Stupid cows. For a smart woman, you're being incredibly dense, Katy. Don't you get it?"

"Carmen. I didn't know ... about your mother, I mean ..."

I felt faint. Hold on, hold on. It wouldn't do to pass out now, she'd shoot me for sure. I took several deep breaths.

"Carmen," I said again. "are you saying all this, everything that happened, it was all because you and Nigel ..."

"You wouldn't understand," she snapped.

My stomach turned flip-flops. "You're right. I've been as thick as two short planks. It's all been right there in front of me, hasn't it? You and Diana were never lovers — it was Nigel all along. You killed Marion to keep Nigel for yourself. And you stabbed Nigel, too, didn't you?"

Unexpectedly, Carmen's eyes filled with tears. "I had to!" she cried. "I didn't know about Rose, until ..."

"Until that night at my house, when I told you she was pregnant," I finished for her. "And when you realized who the father must be, you took that taxi straight to Nigel's house, didn't you?"

She nodded, her face drained of colour. "That bastard. That bastard. He deserved it."

"What happened, Carmen? Tell me."

"It was so quick. He was standing there in the kitchen, laughing at me. I couldn't help it, I just grabbed the first thing that came to hand, and I went for his throat. He wasn't expecting it, he didn't realize what I was doing at first. And once I got the first cut in, it was so easy — I just kept pounding at him until I was sure he was dead. Then I washed the knife off and put it away."

"And then Diana came home," I supplied. "And she found him lying there, covered in blood. She got scared, and ran — straight over to your place. She thought she could trust you, because she'd helped you dry out. You owed her. Did you tell her you'd killed him?"

Carmen shook her head. "I couldn't."

"So ... what? You hid her, and let her think you were her friend? And you let the police, me, everyone think she'd done it?"

"I knew you wouldn't understand. You've never really loved someone, not the way I loved Nigel. If you had, you'd know."

"Love? This by you is love? Killing some poor woman to get her out of the way is love? And if you loved him so damn much, why'd you kill him? Carmen, you're a sick puppy. You need help."

"Shut up! Shut up! You don't know anything about it!" She waved the gun at me, and I took an involuntary step backward. Her gaze was fierce, concentrated. "Nigel and I were going to be happy together. All I wanted to do was make him see that Marion wasn't the woman for him. It's not my fault it all went wrong!"

"Yeah, I'll say it went wrong. So why did you kill Diana? I suppose you knew she'd eventually figure it out about you and Nigel, right? So you helped her hide out until things got better. Pretended to be her friend. What did you do, star in one of Nigel's little home videos? Did you say something stupid on tape? Like,

'Oh, Nigel, honey, now that bitch Marion's out of the way, you're mine, all mine.'"

I mimicked Carmen's fluttery little-girl voice, and she winced. I was being cruel now, and I didn't care. I took a step toward her. She backed away, though she still had the gun trained on me. I couldn't make out the expression in her eyes. Was it fear? Shame? I was past caring.

"That's why you couldn't leave, isn't it? You had to come back here to get the tapes from Diana, to make sure no one knew you'd been screwing her brother. Well, guess what, Carmen? You wasted your time. Diana gave all the tapes to Peter last night. By now, everyone knows about you and Nigel." The lie tripped off my tongue easily. "And now you're going to kill me, for what? You're going to kill someone who's been your friend all your life, just to save your own pathetic skin, aren't you? I'm nauseated, Carmen, you make me want to puke!"

As I spoke, I kept advancing on her, staring her down, forcing her to meet my eyes. The gun must have been heavy in her small hands, for it trembled violently, wavering back and forth. I wasn't afraid now, I was blistering mad, so full of rage that if she had pulled the trigger, the bullet would have bounced off me.

"Get back, Katy," Carmen was saying, but I just kept bearing down on her.

"*Get back, Katy*," I mocked. "Give me a good reason, Carmen. Does it matter to you whether you shoot me at point blank range or not? Why don't you just go ahead, murder me now — I can't stop you. What the hell do you care? You've already killed three people, what's one more? What difference does a lifetime of friendship make to someone like you? Go ahead, shoot me — blow my brains out, just like you did to Diana last night. What's one more?"

I was rigid with rage and disgust, towering over Carmen as I pressed her backward, backward. Her face was all squinched up like she might cry, and she kept trying to look away from me, but she couldn't avoid my glare.

Finally, she could go no further; I had backed her up against the front wall of the house. She stood pinned there, the .38 still clutched in her hands, her lower lip trembling. I was only a few feet from her, my shadow completely eclipsing her small frame.

For several minutes we stood staring at one another, our breath visible in the afternoon chill. The only sound came from Carmen's throat, little high-pitched wheezes.

"Give me the gun," I demanded. I reached for it, and for a moment I thought she was going to hand it over.

Holding the thing still in both hands, she bent her arms, pointed the muzzle skyward. I reached for the butt of the weapon. Then, as my hand froze in mid-air, Carmen squeezed the trigger. The crack was loud, louder than I'd expected, and I yelled and jumped backward instinctively, covering my head with an arm. My recent theory about being bulletproof bit the dust. My heart hammered against my ribcage.

The first bullet flew up and hit the rain gutter that ran along the edge of the roof. I saw the hole later, but they never found the bullet. It must have arced off into the woods somewhere.

Then, in a smooth motion, Carmen calmly brought her elbows in close to her body, still pointing the muzzle of the gun upward. Bowing her head, she fired in the same instant. I didn't actually hear that shot. It seemed to happen somewhere far away from me. I saw, though.

I howled from that faraway place as Carmen's face seemed to blossom into a jagged scarlet flower. She stood tottering against the wall for a few seconds, long enough for me to reach her, catch her, keep her from falling, but there was no point to it.

When Benjamin found us, the December sun had dropped to the top of the grey trees surrounding the property. I was sitting in the snow against the side of the bungalow, cradling Carmen in my arms.

Blood had frozen in the snow all around us, and my ungloved hands were covered in ice and blood. Carmen still clutched the gun close to her chest, as if in an attitude of prayer. I hadn't tried to pry the weapon loose, and now it seemed to be glued there, pointing to the place where her jaw had once been. Fragments of bone stuck out through her flesh. Her face was gone. Just gone.

The only reason I knew for sure it was Carmen I held, out there in the cold, was her coat, her beautifully cut, silk-lined fuchsia wool coat. It was caked with blood and ruined now, but I would have recognized that coat anywhere.

24

A coroner's truck came and removed the body. Benjamin put me in his car and drove me to the hospital, then to the police station. He kept offering me tissues and hot drinks, but I couldn't stop crying and shivering, even after the doctors checked me over and injected me with something to help me relax. I don't think I said much, and of what I did say, I can't swear that anything made sense.

When we got to the station, I had to sign a statement. I told the story in my own words, just like they told me to. Some other detective took it down. Benjamin disqualified himself, saying he had a personal involvement. I didn't really mind.

Later, Benjamin drove me home. He waited while I showered, bundled up my bloody clothing, stuffed it all into a plastic bag to wash later, and found something else to wear. Then he sat with me until Dawn got home from school. I made us coffee, not knowing what else to do. I really didn't want any, but the familiar tasks occupied my hands, filling a void.

Benjamin was still trying to figure out what had just happened.

"What I don't understand, Katy, is why Carmen

kept some of the pills. Why didn't she just throw the leftover ones away when she'd made the switch with Marion's? Why hang onto them?"

Benjamin's forehead crinkled in puzzlement. I took another sip of coffee, watching steam rise from the mug.

"I don't know. Carmen always liked to walk too close to the edge. When we were kids, she was always the one taking dares. And she hardly ever got caught, either."

"So you think keeping the pills was her way of daring someone to catch her?"

I nodded. "And don't forget, she didn't start out trying to actually kill anyone. She thought if she doctored some of her pills, Marion would have a seizure at the party in front of Nigel. Marion would look bad, and Nigel would be turned off. She told me herself, she had no idea someone could die from an epileptic seizure. Plus, if she made the switch while she was out at the church, she couldn't have had much time to do it. She had to find Marion's little dispenser case, stick the right number of pills into each slot, and replace it in Marion's bag. She probably just shoved the leftovers into her purse."

"True enough." My new friend the police detective nodded.

"The funny thing is how guilty I feel about everything," I said.

"What do you mean? You don't have anything to blame yourself for."

"Yeah, right. I could have kept my big mouth shut about Diana, but I was just bursting at the seams to check out my brilliant lesbian affair theory with Carmen. That's what drove her to kill Diana. She realized I'd convinced Diana to turn herself in, and it wouldn't be long before the cops drew the correct conclusion."

"But Katy —"

"And I could have listened to you, gone with you back to the crime scene, instead of getting all huffy and staying at the centre. Carmen might have got away, but at least she wouldn't be dead. I feel like I killed her, Benjamin. I let my anger get the better of me, and I backed her into a corner where she had no other choice."

Benjamin shook his head.

"Carmen did what she did all by herself, Katy. She didn't have to kill Marion, she didn't have to stab Nigel, she didn't have to kill Diana, and she didn't have to pull a gun on you. Those were her own choices."

I said nothing. Maybe he was right, but that didn't make it better.

"She told me something else, out there," I said. Benjamin waited.

"She said Marion turned a blind eye to what Nigel was doing with Rose. To hang onto him, you know. And she said her own mother did the same thing to her. I never knew that."

"Shit."

Benjamin hugged me close, not knowing what to say. His jacket smelled faintly of his aftershave, deep and spicy.

"It doesn't make it better, any of it," I said. "But I just wish I'd known."

"And what could you have done about it?" he countered. "You did the best you could, out there. You know I don't approve of you getting involved in police business, but this one wasn't your fault, Katy. I left you out there. I should have insisted you stay with me. I thought you were wrong, that the killer was already miles away, but I was also just mad that you wouldn't do things my way, so I got stubborn and left you in danger. I was in charge, and I blew it. I'm always going to regret that."

"Don't pull that authoritarian schtick on me, Benjamin. No one's in charge of me. Didn't you just finish giving me a lecture on how people are responsible for their own actions?"

"Yeah, but —"

"I chose to do what I did, and I didn't need your exalted permission. As Dawn used to tell me when she was little, 'You're not the boss of me!'"

Benjamin gave a short laugh. "No, I think we're going to have to work on that one. I'm a little too used to being the boss. Maybe you are, too." Whatever the hell he meant by that.

Dawn came home from Sylvie's and looked appalled to find me resting my head against Benjamin's arm on the couch. Not that we were necking or anything, but Dawn still has residual feelings of resentment over some comments Benjamin made to her last summer. That was something we'd have to iron out, too, I thought. Later.

He stood to leave, and I shocked my daughter even more by allowing Benjamin to give me a kiss on the cheek.

"Mom! What was all that about?" She rounded on me before the front door was even shut.

"That was Detective Benjamin. You remember him, right? You met him last summer."

"I know that. I want to know what he was doing here, slobbering all over you!"

"He wasn't slobbering, we were just having a chat. I've had a long day, Dawn."

Dawn scowled at me and stomped into the kitchen for a snack. I didn't have the energy to argue with her.

Peter called in later that evening, in a dither over the Soldiers story, which had apparently taken on a new twist. He'd just got off the phone with his police contact, who had updated him on the day's events.

"They found out who torched your building," he said. "You were right, Katy – it was the Soldiers. But you'll never guess who was behind it."

I didn't feel like explaining why I was not really up to guessing games at the moment. There would be time to tell him all about it later on.

"You're right," I said. "I can't guess. So why don't you just break down and tell me?"

"It was Janet Tompkins, the city councillor."

"I guessed that already," I said.

"You did?" Peter was aghast. "Why didn't you say anything?"

"Too much happening. I forgot."

Not much mollified, Peter went on. "Well, when they searched her house, the cops found a stash of weapons and explosives tucked in behind the water heater. Apparently they were acting on an anonymous tip they got last night...I'd bet you anything it was Diana!"

"So...Peter, you're saying that the city councillor for the Glebe is some kind of religious terrorist?"

Unaccountably, I was seized with the urge to laugh.

"You got it! Remember I told you there was a link with that treatment centre out in Leitrim?"

My stomach clenched threateningly, but I controlled it through an effort of will.

"Yeah," I managed.

"Well, Tompkins was one of its first graduates, clean and sober for fifteen years. That's before Diana started running the place — her brother was still in charge. Tompkins seemed to feel she owed him a debt of gratitude, and when he was recruiting for the Soldiers, she was one of the first to sign on."

Peter chattered on, delighting in this new plot twist. When he is on the trail of a hot new story, exposing the bad guys, he's like a kid with a new toy. I didn't have the heart to tell him about my day. It would have to wait.

Greg picked me up that evening and took me to his place for a quiet meal. I didn't eat much, and I don't think I was much of a conversationalist, either. I gave him a thumbnail sketch of the last few days. He sat quietly, just listening. When I had talked and cried myself out, he drove me back home.

"Katy, I want you to think about something," he said as we sat in his Audi outside my building. "This isn't the best time, but I have an idea I'd like you to consider. With your office gone, you're going to need help setting up your practice again. I need help too — we're short of consulting psychologists now. If you could come back to the hospital, just part-time for now, I have a place for you."

✦

I didn't give Greg an answer right then, but I have been giving it some thought. Greg is a good friend, he'd be a good boss, and I used to like being a psychologist.

But I'm not ready to give up on astrology yet, and I haven't decided whether it's possible to be both a forensic psychologist and an astrologer. Greg keeps telling me the offer will stand for as long as it takes me to make up my mind. That's a good thing, since making up my mind feels like something I used to be able to do, once a long time ago, but can't master now.

It's been several weeks since Carmen died. I've found myself a new office, a few blocks from Bank Street, in the same general neighbourhood as my old one. My landlady is a genial older woman who owns several cats, wears only purple, and spends her spare time canoeing in Algonquin Park. She doesn't think I'm flaky at all.

Benjamin and I have gone out to dinner a few times, and that's okay with me, though Dawn clearly disapproves. Well, I probably won't like all her boyfriends, either, when that time comes. That's just the way it goes, I've decided. Besides, it's not like Benjamin and I are serious, we just like one another's company. I take it back about him not being my type.

The police investigation into Nigel Farnsworth's church continues. Janet Tompkins is up on arson charges and the case has been attracting a lot of attention. Peter has been covering both cases closely, but I try to keep my ears closed when he talks about them. I know all I need to know.

Phil Stanley has not yet charged me with kidnapping his daughter. Or with letting her die. In fact, no one has heard from him since the funeral. I don't think he's missed.

Sometimes I think about Carmen, and when I do, I try to think of the way we used to be. I try not to remember the bone fragments poking jagged through raw flesh and blood. That image comes to me each night when I sleep, and every morning I put it away, file it with the rest of my dreams, try to get on with my day.

No, when I am awake, I try to think about walking to school with Carmen on brilliant February mornings like this one, or sitting with her in my mother's kitchen, dipping crisp *mandelbrot* in our milk. I think about her fuchsia wool coat, her gold watch, her tiny manicured hand passing me tissue after tissue when Brent and I broke up. I think of suppers shared, and the way she would straighten my jacket for me and buy me fancy silk scarves I never wore. I think about how she always wanted to redecorate my office, how she always chose romantic movies, while I wanted comedies. I think about how little I really knew her. She was my oldest friend, you know.

Thanks to my publishing dream team at Polestar/Raincoast: Publisher Michelle Benjamin, Managing Editor Lynn Henry and Marketing Manager Emiko Morita. No author could ask for better.

My family, as always, makes it all worthwhile.

Jane Barth, Arline Chase, Mary Keenan, Bob Legleitner, Judy Ludlum, Kate Maguire and Jennifer Wright have been wonderful supports and deserve thanks for bearing with me as this book evolved. Jane and Maire, especially, gave some solid writing advice that helped me immensely.

And, of course, thanks to my Montreal "agents," Zay-Za Unlimited, whose promotional and reconnaissance efforts continue to make this all so much fun!

KAREN IRVING is the author of *Pluto Rising*, the first Katy Klein mystery, which was nominated for the Arthur Ellis First Mystery Novel Award. She lives with her family in Ottawa, Ontario, where she writes full-time. She has been writing and studying astrology for over twenty years, and is hard at work on the third Katy Klein mystery.